Flowers

Are Better Than

Bullets

a novel

RODNEY DILLMAN

To Laura, my wife and so much more. Without you this story would have never been told. This book is a testament to our journey, our love, and the indelible mark you've left on every page.

AND

To the memory of Allison Krause, Jeffrey Miller, Sandy Scheuer, and Bill Schroeder—the four bright souls whose lives were tragically cut short on May 4, 1970. Your spirits remain undimmed, echoing through the annals of history and reminding us of the cost of freedom and the importance of peaceful protest.

To Alan Canfora, John Cleary, Tom Grace, Dean Kahler, Joe Lewis, Donald Mackenzie, James Russell, Robert Stamps, and Doug Wrentmore—the nine wounded students whose lives were forever changed that fateful day. Your resilience and courage serve as a testament to the enduring human spirit and the power of hope.

This novel is dedicated to you all. May your stories continue to inspire generations to come, reminding them of the sacrifices made for justice, peace, and a better world.

CONTENTS

Introduction

"What's the matter with peace?
Flowers are better than bullets."

Allison Beth Krause
April 23, 1951–May 4, 1970

Vietnam was a war America couldn't win.

In the early stages of the Vietnam War, 1956–1964, 416 American troops died. In 1968, at the height of America's involvement, 549,500 U.S. military personnel served in Vietnam and by the end of 1969, American casualties had skyrocketed to 48,320. Anti-war sentiment in the United States was white hot.

As 1970 began, over 400,000 troops remained in Vietnam. Morale was low, anger and frustration were high, and drug and alcohol use were rampant. Hundreds of young men were still being drafted every day. President Richard Nixon began to deliver on his campaign promise to de-escalate America's role in the war, but on April 30, 1970, he announced on national television that the U.S. had invaded neutral Cambodia in pursuit of the Viet Cong. This announcement sparked protests in cities and on college campuses nationwide, including the Kent State University campus in Kent, Ohio.

Flowers Are Better Than Bullets is a story told in three rotating timelines and reveals what happened at Kent State during the first week of May 1970 through the eyes of Johnny, an eighteen-year-old freshman from Lima, Ohio.

The **Teens and Dreams** timeline follows Johnny into his teen years from February 8, 1964, to September 19, 1969, as he endures adolescent angst with girls and dating and develops political awareness of the war in Vietnam.

The **Life and Love** timeline describes Johnny's life as a freshman at Kent State from September 20, 1969, to April 30, 1970, as he matures academically and socially and finds his voice politically as an anti-war activist.

The **Bayonets and Bullets** timeline portrays Johnny's participation in the tragic events of May 1, 1970, to May 4, 1970, at Kent State in response to the U.S. invasion of Cambodia.

Flowers Are Better Than Bullets takes you on a historical journey of life, love, and political activism. It is a testament to the brave students who stood up for their beliefs at Kent State and to the 58,220 U.S. soldiers who made the ultimate sacrifice in Vietnam.

1

Monday, May 4, 1970

Vietnam. This fucking war. I'm pinned down on the side of a hill with bullets flying all around me. A few minutes ago, we thought they were in retreat. They had crested the top of the hill, then turned and fired. We never saw it coming.

I feel a bullet whiz past my ear and hear another hit a piece of metal nearby. I hit the ground as I see bodies fall. The shooting has stopped. I cautiously look up and see a field of 18- and 19-year-olds lying face down on the ground. I can't tell if they've been shot or are waiting to see if another volley of bullets is coming.

I stay down and start to belly crawl toward a guy a few yards uphill who's been shot. He got it bad. Took a bullet in the chest. His blood runs down my leg and pools on the ground below me, but he's conscious.

"It's okay, man. I'm going to get you some help." I rip off my shirt and try to staunch the flow of blood. "What's your name?"

"John." He can barely speak.

"Okay, John. Stay with me. My name is also John, but my buddies call me Johnny. Hang in there. We're going to get you some help." I think, but for the grace of God, I could be the "John" lying in this pool of blood.

A guy on the hill just below me is moaning in agony. He's also been shot. Someone crouches down beside me and whispers, "I can help this guy. I know first aid."

"Okay. This is John. Stay with him until he gets medical attention."

I stay low and run to the guy a few yards downhill. His shoe is gone. He's been shot and part of his left foot is missing. Bones stick out from the bottom of his foot.

"Let's get out of here before they start shooting again," I tell him. "What's your name?"

"Tom."

"Okay, Tom, I'm Johnny. I'm going to take you to someone who can help you." He's bleeding heavily and needs help fast. I grab him, put him over my shoulder face down in a fireman's carry, and shuffle him down the hill. I see more casualties.

I get him to a safe place with cover and others rush to his aid. As I lay him down someone says, "He needs a tourniquet. Give me your belt!" I quickly pull off my belt and watch as it's wrapped tightly around Tom's lower leg. The blood flowing from his foot starts to slow, but he is fading in and out of consciousness.

"This is Tom," I tell them. "Others have been shot, and I'm going to see if I can help them."

"Okay. We'll stay with him."

The attack has stopped. The acrid smell of gun smoke assaults my nostrils. Those who can slowly get up off the ground and help the wounded.

Suddenly, I hear a cry for help. I whip around and run back up the hill toward the frantic plea. Someone is kneeling by a guy who's face down in a pool of blood. As I get closer, I see he's been shot through the mouth. I stare at him in disbelief. My God. It's Jeff. A few minutes ago, he had been full of life. Now, he's not moving, and there is so much blood. I know he is dead.

I turn away and look up at the top of the hill and then at the carnage all around me. This damn war. When will it ever end?

Bayonets & Bullets

2

Spring has finally arrived after a cold, harsh winter. Despite a rough start, I now feel like I belong here.

Kent's academic terms are quarters instead of the semesters like most universities. I made the Dean's List for the fall and winter quarters, and the *Lima News* reported my accomplishments. It surprised a lot of people, including myself. My dad had always told me I was stupid and a dummy, and I believed him. Once I overcame my inferiority complex and started to excel, I realized I was more intelligent than most of my fellow students.

Compared to a year ago, when I was waiting to hear from Kent State, I feel pretty good about myself. My backup plan, if you could call it that, was to enroll at the Ohio State University branch in Lima. The problem was that I had not applied, had no money to pay tuition even if I was accepted at the "Branch," and had no money for living expenses.

I've only been back to Lima once since September when I took a bus home for Christmas break. It was torture. Nothing had changed. My dad was still a mean son of a bitch. I couldn't wait for the new year to arrive so I could return to campus. I took the first bus I could and was back in Kent on Saturday, January 3, 1970, when the dorms opened for the winter quarter. It was the beginning of a new year, a new decade, a new life. I vowed I would never live at home again.

The sun shines brightly shortly after 7:00 as I walk into the Eastway cafeteria for breakfast. To the right of the entrance is a stack of the *Daily Kent Stater*, the campus newspaper. I grab a copy, pick up a tray and look over the breakfast options. Students complain about the cafeteria food, but I think it's a great deal. I can eat whatever I want and as much as I want. Pancakes, eggs, bacon, cereal, toast, and more are available daily. For a kid whose motto at home when going for the food on the table was "if you snooze, you lose," the cafeteria food is like manna from heaven. I never had a weight problem when I lived at home, but now I am well on my way to gaining the "freshman 15." I select pancakes, bacon, and orange juice, settle at a table by the windows and open the *Kent Stater*.

GUARDSMEN, STUDENTS CLASH AT OSU announces the headline. Three days earlier, on April 28, 1970, U.S. troops invaded Cambodia. Everyone, except the Nixon administration, saw this as an expansion of the war in Vietnam. Last night on the TV in the Clark lounge, I watched Nixon try to explain that troops in Cambodia were needed to cut off Viet Cong supply lines. I see it as increasing the likelihood that three years from now, after graduating from KSU, I will be drafted and heading to Vietnam. My earlier feeling of contentment quickly evaporates.

The students at Ohio State University were protesting the invasion of Cambodia, despite President Nixon asserting that it was not an invasion. Governor James Rhodes called in the Ohio National Guard to shut down the student demonstrations. The *Daily Kent Stater* reported that "screaming students and National Guardsmen, bayonets at the ready, clashed repeatedly on The Ohio State University campus Thursday in a second day of violence. Tear gas was used to break up crowds of students who chanted, 'Pigs off campus' and 'Pigs go home.'" Classes were canceled, a curfew was imposed, and nearly three hundred demonstrators were arrested. Four people were hospitalized, three with gunshot wounds.

Governor Rhodes announced that the number of guardsmen on riot duty at OSU would increase from twelve hundred to eighteen hundred Thursday evening, with troops to remain "until there is no longer any threat of violence." He further declared, "We are protecting the forty thousand students who want to get an education against the relative few malcontents who are causing the trouble."

What a dick! Governor Rhodes sent in the National Guard to occupy a college campus. Some of those guardsmen probably aren't much older than me and joined the National Guard to avoid getting drafted and going to Vietnam. Now they're pointing their rifles at students who thought the same way they did about the war in Vietnam. It sucks.

Could something like that happen here at Kent State? I don't think so. While Kent State is a liberal community, few are real radicals. Students for a Democratic Society (SDS), the most far-left group, was officially barred from campus by the KSU administration last year, but twenty to thirty students are still active in SDS. However, many students, like me, hate the war in Vietnam and want our voices heard that the invasion of Cambodia is not okay. A group of KSU graduate students known as WHORE, World Historians Opposed to Racism and Exploitation, announced a rally on the Commons at noon today beside the Victory Bell to protest the invasion of Cambodia and bury the U.S. Constitution. I'm going to attend. I want the war to end now! Sending troops into Cambodia is madness.

I finish breakfast and head to my 7:45 calculus class. Most of my friends think I'm crazy for taking a class at that hour, but I like it. I do my best work in the morning, and the early sections are always small. Today's class is even smaller than usual. Since Thursday is the unofficial start of the weekend at KSU, many of my classmates were likely out partying last night.

After calculus, I hustle to my 8:50 History of Ohio class, a ten-minute walk to Bowman Hall. My last class is English 162, just across the road in Satterfield Hall at 11:00.

English was my nemesis at Lima Senior High and still is at Kent State. I received my only C during the winter quarter in English 161. Every other grade had been an A. I had no clue how to write a book report or any other paper. That changed at the beginning of spring quarter. My girlfriend, who received an A in both English 160 and 161, offered to give me a writing tutorial.

She started with the basics, reviewing the parts of speech: nouns, pronouns, verbs, adverbs, and adjectives. Then she moved on to a paper's organization: introduction, body, and summary. Suddenly, everything clicked into place. I'm unsure why English never stuck at Franklin Elementary, Central Junior High, or Lima Senior. Maybe the teachers hadn't taught it, or more likely, I had not paid attention to the lessons on organizing a paper. Now it all made sense. So easy, yet I had been so clueless.

After English, I head to the Commons to attend the WHORE rally. I hope it will not be like political activist Jerry Rubin's speech on Front Campus a few weeks earlier. Rubin, the leader of the Youth International Party or Yippies, a radical counterculture group, told us that a revolution was needed and that to start it, we had to quit being students, burn our books, and kill our parents. Really? *What a waste of time* seemed to be the general opinion of most of the fifteen hundred students who attended. Did Rubin really think we would go out and start killing people? It is safe to say that not many Yippies attend Kent State. In fact, I don't know any, and if they are here, they're most likely also members of the SDS.

The Commons, in the center of campus, is a ten-minute walk from Satterfield Hall. It's a beautiful sunny day with the temperature in the mid-seventies. I meet my girlfriend at noon at the Victory Bell on the east end of the Commons. She's stunning with her long auburn hair, white short shorts, and gauzy blue blouse. We sit on Blanket Hill, which forms a natural amphitheater and faces the bell and the remainder of the Commons. On warm spring days, my girlfriend and I, and a thousand of our closest friends, bring our blankets to the hill and bask in the warm sun, throw Frisbees, read a book, do homework, or just enjoy the life of a student.

About five hundred students sit on Blanket Hill facing the Victory Bell. Students typically ring it to celebrate a KSU Golden Flashes football victory, but today it's being used as a rallying call to protest the war in Vietnam and the invasion of Cambodia. Both are wars that the U.S. Congress has not approved; therefore, they are illegal and, in fact, unconstitutional. The rally is well organized, and a battery-powered portable megaphone has been provided for the speakers. My girlfriend and I clap loudly for each one.

It is a peaceful protest. No violence, no tear gas, no National Guard, no police, and no one telling us we must disperse, unlike what happened at Ohio State. After an hour, the rally ends next to the Victory Bell with a ceremonial burying of the U.S. Constitution, which a student leader has ripped out of a history textbook. Finally, a speaker tells us that there will be another rally on Monday, May 4, at noon to protest the invasion of Cambodia. No one even suggests a rally on Saturday or Sunday, May 2 or 3, since weekends are reserved for partying or going home to see family.

The rally confirms that I am not alone in thinking that the invasion of Cambodia is an expansion of the war in Vietnam. More young men will be drafted, and more young men will die. Hundreds of eighteen- to twenty-year-old men die in Vietnam every month, yet not one has the right to vote for a president or a congressman. I'm no radical, but I am pissed off at President Nixon, who promised to end the war but is now expanding it across Southeast Asia.

After the rally, my girlfriend and I linger on Blanket Hill. "I want to attend the rally on May 4," I say.

She nods. "I agree. We need to stand up and be counted as opposing the invasion of Cambodia. This war is never going to end if we don't protest."

"I don't think either of us wants to be involved in a riot like the ones occurring at Ohio State and other campuses around the country, but at the same time, we can't remain on the sidelines."

She nods again. "Let's definitely go to Monday's rally."

As we leave Blanket Hill, we see a handmade sign hanging from a tree that reads: WHY IS THE ROTC BUILDING STILL STANDING? ROTC is the Reserve Officers' Training Corps, a university-sponsored program for students interested in a military career.

I turn to my girlfriend. "I'm not sure I agree that ROTC is bad. The program is voluntary and provides scholarships for students to study at KSU. But I can see how the ROTC building symbolizes the Vietnam War. I see both sides of the issue, and I'm unsure where I stand."

"I agree. Whether ROTC should be on campus is a difficult issue. We do need soldiers to protect and defend our country, and ROTC helps train the leaders of those soldiers."

As we walk down Blanket Hill, we decide that since neither of us has any classes the rest of the day, we will do what most KSU students do on Friday night—head downtown to a bar, listen to music, and drink beer.

I meet my girlfriend at her dorm at 8:30. We go up to her room to have our own pre-party. Her roommate has gone home for the weekend, so we have the room to ourselves. We do what all college students do, and it is a beautiful thing. Far out, man!

The weather was unseasonably warm today and it's a pleasant spring evening. We arrive downtown around 9:45 after a leisurely fifteen-minute walk.

I'm surprised at how crowded it is on North Water Street. Some of the people hanging out don't look like students. Of course, that is true every Friday night. Kent is the hottest music scene in Northeast Ohio. At least twenty bars, including Kove, JB's, Water Street Saloon, Deck, Fifth Quarter, Dome, and Exit, are on the "strip" and most feature nightly entertainment. We go to Big Daddy's Pizza on North Water Street. We've been there before and know they always have a great band, good pizza, and cheap beer.

A guy checks our IDs at the door. If you are twenty-one or older, the guy stamps your hand with HI meaning you can buy any kind of alcohol. If you are between eighteen and twenty-one, he stamps your hand with LO and you can only buy "low" beer, which contains 3.2 percent alcohol. My girlfriend and I show our driver's licenses indicating we are eighteen, but it is a bit of a joke. An Ohio driver's license is printed in black on a white paper card with no photo. It is common knowledge on campus that for ten dollars, you can purchase a fake driver's license with a birthdate that shows you're over twenty-one. The guy stamps our right hand with LO, and we walk into the bar.

Given the number of people outside, I'm surprised the bar isn't full. We find an empty picnic table and sit down. I order a pitcher of Carling Black Label low beer and a large pepperoni pizza.

The band members walk back on the stage after a break, and the lead guitarist introduces them as *Mum's Cameo.* The honky-tonk band plays an eclectic mix of prohibition-era oldies, country, folk, and rock, and bar patrons sing along. As the night progresses, the bar fills up, and other students join us at the picnic table. You can only get slightly buzzed from low beer, so very few in the crowd are crazy drunk. It's a beautiful spring night with my best girl, pizza, and beer. What more could I ask for?

At around 11:00, things start to change. First, I hear what sounds like a drag race in front of Big Daddy's. A few minutes later, I hear it again.

"Are you okay if I go outside and check out what's happening?" I ask my girlfriend.

"Go ahead," she says. "I'll hold our seats."

As I step outside, a red, white, and blue muscle car blows by, tires screaming and running flat out. A motorcycle gang races up and down North Water Street, with some guys doing wheelies. It's quite a sight, and I wonder where the cops are. A couple of hundred other people are standing on the sidewalks watching the spectacle and cheering.

A guy from the motorcycle gang pulls a trashcan off the curb, dumps it into the middle of the road, flips the top on his silver Zippo cigarette lighter, and torches the paper in the trash can. A bonfire erupts, and everyone claps and cheers. Another guy empties a second trash can onto the blaze, and again everyone cheers and starts moving into the street, dancing like this is some wild ritual. I know the police will be here shortly, and I want no part of that confrontation, so I rejoin my girlfriend inside Big Daddy's.

"What's up?" she asks. I tell her what happened and that I think we will be okay if we stay inside the bar until the police clear the streets. Rowdy partying continues outside, but the music and company are good, so we stay inside.

Just before midnight, while the band is still playing, all the lights in the bar come on, and someone shouts, *"Big Daddy's is now closed."* I turn around and see a line of five cops in riot gear standing at the back of the bar. The head cop shouts again, *"The bar is closed. Kent is under immediate curfew. All bars are ordered closed. Everyone, go home now! Students head back to campus. Anyone failing to leave downtown immediately will be arrested."*

I look at my girlfriend, she nods, and we head outside.

The same thing happens simultaneously at all the bars along North Water and Main Streets. Suddenly, instead of a couple of hundred people, a thousand are now outside. The cops and bar patrons yell at each other. People throw bottles and cans at the cops. The sound of breaking glass can be heard over the din. I grab my girlfriend's hand and shout, "Let's get out of here."

We weave in and out of the crowd trying to get away from the melee. Just before we get to Main Street, rocks shatter the plate glass window of Revco Drugs, and another rock crashes through the window of the Home Savings and Loan. A beautiful spring evening has turned into a full-blown riot. Students yell:

"Fuck pigs!"

"Out of Cambodia!"

"U.S. out of Cambodia!"

"Down with Nixon!"

People loot several stores with broken windows. One guy takes a Scotts lawn spreader from the hardware store, walks across the street in front of us, and throws it through the window of Portage National Bank. People steal shoes from a shoe store. A rock sails through the air and smashes the window of Hickman's Jewelers. Looters quickly grab jewelry from the nearest showcase.

The cops move in on the people throwing rocks and looting. We hurry up Main Street toward campus.

When we get to the corner of Main and Lincoln streets just across from Prentice Gate that leads to campus, a crowd of about a hundred students shouts at the cops on the scene. We quickly cross to the other side of the street, walk toward the Robin Hood Inn, and move behind the protestors. As we continue up Main Street, I look back and see the cops fire tear gas into the crowd, which immediately starts to disperse and move onto campus.

We stop to catch our breath after we are safely away from the chaos. We're both panting. I look at my girlfriend, and see she is worried. "Are you okay?"

"Yes, but I was startled by how quickly the crowd turned on the police," she says between breaths.

"I know. One minute, we're listening to good music at Big Daddy's. The next minute, we're in the middle of a riot. It makes no sense. How can things deteriorate so rapidly?"

We both agree that the cops overreacted, and their tactic of clearing the bars unintentionally brought more people into the streets, resulting in a situation they could not control.

We make it back to campus without witnessing any more incidents. Despite being outside of official hours for coed visitation, we spend the night together in her room. Recently it has become clear that the posted visitation hours are little more than a suggestion. Provided you don't flaunt it, the resident advisors are not checking rooms, and overnight stays by members of the opposite sex are commonplace.

After what happened tonight, who cares about visitation rules.

Teens & Dreams

3

Saturday, February 8, 1964 • Lima, Ohio

"**J**ohnny Joe, where are you?"

"Over here," I yell.

"You boys watch out for those trains," Mom shouts.

"We will hear them," I shout back.

I stand at the top of the hill holding our well-worn red Flexible Flyer. The paint is chipped, and some wood slats have gouges in them, but it works just fine. It snowed last night, and we have six inches of fresh snow to slide on.

We live at the end of Truman Street in Lima, Ohio, a dead-end street next to the Pennsylvania Railroad tracks. Lima is a blue-collar town that has seen better days. It is named after the capital of Peru, but the *i* is pronounced with a long *i* rather than the long *e* sound used in Peru.

A rusty guardrail marks the end of our street. Its last paint job was probably before I was born. On the other side of the guardrail and down the hill from our house are two sets of tracks: one eastbound, one westbound. I march with my two younger brothers down the snow-covered dirt path to the railroad tracks. The tracks are our playground. With the new-fallen snow, we build a snow ramp like the one for ski jumping on ABC's *Wide World of Sports*. You know, the ad they play on TV where the skier flies off the ski jump and crashes in the "agony of defeat." It's going to be so cool.

We pack snow on it hard, then smooth it down to and up against the nearest rail of the first set of tracks. It's ready.

Henry says, "I want to go first. I did the most work."

Kevin says, "I'm the smallest. I should go first."

Holding the sled, I say, "No way. I'm the oldest, and I'm going first to make sure it works, and you guys don't kill yourselves. Now, give me a shove."

I sit on the sled and Henry and Kevin push hard on my back, and down I go. I hit the ramp at the first rail and fly over the tracks, landing between the eastbound and westbound tracks. That was way cool, and I want to do it again, but I wait for Henry and Kevin to take turns. Henry is nine, Kevin is seven, and they are both brats.

Each of us tries to outdo the other to see how far we can fly over the tracks after we hit the snow ramp with our sled. Kevin barely makes it over the first set of tracks. Henry and I usually land somewhere between the two sets of tracks.

Passenger and freight trains pass by often on their way west to Chicago or east to Cleveland. The conductor blows the whistle at each street intersection, but since our street is a dead end, I listen for the whistle when the train reaches the intersections before or after Truman and hope the conductor does not forget to blow it.

It's my turn again. I really want to show Henry and Kevin that I can go a lot further than either of them, so this time I take the sled in both hands, get a running start and dive onto the sled headfirst down the hill. I hit the snow ramp much faster than before and fly. Up and over the eastbound tracks I soar and slam into the closest rail of the westbound tracks. The sled stops, but I don't. I crash face-first into the second rail and roll down the embankment on the other side of the tracks. "Goddamnit, shit, mother fucker," I mumble.

My lip is bloody, and I spit out the corner of my front tooth. I am trying to figure out if anything else is broken or hurt when I hear a train whistle. I look down the tracks to the east and see a big black engine coming straight at me. I have just enough time to grab the sled and get a few feet up the far hill before the train gets here. I bend down to pick up the sled, but one of its runners catches the rail. Once again, down I go, face-first into the snow. Of course, my brothers think all this is great fun and are laughing at me. The train is less than half a block away, and I again grab the sled. Fortunately, it comes free this time, and I scramble up the hill across from our house to wait for the train to pass. That was a close call. My brothers are pointing at me and still laughing so I give them the middle finger salute just before the train arrives.

As I lie there out of breath, I roll my tongue over my fat lip and chipped tooth. My front teeth grew in crooked and now one of them is chipped. We have no money for a dentist. I'll just have to live with it.

The freight train is long, well over a hundred cars. My lip is bleeding, so I wipe it gently with the back of my knitted glove and then make a snowball and hold it against my lip while waiting for the train to pass. I worry about what my dad will do if he sees my bloody lip. He'll probably think I've been fighting. If he's been drinking it could be bad. I've learned over the years to be wary of him. With six kids in our family, five of them boys, it takes little to set him off on a whipping frenzy. If he doesn't like what one of us is doing or if he thinks we've been fighting, he'll strip the belt from his trousers and start whipping whoever is closest to him.

As I wait for the train to pass, I pray that my dad will not be home and that only my mom will be there to help stop the bleeding from my upper lip. Mom never hits us. Even her verbal lashings seem to be more to protect us than hurt us.

Finally, the train passes. I cross the tracks and trudge up the hill, dragging the sled toward our house. Henry and Kevin laugh as I wipe the blood from my lip with snow.

Henry says, "I thought you were going to be smashed to smithereens by that train."

Kevin joins in. "Yeah, you would have been squashed like a bug."

"No such luck. Come on knuckleheads. I need to have Mom

look at my lip." I glance toward our house to see if Dad's car is there. It's not. At least something is going right today.

We live in a small, run-down, three-bedroom house. It has only one bathroom with a tub but no shower. My mom and dad have their bedroom. My older sister, Susie, gets a bedroom to herself, leaving my four brothers and me to share the last one. It has space for only one set of bunk beds. My oldest brother, Dennis, a senior in high school, gets the top bunk. That means I'm stuck on the bottom bunk with Henry, Kevin, and my youngest brother Brian, who is two years old. It sucks, but there is nothing I can do about it. There is nowhere else to sleep in this crappy little house. At night Henry and I are at one end of the bed, and Kevin and Brian are at the other.

Last night we had one of our epic foot fights. "Don't make me come in there," Dad yells from the living room.

Kevin kicks me in the balls. "Ouch," I groan. "What did you do that for?" I get in a few good kicks, but then Kevin and Brian start crying. Without another word Dad comes into the room. He already has his belt off and starts beating me good. My brothers move far away from the blows. I cover my face with my hands, but one hit gets me good and hurts like hell. I start crying, and he threatens, "Goddamnit, I'll give you something to cry about!" He hits me again and again until Mom comes in the room and holds his arm. I hate him, and every time he hits me, I hate him more.

I arrive home with Henry and Kevin bringing up the rear. I look at our shabby house with its faded siding and sagging porch and wonder what it would be like to live in one of the nice houses being built on the west side of town away from the railroad tracks.

As I open the front door, Mom reminds us, "Take those boots off outside and leave them on the porch. I don't want you boys tracking snow in the house." Mom is only thirty-eight, but I already think of her as old. She always looks tired. She's a little fat around the middle, probably something to do with having six kids.

"Okay, Mom," I say.

Taking my boots off is no easy task. They are hand-me-downs

from Dennis and about two sizes too small for me. They are made of hard black rubber and have a metal clasp every couple of inches. The snow has frozen the clasps tight, and I struggle to pry each one up. I have to take off my gloves to pry up the clasps and now my fingers are sore and cold. I'm finally able to unfasten the clasps, but I still can't get them off.

"Henry," I say, "help me take off my boots." While Henry pulls on the heel, I try to pull my foot out. It takes a few minutes, but we finally force each one off.

Mom tells us to put our wet gloves over the furnace vent in the living room. I do as I'm told, then go to the kitchen and show Mom my busted lip and tooth. The bleeding has slowed to a trickle. Mom looks at my face and says, "You have the prettiest blue eyes."

"Mom, what about my lip and tooth?"

"Let me have a look. What did you do?"

"I crashed into the railroad track with my sled and went flying off into the iron rail on the other side of the track."

"Well, you should be more careful." She inspects my lip and pronounces, "You'll live." She cleans up my wound with a wash rag and puts some mercurochrome on it.

"Ouch!" I pull away. Then I show her my chipped tooth again.

"You can hardly see the chip. You'll be fine. What about Henry and Kevin? Are they okay?"

"They're good. They're sitting on a furnace vent in the living room, trying to warm up."

I'm almost at eye level with Mom. I must be in the middle of a growth spurt. She is only five foot three, and when she measured me with her sewing tape measure last week, I was five foot one. She tousles my brown hair and says, "Go check the coal furnace, honey. It's getting a little chilly in here." I feel the chill, too, being just a skinny twelve-year-old kid weighing all of ninety-one pounds.

We had a new coal furnace installed in the basement two years ago. Before that, the only heat in the house came from the coal stove in the middle of the living room that vented its smoke through a tall metal flue in the ceiling. "Checking the furnace" means that I must walk downstairs into the dark, unheated, dirty basement, make sure enough coal is inside the furnace to last a couple of hours, and haul out the burnt ash. I hate this job. The furnace looks like a huge blast oven and takes up most of the space. Lump coal, each piece weighing a couple of pounds, is stored in a bin next to the furnace. I put on the heavy leather gloves that hang on a nail on a wooden post next to the furnace, open the furnace door, toss in six lumps, then open the bottom drawer and shovel the burnt ash into a metal pail. Some spills on the dirt floor. I don't bother to clean it up.

We are the only home I know that still burns coal for heat. All our neighbors have switched to natural gas, but I guess we're stuck with coal. My dad's father was a coal miner from the hills of Kentucky, so I don't think it's likely that we will get natural gas anytime soon.

I make my way up the basement stairs and hear my dad yell, "Whose goddamn boots are in front of the door? I just about killed myself getting inside." As I enter the kitchen, my dad spots me and, says, "Are those your fucking boots in front of the goddamned door?"

I nod, and he says, "You stupid son of a bitch, go move those goddamned boots before someone falls over them and breaks their neck."

As I walk by, he says, "What happened to your fucking lip? Who'd you get in a fight with?"

"No one, I busted it on the tracks sledding."

"You sure as hell better not be lying to me. If I hear you been fightin' with your brothers, I'll whup your ass."

"No fighting, just sledding."

"Get the fuck out of here and move those boots."

It's unusual for Dad to be home on a Saturday morning. He doesn't seem drunk, just his usual foul self. Even so, I can tell he has been to a bar. I smell fried food and beer on his clothes.

Dad doesn't work but always has enough money for a bar and cigarettes. Seven years ago, he had an accident on the job. He drove a truck for a local beer distributor, delivering beer to bars and restaurants. One day he was taking several cases of beer down to the basement of a local bar when the stairs gave way. He fell through to the basement floor and injured his back. He's had several operations to try and fix it, but the injuries were severe enough that he receives disability checks from the Veterans Administration and Social Security, even though he is only forty-two.

Dad is not a cripple and doesn't look like he has any disabilities. His walk is normal, but occasionally he complains of a stiff back. Yet he doesn't work, and I've never heard him talk about looking for a job. Maybe Mom wouldn't have to work so hard cleaning hospital rooms eight hours a day, five days a week, if he had a job. He looks like a normal five-foot-eight guy. With his brown hair and blue eyes, everyone says that I look like him, but I don't see it, and I hate it when people say that to me. The last thing I want to be is like my dad.

I move my boots over to the far-left side of the front porch. I guess it was stupid of me to leave them there, but wouldn't it have been easy for Dad to move them before he entered the house? As I walk back inside, Dad comes out the front door.

"Get out of my way, you stupid son of a bitch," he sneers. He stomps down the steps, gets into his car, and drives off. I'm not sure where he goes on Saturday mornings, and I don't care. He never asks if I want to go with him, and I never ask to go. We never do any of the father and son stuff you see on TV or other kids doing with their dads. He is no Ward Cleaver, and as much as I want to be like the Beaver, we are as far from that kind of father-son relationship as you can get. We share no football, no baseball, no basketball games, nor any fishing or hunting outings. I exist. I am his son. I'm not starving. That seems to be all that is required to fulfill his role as my father. I hear that I am a "stupid son of a bitch" so much that I believe it. I can't ever do anything right when I'm around my dad. Some people are born Jewish, some are born Italian, some are born French. I guess I was born a stupid son of a bitch.

I go back inside and head for the kitchen. It's Saturday, and while we were sledding, Mom did her weekly grocery shopping. She always brings home goodies, like slightly green bananas and Little Debbie Cakes. I grab one of each. With six kids in the house, they will likely be gone by early afternoon.

I settle on the couch to watch my favorite Saturday morning TV shows, *Fury,* and *Sky King.* I like nothing better than watching a horse named Fury and a pilot named Sky King show me what is right and true in America. Only a boy, Joey, who is about my age, can tame Fury, a wild stallion, and only Sky King can find the bad guys and bring them to justice. I look to those TV programs rather than my father as a guide to right and wrong and as examples of courage and grace.

This morning, before sledding, I was up before sunrise to deliver the *Lima News.* Dennis gave me his paper route of forty-three customers last year after he took a job at Ernie's, the neighborhood grocery store. Even though I have to deliver papers when it's cold and dark like today, the job keeps me in spending money. Monday through Friday, it's an afternoon paper, but on Saturday and Sunday, it's a morning paper. I drag the bundled papers into the living room and cut the twine around them with a kitchen knife. I roll each paper into a tight spiral, double wrap it with a rubber band, pack them all into a two-sided canvas delivery bag, and hoist the bag over my head and onto my shoulders.

My route starts four blocks from our house and covers eight city blocks. With the new-fallen snow, the going is tough, but there's no use in bitching and moaning about it. If I want the money, I have to do the work. The sidewalks and roads have yet to be shoveled or plowed, but by 7:00, I am on my way. The Saturday paper is usually light, so carrying forty-three papers isn't too bad. Sunday is the worst. That paper is three times the size of all the other days. The loaded bag on Sunday weighs so much that I often can't lift it over my head. When that happens, I set the bag on the floor with the loaded papers on each side. I crawl under the middle of the bag, put my head through the hole, and stand up with the bag resting on my shoulders. I can only walk for a block before bending over and letting the blood rush back into my head. I repeat the recovery process every block until I start unloading some of the weight.

After my paper delivery today, I head to the *Lima News* offices. This is a cash business. I collect the weekly amount due from my customers on Thursday or Friday and then pay my bill at the *Lima News* office every Saturday morning. I get to keep the money that's left after paying my bill. I've saved enough money to buy a new shirt and a new pair of pants rather than wearing my brother's hand-me-downs. I like the independence that money in my pocket brings, and I dream of the day I can leave Lima and my dad far behind.

On the way home, I stop by the lunch counter at S. S. Kresge for my favorite breakfast. The waitress in her black dress and white apron asks, "What can I get for you, hon?"

"I'd like a stack of pancakes and a Coke."

She smiles at me. "That's a right fine breakfast. I'll put that right in for ya."

Breakfast costs me twenty-five cents, but it's delicious and worth every penny.

After breakfast, I look at the shirts and pants for sale at Kresge's but don't see anything I like. I walk a block south on Main Street and enter J.J. Newberry's five and dime. In the Boy's Department, I find a red and blue madras plaid shirt and a dark blue pair of slacks. They look great together and the price is right, so I buy them.

After my perfect breakfast, sledding, and watching *Fury* and *Sky King*, it's time for lunch. I'm always hungry. I could make myself a bologna and mustard sandwich, but what I really want is a hamburger, french fries, and Coke. Ten minutes later I'm at the Red Barn and give my usual order, which costs me forty cents: fifteen cents for the burger, fifteen cents for the fries, and ten cents for the Coke.

I trudge home over snow-covered sidewalks and arrive just in time for *American Bandstand.* I love watching teenagers strut their stuff. My sister, Susie, a junior in high school, is home.

"*American Bandstand* is getting ready to come on. Do you want to watch it with me?" I ask her. Susie is usually too busy doing girl things, but sometimes she also likes to watch *Bandstand.*

"Sure, Squirt, just let me finish washing these dishes." She still calls me Squirt even though she is only a few inches taller than me. Most of the time, she's a swell sister.

American Bandstand is cool. I listen to the latest hits, learn cool dances, how cool kids dress, and how to do a cool review of a new record: "It's got a good beat, and you can dance to it." That afternoon Jackie DeShannon sings "When You Walk in the Room," and Dick and DeeDee sing "Turn Around" and "All My Trials."

For sixty minutes, I can dream of being one of the cool kids, even though I live on a dead-end street in a dying town with a deadbeat dad.

Life & Love

4

My prayers have finally been answered. I'm excited to be heading to college this morning. It's a new beginning. Six months ago, I applied to and was accepted at one college, Kent State University. I had two reasons that drove me to apply to KSU: I wanted to get as far away from my dad as possible and I did not want to go to Vietnam. Attending Kent State puts 168 miles between me and my dad and gives me a beautiful 2-S student deferment from the military draft for four years.

Perhaps a third reason for applying to KSU is to get a fresh start. At Lima Senior High I always felt like an outsider looking in. I didn't play sports, sing in a choir, or participate in other school activities. I've been self-sufficient since I was twelve, earning spending money from my paper route and after-school jobs.

Kent State is in northeastern Ohio, south of Cleveland, east of Akron, and far enough away that I know my dad will never step foot on campus. From the time I was twelve, I prayed to God to take me far away from him. I will never forget the beatings or the belittling he inflicted on me. When I was accepted at KSU and received enough grants and loans to attend, I knew my life's path had changed forever.

My trip to Kent is without family or friends and that is okay with me. Neither my mom nor my dad offered to take me, and I didn't ask them. I'm getting a ride to campus with a guy who is the only other student from my high school class admitted to KSU. His mom is driving us. Freshmen are not permitted to have cars on campus, so as much as I love my 1964 Chevelle, it must stay home.

The anticipation during the drive to Kent gives me the jitters. It's almost straight shot across Ohio to Kent. I watch the cornfields pass by, farm after farm, in the flat landscape of northwestern Ohio. Houses are few and far between. We slow down through several small towns that dot the route, and for the families living there I wonder what their lives are like. I hope not like mine. I wonder what my life will be like when I'm far away from my dad and no longer subjected to his outbursts. I hope my younger brothers and my mom will be okay.

After the three-hour drive, I'm standing in front of Clark Hall holding a single suitcase. I check in at the office on the first floor, get my room key and go upstairs to room 301. Clark is an all-male freshman dorm, and all rooms are triples. I look around my room and see that it's clean but spartan. Off-white vinyl tiles cover the floor, a set of bunk beds lies against the wall to my left and a single twin bed is to my right. Three chests of drawers and three desks with straight-backed chairs, and three grey metal desk lamps round out the furnishings. All the furniture is plain beige-colored oak. That's it. I walk down the hallway and into communal bathrooms and showers that look a lot like the ones I used for gym class at Lima Senior. My roommates have not arrived, and I have no idea how the beds are assigned, so I put my suitcase temporarily on the twin bed.

Clark is directly across a large grassy area from Allyn Hall, the freshmen girls' dorm. In prior years, visitation in dorms by members of the opposite sex was limited to the lobbies but the sexual liberation movement has finally reached KSU. Members of the opposite sex can now visit dorm rooms on Friday nights from 5:00 to 11:00 and on Saturday and Sunday from noon to 11:00.

Everything at Kent feels new and daunting. Coming from a high school with only one building, I am overwhelmed by a campus of over a hundred buildings covering eight hundred acres and attended by twenty thousand students.

Rather than waiting for my roommates to arrive, I venture out to explore the campus and immediately get lost. I didn't bring a campus map with me. *What guy needs a map*? I walk back the way we had driven to Clark Hall until I get to Loop Road. I turn right and walk, and walk, and walk. After an hour of walking, I reach Front Campus, and it finally occurs to me that Loop Road winds around the campus perimeter. Front Campus is beautiful. The original buildings sit at the top of a hill and overlook a wide Kelly-green lawn dotted with magnificent old-growth trees.

I know there must be a shortcut back to my dorm, so I walk up Hilltop Drive, pass between the Administration Building and Kent Hall, and run smack-dab into a kiosk with a campus map. Perfect! I cut across the Commons, a sweeping green lawn running through the center of campus, and up the hill on the other side. Fifteen minutes later, I'm back in my room. Lesson learned.

My roommates arrived during my trek across campus. I shake hands with Carl and Randy. Carl is a goofy-looking skinny white kid from Massillon, Ohio, and Randy is a cool, hip black guy from Cleveland. Of course, I am the poor white boy from Lima who knows *nuthin* about *nuthin*. Carl and Randy assume I've claimed the single bed where my suitcase still sits, so they flip a coin to see which one will get stuck with the top bunk. Randy loses.

Randy is about six-foot tall, and I am slightly taller at six foot one. Last year, I grew five inches. I guess to Randy, I look like a strait-laced white kid with my smooth brown hair just covering the top of my ears. No one is going to mistake me for a hippie.

After we unpack our stuff, I say, "How about if we check out the Eastway Recreation Center and get some lunch at the cafeteria?"

Randy says, "That's cool."

Carl just nods his head and so we take off to explore the Eastway Recreation Center. We soon discover that Eastway is in the middle of a four-dorm complex comprised of two boys' dorms—Clark and Manchester—and two girls' dorms—Allyn and Fletcher. We walk directly into Eastway from Clark through a connecting hallway. It's very cool. The first floor has a bowling alley, pool tables, ping pong tables, a TV lounge, and a snack bar. On the second floor is Eastway cafeteria, where we grab lunch using our school-issued meal cards. I am astonished by the choices I have but stick with my usual: a hamburger, french fries, and a Coke.

The cafeteria is enormous, so it's easy to find a table. I ask Randy, "Do you have any brothers and sisters?"

"I have two younger brothers. How about you guys?"

Carl says, "I'm the only kid in my family, no brothers or sisters."

I say, "I've got three younger brothers and an older sister and brother.

Randy says, "Whoa! Man, your mom don't know how to say *no*. That's a lot of kids to feed."

"You're right about that. About five too many kids." They both laugh.

We share other details about our families and intended majors. We learn that we all are the first in our families to attend college. We talk about the freshman week schedule. Tonight, we all plan to attend a movie in Bowman Hall.

After lunch, we head back up to our room and unpack. The first thing Randy does is set up a turntable and speakers on top of his chest of drawers. It looks like a pretty good system. He owns a large album collection that he places beside the stereo.

It only takes me a few minutes to unpack my suitcase and put everything in my chest of drawers. Randy's stereo system looks cool. I start flipping through some of his albums and then lift the arm on the turntable to look at the needle.

Randy says, "Hey, man. I don't like nobody touching my stuff."

"Oh. Okay," I say and put the arm back down and step away from the stereo. I look over at Carl, but he has his head in a book and says nothing.

"I'm going to check out the Eastway bowling alley," I say. "I'll see you guys later."

Randy gives me a slight nod. Carl just keeps on reading.

Bayonets & Bullets

5

My girlfriend is still sleeping when I wake up beside her in her twin-sized bed. "Good morning," I say, sliding the hair from her face. She opens her eyes and kisses me. "Good morning."

I sit on the edge of the bed. "The riot last night in downtown Kent was crazy. One minute we were having beers at Big Daddy's, and the next minute we were in the middle of a riot. I'm going to my dorm to change and then downtown to see the damage before I go to work."

"Okay, I'm going back to sleep." She leans toward me, and the bedcovers fall away giving me a great view of her naked body.

I kiss her goodbye, resisting the urge to crawl back into bed. Instead of going back to my dorm, I decide to head straight downtown. A police car sits at the corner of Main and North Water streets. Trash and glass are everywhere but people are sweeping it up and boarding windows.

"I'm here to help clean up," I tell the cop sitting in the patrol car. He waves me through, and I walk toward the mess. I enter Getz Hardware Store and ask one of the guys cleaning up, "What can I do to help?"

He looks at me, skeptically but says, "Thanks. You can start by sweeping up the broken glass and putting it in that trash can. A broom and dustpan are over there." He points to the corner by the front door.

For the next hour, I sweep up glass inside Getz and the adjacent store then help them place plywood over the windows. Other businesses are doing the same, and quite a few people are helping.

Around 7:45, I tell the owner, "I have to go to work. Sorry that I can't stay longer."

"I didn't expect any students to show up here today. Thanks for your help."

As I walk back through downtown, about fifteen businesses have smashed windows. Why did students damage businesses? The owners have nothing to do with the war in Vietnam or the invasion of Cambodia. It makes no sense.

I arrive at my Work-Study job right on time at 8:00. Films that had broken during class showings the previous week are sitting in a rack, ready to be repaired. I sit on a stool in front of the splicing machine and get to work.

Splicing is easy but repetitive. I load the film reel onto a spool on the right side of the machine, then feed the film through the splicing apparatus to the left side and onto an empty film reel. I flip on the switch, and the film speeds through the splicer and onto the empty reel until I find a break. I stop the reels, feed each broken end through the splicer, clip off any jagged edges, overlap the two ends in the splicer, add some glue, and the machine does the rest. Unless you look very closely, you can't even see the splice.

A radio station is playing hit tunes. It's relaxing to listen to some music while I work. At noon, the midday news comes on, and the reporter announces:

"Students rioted last night in Kent, Ohio, home of Kent State University. Around midnight in downtown Kent, students started a fire in the street, broke windows, and chanted antiwar slogans. Police estimate there were over a thousand students in the streets. The police closed the bars and ordered the rioters to disperse. We have been told that several students

were arrested, but no injuries have been reported. The police informed us that by 2:00 a.m., the situation was under control, and all students had been moved back on campus.

"We have confirmed with Kent Mayor LeRoy Satrom that he telephoned Governor Rhodes about getting assistance from the Ohio National Guard but has not yet made a formal request. The mayor also stated that he believes outside instigators were responsible for last night's disturbance. He was informed that twenty to thirty Weathermen, an offshoot of the SDS, were involved. We have not received confirmation from the governor's office whether he will send Ohio National Guard troops to Kent or the university. Stay tuned for further developments."

I stop the splicing machine. I can't believe the mayor called the governor about the Ohio National Guard. Kent State is not Ohio State. There are no riots on campus. Things turned ugly last night downtown, but in no way is the National Guard needed. The local police were able to get things under control. It probably was an isolated incident. No need to overreact. President White or someone else from the KSU Administration needs to step up and calm things down.

I finish my shift and walk back to my dorm.

Teens & Dreams

6

Sunday, February 9, 1964 • Lima, Ohio

Waking up before sunrise, I kick off the blankets and leave Henry, Kevin, and Brian asleep in our lower bunk. It's cold in the house. The furnace must have either burned out or is low on coal. I dress quickly and go down to the basement. A few small coals glow red in the furnace, but no fire is burning. I load in more coal, make sure it lights, head back upstairs, and retrieve my Sunday newspapers from the front porch.

The papers are in two stacks: the newspapers and the advertising inserts, which are almost as big as the newspaper. I stuff each paper with the insert, fold it in thirds, and put a rubber band around it. I load them into my carrier bag, hoist it over my head, and go outside. It's just after 7:30 and well below freezing. Most of the snow from yesterday is still on the ground. Some sidewalks are shoveled and cleared of snow, but many are not. Getting to the start of my paper route four blocks away is treacherous. On weekdays I can finish delivering the papers in about an hour. Sundays always take longer because of the heavy load. Today I finish at 9:00 and trudge home.

Mom makes us breakfasts on school days, but on Saturday and Sunday, we fend for ourselves. I grab the box of Sugar Crisp cereal, shake it into a bowl, and pour milk over it. I only eat the cereal and leave the milk. My dad always scolds me, saying, "You are goddamned wasting milk and throwing good money down the drain." I hate the taste of milk, so when I finish eating the cereal, I do throw the milk down the drain in the kitchen sink.

We are not a regular church-going family. Mom reads the Bible occasionally, and we celebrate the major Christian holidays, but I've never seen Dad set foot in a church. Mom will take us to the Central Church of Christ on North Street when she can muster up enough energy to get us all out the door and up to the church, but today is not one of those days.

After breakfast, Henry, Kevin, and I decide to build a snow fort, and Mom tells us to make sure we wear our hats and gloves.

We run out the back door into our yard. The snow is wet and perfect for packing. We start with a snowball and roll it in the snow until it's the size of a bowling ball. We place these big snowballs beside each other in a row about five feet long. We do this on three sides. We place more snowballs on top of the existing snowballs and fill in the cracks with more snow until the three-sided fort is up to my waist.

Now it's time for a snowball fight. We each make a pile of snowballs. I let Henry and Kevin use the snow fort first. They start by standing up and throwing snowballs at me and then ducking down below the fort walls before I can throw snowballs back at them. I then try lobbing the snowballs up and over the wall of the snow fort so that Henry and Kevin get hit from above, but only a few find their mark. I finally decide to charge the fort and blast them with snowballs standing right next to the fort walls. That works. I take a few hits, but they take a lot more, and they finally call "uncle," meaning they surrender. I win! By then, our cotton gloves are soaking wet, our cheeks are cherry red, and our toes are almost numb, so we go inside.

As we enter the back door, I see our dad sitting at the kitchen table, sipping a cup of coffee, and smoking a cigarette. We start to walk through the kitchen when he yells, "Goddamnit. Don't track that shit into the house, you sons of bitches. Take all that goddamn wet stuff off and leave it by the back door."

We do as we are told, and then we find a floor register vent to sit on to try and warm up with the heat from the furnace.

Dad's mood does not improve after his coffee. He sees me sitting over a register in the living room and says, "You stupid son of a bitch. You're twelve years old, you simpleton. You should know better than to track goddamn snow into the kitchen." He isn't looking for a response, and I don't give him one. He grabs the newspaper, lights up another Kool cigarette using a book of matches stuck in between the cellophane and the cigarette pack, and starts reading. Both he and Mom are two-pack-a-day smokers. It's unusual for either of them to be without a cigarette in one hand. Dad chain smokes by lighting a new cigarette from the end of the one he's just finishing. The house smells like cigarette smoke, I smell like cigarette smoke, and my clothes smell like an ashtray. The first thing I notice after coming in from outside is the smell of cigarette smoke. I hate that smell.

Mom always makes Sunday dinner, which is usually the best meal of the week. Today she serves us meatloaf, mashed potatoes and gravy, green beans, and dinner rolls. Mom is not much of a cook, but this is one of her better meals.

Mom was raised on a farm near Fordyce, Arkansas, where her father was a sharecropper. Dad is a hillbilly from Middlesboro, Kentucky, in the southeast corner of the state near the Cumberland Gap. His daddy was a coal miner. Their Southern roots sometimes have Mom preparing "delicacies" like wilted lettuce, turnip greens, dandelion greens picked from the backyard, black-eyed peas, pickled eggs, or pickled pigs' feet. All of it stinks up the house. Now that I have my paper route money, whenever Mom makes any of those things for dinner, I enjoy eating a hamburger and a Coke at the Kewpee downtown.

Shortly after Sunday dinner, Dad drives away in his 1959 Ford Ranch station wagon. I always feel relieved when he's out of the house, as though a weight has been lifted off me. Dad has a drinking problem, and every couple of months, he will make a 335-mile run in the station wagon to Middlesboro, Kentucky where he will get two or three cases of homemade moonshine from his brother-in-law. Each case has twelve jars. He sells most of them, which will keep him in drinking money until his next run, but he keeps several jars for himself. He is always mean and angry, but after a moonshine run, he sometimes goes on a drinking bender and will be gone for several days until he dries out. I don't know where he goes, and Mom does not know how long he will be gone. She says, "We will be fine without him," and we always are. From my point of view, we are better than fine.

Dad comes home in the afternoon, around 4:00, and staggers into the house. I can tell he's been drinking. When he comes in the front door, Henry and Kevin are in the middle of a fight about a book that Kevin had been reading, and Henry took it away from him, claiming it was his book. Dad sees the two of them pushing each other and says, "Goddamnit. I'll whup the fight out of both of you." He then unbuckles his leather belt, strips it from his pants in a single motion, and folds it in half. He grabs Henry's right arm and starts hitting him as hard as he can with the belt, first on his back and butt, and then as Henry tries to break away, he hits him on his arms and legs. Henry screams, and Dad says," I'll give you something to cry about," and whips him again and again and again. Henry continues to cry, and Dad continues to hit him with the belt as hard as he can.

Mom finally steps in, puts her hand on Dad's arm with the belt, and says calmly, "That's enough." Dad starts to hit Henry again, but Mom repeats, "Enough."

Dad lowers his belt and glares at Henry. "That should learn ya. There's no fuckin' fightin' in this house." He then warns Kevin, "It'll be your turn next if I see you fightin' again." Kevin cowers and says nothing. They both run to our bedroom and hide.

I'm not old enough or big enough to stop him when he is in one of these whipping rampages. I just stand there and watch, feeling helpless. The hate builds in me every time this happens, whether one of my brothers or I get the beating. As he puts his belt back on, I start walking away from him toward the kitchen. He sees me and shouts, "Where the fuck are you going, you stupid son of a bitch?"

I turn and say, "To the kitchen," and as I turn back, I bump into a table lamp, knocking it over, and the light bulb explodes. That sets him off again, and he comes after me. I move toward the kitchen, but he catches me by the shirt.

"You fuckin' broke the lamp, you stupid son of a bitch!" Then, he does something he's never done before. He hauls back with his fist and takes a swing at my face. I duck just before his fist connects with my head and punches through the drywall where a wooden stud stops it. I look at a five-inch hole in the wall. Blood is dripping from Dad's knuckles. I look at the hole, then at him, and then back at the hole. I'm stunned. I cannot believe he almost slugged me. He doesn't say a word, and neither do I. I turn around, grab my coat, and walk out the front door.

I walk up to Spykers Restaurant directly across from my school, Central Junior High, and order a tenderloin sandwich and fresh lemonade from the takeaway window. Good food always seems to help settle my nerves, and deep-fried pork tenderloin from Spykers is the best sandwich in town. I walk while eating and try to calm the emotions running through me. That swing could have killed me or, at the very least, knocked me out. What is wrong with him? Why is he so mean?

It's now dark outside, and though I'm still emotionally drained from the confrontation with my Dad, I have no place else to go, so turn toward home. Staying out past dark isn't a problem. Neither my mom nor my dad care what I do or where I go, provided I don't get into trouble and I'm home by 10:00 on school nights. I walk in the front door, expecting another clash with my dad, but see just my mom sitting on the couch. The door to their bedroom, just off the living room, is closed. Mom motions me over and asks in a low voice, "Are you okay?"

"Yeah," I reply. "I just got something to eat and walked around downtown."

"Dad is in the bedroom sleeping it off, so try not to wake him."

I nod and head to the kitchen, although if I was bigger, I'd wake him up and beat the shit out of him with his own belt.

Dennis is sitting at the kitchen table eating a ham sandwich. "I hear you had a little problem with Dad," he says, looking at the gaping hole in the wall where Dad's fist landed.

"Guess so. How was work?"

"Pretty good. I just got off work at 6:00 because we close early on Sundays." Dennis has worked at Ernie's, the neighborhood market, for the past two years. He's now a senior in high school. He sleeps in the same bedroom with the rest of us boys but has the top bunk to himself. That is a sweet deal and I fully expect that when he moves out, I will get the top bunk to myself. I can't wait to sleep without my bratty brothers' stinking feet in my face.

"How's the '57 Chevy running?" I ask.

"Great!" Dennis's car is a cherry red 1957 Chevrolet Bel Air convertible with a white top, white tail fin inserts, and lots of chrome. It is a sweet ride, and I feel on top of the world when he takes me for a spin. It has one neat feature: on the passenger side is an under-dash-mounted 45 rpm record player. Really cool.

Dennis nods toward the hole in the wall and says, "Just stay away from him."

I look at the hole. "Yeah, I plan to," I mumble. Except it's easier said than done in a nine hundred-square-foot house.

Dennis says, "Hey, The Beatles are going to be on *Ed Sullivan* tonight."

"Yeah, I know. Five thousand screaming fans, mostly girls, greeted them at the airport in New York City a couple of days ago. Some girls fainted when John, Paul, George, and Ringo waved to them. Pretty cool!" I say, nodding my head in admiration.

Dennis says, "Let's see if we can get it on the TV."

We have a good-sized floor model, color TV with a "rabbit ears" antenna. We've had it since last September. It was a replacement for our old black and white TV that always seemed to blow a tube. Lima has only one TV station, WIMA, UHF Channel 35, so it's the only station we receive. It broadcasts programming from all three major networks: NBC, CBS, and ABC. If it isn't on WIMA, we don't get it. It doesn't matter since we don't know what we might be missing.

We watch the NBC broadcast of the *Huntley-Brinkley Report* every weeknight with Chet Huntley and David Brinkley reporting the world news. I am always fascinated to learn what is going on outside of Lima.

Last year on November 22, our president, John F. Kennedy, was shot in Dallas, Texas, and rushed to a nearby hospital. It seems like the world stopped that day. Our seventh-grade civics teacher brought a TV set into our classroom, and thirty-two of us watched and waited with the rest of the world for news of the president's fate. We sat in stunned silence when, with tears in his eyes, the reporter told us that President Kennedy had died on the operating table. Several girls started to cry. Within an hour of the president's death, the principal of Central Junior High School dismissed all classes for the rest of the day.

Now, less than three months after that tragic day, the world has moved on. It's a new year. Vice President Lyndon Johnson is the thirty-sixth president of the United States. Huntley and Brinkley report that the Communists are trying to take over Southeast Asia. They've already gained a foothold in North Vietnam, and if we let them also take South Vietnam, there could be a domino effect causing the rest of Southeast Asia and then the rest of the world to fall to communism. President Johnson is trying to stop communism by sending additional military advisers to South Vietnam. I watch the evening news and believe with the rest of America that we need to stop the Communists.

Tonight, WIMA will be broadcasting *The Ed Sullivan Show* from the CBS network. They do every Sunday at 8:00, so why would tonight be any different?

Dad is still sleeping, so I tell Dennis we have to keep the volume down. Susie, a year younger than Dennis, joins us, as do Henry and Kevin. Mom wants to see what all the fuss is about, so after putting two-year-old Brian to bed, she joins us. I sit on the floor with my back against the couch. The announcer says, "Live from New York, *The Ed Sullivan Show*!" and the screaming starts. Ed Sullivan tells us that The Beatles received a telegram from Elvis Presley this afternoon wishing them success during their U.S. tour. "Very cool," I say.

After several commercials, Ed Sullivan introduces The Beatles, and the teenage girls in the live audience go crazy. The band opens with "All My Loving," which they pronounce "lovin" in their British accents. The camera cuts to the audience. Several girls look apoplectic, some girls look like they are in love, and others look like they're going to faint. The Beatles then mellow things out with "Till There Was You," a love song that leaves the girls swooning. While they are playing this song, the television network superimposes the name of the band members on the screen as the camera zooms in on each one so that we can recognize John, Paul, George, and Ringo. Under John's name, a caption reads, *Sorry girls, he's married*. The final song of their first set is "She Loves You," which really cranks up the crowd.

Waiting for the Beatles to play their final set, we suffer through several other acts. Lucky for us, a freight train passes by now rather than later. When a train goes by, the TV reception is lousy. The picture gets fuzzy, and the sound fades in and out. This is a long freight train that takes at least ten minutes to pass. The TV picture clears, and The Beatles come back on. They sing "I Saw Her Standing There," and again, the girls go crazy. Their final song and biggest hit, "I Want to Hold Your Hand," sends the girls into a frenzy.

The Beatles wear long hair over their ears, tailored black suits, white shirts, and skinny black ties. They all look swell, and, of course, with girls fainting at their feet, who wouldn't want to be a Beatle?

Susie says, "They look and sound really cool."

Dennis says, "I like the music, but I'm not sure about the long hair."

Henry and Kevin, ages nine and seven, don't see what all the fuss is about. Mom seems amused by the hoopla, but as we excitedly talk about the band, she warns, "Don't you boys think for one minute that I'm going to let you grow your hair that long."

I know that The Beatles will be the only thing everyone will talk about at school tomorrow.

Life & Love

7

Today is my first day of college classes and I'm feeling both intimidated and ready for something new.

I attended freshman orientation for the past several days. It was heavy on fun and light on orientation but did little to calm my fears. What if I can't make it? What if everyone thinks I'm stupid? What if I flunk out and get shipped to Vietnam, or worse, go back to Lima and live with my dad? I have no answers and no one to tell me everything will be okay. I'm on my own. Failure is not an option, but the what-ifs keep popping up.

Last Monday, the dean of students told us, "Welcome to Kent State University!" He said we would have a unique experience at KSU and encouraged us to try as many new things as possible. As we leave the auditorium, we are given the standard blue and gold beanie hats to wear during Frosh Week. We are supposed to wear the hat and remove it, *dink,* upon demand by an upperclassman. It seems an antiquated and stupid tradition. I put mine on as we leave but take it off on the way to my dorm, vowing never to wear it again. This is a tradition well past its time.

In addition to official orientation events like movies and mixers, unofficial events occur after hours in the dorms. Smoking is not permitted, which is fine with me, but late last Monday night, I'm sitting in my room talking with my roommates and smell something burning. I look at Randy. "What is that awful smell?"

"Man, you *is* a white boy from the sticks. That is Mary Jane, pot, grass. You know, marijuana."

Of course, I had heard of marijuana, but I didn't know anyone who used it. I try to play it cool and say, "Yeah, okay." I'm sure I fail miserably because Randy laughs and goes back to playing records on the stereo system which he had declared off limits to Carl and me.

Last Tuesday's freshman orientation was more of the same, but late that night, the third floor of Clark Hall got wild. I am with a group of guys in the hallway talking about the orientation events that day when one of the guys, Jay, suggests, "You know, this hallway is nice and slippery. It will make a super Slip 'N Slide." Everyone on our floor knows what he's talking about. Slip 'N Slide is a sixteen-foot-long strip of yellow plastic that you set up in your backyard and wet down using a garden hose. You take off running, hit the plastic on your butt or stomach, and slide to the end.

The dorm hallway floor is made of hard vinyl tile that is waxed and very shiny. But we don't have a garden hose. Jay goes to the end of the hallway, where a maid's closet has a water basin on the floor and hot- and cold-water faucets above the basin. Jay finds some old towels in the closet, stuffs them in the drain, and turns on both faucets simultaneously. The basin quickly overflows, and water spreads down the hallway.

Jay strips down to his whitey-tighties, runs, and dives headfirst onto the hallway water slide. He glides down the hallway and stops before he flies down the stairs. We all strip down to our underwear, take off running, and hit the water-covered floor on our very own Slip 'N Slide. We do it over and over until someone on the ground floor sees water cascading down the stairwell and alerts a resident advisor, who comes upstairs and puts a stop to our fun. We spend the next hour mopping up the mess.

Wednesday, during orientation week, is mass registration day when everyone on campus registers for fall quarter classes. It's organized pandemonium. Each student is given a number and approximate time to enter Wills Gym, where registration occurs. First, you go to University Auditorium to check two big white boards on the stage that indicate which course sections are closed. When your assigned number is posted, you can enter the gym. Ten stations are set up where you must pick your classes and complete registration. It's a trial-and-error process. By the time you decide which courses and section times you want, and try to register for them, inevitably, some are no longer available. So, you start all over. If you successfully make it through all ten stations, you win and are registered for classes, which start the following Monday.

Our freshman orientation student leader tells us that 20,913 students will go through mass registration today and that 7,428 are freshmen. The organizers post a range of numbers indicating that my assigned number is ready for registration. I enter Wills Gym and go through the process. I have difficulty getting a geography elective for my social studies major. I find an open section of Geography of Europe and successfully register for it. Finally, I'm done. Our orientation leader tells us that we might be back again next Saturday for Drop and Add in case we want to change classes. He warns us that only those classes still having open seats will be available.

After a long day of battling mass registration, I am ready for some fun. Word has circulated throughout Clark Hall that tonight, we will do a panty raid on Allyn, the girls' dorm just across the lawn. Shortly before 9:00, I join about a hundred other guys outside our dorm. Each room in Allyn has a stationary picture window and two side windows that crank open. News of our impending raid must have gotten out to the girls because we can see several of them standing in front of their open windows.

At 9:00 on the dot, one of the guys from Clark yells, "*Ready, set, go!*" and we all run across the lawn to Allyn, yelling, "*We want panties! We want panties! We want panties!*" This continues until two girls from the fourth floor throw lacy panties from their windows. We jockey for position in a frantic scrum to catch them. The chant once again goes up, "*We want panties!*" Soon, many girls are tossing panties to the guys. I catch a black lace pair and think I've gone to heaven. The panty raid ends, and we return to Clark, showing off our bounty.

It's now Monday morning, and time for my first day of classes. I signed up for five courses: Calculus I, Geology 101, Geography of Europe, History of Mesopotamia, and English 160. I've been warned that it's a heavy schedule for a first-quarter freshman, but I think I can handle it.

I have all my classes today except English 160. I make it through calculus okay. It's a small class. The professor talks about her expectations and then hands out the syllabus. I've never heard the word syllabus and have no idea what it is. I soon learn that it is a schedule indicating the topics to be covered and listing the required books, assignments, and test dates.

I walk a short distance to my Geology 101 class, the size of which is the opposite of my calculus class. It's held in University Auditorium on Front Campus. Five hundred fellow students and I are trying to satisfy our science requirement. I've heard that Professor Glenn Frank is one of the best professors on campus. He is entertaining and informative, and his classes are engaging and always well-attended. Today, he is projecting slides onto a large movie screen at the front of the auditorium. I sit in the front row to focus on the professor and avoid any distractions. If I sit in the middle or rear of the class, I will likely focus on watching the girls more than the professor. Professor Frank discusses the differences between igneous, metamorphic, and sedimentary rocks and somehow makes the subject interesting. Go figure.

Next up is the Geography of Europe. I find the classroom in McGilvrey Hall and take a seat down front. As the professor starts his introduction, I immediately dislike him. He is pretentious, and whenever he opens his mouth, I cringe. At the end of class, I conclude he is a pompous ass. I will need to visit Drop and Add on Saturday.

After geography, I walk to Bowman Hall across the street from Satterfield and find my History of Mesopotamia class. I tried to get an introductory history course during mass registration, but none were available, so I selected this 200-level class. Most of the students in the class are sophomores and juniors. The professor quickly gets through the logistics and syllabus and starts lecturing on substantive material. Other students pull out spiral-bound notebooks and write down some things the professor says. I wonder why they're taking so many notes. I had purchased a single steno pad with spirals at the top that I thought would be sufficient for all my classes, and I have yet to write anything down.

I never took any notes in my classes at Lima Senior High and never brought home any books. I listened to the teacher and then did homework in a study hall, or if I didn't complete the reading before class, I would read the material as the teacher was teaching. It was never a problem. Most of the time, I got Bs, but sometimes I also got Cs and a few As. It was also never an issue at home. If I didn't bring home an F, nobody seemed to care what grades I received. Neither my mom nor my dad ever asked me about home-work. One time, in junior high, I did bring books home, and my dad warned, "Make sure you take care of those goddamn books. I sure the fuck am not paying for any damage you do to those books." So, it was clear to me that I should not bring any books home from school.

The history lecture is boring, but I take a few notes mostly to conform to what everyone else is doing. I only have about half a page of notes in my steno pad when class ends, and they are mostly indecipherable.

After my history class, I head back to the dorm and find Randy packing his suitcase as I enter the room.

"You're not dropping out already, are you?"

He laughs. "No, I'm switching rooms. A guy I know just lost his roommate, so I got approval from Residence Life Services to change rooms. He has a double, so I'm gonna leave you two white boys and room with a Brother in Tri-Towers."

I am a little surprised but not shocked. Neither Carl nor I have anything in common with Randy. He seems streetwise and worldly, and we are just two white boys from the sticks. I tell him, "Good luck with the new roommate. See you around."

I leave my room and wonder if I had done something to cause Randy to want to move. Besides the stereo incident and the fact that he is black, and I am white, nothing specific comes to mind. Randy is a cool dude, to be sure, and maybe the two hicks from the sticks are damaging his image. I don't have a clue. I decide I can't do anything about it, but the upside is that our triple room has just become a double. Residence Life might move someone else into our room. We'll have to wait and see.

I need to purchase my textbooks, so I walk back toward McGilvrey Hall and across Lincoln Street to DuBois Book Store. Some upper-class student leaders told me during orientation that this was the best place to buy textbooks. They also recommended buying used books whenever possible because I could save twenty-five to thirty-three percent versus the cost of new ones. I had budgeted $75 for books because I knew they would be expensive. My tuition, room, and board total $495 per quarter. KSU awarded me a federal Basic Education Opportunity Grant, which will cover those costs. I also took out a $300 student loan. I hope all of that will get me through this academic year. I buy all used books for $61.20. I am below budget.

KSU has also offered me the Federal Work-Study program, which will provide me with additional spending money. I've been assigned to work in the audiovisual (AV) department and have my first meeting with them this afternoon at 4:00 to understand more about the program and what kind of work I will be doing.

Back at my dorm, Randy and his belongings are gone, but Carl is there, and I tell him about Randy moving to a new dorm. Carl is about as low-key as they come and seems nonplussed about the whole thing.

After cleaning up a bit, I walk over to the Education building on Front Campus, where the AV department is located, and meet with the department head. He tells me I can work up to fifteen hours per week and will be paid $1.45 per hour.

"We have a film library in the back, which I will show you in a moment," he says, pointing over his shoulder. "Most of the time, you will be repairing and cleaning movie film. In addition, you may be asked to set up overhead projectors or movie projectors and load movies onto the movie projectors. Does that sound good to you?"

"Sure," I reply. "I'm looking forward to working here. Thanks for the job."

He shows me the back room where the movies are stored. There are thousands of them in round metal canisters labeled with identification numbers. Most are documentaries or technical films for specific college courses. A printed master catalog lists every movie by name and its location in the film library. He also shows me the large splicing machines and asks one of the workers to demonstrate how to piece together two sections of broken film. It seems straightforward, so I don't think I'll have a problem doing this work.

We look at my class schedule to determine what hours I can work each week. All my classes are in the mornings, so I am free every afternoon. I agree to work Tuesdays, Wednesdays, and

Thursdays from 2:00 to 5:00. On Saturdays when I have no classes, I will work from 8:00 to 2:00. No sleeping in for me on Saturday.

I will earn $21.75 per week, or about $18 after taxes, which will be enough spending money to get me through each week. I start this Wednesday.

Life & Love

8

Drop and Add last Saturday was our final chance to change our schedules. I knew I had to do something about my Geography of Europe course. Carl tells me he also needs to go to Drop and Add, so we head to Wills Gym and prepare for another course selection battle.

Before coming to KSU, I decided that I wanted to teach math or history, so I enrolled in the School of Education. I'll work toward a Bachelor of Science in Secondary Education with a double major in math and social studies. I'm already thinking about job prospects after graduation. Having a double major will double my chances of finding a teaching position. I need a geography elective for my social studies major, so I want to drop the horrible geography class I'm in now and add a different geography course with a different professor.

Wills Gym is a madhouse. Hundreds of students are sitting on the floor staring at a two-story, fifty-foot-wide board with cards listing every available class. After much trial and error in switching classes, I am ready to add Geography of U.S. and Canada and drop the other class. I visit several stations in the gym to get stamped approvals and successfully make the change.

It's Monday and the beginning of my second week of classes. I hope I made a good choice in Drop and Add. I have no more opportunities to change classes.

I go to my calculus and geology classes. Next up, Geography of U.S. and Canada. At Drop and Add, I was able to get the same time slot as the class I dropped, so nothing changed in my schedule. It's a short walk to McGilvrey Hall. The classroom holds about sixty students and has unbroken rows of long tables with chairs behind them. I walk toward the front of the classroom and, in the second row, see the back of a girl with shoulder-length, dark brown hair. She turns, sees me, and smiles. That is all it takes. I sit in the chair beside her. She is beautiful. I think to myself, I could really get into that.

We start to talk, and it's an easy conversation. I tell her, "I'm Johnny, John."

She asks, "Well, which is it, Johnny or John?"

"My friends call me Johnny."

"I'm Katie, and most of my friends call me Katie."

I laugh. "Hi, Katie, it's good to meet you."

We have a few minutes before class starts, so I ask, "Where are you from?"

"Cleveland, and you?"

"Lima. It's a blue-collar town of about fifty thousand in the middle of corn and soybean fields in northwestern Ohio." I think, small-town guy meets big-town girl.

She smiles at me again, and I know I am smitten. She has the warmest smile and the brightest blue eyes I've ever seen. She's about five foot seven and slender but with curves in all the right places.

The professor starts the class and says something about the syllabus and what we will cover, but paying attention to what he is saying is tough. I glance at Katie, then back at the professor, then back at Katie, and then repeat. Finally, and mercifully, the class ends.

"Are you heading to another class?" I ask.

"Yes, English at Satterfield Hall."

"I'm heading to Bowman Hall for a history class. I think Bowman is close to Satterfield. Do you mind if I walk with you?"

"Not at all. Maybe you can keep me from getting lost."

"Or maybe we'll just get lost together." We both laugh.

Having studied the campus map the night before, I have a pretty good idea of where we are going, and Katie also seems to know the right direction.

"What's your major?" I ask.

"Nursing. What's yours?"

"Secondary Education with a double major in math and social studies."

Her eyes open wide. "That sounds like a lot of work."

"Maybe, but I think I can do it," I say. "What dorm are you in? I'm a freshman and live in Clark."

She says, "I am also a freshman and live in Terrace Hall."

I have no idea where Terrace Hall is, so I ask, "Is that part of small group housing where all the jocks live?"

She laughs. "No, it's near Front Campus over by the Education building."

As we walk to our classes, our conversation is easy. I learn that Katie lives with her mother and older brother at her grandmother's house on the west side of Cleveland. Her brother just recently completed a four-year tour with the Navy and is now a surgical assistant at a suburban hospital. Her mom and aunt own a beauty salon in downtown Cleveland. I tell her that my older brother, Dennis, is in the Navy, serving on USS *Joseph P. Kennedy*, a destroyer. I tell her about my three other brothers and older sister.

I walk with Katie to Satterfield Hall but don't want to leave her, so I say, "Would you like to get some lunch at the Student Union after you finish your classes?"

To my surprise, she says, "That would be great." We agree to meet at the Student Union near Front Campus at 1:00.

Shortly before 1:00, I head over to the Student Union. My mood changes dramatically as I think about the beautiful girl I will see. It seems too good to be true that I meet the perfect girl after only a week of classes.

Katie is waiting for me just outside the entrance. Man, is she hot. Long auburn hair, crystal blue eyes, and a great body. I'm in trouble. She's early. Nice. We go inside and get in line. I order a cheeseburger, fries, and Coke. Katie orders a grilled cheese sandwich and Sprite.

We find a table. "How was your English class?" I ask.

"It's going to be good. I like the professor. She's new and seems very excited about teaching. Plus, I've always done well in English. How was your history class?"

"I'm a little concerned. It's an upper-level class with sophomores and juniors. I guess I'll have to see how it goes."

"Well, at least it's a class in your major, so it should be interesting."

"Where did you go to high school?"

"Magnificat, an all-girls Catholic school in Rocky River, west of Cleveland."

"It must have been tough socially going to an all-girls school."

"Not really. St. Joseph's, an all-boys Catholic high school, isn't far away. The two schools get together for social events."

"Did you bring any of those St. Joseph guys with you to Kent?"

She laughs a bit. "No, but I've been seeing a guy from St. Joe's. He still lives in Cleveland."

"Oh, I guess I have some competition."

Katie looks at me with those blue eyes and smiles. "I guess so."

I think, she must like what she sees. Otherwise, she would just tell me to take a hike. I won't let some guy in Cleveland stop me from talking to Katie. There's no ring on her finger, so it can't be that serious.

The rest of lunch could have been awkward, but it isn't. I am still very interested in getting to know Katie, and she seems interested in getting to know me. The conversation flows freely, and we talk about our hometowns, our friends, our faith, and how we came to enroll at Kent.

When we part ways two hours later, my infatuation with Katie has only increased. We say our goodbyes, and I tell her, "See you in geography Wednesday."

She smiles. "I'm looking forward to it."

Bayonets & Bullets

9

Saturday afternoon, May 2, 1970 • Kent State University, Kent, Ohio

Back in my dorm room after my shift at the AV department, I keep feeling like I am missing something. I don't understand why anyone would think the Ohio National Guard is needed in Kent or at KSU. My roommate, Carl, is a quiet guy, but he seems to have a good network of friends who know what is happening on campus.

I ask him, "Have you heard anything about the governor sending the Ohio National Guard to the Kent or the campus?"

"No, I haven't. What's happening?"

I tell him about the news report on the radio earlier this afternoon, which stated that the mayor had spoken to the governor's office and was considering making a formal request for assistance from the Ohio National Guard.

"I didn't hear anything about the Guard, but I did hear from a friend of mine that there is going to be a rally tonight at 7:30 on the Commons."

"What's happening at the rally?"

"I don't know exactly, but my friend said says a lot of people are talking about the ROTC building and feel that ROTC should not be on campus."

I tell Carl I am heading to the cafeteria to get some lunch and that I will see him later.

After lunch, I phone my girlfriend's room and ask her if she wants to get together later that afternoon. We agree to meet at The Hub at The Student Union at 4:00. When I arrive, there seem to be many more people than normal for a Saturday afternoon with nothing special going on. I find my girlfriend at a table with two chairs.

I kiss her and sit down across from her. "Have you heard that the mayor is considering calling up the Ohio National Guard?"

"No. What for?"

"After what happened last night downtown, he thinks outside instigators are coming into Kent and on campus to cause trouble."

I tell her about what I heard on the radio. She says, "That sounds crazy. Nothing has happened on campus. We don't need the National Guard."

A few minutes later, a student comes into The Hub and starts passing out flyers from Robert E. Matson, vice president for Student Affairs, and Frank Frisina, student body president. It reads:

STUDENT INFORMATION SHEET

BETWEEN THE HOURS OF 11:00 P.M. AND 3:00 A.M. LAST NIGHT, THERE WERE DISTURBANCES ON NORTH WATER STREET AND MAIN STREET WITH THE TROUBLE STARTING AROUND J.B.'S AND ENDING AT THE ARCH ON CAMPUS AT LINCOLN AND MAIN. DUE TO PROPERTY DAMAGE AND PERSONAL INJURIES, THE MAYOR OF KENT HAS PLACED A CURFEW ON THE CITY OF KENT.

CURFEW IS HEREBY DEFINED AS A PROHIBITION AGAINST ANY PERSON OR PERSONS WALKING, RUNNING, LOITERING, STANDING, OR MOTORING UPON ANY ALLEY, STREET, HIGHWAY PUBLIC PROPERTY OR VACANT PREMISES WITHIN THE CORPORATE LIMITS OF THE CITY OF KENT, EXCEPTING

PERSONS OFFICIALLY DESIGNATED TO DUTY WITH REFERENCE TO SAID CIVIL EMERGENCY.

NOTE: THE POLICE DEPARTMENT OF KENT HAS SAID THAT MOTORISTS PASSING THROUGH KENT FOR A GOOD REASON MAY BE STOPPED BUT WILL NOT BE ARRESTED.

ANY PERSON VIOLATING THE PROVISIONS OF THIS ORDINANCE OR EXECUTIVE ORDER ISSUED PURSUANT THERETO SHALL BE GUILTY OF AN OFFENSE AGAINST THE CITY OF KENT AND SHALL BE PUNISHABLE BY A FINE NOT EXCEEDING $100 AND OR IMPRISONMENT IN THE CITY JAIL NOT EXCEEDING THREE MONTHS. (FROM THE MAYOR'S ORDER).

THE CURFEW IS IN EFFECT FROM 8:00 P.M. TO 6:00 A.M. EVERY NIGHT UNTIL THE MAYOR LIFTS THE CURFEW.

LIQUOR, BEER, AND WINE SALES ARE PROHIBITED BY LAW IN KENT.

STUDENT LEADERS AND FACULTY MEMBERS SHALL BE COMING AROUND THIS EVENING TO DISCUSS THE CURRENT SITUATION. THERE IS A CENTER FOR INFORMATION AT 672-2840, 7887, 2525, WHICH YOU SHOULD CALL IF YOU WANT TO CHECK OUT THE TRUTH OF A RUMOR.

THE COURT HAS ISSUED AN INJUNCTION WHICH APPLIES TO ALL PERSONS, STUDENT AND NON-STUDENT, ON THE MAIN CAMPUS OF KENT STATE UNIVERSITY WHICH IN EFFECT WILL MAKE IT

CONTEMPT OF COURT TO PARTICIPATE IN DESTRUCTIVE ACTIVITY ON CAMPUS.

THE FOLLOWING ACTIVITIES ARE ON CAMPUS TONIGHT:

1. BAND IN UNION – 7:00 TO 12:00
2. TWO BANDS AND FOOD IN TRI TOWERS –7:00–12:00
3. SAB FLICK IN BOWMAN HALL, LECTURE B, 'THE DEVIL AT 4 O'CLOCK' 6:00 P.M.–9:00 P.M.
4. FILM FESTIVAL IN UNIVERSITY AUDITORIUM.
5. BAND AND RECREATIONAL ACTIVITIES IN EASTWAY AT 8:00 P.M.
6. FOLK MUSIC – BEALL LOUNGE – 8:00 P.M.
7. SCHOOL OF MUSIC – DENNIS LANG – PIANO: 8:30 P.M. M&S RECITAL HALL

We finish reading the flyer and I look at my girlfriend. "Sounds like they don't want a repeat of what happened downtown last night."

She says, "It sounds serious."

The Hub is crowded, and the noise level has suddenly increased with the distribution of the flyer declaring a curfew.

Mayor Satrom was first elected to office last November. Imposing a curfew and calling the governor about the National Guard seem like overreactions. The Kent Police handled it last night. We have no reason to think they can't keep the peace. I think the mayor's lack of experience is showing.

We also hear some talk about a rally on the Commons this evening. No one seems to know who organized it or why other than to protest ROTC on campus.

My girlfriend says, "After what happened downtown last night, I'm going to stay in my room tonight."

I say, "That's probably a good idea. I may go to the Commons to see what is happening, but I have mixed feelings about ROTC, so won't participate in any anti-ROTC activities."

She says, "Okay but be careful. You saw how quickly things can turn nasty when everyone gets riled up."

I say, "Don't worry. I'm not going to be a part of any craziness."

We continue to talk and listen to good music being broadcast over the P.A. system by WKSU. Around 5:00, we hear a special news report:

"Mayor LeRoy M. Satrom has declared an 8:00 p.m. curfew for tonight. The mayor says he wants all citizens, including students, to be off the streets by 8:00 p.m. Here are the specific rules as ascertained by WKSU radio after consultation with the Kent City Police and the Kent State University Police:

1. *"Nobody may walk on the streets within the city limits of the Town of Kent after 8:00 p.m. this evening.*
2. *Citizens and students may drive through Kent only if they are headed for a specific destination.*
3. *You may not drive in Kent if you simply plan to 'loiter in your car' or drive around to see what is going on.*
4. *Kent City Police will be stopping any car which looks suspicious and checking out its passengers tonight.*
5. *If individuals are found to be in violation of the above city-wide curfew rules, they will be brought to the Kent City Police Station and charged with curfew violation.*
6. *All bars, stores, movie theaters, and places of business will close at 8:00 p.m. this evening.*
7. *Police do not want to see anyone on the streets of Kent after 8:00 p.m. this evening.*
8. *At this time the above rules do not apply for students remaining on the Kent State campus. There is no curfew on the KSU campus, and students will have the same freedom as always. But only while remaining on campus. Students may not walk on City streets.*

"Once again, that curfew goes into effect at 8:00 p.m. this evening. If you have any questions concerning these regulations, please do not call the police. We will repeat them every half hour."

The WKSU announcer gives us a few more details about the curfew, but since neither my girlfriend nor I have a car on campus, we aren't going to be doing any driving around town. So, we are confined to campus for the indefinite future. With that sobering news, we both head back to our dorms.

Before I leave, she says, "Please be careful tonight. The police are on edge from what happened last night, and anything could set them off."

"I'll be careful. See you tomorrow."

"Please call me tonight when you get back to your dorm room. Even if it's late."

"I will. Don't worry. I'll be okay."

When I return to Clark Hall and enter our dorm room, it's hot and stuffy inside. I open the windows and the warm spring air seems to give me a fresh perspective on everything.

Carl is sitting at his desk reading a chemistry textbook. I sit at the desk next to him and ask if he has heard anything new.

"I've been in our room all afternoon and haven't heard anything," he says.

Carl can be a bit of a nerd, so I tell him about the town-wide curfew and what I'd heard at The Hub about tonight's rally on the Commons.

Carl says, "Anything could happen tonight. If you go out, you'd better be careful."

"Yep, it could get ugly. I hope no one at the rally does anything stupid."

We head to Eastway cafeteria for dinner. Just before we get in line, on a side table I spot copies of the flyer I saw earlier this afternoon at The Hub. We get our food and find a seat.

Carl asks me, "Have you heard any more about whether Governor Rhodes will send the Ohio National Guard to Kent?"

"No, but the mayor thinks Kent is being invaded by the radical Weathermen and other outside agitators. I haven't noticed anyone like that on campus. He probably thinks the governor's office is a lifeline. I just hope his inexperience doesn't cause more problems."

Teens & Dreams

10

Saturday, June 19, 1965 • Lima, Ohio

At 2:00 in the morning. Mom jostles me awake and says it's time to go. She's done the same to Henry, Kevin, and Brian, who are sleeping on the bottom bunk. We are leaving for our annual trip to Fordyce, Arkansas, to see Grandma and Grandpa. Mom has three sisters and a brother living in Arkansas, so we will likely also see my aunts, uncles, and cousins.

We've taken this trip for as long as I can remember. It's eighteen hours, and we will drive straight through, only stopping for gas and bathroom breaks. Dad will do all the driving. Mom offers to drive, but he never lets her. Mom packs enough food and water so we don't have to stop at a restaurant. We leave in the middle of the night to arrive before sunset the next day, so we don't have to stay at a motel.

Dennis is not going with us. He graduated from Lima Senior High last year and had been living at home and working at Baldwin-Lima-Hamilton, a heavy construction equipment manufacturer. Dad told Dennis that after he turned eighteen, he would have to pay rent or move out. Dennis had been paying rent, but two months ago, he was laid off and hasn't found another job.

Dad told him, "You still got to pay goddamned rent. There's no free rides here. You're eighteen. Either pay rent or get the hell out!"

"I'll pay the back rent when I find a new job," he told Dad.

"Pay it now or pack your stuff and get out." Dennis couldn't pay, so Dad kicked him out of the house last month. Dennis has been staying at a friend's house. It was a sad day when he left. Mom was crying, Susie was crying, and I saw tears in Dennis's eyes. I was sad too and hated my dad even more if that's possible.

Susie is also not going with us. She graduated from Lima Senior High last week and is a cashier at Pangles, the local supermarket chain. Susie will turn eighteen in August, but Dad hasn't said whether he will start charging her rent.

Mom loads the Ford station wagon with the supplies. She lays the third row of seats flat and covers the area with long pieces of yellow foam that look like they came out of a sofa bed. Henry and I grab our blankets and take the second row. Kevin and Brian lie on the foam pads. Mom lays a blanket over each of them, and they are asleep before we pull away. On trips when we were younger, I remember that both sets of rear seats would be folded down, and all six of us kids would lie in the back on the foam pads.

By 2:30, we are on the road. It is dark, so we can't see anything interesting out the window, and I fall asleep quickly. When I wake up, the sun is shining.

"Mom, where are we?" I ask, rubbing my eyes and squinting.

"Kentucky. We just went through Indiana. We're making good time."

Shortly, everyone else wakes up, and we all need to use the bathroom. Mom says, "Hold it a little longer, and we'll stop at a roadside rest area."

About thirty minutes later, I plead, "I really have to go." Dad reluctantly pulls to the side of the road. All four of us boys jump out of the passenger side, drop our pants, and start watering the weeds on the side of the road.

We no sooner pile back in the car when Kevin whines, "I'm hungry."

"Me too!"

"Me too!"

"Me too!" says each of us in turn.

Mom gives us each a fried egg sandwich on toasted Wonder Bread she made the night before. She also gives us a thermos to share filled with orange juice, the kind that comes as canned frozen concentrate, and you mix it with a can of water. The orange juice is still cold and delicious. Mom also gives Dad an egg sandwich, and we are back on the road within ten minutes.

Mom navigates using a paper map. Sometimes we are on one of the new interstate highways, but most of the time, we are on two-lane roads and pass through small town after small town. To me, one looks like the other.

Some kids at school said they must wear seatbelts when riding in their cars. I ask Mom, "Why doesn't our car have seatbelts?"

Mom explains, "When you buy a new car, seatbelts are an option, but since we don't use them, we don't need them. Anyway, Dad bought a used station wagon that came without seatbelts. You boys will be safe enough without them."

Around noon Dad stops for gas, and we all get a real restroom break. Mom passes out boiled ham and mustard sandwiches on more Wonder Bread. We each take sips from a jug of water to wash down the sandwiches. Dad also eats, and in short order, we are back on the road again.

The four of us boys have been quiet for most of the trip. We know Dad doesn't like it when we fight or argue in the car. After lunch, we start to get antsy, and it isn't long before Dad shouts, "You boys shut the fuck up and stop all that goddamned noise. If I have to stop this car to put a stop to it, I'll whup your sorry asses!"

We are quiet for a little while, and then the arguing about everything and nothing starts up again. I hear Dad say to Mom, "Hand me my jar." Mom looks at him and then reluctantly hands Dad a Mason jar half full of clear liquid. Dad unscrews the lid, takes a sip, screws the cap back on, and sets the jar between his legs while driving sixty to seventy miles per hour. He unscrews the lid every ten or fifteen minutes and takes another sip. Neither Mom nor Dad says anything about what he's drinking, but I know it's moonshine. I saw cases of the stuff in the back of the station wagon after Dad made one of his trips to Middlesboro, Kentucky.

We are in Tennessee and will go through Nashville on the way to Arkansas. Dad and Mom are both country music fans, so Mom finds a country music station on the AM radio.

"Are we going to stop in Nashville and see one of those country music singers, like Hank Williams, you are always listening to on the radio?" I ask

"You goddamn, stupid son of bitch, Hank Williams is dead. How do you suppose we are going to see him?" Dad growls.

I didn't say anything. After a while, Mom says quietly, "We need to keep drivin' so we can get to Grandma's before dark."

Just as the sun starts to set, Dad pulls to a stop, and Mom announces, "We're here!" I look out the window to see a familiar two-story, white house with a wraparound front porch.

Soon, Grandma is hugging us and giving us kisses, which I shy away from. Grandpa is a tall man but solid. He looks at each of us, tousles our hair, and says, "Y'all are sure growin' like weeds. Come on in. Ma has some iced tea waiting for y'all."

I pass on the iced tea. I had tried it on previous visits and did not care for the taste. Grandma hands me a glass of ice water instead, and says, "Johnny Joe, look at you. You're taller'n me and growin' up to be a handsome young man." I smile and thank her for the water. Almost everyone is taller than Grandma. She is short by any standard, definitely under five feet.

Grandma asks if we're hungry. Mom laughs. "Those boys are always hungry!"

Grandma brings out a platter of cold fried chicken along with potato salad. She puts out a stack of plates and silverware and tells us to help ourselves. She doesn't have to tell us twice. We each grab a piece of chicken and start inhaling the food.

After dinner, Mom says, "You boys been sittin' too long. Run along and burn off some of that energy you got bottled up."

I ask Grandma if she has an empty jar with a cap we could use. "Come on," I tell my brothers. "Let's go catch some fireflies." I race out the front door holding tightly to the jar, with Henry, Kevin, and Brian close on my heels.

When we come inside about an hour later, Grandma shows us where we will be sleeping. She has put a couple of mattresses on the floor of her sewing room with a blanket and pillow for each of us. The four of us have plenty of room, more than in our bunk at home, so we settle in, and I soon fall asleep.

Teens & Dreams

11

Sunday, June 20, 1965 • Fordyce, Arkansas

The mouth-watering smells of bacon frying and something baking in the oven wake me up and I rush downstairs. Grandma is at her stove, and Mom is at the kitchen table drinking coffee.

"Breakfast will be ready *dreckly*," Grandma says with her Southern drawl. "Orange juice and ice water are on the dining room table. Help yourself."

"What are you baking, Grandma?" I ask.

"There's biscuits in the oven, and I'm cookin' bacon and eggs. That sound good?"

"It all smells delicious." I sit at the dining room table, pour myself a glass of orange juice, and Grandma brings out a plate of the biggest homemade biscuits I've ever seen. I grab one and slather it with butter. "Grandma, these are the best biscuits ever," I say.

She smiles. "Thank you, hon. The bacon and eggs are almost ready."

The best part about being at Grandma's is that Dad is never around. I'm not sure where he goes or what he does, but I rarely see him before bedtime. He is not there to yell at me, and I can't remember when he ever whipped us while we were at Grandma's. It almost seems like it is a vacation from Dad. Perfect.

After breakfast, Mom takes us boys to a public park with

swings, monkey bars, and a merry-go-round. At thirteen, soon to be fourteen, I am a little old for the park, but I go along anyway because I know Henry, Kevin, and Brian will have fun. I remember coming to this park when I was seven or eight. It would have been shortly after I learned how to read because I saw a WHITES ONLY sign over the drinking fountain. I asked Mom what that meant, and she said, "The coloreds can't use this fountain, only white people are allowed to use it."

"Where are the coloreds supposed to drink?"

She pointed to a drinking fountain at the park's other end, far from the playground. "Over there."

"It's not that way at home. Why's it that way here?"

"It's just always been that way. Now off ya git. Go on and play."

It's 1965. A lot has changed in Arkansas in seven years. I look around the playground and don't see any WHITES ONLY signs. All the fountains and restrooms are now open to everyone. Everything about Arkansas has always interested me. I learned in my eighth-grade history class last year that President Eisenhower brought in the Army to enforce the integration of Central High School in Little Rock. We also learned that April 9 this year marked the one-hundredth anniversary of the end of the Civil War. People that were slaves during the Civil War might still be alive. They would be over one hundred years old. If I knew one of them, I could talk to someone living during the Civil War. Amazing!

Mom had arranged with her sister for me to stay at her house for a few days and have some fun with my cousins, Ronnie, and Jim Bob. After visiting the park, Mom drops me off at their farm, and I imme-diately run off with my cousins. They show me their horses, and Ronnie says, "We can ride 'em if you want."

"I've never ridden a horse but would love to learn."

"Okay, let's saddle 'em up and I can show you the rest of the farm."

"Great!"

Ronnie asks, "Do you have a pair of blue jeans or just those cut-offs you're wearin'?"

"I just have the cut-offs. Why?"

"Well, you may get a little chafed wearin' those while you ride."

"I don't care. Let's go.

We saddle the horses, and Ronnie shows me how to get on by putting my left foot in the left stirrup and hoisting my right leg over the saddle. Ronnie, Jim Bob, and I ride over to the pond.

"That pond is full of crappie, and we can go fishin' later if you like," Jim Bob says. "The fish really bite just before sunset."

"I love to fish. I'm ready when you are," I tell him.

Jim Bob replies, "Okay, we'll do that later this afternoon."

We ride over to the chicken coop, and Ronnie shows me how to retrieve the eggs without disturbing the chickens.

Ronnie warns, "Always shut the chicken coop door when ya leave. A lot of coyotes are in the woods, and they could kill all the chickens in a single night if the door is left open."

I nod my head in understanding. "Okay. Not a problem."

"We also need to slaughter a chicken for Sunday dinner today, and I can show ya how we do that."

I look at Ronnie, wide-eyed. I've never seen a chicken slaughtered before, and I'm not sure what it involves, but I tell him, "Okay."

After we've ridden for about half an hour, Ronnie asks, "You ready to run these horses?"

I hesitate. "Sure, I think so."

Ronnie laughs. "We'll start with a trot first, then break 'em into a gallop and let 'em run. Just say giddy-up and shake the reins loose."

Ronnie and Jim Bob do just that, and their horses trot away. "Giddy-up," I say and let the reins go loose. My horse obediently follows Ronnie's in a trot. The up-and-down motion of the trot is uncomfortable and painful.

Ronnie sees me grimacing. "You should use the stirrups when you trot to take the pressure off your butt." He shows me how, and I try it, but it only helps a bit. Both my butt and balls still hurt, just not as much.

Ronnie says, "Enough trottin.' Let's get 'em gallopin' and let 'em run. First, say 'Giddy-up' again, let the reins loose, and give a light kick to the horse's sides with both heels. Then hold on to the saddle horn with one hand and your reins in the other."

Ronnie demonstrates, and his horse breaks into a run. He looks like a cowboy racing after the bad guys. Jim Bob takes off and does the same. I try to do what Ronnie did, and my horse takes off into a gallop, just not as fast as Ronnie's horse, which is good because I am holding onto the saddle horn with both hands. It's like we are flying. The horse seems to glide over the ground. Why would anyone trot when they could gallop? The pain in my haunches immediately goes away as my horse breaks into a run. It is both frightening and exhilarating!

Soon Ronnie pulls back on his reins, saying, "Whoaaaa!" Jim Bob and I do the same, and our horses come to a stop.

"Wow! Can we do it again?" I ask.

Ronnie says, "We can let 'em gallop a couple of times, but we don't want to overheat 'em in this hot weather. It will take 'em a lot longer to cool down after they been a'runnin'.'"

We gallop some more and then walk the horses back to the barn. Ronnie shows me how to give them water and make sure they have completely cooled down before putting them in a stall.

After we put the horses away, Ronnie says it's time to get one of the chickens ready for dinner. I watch in awe as Jim Bob catches one. Ronnie cuts off the head with an axe, drains the blood, puts it in boiling water to loosen the feathers, and then has Jim Bob pluck them. Jim Bob then takes the chicken to his mom so that she can prepare Sunday dinner.

We go inside and wash up. The TV in the living room is broadcasting a news report about the war in Vietnam. I've been paying close attention to the Vietnam War. My brother, Dennis, registered for the draft when he turned eighteen last year, and I am afraid he might soon be drafted and shipped to Vietnam. The reporter says the first combat troops—thirty-five hundred marines—arrived in Vietnam on March 8. President Lyndon Johnson then authorized increasing the troops in Vietnam to seventy-five thousand and increasing the draft to seventeen thousand men monthly. The report says that General Westmoreland, the commander in Vietnam, has requested that President Johnson increase the number of troops to one hundred twenty-five thousand and the draft to thirty-five thousand men per month. I am sure Dennis will be drafted and sent to Vietnam.

I know what could happen to Dennis in Vietnam, and it frightens me.

Life & Love

12

Monday, October 20, 1969 • Kent State University, Kent, Ohio

Last week was a wake-up call for me. I reflect on it as I walk to my 11:00 class at Bowman Hall.

A week ago, I took my first midterm college test in History of Mesopotamia. I had never taken a test like this before and didn't know what to expect. We were told to bring a blank "Blue Book" to the test.

I've never heard of a "Blue Book," so I go to DuBois bookstore and ask if they have any. The clerk directs me to the aisle with tall stacks of them. Each blank booklet has a blue cover and twenty pages with wide-ruled lines. On the front cover are the words "Blue Book." I'm sure I will need these for other exams, so I buy five of them.

The history professor passes out a single sheet containing five essay questions. We are directed to write each question in the "Blue Book," followed by our answers. The questions are very specific regarding events that occurred in the early history of Mesopotamia. I've been to every class but haven't taken many notes. I did the readings, but there were many pages to read, so I skimmed over much of the material. I knew other students studied for exams, but I wasn't sure what or how to study. I thought I was ready for the test. I am now faced with answering questions about material I know we covered in class, but I have few details to enhance my basic answers.

Each of my answers fills less than a page. As I finish the exam, I look around and see that the other students are still writing and using multiple pages for each answer. I'm concerned.

Last Friday, the professor returned our graded exams. On the front cover of mine is a big red D- with a fat red circle around it. My jaw drops, and my heart sinks. I'm in trouble, big trouble. I know I must maintain at least a 2.0 GPA to stay at KSU. If I flunk out, I will lose my 2-S deferment from the draft. Within months I will be drafted and heading to Vietnam. What I am doing is not working. I need to change the way I study and prepare for tests.

I have no one to talk to about it, so I need to fix it myself. On Saturday, I go back to DuBois and purchase a full-sized spiral notebook for each class. Instead of scanning the required text reading over the weekend, I closely read the material that will be covered in my next class. Some of the sentences in my used textbook have been highlighted with a yellow marker. Those passages must have been important to the prior owner of the book. So, I purchase a yellow highlighter, and as I am reading, if something seems particularly important, I highlight it in yellow. Two things happen: I am reading these passages twice, once when I read them the first time and again when I highlight the passage; and the highlighted passages will help me review the material when it is time to study for an exam.

Back in my History of Mesopotamia class, I closely watch other students take notes. When they write down something the professor says, I write down the same thing. Then I write down even more. As often as I can, I write down what the professor says. If the professor is lecturing on something, it must be important since he can't possibly lecture on all the material in the book. After a while, I realize I do not have to write down every word the professor speaks, only the concepts and enough detail to jog my memory about the material he covered. Instead of a half page of notes in a steno pad, at the end of class, I end up with seven pages of notes in my full-sized spiral notebook. I hope I am now on the right track.

Katie and I continue to sit next to each other in the second row of Geography of U.S. and Canada. We chat before the start of lectures and occasionally write notes to each other during the lectures.

This morning, shortly after the lecture starts, Katie notices my new notebook and writes at the top of the first page: You have a new notebook. Are you tired of taking shorthand on your steno pad?

Under her note, I write: Yep, I have a new study plan and need to take a lot of notes.

Great, you can take notes for me too.

My notes will cost you.

How much?

A Coke at The Hub in the Student Union.

You come cheap. She looks my way and smiles.

I write on her notebook: You're distracting me. She smiles at me again and then looks back at the professor.

I am totally infatuated with Katie. I know she has a boyfriend back home, and his name is Chuck something. It doesn't matter. For almost every class, we arrive early and talk, and then after class, I walk her to her next class. So, I see her at least three times a week, and my heart fills every time. I know I can't ask her out on a date, but I can feel the sparks fly each time we are together, so something is happening. We talk about everything. As we walk to our next class this morning, I tell her about my date last Sunday with Carol.

I met Carol a couple of weeks ago while bowling with Carl at Eastway Center. Two perky, pretty girls are bowling in the alley next to us. While waiting for Carl to bowl, I sit down. One of the girls from the next lane is sitting directly behind me. Our seat backs touch each other.

I say, "Hi," and she says, "Hi," and soon we are chatting. I find out her name is Carol, and she is from Bay Village on Lake Erie, west of Cleveland. After bowling, I ask her if she wants to shoot some pool in the room next to the bowling alley.

"Sure," Carol says, "but first let me tell my friend what I'm doing," I tell Carl what is happening, and he heads back to our dorm. Carol returns and says, "I have to warn you, I'm not very good."

"No problem, neither am I." We have a good time, and I find out she lives in Allyn Hall across from my dorm. Over the next week, we meet for lunch a couple of times in the Eastway cafeteria.

Carol is interesting and very nice, so I ask her if she wants to go to the Donovan concert with me at Memorial Gym on Sunday, October 18. She says, "That will be nice. I like his music." So, it's a date. I feel attracted to Carol, but I have yet to feel the sparks with her that I do with Katie.

As I walk Katie to class, I tell her about the concert. It was the first one I'd been to on campus, so I was excited about going. It was also only my second concert ever. I saw The Supremes in Dayton, Ohio, last year.

I had previously told Katie about meeting Carol, but the concert was our first actual date. I tell Katie, "The concert started at 8:00, and we arrived about 7:30. It was packed. We had reserved seats close to the stage, about halfway up on the side of the gym. There was no warm-up band, so Donovan came on solo. He told the crowd in a mellow voice, 'We are going to get a natural high tonight.' Many people sort of nervously laughed about that. I think much of the crowd was already high before Donovan came out."

I look over at Katie and can tell she is listening intently. So, I continue, "For the first set, it was just Donovan and his guitar. He sang 'Jennifer Juniper' and 'Sunshine Superman.' Then he sang some songs I'd never heard. It was all good and very laidback. After about an hour, the first set ended, and he took a break."

Katie says, "It sounds like it was great. I've never been to a rock concert."

"Well, we should go sometime," I reply. She looks at me funny, and I realize what I said. "As friends, I mean. We can go Dutch if you like."

She again looks at me like she wants to say something, hesitates, then says, "Maybe. We'll see."

That is her way of telling me we are in uncharted territory here. I don't pursue the matter further, but instead, tell her about the rest of the concert. "After a thirty-minute break, Donovan returned accompanied by a guy playing a flute. They played some excellent easygoing music together. His last song of the night was 'Mellow Yellow'. It was cool."

Katie asks, "How did Carol like the concert?"

"She was grooving to the music and said it was great, so I think she enjoyed it."

"And then what happened?"

I look at her. "What do you mean?"

Katie says, "Well, did you go someplace else after the concert?"

"Oh, no, we just headed back to our rooms."

Katie says, "You seem to like Carol a lot."

I know I need to be careful here. "Yeah, having someone to go out with is fun." I do not go into further detail with Katie, but Carol and I shared several kisses and had a bit of a make-out session after we left Memorial Gym but before we got back to our dorms. She's a good kisser, and I think we both ended the night expecting to have more dates.

I walk Katie to Satterfield Hall and say goodbye. Every time I leave her, it is painful. If I could only tell Katie my true feelings, she would understand that neither Carol nor anyone else matters. I don't think I can have that conversation with Katie, at least not yet.

The war in Vietnam continues to rage and opposition to it continues to grow. Last Wednesday, October 15, 1969, was a nation-wide Vietnam Moratorium Day. Washington, D.C., and most major cities and college campuses planned protests, including Kent State. President White stated that classes would be optional so that those who wanted to attend the day's activities could do so, and those students who wanted to attend class could go to class.

I go to my 7:45 calculus class, then cut my other classes and attend the Moratorium activities that start at 9:00 on the old football field across from Bowman Hall. When I arrive shortly before the program begins, I'm not alone. Thousands of students stand in the bleachers talking. It's hard to estimate the actual number, but a good guess is around three thousand. A temporary stage and podium have been set up with a microphone and loudspeakers.

The activities start with a prayer followed by everyone singing the chorus to "Give Peace a Chance." After each of the anti-war speakers, students applaud and chant, *"Get out of Vietnam!"* and *"Bring the troops home now!"* One notable speaker, University Vice President and Provost Louis Harris, states he is not speaking on behalf of the University but rather as a private person, and he is against the war in Vietnam. This feels like an endorsement of my participation in this rally. I am not a radical, but I am against the war in Vietnam, and that voice needs to be heard. If my presence, along with thousands of others, can lend credibility to that cause, that is why I am here.

The speakers take a couple of hours and then announce that we will march peacefully through campus, down Main Street into downtown Kent, and return the same way. We march across campus toward Midway Drive, exit campus, and take a left on Main Street. I am concerned that the Peace March might turn violent, and I am prepared to leave if that happens. It is indeed peaceful. Marchers frequently sing the chorus to "Give Peace a Chance" and spontaneously erupt in chants of *"Get out of Vietnam now!"* and other slogans. Many of the marchers are holding protest signs. A banner stretching across the street reads in blood red letters: BRING ALL THE TROOPS HOME NOW! Other signs read: STOP THE WAR MACHINE, GIVE PEACE A CHANCE, STOP THE DEATH MACHINE, PEACE IS PATRIOTIC, and WHY WAR? Peace is

Patriotic captures my feelings. I love America. I know that many of the young men in Vietnam have been involuntarily drafted and would not be there if given a choice. Protesting for peace is my patriotic way of honoring our servicemen.

The only negative part of the Peace March occurs as we pass the Army recruiting office downtown. Protesters boo loudly and chant against the war, but then someone throws a rock through the front window. Everyone is startled by this incident, but it does not escalate into something more extreme. Several policemen following the march immediately position themselves in front of the recruiting office, and the march continues until we return to campus.

I feel good about my presence at the Vietnam Moratorium Rally and participation in the Peace March. If this march can prevent our troops from being killed in an unjust war, I have done my patriotic duty for my country.

Bayonets & Bullets

13

It's still daylight at 7:30 as I head over to the Commons to see if the rumor is true that there will be a rally tonight. It won't get dark until around 8:30, and I doubt anything will start before then. A couple of hundred people are standing around the Victory Bell at the east end of the Commons, but it doesn't look like anything organized is happening.

If the rally's purpose is to protest the invasion of Cambodia and the war in Vietnam, I want to be here. The world must hear that U.S. involvement in Vietnam and Cambodia is not okay. I want our soldiers to stop dying in Southeast Asia. I want our soldiers to come home. I want the draft to end now.

Around 7:45, several students chant, *"Down with Rotsee! Down with Rotsee!"* We all know that "Rotsee" is the colloquial way of pronouncing ROTC. That chant seems to energize the crowd, and someone decides to march to the dorms to recruit more people. Even though I'm still not convinced ending ROTC on campus will help the anti-war effort, I follow along toward Prentice and Dunbar halls, Tri-Towers, and then around the Eastway Center dorms, including mine.

At each stop, the crowd calls, *"Come and join us! Come and join us! Come and join us!"* Just before we arrive at Manchester Hall in the Eastway Complex, one of the leaders rushes ahead through the door into the lobby of Manchester and pulls the fire alarm to get students to come outside and join us. More do, and the crowd surges toward Johnson and Stopher halls and back toward the Commons. At each stop, more people join us. I hear one of the leaders tell a couple of students, "We're going to burn that fucking ROTC building to the ground. Let's go!"

At dusk, the crowd returns to the Commons, stopping at the west end next to the ROTC building, a decrepit wooden World War II barracks building that had been repurposed for use by the ROTC. The crowd, now numbering about a thousand, chants, "*One, two, three, four, we don't want your fucking war.*" I join in. The chant continues until someone starts a new one, "*Get it! Burn it! R-O-T-C has to go! Get it! Burn it! R-O-T-C has to go!*" I don't join in.

I'm standing at the back of the crowd on the west side toward Front Campus. Many present, like me, want to see what's happening, but the students in the front seem to be there for something more nefarious. I, too, want the fucking war to end, but I don't think burning down a building will make that happen.

Right after dusk, some guys at the front of the crowd throw rocks at the ROTC building, breaking a few windows. A guy lights a railroad flare and tosses it through a broken window. The building smolders. A student at the front of the crowd runs to a nearby motorcycle, removes the gas cap, pulls the bandana from around his head, and dips it into the gas tank. He runs with the dripping, gas-soaked bandana back to the ROTC building, sets it on fire with his Zippo lighter, and throws the flaming bandana through a broken window. Almost immediately, fire flares up inside the wood-framed building.

The crowd is riled up now and cheers as the building starts burning. No campus cops, local police, or highway patrol are in sight. The crowd senses that it has unlimited power. A couple of guys in business suits are watching everything, but neither they nor anyone else is trying to stop the crowd from burning down the ROTC building.

About ten minutes later, the Kent fire department arrives. Some students throw rocks at the firemen who are just doing their jobs trying to save the entire campus from burning. No one seems to care about that. The firemen turn on their hoses, and within a couple of minutes, one student and then another stab and slash the fire hoses with pocketknives. Unbelievably, another student pulls out what looks like a machete and starts hacking at a hose. I continue to stay and watch, but I don't get it. Why are students throwing rocks at the firefighters? Do they really want the whole campus to burn?

About thirty minutes later, the fire appears to have been doused. Some students still pelt the firemen with rocks. Rather than inspecting the building to ensure the fire is out, the firemen pack up their gear and leave. The building is still smoldering, but no flames are visible. I'm thankful it looks like none of the firemen are seriously hurt. With the ROTC building visibly damaged, I'm hoping that's enough to satisfy the crowd, and we can continue protesting the invasion of Cambodia. I talk to a couple of guys I know from Clark Hall, and they, too, hope this is the end of the violence tonight.

Just as the mob's energy seems to dissipate, the Kent police arrive in full riot gear and shoot tear gas canisters into the crowd. The students fall back, but the arrival of the police reenergizes everyone, and now no one is going home. The ROTC building, though damaged, is still a symbol of the Vietnam War. The mob pulls down a fence surrounding the tennis courts at the west edge of the Commons. They break the windows of the KSU Information Center. Then someone sets fire to a small archery equipment shed. It's like the protesters are on a rampage, tearing down everything in their path.

Suddenly, and without any more student involvement, the ROTC building reignites and is now fully engulfed in flames. The crowd surges back toward the burning building like moths to a flame. Sirens announce the return of the fire department, but this time they are escorted by Kent police in riot gear. The firemen once again set up their hoses, but it looks like they may be too late. The wooden building is ablaze. Firemen blast water into the inferno with little effect. Smoke fills the air, and fire lights up the night sky. The ROTC building can't be saved this time. The symbol of war has been removed from campus.

The protestors seem unsatisfied and want something more to burn. From my vantage point, I see police reinforcements arrive from the direction of Front Campus. As they get closer, I see it's not the police but a squad of soldiers carrying M1 rifles with bayonets fixed on the end of the barrels. The Ohio National Guard has arrived. They take up a position around the ROTC building with their M1s across the fronts of their shoulders. It is clear they mean business.

"Students are ordered to disperse or face immediate arrest. Go back to your dorm rooms now," commands a guardsman with a bullhorn. His voice is forceful but eerily calm. He doesn't wait for students to disperse but immediately orders the soldiers to shoot tear gas canisters into the crowd.

I've seen enough. I head back to my dorm, but with all the tear gas, I have no easy way to get there. My eyes burn as I run toward the Victory Bell at the other end of the Commons, up Blanket Hill, past the Pagoda next to Taylor Hall, and past Prentice Hall. As I cross Midway Drive, I blink to clear the tears and look to the left toward the campus exit to Main Street. An army tank and guardsmen are stationed around the entrance to campus. Clearly, no one is getting on or off campus tonight.

I make it back to my dorm room without any further encounters with the national guard. Around 11:15, I call my girlfriend. She answers the phone right away. "I'm so happy you called. I've been worried about you. I was visiting a girlfriend in her room across the hall from mine and we could see that something was burning. It lit up the night sky. Are you okay? What happened?"

"I'm ok. The mob set fire to the ROTC building. Once the fire took hold, the mob lost all sense of reason and started destroying everything in sight. Then the Ohio National Guard shows up with their rifles and bayonets and gives an order to disperse. Without waiting the Guard fired tear gas into the crowd. That's when I took off and made it back to my dorm. The crowd just went crazy. They were totally out of control."

"I'm so glad you're okay."

We continue to talk for another fifteen minutes, and I fill her in on the details of what happened. With the Ohio National Guard on campus, I don't know what will happen next.

Teens & Dreams

14

Thursday, March 10, 1966 • Lima, Ohio

School is different now. I'm in ninth grade at Central Junior High, and until a couple of weeks ago, I had a regular class schedule. I walked to school in the morning, arrived by 8:00, and the school day was over at 3:15.

On Sunday morning, February 27, 1966, everything changed. Around 10:30, I see smoke billowing into the sky from the direction of downtown Lima.

"Hey, Henry! Let's go see what's going on!"

Henry looks at the smoke. "Do you think the post office is on fire?"

"We'll see soon enough. Mom! Henry and I are going out."

We bolt out the front door and run toward the smoke. Within a few blocks, we can tell it's coming from our school building. We only live six blocks away and are at Central within a few minutes. The building takes up an entire city block, so we follow the smoke around to the east side of the building and see flames shooting through the roof. Firemen are setting up their hoses and tell us to move across Pierce Street and stand next to the post office.

I look at Henry. He looks back, and we both smile. "No school tomorrow," I whoop.

Henry grins. "Nope!"

"Give me some skin," I say, and we slap hands.

The sixty-one-year-old structure has old wooden desks bolted to the original wood plank floors. Perfect kindling for a fire, along with all the books and papers. Lima Central Junior High and Franklin Elementary used to be separate schools but were connected years ago. Everyone just calls the combined school building Central.

As the firemen shoot water through their hoses onto the blaze, more fire trucks arrive. Soon, windows blow out, and flames leap through the openings. It is cold outside but not freezing, and no snow covers the ground. We are mesmerized by the fire and do not even feel the cold. It looks like it started somewhere on the second floor, maybe in the cafeteria or band room.

I play cornet in the Central Junior High Band and have class in the band room on Tuesdays and Thursdays. I left my cornet in an instrument storage locker in the Band Room last week. I'm not a very good cornet player. In fact, I'm terrible. Outside of school, I never practice because my dad had said, "I don't want to hear that goddamned thing in this house. Take it outside." The only place to practice outside was either on our rear steps or out back in the old horse-drawn milk wagon missing its wheels that we used as a club-house. Both places are too cold to practice during the winter. So, I don't practice, and, therefore, I don't get any better.

The band room is now fully engulfed in flames, so bye-bye to my cornet. We have no money to replace it, and I lost interest long ago anyway.

The entire roof suddenly erupts in flames, so we move around the corner to High Street and stand across from the stone steps that lead up to Central's entrance. The roof above the arch over the school's large clock is now ablaze, and water from a fire hose shoots up and over the third story, and onto the roof. With a great *woosh* and a deafening *crash*, the entire roof collapses inward.

After several hours, the blaze seems under control, but the only things left standing are bare brick walls that flames have scorched. We can see through the blown-out windows to the other side of the building.

We walk toward home and see that much of the North Street

side of the building has been saved. Henry and Kevin attend Franklin Elementary School, located on that side of the building.

Dad is watching TV when we get home, and we are not about to interrupt him, so we excitedly tell Mom all about the fire. We are elated about the prospect of no school tomorrow, and maybe longer. When we finish, Dad growls, "I better not hear that you goddamn boys got in the way of those firemen."

"We didn't," I assure him.

"And stay the hell away from that school building." He adds, pointing a finger at us.

"Okay," we say in unison. He never has a good word to say to any of us, and today is no different.

The next day, the *Lima News* reports that seventy-two fire-fighters battled the 1.4-million-dollar blaze for seven hours. The fire did start in the band room and is under investigation. The band room, cafeteria, and thirty-one classrooms were destroyed, but fire-wall doors saved most of the building's north side, including Franklin Elementary School. However, the entire building suffered damage from smoke and water. There will be no school next week, and no one can say when school will start again for students at either Central or Franklin.

To my great disappointment, Superintendent of Schools Dr. Earl McGovern quickly comes up with a plan to put Central Junior High students back in the classroom. Starting Monday, March 7, 1966, Lima Senior High will operate in two shifts. The morning shift, 7:00 to noon, will be for the Lima Senior High Students. By 12:30, all senior high students and staff will leave the building. It will become Central Junior High, with classes running from 1:00 to 6:00. The plan also allows the students attending Franklin Elementary to go to Horace Mann Elementary. So, Henry and Kevin will go to Horace Mann, and I will go to Lima Senior.

It is strange, but it works. Well, it mostly works. I go to study hall instead of band, and I have no instrument and no interest in having Mom buy or rent me a new one. Classes are shorter, but everyone tries to make it work in the best way possible.

At home, things are different. Mom always works during the day, and Dad has never worked, at least not since I can remember. Mom cleans St. Rita's Hospital rooms from 7:30 in the morning to 4:30, Monday through Friday. She also cleans our house, cooks our meals, and does our laundry. Dad does nothing, and I mean literally nothing, except collect Social Security and veterans' disability checks and pull off his belt to beat the shit out of us boys.

Shortly after the new Lima Senior/Lima Central school schedule starts, I realize I will be home alone from 8:00 to noon almost every day. Mom goes to work and drops Brian off at our aunt's house. Henry and Kevin go to Horace Mann Elementary. Dad takes off every morning around 8:00, and most days does not return home until sometime after I leave for Lima Senior at noon. I have no idea where he goes, and I don't care. I'm happy he's not home when I am. One time, I asked Susie where he goes in the mornings, and she said, "Downtown to either Louie's Bar or Lombardo's Bar." I guess those bars are as good a place as any for an alcoholic.

It takes me thirty minutes to walk to school now instead of ten. Dad never offers to take me, and I never ask. Every morning he drives away, and I have the house to myself for four hours. It is strange and somewhat freeing. In a family of six kids and two adults, I've never been alone in the house.

Now, after several days of being by myself in the mornings with nothing to do, the uniqueness of my situation has begun to wear off. I decide to explore the only part of the house that has been off limits. Mom and Dad's bedroom. In the nightstand drawer beside the bed, I find a handgun. I don't know much about handguns, but I am curious and pick it up. It is much heavier than I expected. I don't know if it's loaded and don't know how to tell if it is. I don't want to accidentally shoot myself or anything else in the house, so after practicing a couple of quick draws from the side of my hip, I put it back.

There's also a rack above the bed containing three long guns. I stand on the bed to reach them and take down a rifle. Dad had talked about using a .22 caliber rifle for rabbit and pheasant hunting, so this might be the twenty-two. It looks old and has a bolt action mechanism that I've seen in TV shows. I move the bolt action up and down but can't tell if it's loaded, so I put it back on the rack. Next, I pull down a double-barreled shotgun. It is heavy. Dad has never taken me hunting or even offered to show me how to shoot a gun, so I have no idea how to check to see if the shotgun has shells in it. I put it back on the rack. The last gun is another rifle and is longer than the twenty-two, but I don't know what caliber of bullets it takes. I take it off the rack and aim it toward my reflection in the mirror over the chest of drawers. I am tempted to pull the trigger but don't since I don't know if the safety is on or not. I put it back on the rack.

With some trepidation, I move to the chest of drawers with the mirror and start going through each drawer, beginning at the top and working my way down. Little of interest is in the drawers. Some knick-knacks and a few mementos Mom has kept, and a lot of clothing. The bottom drawer is Mom's and contains a lot of her underwear, including a girdle. I know from TV that some women wear these things, but I don't understand why they would want to. It is made of thin rubber, is an off-white dingy color, and looks more like a torture device than anything else. I pick it up to feel the weight of it, and underneath the girdle is a book: *Sex Without Fear* by S.A. Lewin, M.D., and John Gilmore, Ph.D.

Neither Mom nor Dad has ever talked to me about sex or even mentioned the word sex. The only things I know about sex are from other boys at school, and it is all very confusing. I heard older boys claim, "I'm going to get me a piece of ass." I know the reference was related to sex, but I thought why would you want to take a piece of a girl's butt? It makes no sense to me, and there is no one to ask without looking stupid. I also heard older boys say, "I'm going to eat me some pussy." I know that pussy is slang for a girl's private parts and that a girl's privates are different from mine, but I have no idea why or how it is possible for a boy to eat a girl's privates. Wouldn't that hurt the girl? I know sex has something to do with making babies. I can remember when my mom was pregnant with my youngest brother, Brian, and how big her belly got just before he was born. It is a mystery to me exactly how a baby is born. I assume that when her belly gets big enough, somehow it opens up and the baby comes out.

In my own body, things are starting to change. I am now five foot six, and I have hair starting to grow down there next to my penis. Almost every morning, I wake up, and my penis is hard. I have no idea why these things are happening. I know I will learn answers to some of these things in high school next year. Sophomores are required to take health education, where, apparently, we will learn about sex. The boys and girls have separate health ed classes. Next year seems a long way off when things are happening to me now.

I pick up the book on sex. I didn't know such a book even existed. I open it and see illustrations of couples engaged in acts that are beyond my imagination. The table of contents gives me an idea that many of my questions about sex will be answered by this book. Why do Mom and Dad, who already have six kids, need a book about sex? It is a question I can't answer. I carefully take note of where the book has been placed in Mom's underwear drawer, take the book into the living room, sit on the couch, and start reading.

Every few minutes, I look up to make sure Dad is not pulling up in front of the house. He never does. I read and re-read the book and study the illustrations. Things start to make sense. Getting a "piece of ass" means having sex. "Eating pussy" is oral sex. The biggest revelation, however, is how babies are born. The book illustrates a woman's genitals, but when I read that a baby is born by coming out through those genitals, I lurch forward in my seat. "No fucking way!"

Oh, and I now know what fuck means, even though I have been hearing my dad say the word for the last fourteen years.

Teens & Dreams

15

Saturday, April 30, 1966 • Lima, Ohio

I'm up at 7:00 to retrieve the *Lima News* from the front porch and start rolling them. Delivery will be easy today. I purchased a new three-speed Schwinn Racer touring bike last week from the bike shop on Wayne Street. The regular price was $51.95, but since it was last year's model and newer models were arriving in a few days, I bought it fully assembled for $41.00, taxes included. Groovy. It's the first new bike I've ever owned and takes almost my entire savings. I had hand-me-down kid clunker bikes in the past but never had a bike of my own. All the kids in the neighborhood are lusting after one of the new banana-seat Schwinn Stingray bikes. It's a cool bike, but I was looking for something I could use on my paper route and ride around Lima without it looking like a kiddie bike.

After rolling the newspapers, I lift the delivery bag onto my shoulders and take off on my Schwinn. Sometimes, I can throw the papers from my bike, but many of my customers live in apartments or two-family homes, so, I need to get off my bike and put the paper in front of their door. Even so, it takes less than half the time to deliver my papers than it took before. To me, it feels like a big deal. I purchased a bike with my own money, and I am now mobile.

After finishing my route, I head downtown to the *Lima News* offices on High Street to pay my bill. It is cool how much time I save by riding my bike rather than walking. I pay my bill then go to S.S.

Kresge's for my usual breakfast: pancakes and a Coke. Wheaties may be the official "Breakfast of Champions," but you can't beat pancakes and a Coke from Kresge's.

I'm only fourteen, but recently, everything seems more important to me, and many things weigh heavily on me. Two months ago, Dennis received his draft notice. Rather than waiting to be assigned to the Army and be deployed to Vietnam, Dennis joined the Navy to see the world. I think that was a good move. He might still get to the waters off the coast of Vietnam, but at least he won't be in the jungles fighting the Viet Cong. Dennis recently finished basic training at Naval Station Great Lakes near Chicago and is stationed on the destroyer USS *Joseph P. Kennedy*. He can't tell me exactly where they will be going, but it's somewhere in the Middle East.

The war in Vietnam continues to rage. Almost every week, the *Lima News* reports that a soldier from Lima was killed in action or wounded. General Westmoreland keeps telling President Johnson he needs more troops to win the war. Last night on the *Huntley-Brinkley Report*, the news anchor announced that the president had ordered the number of troops in South Vietnam increased to two hundred and fifty thousand. A quarter of a million young guys, mostly eighteen and nineteen, will fight this war. I keep wondering, when will this war end? And what are our soldiers fighting for? To defeat communism? That seems unlikely. More than one billion Communists live in China and Russia. They are not going anywhere. Protest marches against the war are happening in major cities across the U.S., but it doesn't seem to matter. More and more troops are headed to Vietnam. Watching the news and seeing body bags loaded onto a transport plane every evening is sad.

It seems like something changes every day. Last Saturday, Susie moved out of the house and into an apartment on North Street across from Frisch's Big Boy Drive-In. After delivering my papers last Wednesday, I stopped by to see her new place. Everything is clean and new, plus it has natural gas heat. No coal to worry about. It's much nicer than Truman Street, definitely a move up. I wish it were me living there. Susie's boyfriend stopped by, and I saw his new 1966 white Corvette Stingray convertible with a red leather interior. It's sweet.

My interest in girls is also changing. It has increased dramatically. Now at school, I notice which girls have breasts and which do not. Girls with breasts are definitely more interesting. I dress more carefully and make sure my hair is combed before I go to school.

Two Saturdays ago, some of the neighborhood guys and I decided to go to a teen Sock Hop at the Armory sponsored by WCIT, the local AM top 40 radio station. Since I watch *American Bandstand* every Saturday, I thought I knew what to expect.

Everyone must remove their shoes inside the Armory, so we don't scuff up the gym floor. Now I understand why it's called a Sock Hop. Everyone is in their socks. And I see firsthand how awkward everything is with girls. A few couples are dancing, but for the most part, guys are on one side of the gym, and girls are on the other. Neither side wants to take the risk of being rejected after asking someone to dance. Except for a few brave boys, the status quo remains unchanged for the entire dance. I am not one of the brave. I see several girls I would like to ask to dance, but I don't have the courage to walk across the gym. The fear of rejection is stronger than the possibility of losing out on meeting a new girl. I get to watch some new dance moves, though, and file those away for future use.

At school, I overhear a couple of the guys in my class talking about a birthday party that one of the popular girls had at her house on Saturday night. She lives in one of the big fancy houses at the far end of Market Street. Apparently, her dad is a bigwig at a local bank. One of the guys says there was a live band at the party and that "everybody who is anybody was at the party." I was not at the party, and until just now, had not even heard about it. I am a nobody, and it hurts. I am not part of the in-crowd. I live on a dead-end street next to the railroad tracks with a deadbeat drunk dad. I'll never be part of the in-crowd.

As I finish my pancakes and Coke at Kresge's, I stop reflecting on all that has happened the past few months and think about what to do next. I decide to go home and watch *American Bandstand.* I pay for my breakfast, get on my Schwinn, and pedal home.

Dad's 1960 Chevy Biscayne is parked in front of the house when I arrive. That's strange. He usually doesn't hang around on Saturday mornings. I open the front door and step inside. Dad immediately barks, "Where the fuck have you been?"

I just look at him for a moment and then say, "Delivering papers and paying my bill."

"I don't need no fuckin' attitude from you," he says.

I look at him again, then walk toward my bedroom.

"Goddamnit, I'm talkin' to you. I can still take my belt off and whup you."

I look straight into his eyes and say, "You can try." I am now just a couple of inches shorter than him. During the last several months, I've gone through a growth spurt and am no longer a little kid. He still outweighs me by about twenty pounds, but I've developed some muscles and know I am much stronger than I was last year.

"So, you think you're big enough to take me on?"

I don't say anything but continue to look him in the eye.

"Go on, you stupid son of a bitch," he says.

I go to my room. Since Susie moved out, I have had her old bedroom to myself. I close the door and stand there for a moment. The old man just backed down. I stood up to the bully, and he blinked first. I've never forgotten the fist he threw at me and the hole he punched in the kitchen wall when he missed. In fact, that gaping hole is still there. Dad never repaired it. So, every time I enter the kitchen, I see it and get angry.

Susie left me her small portable TV when she moved out, so I don't need to go into the living room where Dad is sitting to watch *American Bandstand*. I turn on the TV, kick back on my bed and start watching. It has a black and white screen rather than the color one in the living room, but that is okay with me.

Bandstand doesn't come on for another hour. A news show talks about the *Time Magazine* cover that came out earlier this month. In large, bold letters, it asks, "Is God Dead?" The story focuses on the decline of religion among American households. Fewer people are attending church. Some blame it on rock 'n roll and The Beatles. Last month when an interviewer asked John Lennon from The Beatles about their popularity in America, he replied, "We're more popular than Jesus now." That did not go over well with the Christian community, and since then, bonfire rallies have burned anything related to The Beatles. TV newscasts have shown kids burning their records, magazines with the band on the cover, and anything else related to Beatlemania. I don't think God is dead. God is alive and well and resides in our hearts.

American Bandstand finally comes on. The record reviews— "It has a good beat" and "You can dance to it"—are the same every Saturday. I watch Jackie DeShannon sing "What the World Needs Now is Love." Then Bob Kuban & The In-Men sing "The Cheater." Dick Clark does a cool phone interview with Brian Wilson of The Beach Boys.

The dancing is cool, and the girls look better each week.

Life & Love

16

Monday, December 1, 1969 • Kent State University, Kent, Ohio

Thanksgiving break is over, and everyone is back. I stayed on campus for the long weekend. I was tempted to take a bus home, but I would have had to deal with my dad. I miss my mom, but if I never see my dad again, that's fine with me.

To be sure, Thanksgiving on campus is different. No one I know stayed, but I am not alone. A few hundred of us are here. Tri-Towers has the only open cafeteria, so I trek over there for my meals. The holiday menu is pretty good. No turkey, but we are treated to Porterhouse steaks. It is the first Porterhouse I've ever eaten, and, man, is it good. Tender and juicy. It's served with mashed potatoes, gravy, candied yams, corn, green beans, cranberry relish, and pumpkin pie. All delicious. I eat by myself, and it is a bit lonely. During the rest of the long weekend, I watch TV in the Clark Hall lounge and catch up on reading in my classes. Finals are only a couple of weeks away, and I want to be ready.

Carol and I are still dating, but I am careful not to let it progress too far. I am still hoping that Katie might break up with Chuck, her boyfriend back home. I think that might happen when she's home this week. Katie and I have not discussed the possibility of a breakup, but we talk a lot about everything else and have become close friends. Nothing physical has happened with Katie, but I hope she can sense how I feel about her.

Today is the first day of classes after the break. I'm headed to Geography of U.S. and Canada class and am excited to see Katie. I thought a lot about her while I was alone over the weekend, and the more I thought about her, the more I convinced myself that she would break up with Chuck when she was home. Walking into geography class, I see Katie at our usual spot in the second row. She looks spectacular but has a worried look on her face.

"Hi, how was your Thanksgiving?" I ask.

She says, "Great, how about yours? Were you the only one here during the break?"

"No, there were a few of us here." Sitting down, I see her left hand resting on the desk. "What's this?" I ask, picking up her hand.

"Chuck proposed. I got engaged over Thanksgiving."

I am dumbstruck. I look at the diamond engagement ring on her finger and all I can manage to say is, "Oh."

"It was a surprise. I had no idea he was going to propose."

I say, "Uh-huh." An engagement is the last thing I expected, and I have no words. Literally, the girl of my dreams is now taken. The professor enters the room, and Katie says, "Let's talk after class."

I'm numb but mumble, "Okay."

During class, I keep looking at the engagement ring on Katie's finger and then look at Katie and then look back at the engagement ring. This repeats several times then I try to focus on what the professor is saying and take some notes. After a few minutes, I find myself again looking at the engagement ring. I feel a bit nauseous. Then I feel sad. Then I look at the ring and feel nauseous again. Mercifully, an hour later, class is over.

We leave the classroom and walk a short distance. In a protected alcove behind Kent Hall, Katie stops and faces me. "I'm sorry. I know you are surprised by this. I was surprised too. I care a lot about you, and I'm sorry if you are hurt by this."

I look at Katie and decide I have nothing more to lose. I waited too long to tell her my true feelings. "I guess I shouldn't be surprised that Chuck asked you to marry him. You're beautiful. You're intelligent. It's fun to be with you. I love talking with you and exploring new ideas with you. I think you know I'm attracted to you, and I thought you also felt something for me. I want us to be together. I want to take you to concerts, to the movies. I want to take you to my room. I want to fall in love with you."

Katie's shoulders slump, and she looks deep into my eyes and says, "I want those things too, but I didn't think that was possible. You started dating Carol, and I thought you felt something for her."

I look into Katie's eyes. "I was dating Carol because I thought I could not date you. Was I wrong?"

Katie lowers her gaze. "I guess not."

"I didn't allow things to progress with Carol because I hoped that something would happen between you and me. I thought I would sit down beside you in class today, and you would tell me you had broken up with Chuck. I guess I was just dreaming."

Katie looks at me dejectedly. "Things are such a mess. I don't know what to do. I'm sorry."

"I'm sorry too. I should have let you know how I really feel about you." There is nothing more to say, and I am really hurting inside. I tell Katie goodbye, and we go our separate ways.

Walking alone to my next class, I feel down and force myself to think of something besides what just happened. I don't know why, but my thoughts turn to the war in Vietnam, and I get angry. The fucking war seems like it will never end. During his campaign, President Nixon promised to bring the troops home. He's been in office almost a year and reduced the troops by only fifty thousand. Over four hundred thousand soldiers remain in Vietnam. More than eleven thousand men have already been killed in action this year.

The first draft lottery is being held later today, and anyone turning nineteen by December 31, 1969, will get a number. I don't turn nineteen until next year, so I won't get my number until the second lottery. That number will stay with me and be my draft number when I finish at Kent State.

The draft lottery works this way: Each of the 366 possible birthdates for men ages eighteen to twenty-six is printed on a slip of paper and placed inside a blue plastic capsule. The capsules are mixed in a shoebox, dumped into a water-cooler-sized glass cylinder, and withdrawn one at a time. The date in the first capsule is lottery number one, the date in the second is number two, and so on. I will not know my draft number until the second lottery in July 1970. Even then, it will be unclear whether I will be drafted because it will depend upon the number of men killed in action in Vietnam, the number of men the president thinks we need to fight this war, and my lottery number.

Two weeks ago, it was reported that more than three hundred unarmed Vietnamese men, women, and children had been massacred by U.S. troops a year ago in and around the village of My Lai, South Vietnam. Young girls and women were raped and mutilated before being killed. Twenty-six U.S. soldiers, including their platoon leader, Lieutenant William Calley Jr., were charged criminally for the massacre. The brutality and official cover-up of the crime are stoking the fire of anti-war sentiment. On November 15, 1969, two hundred fifty thousand people participated in the March Against Death in Washington, D.C., protesting the war. Can't Nixon see that the war is destroying everything America stands for?

After my last class, I have lunch in Eastway cafeteria and focus on more positive thoughts. I know from living with my dad for eighteen years, that if I dwell on everything that is wrong in the world and my life, I could quickly spiral downward. I have learned that when that happens, I need to think about the good things in my life and move in a new direction.

First, I think about what my grades were in October and what they are now. I received a D- on my first midterm for History of Mesopotamia. I changed how I took notes, read my material, and studied for exams, which has paid off. Last week, I got back my "Blue Book" exam for the second midterm and received a B-plus. In calculus, I have an A average on exams. In English, I have a B average on my papers, in geology I received an A on both mid-term exams and in geography I received an A on my midterm. I am feeling good about my grades. I still have finals, but I no longer worry that I will flunk out and be shipped to Vietnam.

My thoughts then turn to Katie. In our conversation, Katie confirmed she has feelings for me. She is engaged, but she isn't married yet. Being upset with Katie is not going to bring me closer to her. I need to stay positive and show her what a relationship with me could be. I think of things we could do together without going on an official date. So far, our time together has been limited to geography class, walking to her English class, and having an occasional Coke at the Student Union. I need to step up to the plate and take a big swing.

I call Katie's room. She answers the phone on the first ring. "Hi," I say.

"It's good to hear from you." She pauses. "I thought you might not want to talk with me."

"Not a chance. I always want to talk with you," I assure her.

"That's good. I like talking with you too." I can hear a smile in her voice.

"Tomorrow night on Front Campus by the administration building, the university is hosting a Christmas tree lighting ceremony, and the KSU Chorus will sing Christmas carols. It should be fun. It starts at 7:00. Would you like to meet there and watch the festivities?"

Her voice is eager. "That does sound like fun," she answers. We agree to meet at the bottom of the steps that lead up to the administration building at 6:45 tomorrow night.

I have one more thing to do today if I am going to do everything I can to win Katie over. I call Carol, and we agree to meet at

Eastway at 4:00. We find a table, and I get us each a Coke and sit down.

"How was your Thanksgiving?" I ask her.

Carol says, "It was good. My entire family was there, including my grandparents on my mom's side. Did you stay here for Thanksgiving?"

"Yes, but it was pretty quiet."

Carol nods her head. "I bet."

I look at her, hoping I can deliver the words I have to say gently. "There's something I've wanted to talk with you about. We've been on some dates, but I know you can tell I've been holding back. I know you want us to get closer, but that hasn't happened. I haven't been dating anyone else, but there has been someone else on my mind, and that's why I haven't asked you to be my girlfriend. That was unfair to you, and I'm sorry. I know I can't keep you in limbo, so I think it's best if we stop seeing each other"

Carol's eyes tear up and with a quivery voice, she says, "I knew there was something holding you back. I just didn't know what it was. I like you a lot, but it looks like it won't happen for us." She gets up, and without saying another word, leaves Eastway.

I feel bad but know that I need to let Carol go if I have even the slightest chance of getting Katie to change her mind about her engagement.

Teens & Dreams

17

Sunday, August 14, 1966 • Lima, Ohio

The Sunday edition of the *Lima News* is the worst. After stuffing the advertising circulars, each paper weighs at least a pound. I'm glad I can ride my Schwinn to help carry the weight of forty-three papers. It still takes me twice as long as any other day, but I get it done and I'm back home by 8:30 in time to get ready for church.

Last year I started attending the Grand Avenue Church of the Nazarene. Our neighbors asked if we wanted to go with them, and I was the only one to take them up on their offer. I would do anything to get away from my dad. Every Sunday morning, I go with them to the 10:00 service. The members of the Church are welcoming, and the weekly sermons are inspiring. Last year, one of the deacons presented me with a Bible for my fourteenth birthday. I've been reading a few passages almost every day. This past spring, a deacon sat me down and told me the church would like to sponsor me at church camp this summer. They will arrange for transportation and pay all fees. With a smile, I said, "I would love to go. Thank you!"

On Saturday morning, June 18, 1966, I join five other teenagers from the church for the two-hour ride to church camp southeast of Lima. We check in at the main lodge, where I get my cabin assignment. Of course, boys and girls are in separate cabins, each grouped by age. I'm in a cabin with five sets of bunkbeds and nine other thirteen- and fourteen-year-old boys from all over western Ohio. We are told to be at the main lodge for lunch at 12:30. It's only 11:30, so after unpacking, I set off to explore camp with another boy in my cabin from our church.

The camp fronts a beautiful lake. We walk a well-worn path down to the docks to check it out. The wide beach is sandy, and a large square raft hovers on the water about forty feet from shore. Float lines encompass the perimeter of the swimming area, which looks almost as long as my street. Rowboats and canoes are arranged in a neat row at the far end of the beach. I've never been in a rowboat or a canoe, so I'm looking forward to trying both.

A circular area in the grass at the end of the lake has a firepit in the middle surrounded by large, split logs for campers to sit on. They must have had a campfire last night because I can smell the smoky dampness that comes from a fire that has been doused with water. Picnic tables fill an open pavilion nearby. I bet it's used for outdoor church services and other group activities. Hiking trails wind around the lake. A softball diamond has been marked out in a large open field, and another field has bullseye targets set up for archery. So many new things to do here. This week is going to be swell. We head back to the main lodge for lunch.

After we wolf down hotdogs, baked beans, potato salad, brownies, and fruit punch, we get our schedule of daytime and nighttime activities for the rest of the week. We will attend Church services on Sunday and Wednesday and teen Bible rap sessions every day to discuss how the Bible applies to our daily lives.

Sunday service is moving and relevant, and at the end, the minister issues the call to be saved and born again in Jesus Christ. I've heard the call at our church, and several times have been moved, but have never gone forward. I'm not sure what is holding me back. During Sunday service at camp, I feel the call, but again hold back. I think it's not knowing what to expect after I give my life to Jesus Christ that holds me back.

At the rap sessions, most of my questions are answered and at the Wednesday church service, I feel the power of the Holy Spirit come over me. I stand up and walk to the altar, where I give my life to Jesus Christ and am saved and born again. I feel an emotional outpouring like I've never experienced. Anything and everything now seem possible. I no longer feel alone because now I have Jesus by my side. For the first time in my life, I feel loved, and that love comes from Jesus. After being saved, I feel at peace with myself and not so much like an outsider anymore. Everything at camp seems easy.

I learn to row a boat and paddle a canoe. I learn the basics of archery and manage not to shoot myself in the foot. I have a great time with other kids, but I particularly enjoy the teen Bible rap sessions. I learn more about myself and the Bible in that one week than I did in my entire life before church camp.

Now that I've been born again, I want to be baptized. On our next to the last day, I step into the lake with the camp minister and am fully immersed. When I come up out of the water, I feel the Holy Spirit come with me. I leave camp the next morning a much different person than the one who arrived a week earlier.

This August day is scorching hot. After church, I ask Henry and Kevin if they want to go to Schoonover's swimming pool for the afternoon. Schoonover's is a public pool, a thirty-minute walk from our house. I tell Mom where we are going, but it never occurs to me to ask her for a ride and forget about asking Dad. That is not going to happen.

The easiest way to get to the pool is to walk east on the Pennsylvania Railroad, which is what we do. We walk down the hill next to our house, turn right, and walk the tracks. Kevin slows us down a bit, but not too much. We keep our heads down, stepping from one railroad tie to the next over the rocks in between. Within a few minutes, I find an iron spike that has popped loose from a wooden railroad tie. We pass it back and forth, but no one wants to carry it all the way to Schoonover's and back, so we soon lose interest and toss it. We walk for about fifteen minutes when I hear a train coming from the east. I can tell it's still several blocks away, judging from the intensity of the whistle. I tell Henry and Kevin to get off the tracks and up the hill a few yards.

"Watch this," I tell them as I take three pennies from my pocket and place them about six inches apart on the rail closest to where Henry and Kevin are sitting. I scramble up the hill to join them just before the train arrives. Fortunately, it is a short passenger train. We watch the train's front wheel hit the pennies, and they disappear.

The train passes and we scamper onto the tracks looking for the pennies. Henry finds the first one. It is now a bright copper color and still warm from being flattened by the train's massive wheels. It's oval shaped and so paper thin and perfectly smooth that, except for the color, you can't tell it had been a penny. I find the other two pennies and give one to Kevin. "Pretty cool, huh?" They both nod and pocket their souvenirs.

It's hot walking on the tracks, but it cuts about ten minutes off our trip. When we arrive at the pool around 1:00, at least a hundred kids are swimming. Schoonover's is huge and always a blast. It costs thirty-five-cents to get in. Henry has a paper route now, so he pays for himself, and I pay for Kevin and myself. We go to the locker room to change and store our stuff. I change and pin the locker key to my swimsuit, so I won't lose it.

At the pool's deep end are two diving boards: a low dive and a high dive. The high dive is about twelve feet high and looks even higher when I stand at the top looking down at the water. I dive off and swim to the island in the middle of the deep end, an excellent spot to see what's going on all over the pool. For teenage boys, Schoonover's is all about checking out the girls without them knowing it.

After swimming for a while, Henry and I leave Kevin with some kids at the shallow end and go to the fenced-off grassy area where all the girls like to sunbathe. We lay down on our towels, and I take a deck of cards from my gym bag. We play rummy and crazy eights, and of course, I check out the girls.

We stay at Schoonover's until 4:00, then head home the same way we came. We are tired from being in the sun all afternoon, and it's hot, so it seems to take forever to get there. As soon as we get home, we all run to the kitchen for a glass of cold water.

Mom is sitting at the kitchen table. She says, "I have something to tell you boys. Come over here and sit down." We all sit down, including Brian, who is only five years old. I know something is up because this type of family meeting never happens.

Mom looks concerned and says, "Your dad isn't going to be around for a while. He decided to live somewhere else, and I'm not sure if he is coming back." We all look quizzically at her. Dad has left before for a few days but always came home. I knew I had not seen him in a couple of days, but I had assumed it was the same as before.

Henry asks, "Where did he go?"

Mom says, "I'm not sure, but it doesn't really matter. We will be fine, don't you think?"

We all nod, and I think, yeah, who needs a cranky old bastard around who beats his kids? Although, he had not tried to hit me since I challenged him last spring.

Mom says, "Go on and get cleaned up for dinner." And that was that. Nothing more was said about Dad.

Dinner is a pleasant experience for a change. None of us worry about Dad going off the rails and swearing at us for some perceived slight that sets him off. I feel free for the first time maybe ever. At least temporarily, the fear of him is lifted. With my dad gone, everything feels possible.

After dinner, plenty of daylight is left, so our neighbors set up a volleyball net. On a dead-end street, we don't have to worry about traffic. One end of the net is tied to a telephone pole on the west side of the street, the other is tied to a tree on the opposite side. We divide all the kids and adults into two teams. My neighbor, Jack, is my age but is at least six inches taller than me, and I am glad he is on my team. Jack's new girlfriend, Diane, is visiting and plays on our team too. Diane is a real stunner. She is very distracting, but I'm glad she's on our team.

After we play volleyball, Jack, Diane, and I sit on Jack's porch, drinking lemonade. I've not seen Diane before today, so I ask her, "Where do you go to school?"

"Shawnee. I'll be in tenth grade this fall. How about you?"

"Jack and I are in the same grade. We'll be sophomores at Lima Senior."

We talk about school, and other kids we know, and Diane says, "I have some friends from Shawnee and Lima Central Catholic that you should meet. I think you will get along great."

"That would be cool. Thanks." We continue to talk, and it turns out her friends from L.C.C. are all girls and live within walking distance of my house. If her girlfriends look as good as she does, I will be a happy boy. I don't know if it's my dad leaving or something else, but when talking with Diane, my self-doubt evaporates, and I start talking to her like she is my best friend.

We talk about movies and TV shows we have seen. I say, "I really like the new *Batman* series, *The Man from U.N.C.L.E.* and *I Dream of Jeannie*, and I saw previews for the new shows starting this fall. *The Monkees* and *Star Trek* look like they are going to be really cool."

Diane says, "I like *Bewitched* and *Gilligan's Island*."

"*Bonanza* and *Hogan's Heroes* are the best," says Jack.

Diane says, "We should all go see a movie sometime. The Lima Drive-In Theater is close to where I live, and I'm sure I could get my brother to take us. He's two years older than me and has his driver's license. Maybe one of my girlfriends could come with us."

"That would be really cool," I say.

Diane says her brother is coming to pick her up shortly. "See you later, I say. "It was really great meeting you, and I hope I can meet your friends."

"Same here. Bye."

The way Diane talks with me and listens to me makes me feel like I have something important to say. It's a good feeling.

At home, the TV is on. Henry and Kevin are watching a news program that shows the launch four days ago of *Lunar Orbiter 1*, the first U.S. spacecraft to ever visit another celestial body. The unmanned spacecraft will photograph potential landing sites for putting a man on the Moon. So cool. It's hard to believe that soon man will walk on the Moon. The news also shows an architectural rendering of what will be the tallest building in the world—the World Trade Center in New York City. A groundbreaking ceremony was held last week, and construction will start soon.

I go to my room and get ready for bed. It has been a good day. Church, Schoonover's, volleyball in the street, meeting Diane, and best of all, no dad to yell at me.

Teens & Dreams

18

Saturday, January 14, 1967 • Lima, Ohio

At the end of last summer, I met Diane, the girlfriend of my neighbor and friend, Jack. Diane is a godsend. She introduced me to some of her girlfriends who invited me to house parties where I met even more girls. At fifteen, my hormones are raging, and I accept every opportunity to mingle with the opposite sex. We often play "spin the bottle" at these parties. If a girl spins an empty pop bottle and it points toward me, I am "required" to kiss her. It's tough duty, but somebody has to do it. It's then my turn to spin the bottle, and when it points to a girl, she must kiss me. For me, it is a win-win game. It is a lot of fun and leads to extracurricular kisses after the game ends. I am now getting the hang of kissing and want more of it.

Amy is a friend of Diane's that I kissed during a spin-the-bottle game. She's a sophomore at Lima Central Catholic and lives only a fifteen-minute walk from me on McKibben Street. At a recent house party, I talk to Amy instead of talking to the other girls at the party. We spend almost the entire party talking about things we like and don't like about school and shows we like to watch on TV.

Before the party ends, I ask Amy if we can get together with a few of her friends during the week. She likes that idea. So, we start seeing each other after school, usually at one of her friends' houses. When we attend the same party, we stick close to each other. We've had a couple of short kissing sessions which I hoped would lead to longer make-outs, but since we're both fifteen and don't have our driver's licenses yet, we're limited in our time together. I've met Amy's mom and her mom's boyfriend. Her mom and dad are divorced. We watched some TV at her house while her mom was at home.

We're not going steady yet, but I enjoy being with Amy, and I think she enjoys spending time with me. Then last Saturday at a house party, Amy says, "We should see other people."

I am stunned, but say, "Okay. If that's what you want."

She says, "Things between us are just getting too serious, and I'm not ready for anything like that."

"Okay." I walk away, realizing that I've been dumped for the first time in my life. It came out of the blue without warning. I have no idea why Amy thinks things are getting too serious or what that even means.

Jack offered me a ride to another house party tonight since I won't get my driver's license until this summer. He got his license last November. We're picking up Diane on our way, and I hope to get her insight into what's going on with Amy.

However, I have bowling on my mind this morning. My cousin, Jim, who is the same age as me and lives only ten minutes away, invited me to join a bowling league with him at Northland Lanes. He said that the league is for fourteen- to seventeen-year-olds, including girls from schools other than Lima Senior High. We will bowl on the same team with girls from L.C.C., Bath, and Elida schools. Jim told me to be at his house at 9:30 this morning, and his mom will drop us off at the bowling alley. We will finish by noon.

I can bowl a solid 135. Jim is a natural athlete and averages around 170. Of course, neither of us is good enough to even think about rolling a perfect game—300, or twelve strikes in a row.

I walk over to Jim's house, and my aunt opens the door with a big smile. She hugs me and says, "Sugar, how are you doin', today?" She drives us to the bowling alley and tells us to have a good time and that she will be back at noon to pick us up. The ride from my aunt is a sweet deal.

I can't figure out why my dad and my aunt are so different. They're brother and sister but have completely different personalities. My aunt is always sweet to me. I'm not used to hugs or verbal affection, and I always feel a bit uncomfortable because I never get that at my house. Jim's mom is now taking the time to drop us off and pick us up from bowling. I know my dad would never do any of that. He only talks to me when he criticizes me.

Northland is packed with teens, and Jim is true to his word. Most of the girls are not from Lima Senior but from other schools in the area. Three boys and three girls make up each team, and Jim and I introduce ourselves to everyone on our team and the opposing team.

Two of the girls on our team are nice, and then there is Beth. She's sixteen, has her driver's license, goes to Bath High School, and is beautiful. My mouth drops open every time I look at her, and I need to consciously close my mouth so that I don't look creepy.

Jim and I are smitten with Beth. Jim is gregarious, and during the match, he sits down next to her, so I sit on her other side. She is not only beautiful but also intelligent and funny. We're only fifteen but that doesn't seem to bother Beth. She offers to give us a ride home after bowling. We stumble over our words saying yes to her offer. Jim immediately goes to a pay phone and calls his mom to tell her we will not need a ride home. I manage to bowl a decent 140, and Jim bowls a 155. Beth bowls a 125. Our team is in second place at the end of the first league day. We are all happy about that.

As we walk with Beth to her car, she mentions in passing that she has a boyfriend. My heart drops a bit at this news. Then she tells us that he graduated from Bath last year, is now in the Army, and is stationed in Vietnam.

I continue to follow the news about Vietnam and know that

380 thousand U.S. troops are currently in Vietnam and that 6,350 U.S. soldiers were killed there last year. In President Johnson's State of the Union address to Congress last week, he said, "I wish I could report to you that the conflict is almost over. This I cannot do. We face more cost, more loss, and more agony."

Vietnam is a bad situation and getting worse. No end is in sight for this war that has not been legally declared a war. Of course, I say nothing about any of that to Beth. I'm sure she knows the statistics. I tell her, "My brother is in the Navy on a destroyer and will likely be heading to the coast of Vietnam."

Beth says, "I don't know exactly where in Vietnam my boyfriend is located because his letters about what he is doing are always censored." We continue to have a free-flowing conversation with her as she drives us to Jim's house.

After she drops us off, she says, "I look forward to seeing both of you next week."

"Likewise," we say simultaneously, and then say, "Dibs on a Coke."

Beth laughs, waves goodbye, and drives away. After she leaves, Jim and I look at each other and say, "Wow!"

"She is really something else. Do you think it is strange her telling us about her boyfriend?" I ask.

"Yeah, I guess. Or maybe she just wants to have fun but is telling us she can't get serious because she has a boyfriend."

"Could be. I like her anyway and, man, she is built like a brick shithouse."

Jim nods his head in agreement. "That's for sure."

As I arrive home, Mom pulls up in her car after grocery shopping at Pangles. I help her carry the bags into the house and rummage through them until I find my favorite snacks: a chocolate Hostess Cupcake and an almost green banana. I am halfway through my cupcake and peeling the banana as I walk into the living room. Henry, Kevin, and Brian are sitting in front of the TV watching cartoons. "If you snooze, you lose," I say. They see me eating my cupcake and banana, jump up, and run to the kitchen, hoping that enough snacks are left for them.

I go to my room, close the door, and turn on the TV to watch *American Bandstand*. Once again, the teenage record reviewers say, "It has a good beat, and you can dance to it." The reviews are always the same. Still, the teen dancers are cool, and I hope I can mimic some of their moves at the house party tonight. Usually, these parties have a record player, and someone will bring the latest 45s to play. Eventually, everyone starts to dance.

Just as *Bandstand* ends, I hear Dad come in the house and yell at Henry, Kevin, and Brian. "You goddamn boys pick up that goddamned garbage and throw it in the fucking trash can. Do you think you live in a goddamned pigsty?" I hear them scurry to pick up the remains of their snacks and put them in the trash can in the kitchen.

When it comes to Dad, some things never change. He is still a cranky, old bastard. Last August, he moved out of the house, but that had only lasted five weeks. Before the end of September, he moved back home. He was not contrite but picked up as if nothing had happened. He still swears at us at every opportunity he gets and still beats Henry and Kevin with his belt. He never touches his baby, Brian, who is now four years old and can do no wrong. He also doesn't try to mess with me. I stood my ground, and since that time, he has not even threatened me. Also, during the last year, I have grown another three inches, and at five feet nine, I am now taller than him.

I walk over to Jack's house at 6:30, and we drive to pick up Diane. She lives in Shawnee Township, an affluent suburb southwest of Lima, about fifteen minutes from Jack's house. Diane answers the door when Jack knocks. She looks stunning. Her reddish-brown hair falls in waves to her shoulders, and her mini-skirt shows off legs that never seem to end. She has a sparkly personality and welcomes me into her home. She introduces me to her mom and stepdad.

Diane's brother is also home. I had previously met him and

immediately liked him. He knows a lot about popular music and is laid back about everything. Nothing ever seems to bother him.

"How's it going?" I ask him. "Listen to any cool music lately?"

He nods his head. "The Supremes just released 'Love is Here and Now You're Gone.' It's a cool song."

"I haven't heard it yet, but I will definitely listen for it the next time I tune in to CKLW," I say.

We all climb into Jack's car and head to the party.

"I guess you heard that Amy wants us to see other people," I tell Diane.

"Yep," she says, "but don't take it personally. She probably wants to spend time with someone else. Don't worry about it. Just have fun at the party."

"Okay. Thanks."

We arrive at the party, and Amy is already there. She's getting cozy with a guy from Shawnee High School I met at a previous party. I don't know him that well, but he seems okay. I'm beginning to get the picture of how this dating thing works. A girl pays attention to you until she finds a shiny new toy to play with, and then she tells you that she thinks we should see other people. Okay. I get it. Time to move on. No need to get into a funk about it. It's just part of being a teenager. Life goes on. So, I hold my head up and start talking to other girls.

The bottle spins, the 45s turn, and I am back in the game.

Life & Love

19

Since I found out Katie was engaged, my entire focus has been on her and my classes. Nothing else matters.

Katie and I met up at the Christmas tree lighting on Front Campus last Tuesday. Organizers wander through the crowd passing out lit candles to everyone. The candles and lightly falling snow make everything look like a magical winter wonderland. We stand before the large pine tree waiting for the Christmas lights to come on. I take Katie's hand. She looks at me with a bit of sadness in her eyes but doesn't pull her hand away. I smile at her, and we continue holding hands. I want her as much as I have ever wanted anything. She lights up my life. When I see her, anything and every-thing seems possible. When I'm away from her, my only thought is how and when I can see her again.

After a countdown, KSU President White pulls down a lever, and thousands of lights burst forth from the dark evergreen tree. It is spectacular. Katie and I both clap. The KSU chorus sings Christmas carols accompanied by members of the KSU marching band. Volunteers pass out mimeographed copies of the lyrics, and Katie and I sing along. I look at her, and she looks back at me with those big blue eyes, and I feel like there is something she wants to say but holds back. Being with Katie feels so right. She reaches out and takes my hand again. I like that and smile at her. She smiles back, and at least for tonight, I feel we are one.

After the singing ends, we help ourselves to free hot chocolate and sip it as we walk back to her dorm. When we get there, I look into her eyes and say, "Thanks for meeting me. I had a great time."

"Me too. It was a beautiful evening."

"I'm glad we experienced it together."

Katie nods her head and smiles. "Goodnight."

I smile back at her. "Goodnight." As I walk back to my dorm and think about Katie, I feel something between us has changed definitely for the better.

I wake up the next morning and look out my dorm window. Snow continued falling throughout the night, and the campus is covered in a fluffy blanket of white. When I see Katie in geography this morning, I will tell her about my idea for another non-date.

Katie is smiling and seems happy to see me when I get to class. "How did you sleep last night? Did you have sweet dreams?"

"After a perfect evening, I had very sweet dreams."

Katie smiles. "Me too."

"The snow looks wonderful. I'm thinking of sledding on Blanket Hill over by the Commons after lunch. Would you like to join me? We can meet by the Pagoda next to Taylor Hall."

Katie pauses for a moment. "I don't have a sled, do you?"

"Let me take care of that. How about if we meet at 2:00?"

"Okay. Sounds like fun."

After geography, I walk Katie to her next class. "See you at 2:00 by the Pagoda," I remind her as we part.

"I'm looking forward to it."

After lunch in Eastway, I leave with two empty lunch trays under my winter coat and walk to Blanket Hill with my "sleds." The lunch trays are made of heavy fiberglass and are almost indestructible. Katie is waiting for me by the Pagoda wearing a white ski hat and white mittens. She looks like a beautiful snow bunny. I show her the "sleds" and she laughs.

"Are you ready to give it a try?"

"You go first, and if you don't break your neck, I'll follow."

"Just hold on tight to the sides of the tray with your feet in front of you. If you go too fast, dig your heels into the snow."

"Okay. I'll watch you first and see how it's done."

I slide downhill and quickly pick up speed, but slow down with my heels in the snow before reaching the bottom. I turn around and wave at her. She waves back, sits down on the tray, and cautiously slides down the hill. Every few feet, she brakes with her heels so that she doesn't gain too much speed. When she makes it to the bottom, I grin. "Ready to do it again?"

"Yes! And maybe I'll go a little faster this time."

"Let's start together."

The next run is a little faster, and the ones after that are even faster. We have a great afternoon but are cold and wet, so we decide that we have had enough fun for one day.

"Thanks for meeting me for sledding. I really enjoy being with you," I say as she hands me her tray. Our mittened hands touch for just a moment, and I give her hand a reassuring squeeze.

"Me too. I had fun. The cafeteria trays were a brilliant idea." We wave goodbye and turn in opposite directions toward our dorms.

Friday, December 5, 1969, is our last day of classes for fall quarter. Final exams start on Monday. When I get to geography class, I ask Katie if she wants to study together for the exam next Wednesday. She agrees and we plan to meet in the lobby of Rockwell Library, Monday afternoon, December 8, at 2:00.

After class ends, I tell Katie "I'm sad our class time together is over. I'll miss sitting next to you. Do you want to meet at the Student Union for a Coke later this afternoon?"

"I'll miss class with you too," Katie replies. "I can't meet this afternoon. I'm heading home to Cleveland for the weekend and won't be back until late Sunday."

"Oh. Okay. Have a great weekend. See you at the library on Monday."

She says, "You too. See you Monday."

As she waves goodbye, I see the sparkle of her diamond and know, with a twinge of sadness, that she will see her fiancé, Chuck, this weekend.

I study for final exams all weekend and try not to think about Katie. Not thinking about Katie is futile. When I'm not studying, I think about Katie, and when I am studying, I also think about Katie.

I've never studied for a final exam. In high school, I just showed up and took the test. Sometimes the result was good, and sometimes it was average, but I never flunked a test. My first midterm in History of Mesopotamia demonstrated to me that a new approach was required. My new study methods seemed to work for the rest of my midterms. But now I will be tested on the material for an entire quarter. I start with my spiral-bound notebook for each course and read all my notes cover to cover. Then I reread them and then read them a third time. I also review my highlighted passages in each textbook. I feel good about my preparation, but I really don't know what I don't know. My grades on the finals will tell the real story.

I spend most of Sunday reading my class notes again and again. It takes about three hours every time I review my extensive notes.

Monday does not come soon enough. I have my History of Mesopotamia final at 10:00 this morning. I feel as ready as I will ever be. I arrive early with my "Blue Book" in hand. The graduate assistant passes out the test questions. I read all of them before starting. The exam is not easy, but my preparation has been adequate. I can easily write several pages to answer each question. I finish the exam within the allotted time and feel good about the result.

After my exam, I walk to Eastway cafeteria for lunch. It's bitter cold, and the sidewalks are icy. Snow from last week has melted and re-frozen. I pull my ski hat over my ears and walk head down into the howling wind. I am glad to get inside Eastway where it's warm.

I select chicken noodle soup and a turkey on rye sandwich for lunch. The soup helps warm me up. I think about Katie and wonder about her weekend with Chuck. She told me she's been dating him for about three years. That's much longer than the three months we've known each other. Since her engagement, I can tell Katie is conflicted each time we meet. Still, it will be great to see her. I want to be with her, that has not changed.

I venture back out into the cold and fight through the wind to the library. I arrive about fifteen minutes early and sit in the lobby. Ten minutes later, Katie comes through the door, and the room seems to brighten.

She smiles when she sees me, and my heart goes flip–flop. "Hi. I missed you. How was your weekend at home?"

She says, "I missed you too. Let's find a quiet place where we can talk."

We find an empty alcove in the stacks with no one else nearby. I say, "Did you freeze walking over from your dorm?"

Katie says, "Almost. It's colder here than in Cleveland."

"Did you have a good visit with your mom?" I ask.

Katie sighs, "Well, Friday was good, but the rest of the weekend was rough."

"Why, what happened?"

"I saw Chuck on Saturday afternoon and gave him back his ring. We broke up." She holds up her left hand, sans engagement ring, and looks into my eyes. "I'm available if you still want me."

I can hardly believe this has happened. I give her a big smile, take her hand, and look into her eyes. Holding her gaze, I say, "I will want you every day for as long as you will have me."

I see tears in her eyes and lean toward her. Our lips meet, and her kiss is soft and sweet, unlike any kiss I've ever had. I pull back for a moment, look into her eyes, and kiss her again and again and again. I finally break the embrace. "Wow, that was even better than my dreams."

Katie smiles. "For me too."

"You have no idea how long I've been wanting to do that."

"Exactly how long would that be?" Katie asks softly.

"From the first day I met you," I confess.

She says, "I was attracted to you from our first meeting too. I don't know how that's possible."

I lean in, and we kiss again. "Maybe, we are just meant to be together."

Suddenly, Katie looks alarmed and pushes back from me. "Johnny, what about Carol?"

I smile to reassure her and say, "It's okay. I broke up with Carol the day you told me you were engaged. I knew I could not give my heart to anyone but you."

"But you didn't know I would break up with Chuck," Katie says.

"That's true, but I only wanted you. I knew I could not pursue you and date Carol at the same time. You were the only girl in my thoughts."

Katie says, "That's sweet." This time she leans in and kisses me with a little extra. I want to hold her in my arms and kiss her all night long but think I should let her make the next move.

"Why was the weekend so rough after you broke off the engagement?"

Katie answers, "Ohhh, my mom did not approve of my breaking up with Chuck," she says with emphasis on *not*. "She's convinced I should marry him. She loves him like a son and thinks he can do no wrong. When I told her about you, she got angry and said, 'How can you throw away Chuck for someone you just met?' And so, we went back and forth with the same arguments about Chuck and you the rest of the weekend."

"I want to meet your mom."

Katie pauses before answering. "That's sweet, but let's give her some time to get used to the idea of you."

"Okay. Whenever you think the time is right," I say. "I guess we should do some studying for our geography exam."

"I guess so," she says and gives me another hot kiss.

I say, "You keep that up, and we will both flunk the exam."

She laughs, and her eyes twinkle. "I've behaved around you far too long. I'm just making up for lost time."

I laugh and say, "I like your style."

We study some and then agree to meet at the Student Union after dinner. We must eat meals in our assigned cafeteria, hers in Terrace Hall, mine in Eastway, so we can't have our meals together. That's too bad because I want to be with Katie all the time.

I meet Katie at the Student Union, and we kiss as soon as we see each other. And then we kiss again, and again, and again. I finally come up for air, wrap my arms around her and ask, "How is your studying going for your other finals?"

"Okay, but somebody has been distracting me,"

"It must be your roommate."

"I don't think so." She smiles at me and my heart melts.

We talk about her family and mine. Her parents divorced when she was eight, and they were living in California. Her mom, older brother, and Katie moved back to Cleveland and have been living with her grandmother ever since. I tell her about my family, including my screwed-up dad.

"I am not looking forward to going home for Christmas," I admit, "but I don't have any other options. Campus is closed for the Christmas holiday starting Saturday, and I can't get back into my dorm until January 3."

Katie frowns. "I'm going to miss you."

I pull Katie into my arms, "I'm going to miss you too. But I will call you. I know my dad won't let me use our home phone to make long-distance calls, so I will call you from a pay phone."

Katie's face lights up. "That will be nice." Her tone changes. "I'm sure I will have another battle with my mom about Chuck when I get home. That won't be nice."

We continue to talk about anything and everything while holding hands and sharing kisses. "When is your last final?" I ask her.

"Friday. How about you?"

"Also Friday. I'm going to take a bus to Lima early Saturday morning."

Katie says "My uncle is picking me up Saturday morning. Do you want to get together and celebrate the end of finals Friday afternoon?"

"That will be perfect. How about if I meet you at your dorm at 5:00."

"It's a date," she says, giving me a naughty smile.

Life & Love

20

Friday, December 12, 1969 • Kent State University, Kent, Ohio

Katie and I see each other every day for at least a little while throughout exam week. We usually meet at the library and do some studying and some kissing, and some studying and some kissing, and so on and so on. I cannot get enough of her and look forward to our post-exam celebration this afternoon.

Finals for the fall quarter are almost over. Yay! I have one last exam today—calculus. I'm happy but exhausted. I've really put in the work preparing for my finals. My method was: read my class notes, read the highlighted textbook material, and repeat. I did that for each course until I ran out of time. I feel good about how I did on each test, so I think my study technique worked. We shall see.

I arrive at Terrace Hall early. Katie gets off the elevator just as I sit down in the lobby. She looks hot. She is wearing a peach-colored sweater that really shows off her spectacular body. I put my arm around her waist and lean in for a kiss. Her sweater is made of cashmere and seems to melt into her body when I touch her waist. She is so soft, and her kiss says much more than just hello.

She pulls back, and I say, "Wow! It's good to see you too."

She gives me that naughty smile again, and says, "Are you ready to celebrate the end of finals?"

"So ready. I thought we might go downtown and have some pizza and beer at Big Daddy's."

She says, "I thought we might do something else. My roommate already left for Christmas break. Would you like to come up and see my room?"

She doesn't have to ask twice. "A perfect plan," I say. She smiles, takes my hand, and presses the elevator button.

Inside, Katie presses the button for the fourth floor. She puts my hands around her waist and gives me a hot French kiss. She presses her body into mine, and I can feel her breasts against my chest. The kiss continues until the elevator door opens. She takes me by the hand and leads me into her room. Soft music plays on her stereo. A single study lamp is angled away from her bed providing just enough shadow and light to set the mood. I can feel the anticipation of what is about to happen pulse through my body. Katie pulls me over to her bed and gently pushes me down onto it. She lies next to me, takes the lead, and kisses me hard, which immediately makes me hard. Our bodies are pressed against each other so there is no way for her not to notice. I start to tell her how I have longed to hold her, but she puts the tip of her forefinger to my lips. "*Shhhh,*" she says. I immediately get the message. Katie is in charge.

We continue kissing passionately, and then she lightly bites my ear lobe. I kiss the side of her neck and unbutton the top button of her cashmere sweater. I kiss her neck that has been exposed by the button and she takes my hand and places it on her breast. I am breathing heavily, and she is too. I unbutton the second button of her sweater and feel her nipple harden beneath my hand. I brush her nipple through her sweater with my lips and then kiss her lips. She takes my hand and moves it to her other breast, and I feel that nipple go hard when I touch it through her sweater. I undo the rest of her buttons and pull back her sweater. She is wearing a pink lace bra. She looks delicious. The tops of her breasts are milky white. I pull down the edge of her bra and brush her bare nipple with my lips. She sighs and I close my mouth around her nipple and flick my tongue across the tip. She raises her hips and moans.

I pull down her bra strap and expose her entire breast. It is beautiful. I cup her breast with my hand and take as much as I can into my mouth and suckle her breast. Her nipples are rigid, and as I flick my tongue back and forth across her nipple, she grabs the ass of my jeans and says, "Take these off!" I lift up and do as I am told. I then slide the other strap off her shoulder and kiss the underside of her other breast. Katie reaches down and slides her hand inside the front of my underwear and takes hold of my erect penis. She slides her hand up and down inside my underwear. I gasp as she continues stroking me. I reach around her back and unsnap her bra. It falls away and exposes two perfect breasts caressed by the edges of her cashmere sweater. I kiss one breast and then the other. She wears a perfume that seems to intensify every time I touch her.

Katie pulls her hand out of my underwear and starts to unzip her jeans. I gently push her hand away and run my hand slowly down the front of her from her breasts across her belly button to the top of her jeans. I slip my hand inside the front of her jeans until I can feel her lace panties. I lift the front of her panties and slide my hand down and across her pubic hair until I feel her wet vagina. She gasps as I lightly flick the ridge at the top of her clit. I slowly pull my hand out and pull down the zipper of her jeans. She lifts her hips and I slide her jeans off her hips and run my hand up her inner thigh as I pull them the rest of the way off.

She is wearing matching pink lace panties. I can feel and smell her wetness as I kiss the top of her panties and move up across her taut belly. I kiss both breasts before passionately taking her lips on mine. She lifts her hips again and moans. She then takes my underwear and in one swift motion pulls them down exposing all of me to her. She pushes me onto my back and straddles me. She slips off her sweater and her beautiful breasts exposed in front of me send shivers down my entire body. She pulls off my sweater, looks at all of me and moans.

Starting at my neck she kisses both sides of my neck and then slides her hands over my nipples. She kisses one nipple and then the other and gives a flick of her tongue over each nipple after the kiss. She works her way down the front of my body and just before she gets to my penis, she tells me to turn over. The anticipation is killing me, but I willingly obey. She then bends down over my back and brushes the top of my back with her breasts while kissing the back of my neck. The feel of her soft breasts on my back almost sends me over the edge. She then works her way down my back, kissing me all the way down. When she gets to my bottom, she reaches between my legs and grasps my throbbing penis. I arch my back upwards to give her better access and she strokes me from behind. I moan and want more.

She then urges me to turn over to my front. She takes my rock-hard balls and rakes her manicured nails across them. I moan hard and then with no warning her mouth is on my penis, and she is flicking her tongue across the ridge. I am ready to explode, but somehow manage to hold off. She takes my entire shaft into her mouth and moves up and down. I think she knows I'm getting ready to come and pulls her mouth off me.

I make a move to sit up and change positions with her, but she is not having any of it. She pushes me back down and slips off her lace panties. She then guides herself onto my penis and moans. I was already in heaven, and I am now panting with pleasure. She moves back and forth until she finds the right spot, and then moves even faster. I reach up and grasp her nipple with my fingers, and then bring her nipple to my mouth. As soon as my mouth closes over her nipple, she gasps and cries, "yes," and moans loudly as she moves slowly back and forth. She looks at me, smiles, and then kisses me wildly and starts moving faster. Within seconds, I moan and let it go. She smiles again and rolls off me.

I snuggle up next to her and say, "You are amazing. You're beautiful. I cannot get enough of you. It's like I've waited all my life for you and now here you are. I've never said this to anyone else. "I love you."

She smiles, kisses me, nuzzles up against me and says, "Johnny, you are a very special guy. I love you too."

I look at her and whisper, "You were definitely worth waiting for. I love being with you. I love talking with you. I love your eyes, your cute nose, the way you kiss me. I love everything about you. I will love you every day you will have me."

Katie smiles at me and I can see the love in her eyes. "Johnny don't ever let me go. I will love you with all my heart and soul."

We never made it to Big Daddy's that night. Two more rounds of lovemaking push away any thoughts of going downtown. After the last lovemaking session, I know I am spent, and say "That was quite a Christmas present. Thank you."

She smiles. "I liked my Christmas present too. Thank you."

I say, "You are something else. How am I going to spend the next three weeks without seeing you?"

She says, "I know it is going to be tough, but just remember what will be waiting for you when you return from Christmas break."

I smile and say, "No chance of me forgetting that."

We spend the night together, and I kiss her goodbye just as the sun is rising.

Bayonets & Bullets

21

I sleep late on Sunday morning, not waking up until shortly before 8:00. At The Hub yesterday, my girlfriend Katie and I talked about going to the 9:00 Mass at the Newman Center. Katie is not an every-Sunday Catholic, but in times of trouble feels the peace she receives at the Newman Center calling to her. I am a Christian, but not a Catholic, and since arriving at KSU, my churchgoing has been limited to attending services at the Newman Center when Katie wants to go.

I look out my third-floor window to see if any National Guardsmen are posted close by. I can see Allyn Hall, and across the street, Beall Hall. No guardsmen or military vehicles are in sight. Maybe they settled everything down last night and left campus.

I'm meeting Katie at 8:40 at her dorm, and then we will take a short walk over to the Newman Center. I have just enough time for a quick breakfast at the Eastway cafeteria. In line, I hear a lot of talk about the burning of the ROTC building last night and the National Guard still being on campus. A few students I know tell me the Guard is all over Front Campus and is using the old football stadium across from Bowman Hall as a staging area. They say that army jeeps, trucks, and tanks are everywhere. So much for the Guard leaving campus.

I finish breakfast and head over to meet Katie. Army jeeps are lined up along the street next to her dorm. An armored personnel carrier blocks the entrance to Terrace Drive from Main Street. Guardsmen are everywhere but don't challenge anyone walking on or off campus. It's a beautiful morning, and the guardsmen seem to be relaxed and enjoying the warm spring weather. Several of them lean against their jeeps, watching Kent's iconic black squirrels scamper across the grass and chase each other up the trees. Several of the guardsmen look about my age—eighteen or nineteen. Most likely, they are factory workers, auto mechanics, or tradesmen who joined the Guard to avoid being drafted and going to Vietnam.

Katie is waiting for me in the Terrace Hall lobby. I'm dressed in my best outfit: red plaid bell bottoms, a white cable knit sweater, and platform shoes. I look up and see Katie coming toward me. Wow! She looks exquisite. She's wearing a dark blue mini-skirt with a white satin blouse, blue kitten heels, and a pearl necklace. I rarely see her in a skirt. Most of the time she wears jeans and a blouse or sweater, just like all the other girls on campus.

I kiss her and say, "You look ravishing."

"Thanks," she says, smiling up at me.

"Maybe we should go back to your room after church."

She gives me a slight shove. "Behave. My roommate is here."

I smile. "Did you see the National Guard out front?"

"Yes, I saw them from my room. Do you think we'll have a problem getting to the Newman Center?"

"I don't think so. Students are walking on and off campus without being stopped.

"Okay. Let's go. I don't want to be late."

We walk out the front door, turn right on Terrace Drive, and right onto Main Street. Guardsmen nearby look at us. Some of the younger ones smile and nod at Katie. They're just like any other healthy guy my age, I think. We walk by the Midway Drive entrance to campus and are astonished by the number of National Guard vehicles and guardsmen stationed there. Two tank-like armored personnel carriers and at least a dozen jeeps are parked along

Midway Drive. No one confronts us, so we walk past Midway Drive and continue up Main Street.

As we walk by President White's house, another armored personnel carrier and several jeeps are parked in the driveway, where half a dozen guardsmen are talking. I don't sense activity inside the house. We haven't heard anything from President White since the unrest began on Friday night.

Katie says, "The rumor is that President White isn't even on campus. He's at some conference out in Iowa."

"Really?"

"That's what my roommate told me. Our campus is under siege, and he is off on some junket. She doesn't know when he's supposed to return."

Another contingent of National Guardsmen and vehicles is parked at the entrance to Horning Road. Again, no one questions us as we walk toward the Newman Center. We arrive with five minutes to spare. We find a pew, and Katie genuflects and sits down. I don't genuflect but follow her and sit down. The Newman Center is two-thirds full, typical for other 9:00 Masses I've attended. The priest delivers a homily encouraging peace in our country and on campus. It's a timely message. I hope both students and guardsmen will get through this occupation peacefully.

When Mass ends at 9:40, I ask Katie, "What would you like to do next?"

"I want to go back to my dorm and change, and then see what's left of the ROTC building."

"Okay, let's cut through campus on the way back to your dorm."

We walk toward Theatre Drive, past the Music and Speech Center and Nixson Hall, then turn right onto Midway Drive. Several National Guard vehicles are in the parking lots, but no guardsmen are stationed at the building entrances.

We enter the back entrance of Terrace Hall, and Katie says, "I'll be quick. You wait here."

I smile and wink at her. "Do you need any help changing?"

Katie grins. "You're bad. I told you to behave. Stay here."

I hang my head. "Okay."

Five minutes later, Katie is back, and we walk toward the Commons and the ROTC building. We arrive at what is left of the ROTC Building shortly after 10:00. A heavy line of National Guardsmen surrounds the site, standing at attention only a couple of feet apart, holding M1s across their chests with bayonets fixed.

The ruins are still smoldering and the pungent smell of damp, burnt wood lingers in the air.

"It's completely destroyed," Katie utters, her eyes wide in disbelief.

I'm shocked at the sight too. It looks worse this morning than it did last night.

The guardsmen prevent us from getting close to the rubble, so we walk on the Commons and circle around the perimeter to the east side of the cordoned-off site. A motorcade pulls up directly in front of us, and Governor Rhodes accompanied by an entourage of suits emerges from the vehicles. We are too far away to hear anything being said, but I watch the governor point at the ruins of the ROTC building. As the governor continues his tour around the site, more and more students gather on the Commons, gawking at the governor and the smoldering ruins. After a few minutes, the governor and his motorcade depart. A student I know from Clark Hall tells us that he heard on the radio that the governor has a news conference scheduled at 10:15 this morning. I look at my watch. It's 10:15.

We walk back across the Commons toward Front Campus and see the tennis fence that was torn down last night, and the blackened remains of the archery equipment shed. Katie says, "The War is wrong, but destroying our campus is not the answer. We need to get our message across through peaceful protest."

"I agree violence is not the answer."

Just as we turn to leave the Commons, a National Guardsman shouts through a bullhorn, *"Your assembly on the Commons is unlawful, and you are ordered to immediately disperse."*

Katie and I look at each other and say, almost simultaneously, "You've got to be kidding."

Nothing organized is going on here. No protest is happening. No one is shouting anti-war slogans. A bunch of students are quietly looking at the ruins of the ROTC building.

"Johnny, I don't want to be tear-gassed. Let's get out of here," Katie says, with a quiver in her voice.

We quickly head toward the pedestrian gate on Front Campus at the corner of Lincoln and Main streets, known as Prentice Gate, and encounter an almost carnival-like atmosphere. More students are out than you would normally find on a Sunday morning. Some chat with the guardsmen who seem relaxed. Some guardsmen have their helmets off and lean against their jeeps smoking cigarettes. Several jeeps are parked at the corner entrance to Prentice Gate, one is parked across Lincoln Street in front of Captain Brady's café, and another one is parked across Main Street in front of the Robin Hood Inn. Some students throw Frisbees on the lawn. Other students just sit on the grass talking.

No one is protesting. Katie and I wander through the crowd. Everyone just wants to know why the guardsmen are on campus and when they are leaving.

Teens & Dreams

22

Friday, April 28, 1967 • Lima, Ohio

By 7:00, I'm up to get ready for school. We don't have a shower in our one-bathroom house, just a bathtub. With four boys and two adults, baths are not an everyday occurrence for everyone. I am the exception. I need to look good every day, so I bathe every night. As kids, we were not required to brush our teeth, but now as a teenager, I brush them religiously every morning.

Mom makes sure the younger boys have a good breakfast, but I just pour myself a bowl of Sugar Crisp cereal and a glass of orange juice and make a couple of pieces of toast.

Jack gives me a ride to school every day, so I walk across the street at 7:45 for the five-minute drive.

I head to homeroom with Mr. Riker. He's an older teacher and pretty laid back. The sophomore class dynamics are different than they were last year at Central. That's because all the ninth graders from South Junior High have now joined the ninth graders from Central Junior High to form the sophomore class at Lima Senior High. I don't know a lot of the kids because they haven't been in any of my classes. And the girls at Lima Senior are an enigma to me. I have carried my inferiority complex with me to high school, and while I'm okay talking to girls from L.C.C. and Shawnee, I feel stuck, like an outsider looking in, when I talk to girls at Lima Senior.

I have barely spoken to any of them and have not been invited to any parties by any kids in my class. I still feel like I am a nobody at Lima Senior.

My classes are okay for the most part. The exceptions are history with Mr. Bradley and English with Mrs. Granger. Both seem to have it in for me.

Today in history, we are discussing the war in Vietnam. Mr. Bradley tells us that the U.S. needs to fight in Vietnam to keep the peace and stop the spread of communism.

I raise my hand and, when recognized by Mr. Bradley, ask, "What about the large demonstrations against the war in San Francisco and New York City last week? Over ten thousand people protested in each city. And three weeks ago, Dr. Martin Luther King Jr. denounced the war in Vietnam at a Sunday service in New York City. More than six thousand U.S. servicemen were killed in action in Vietnam last year. That seems like a high price to pay for peace in a country that is halfway around the world and not threatening the U.S." I continue, "I recently heard an analogy that is relevant here—fighting for peace is like fucking for chastity."

Mr. Bradley immediately interrupts me. "That's enough. We don't need that kind of language here."

I just look at him and smile. I can tell he doesn't like me at all.

My next class is English with Mrs. Granger. Every class is like a contest of wills between us. I walk into class and Mrs. Granger looks directly at me. Her eyes are like daggers. She is used to intimidating her students, but that doesn't work with me. I stare right back at her and smile. I can tell it infuriates her, so I keep doing it. Every time she calls on me, her intent is to embarrass me. She doesn't know that I've had sixteen years of daily belittling by my dad, so I don't submit to her attempts to intimidate me, which angers her even more.

Two weeks ago, Mrs. Granger sent a letter to my mom. It surprised both of us. No teacher has ever sent a letter to my parents. Mom showed the letter to me and asked what was going on. I am consistently getting Bs on my tests and papers so I knew it couldn't be about my grades. Mrs. Granger wrote that I was a "disruption" in her class and that I would likely "become a juvenile delinquent and end up in jail." The letter went on to request that Mom call the school and arrange a meeting with Mrs. Granger. Mom called the school office and asked that Mrs. Granger call her back. I told Mom she would never call her back and that there would be no meeting. It's been over two weeks and Mom is still waiting for a phone call.

My health class is with Mr. Scranton, who also coaches varsity football. Several boys in my class know him well. We are supposed to learn about sex in this class, but every time the subject of sex comes up, Mr. Scranton refers us to the textbook and assumes that fifteen- and sixteen-year-old boys know all about sex. The textbook contains some basic diagrams of the female reproductive system but does not go into the details about sex that I learned from the book I found in my mom's underwear drawer last year. Without my mom's book, I would still have no idea what sex is all about. We learn everything in health class except how to actually have sex.

Social studies with Mr. Riker, my homeroom teacher, is one of my favorite classes. We talk about current events in the U.S., and what is going on around the world. Our first discussion today is about the unmanned *Surveyor 3* probe that landed on the Moon last week. It took photos of the Earth and relayed them back to mission control. It is very cool to see how the Earth looks from about 239 thousand miles away. We talk about Mohammed Ali, formerly known as Cassius Clay, the world heavyweight boxing champion, and his refusal to be drafted for military service due to his religious beliefs and his opposition to the Vietnam War. We discuss what it means to be a conscientious objector. I feel this is an important discussion. I don't think I am a conscientious objector, but the discussion helps put into perspective how to oppose the war.

My final class of the day, French with Mrs. Spively, is always fun. She greets us in French and talks to us in French as though we understand every word she is saying. Sometimes it's comical because most of us have no idea what she's saying. She helps us dullards along and makes our ineptness funny, without making us feel bad about ourselves. It's a real balancing act and she does it with aplomb.

Jack and I head home after classes are done for the day. We are going to Diane's later to see her new motorcycle, then heading to another house party tonight. At home, I change into something fresh and tell Mom I am going bowling. I always tell her I am going bowling so that I don't have to give her any details about what I'm really doing. Provided I'm back by my midnight curfew, and don't get into any trouble, I don't think she cares what I do.

On the way to Diane's, Jack tells me that Diane's mom gave her a new 50cc Honda motorcycle for her birthday. "It's easy to ride," he says. "I rode it around her backyard last Saturday. It's a blast."

I say, "It sounds cool."

It's a beautiful spring day and feels like it's in the seventies. We meet Diane in her backyard and admire her motorcycle. Diane doesn't have her driver's license yet, so the bike has no license plates.

"It's a neat little motorcycle. Very cool," I say.

"Would you like to learn how to ride it?" Diane asks.

"Sure, if it's okay with you,"

"I'll show you some basics on how to start it and shift gears."

I get on the bike, and Diane gives me instructions. "The clutch is on the left handlebar, and the left leg peg is used for shifting. Pull the peg up with the toe of your shoe for first gear, and access four more gears by pushing down on the peg with the bottom of your left foot. Neutral is in between first and second gear. The rear tire brake is the peg just ahead of your right foot, and the front tire brake is the pull brake on the right handlebar. To give it gas, turn the right handle grip toward you."

"That's a lot to learn for my first lesson."

She says, "Not to worry, just stay in first gear to begin and remember that the brake is just ahead of your right foot. If you are going to stop, let go of the gas, pull in the clutch with your left hand, and it will be like the bike is in neutral."

"Now that I know what to do, let me see you do it first before I try it."

Diane gets on the motorcycle, pulls in the clutch with her left hand, pulls up the gear shift into first, gives it a little gas with her right hand, and slowly lets out the clutch with her left hand. She is off and going slowly around the perimeter of her backyard.

When she comes around, she stops in front of me and says, "Are you ready to give it a try?"

"Sure," I say.

Diane gets off the bike, and I get on. I do exactly what she told me. The bike jumps forward and stalls.

"You popped the clutch," Diane says. "You have to let the clutch out slowly while giving the bike more gas."

"Okay."

I go through the same motions again, and this time, I still let the clutch out too fast but slower than last time, and I still do not give it enough gas, and the bike lurches forward a couple of times, but then smooths out. I stay in first gear and go slow, but I know I am immediately hooked. I want one.

I stop after doing a couple of laps around her yard.

Diane says, "You got it. Now shift into second gear after you pick up some speed."

I take off again, but this time I take off smoothly and don't bunny-hop the bike. I pick up some speed, pull in the clutch with my left hand, and push down the shift peg with my left foot until I hear a click. I let out the clutch and pick up speed. Wow! I am riding a motorcycle.

Jack takes a turn, and then Diane takes a ride. She is the best. Her control of the bike is flawless.

Just before dark, Diane puts the motorcycle away, and we wash up before heading to the party at Barbara's house. On the way over, Diane says to me, "You know, Barbara sort of likes you. You might want to talk with her tonight."

I say, "Really?" I had no idea. Barbara always seems to go for the older guys. "I'm not sure if I'm right for her."

Diane says, "No harm in talking. See how it goes."

"Sure. Okay.

We arrive at the party a little later than usual, and some of the kids are already dancing in her finished basement. Barbara stands by the record player. I go over to her, and we start talking. She has a bit of a reputation. It's hard to know if any of it's true, but her reputation is that she moves fast with guys. Barbara is more mature than most girls her age. She's taller than me and has very generous breasts. After talking for a while, Barbara says, "We need more Cokes. Do you want to help me get them in the kitchen?"

"Sure," I say, and we walk upstairs. When we get to the kitchen, Barbara turns toward me and says, "I've been wanting to kiss you all night."

No further hint is needed. I lean in and start kissing her the way I had kissed the girls during rounds of spin the bottle. Barbara opens her mouth slightly while we are kissing and sticks her tongue in my mouth. It is unexpected but not unpleasant. I do the same to her with my tongue, and suddenly my body wakes up and is on fire. So, this must be what French kissing is all about. I feel myself go hard, but Barbara keeps French kissing me, wraps her arms around me, and leans into me. I can feel her breasts against my chest, and it feels wonderful.

After a few minutes of kissing, she takes my hand and says, "Come with me." We walk down the hallway off the kitchen to a bathroom. She pulls me inside and closes and locks the door. She then starts kissing me even more passionately. Barbara is wearing a button-down blouse with the shirt tail untucked. She takes my hand and puts it under her shirt around her bare waist.

This is uncharted territory for me. I have never French kissed a girl, never felt a girl's breasts against my chest, and never touched the bare skin of a girl's waist. She is really turning me on. We keep kissing, and then I move my hand up inside her shirt and brush her bra with my thumb. She keeps kissing me and doesn't tell me to stop, so I move my hand further up her bra until I feel her nipple through her bra. I brush her nipple with my thumb and then wrap my hand around her breast. She inhales rapidly and moans a little. She suddenly stops kissing me, pulls away, and says, "We'd better get back before someone misses us."

I say, "Okay, but I'm going to need a minute."

She looks down at the erection in my pants. "Oh, okay. You stay here and I will meet you downstairs."

I smile, give her another kiss, and she leaves. It takes a couple of minutes for things to get back to normal.

When I walk downstairs, Barbara is talking with some of her girlfriends. She catches my eye and smiles at me. I smile back and then get myself a cold Coke. My face feels hot. I don't know if anyone has missed me or can see that my face is red. After a while, no one says anything to me, so I don't think anyone noticed us go upstairs.

I talk with Barbara intermittently throughout the evening, but there is no repeat of the earlier events.

At the end of the party, I find her and say, "Thanks for a fun party and for being a great hostess."

She smiles, winks at me, and says, "I hope you enjoyed yourself tonight."

I lean in, kiss her cheek and whisper in her ear, "You know I did. Thank you."

On the drive back to Diane's house, she asks, "Did you have a good time with Barbara tonight? I saw the two of you go upstairs alone."

"Yes, she is really sweet."

"Did you kiss her?"

I can feel the blood rushing to my face, but it's dark inside the car. I say, "We may have had a kiss or two."

Diane looks at me and says, "Good."

Teens & Dreams

23

Today is the last day of the Allen County Fair and the last day of my summer job. I've been on the road for eight weeks working for Nelson Food Service, traveling from county fair to county fair around Ohio.

In early June, just as I am about to finish my sophomore year at Lima Senior, I start my search for a summer job. I need a job to have enough money to buy a car at the end of the summer. The problem is that almost every job has a minimum age requirement of sixteen, and I won't turn sixteen until July. Laws exist about using child labor, and sixteen is the minimum age to avoid running afoul of those laws.

I look at the Want Ads in the *Lima News* under "Help Wanted: Male" to see if anyone will hire a fifteen-year-old. Most businesses want a recent college grad or at least someone with experience. Then I spot this ad: WANTED: HIGH SCHOOL STUDENT TO WORK SUMMER JOB AT COUNTY FAIRS IN FOOD SERVICE. CALL 419-555-1212 TO APPLY.

I call the number and speak to a Mr. Nelson. He explains that his company works the county fair circuit in Western Ohio, selling hotdogs, snow cones, and cotton candy. He provides all the training I will need. He will leave Lima on June 23 and not return until August 19 when the Allen County Fair begins. The job will end when the fair ends on August 24. The pay is $40 per week, and if I stay the entire eight weeks, I'll receive a bonus of $250. I'll be required to work whatever hours each fair is open, which will be Saturday through Thursday for most fairs, plus a setup day for each fair on Friday. Most midways will be open from 11:00 a.m. to 10:00 p.m., and I will be expected to work those hours with thirty minutes off for both lunch and dinner. I am welcome to eat the hotdogs and other food the Nelsons sell, but all other meals will be at my own expense. They will provide a tent and sleeping bag for me to use. Each fairground has communal showers. Mr. Nelson tells me that he is looking to hire three young men for the summer. If I am interested, we can set up a time for an interview.

It is a lot to consider. I will be gone for eight weeks, the entire summer, and will not see any of my friends or family during that time. I like the idea of being away from my dad for eight weeks. The weekly pay seems low, but at the end of the summer, with the $250 bonus, I will have enough money to buy a car and pay for the required liability insurance.

The only time I have been away from home was when I went to church camp, and I didn't miss home at all. I don't think being away for eight weeks will be a problem. Who will I miss? Who will miss me? Not my dad, not my brothers, maybe my mom. I have no steady girlfriend, so that won't be an issue. I will miss going to house parties and hanging out with my friends, but at the end of the summer, I will have enough money to buy a car, and a car means independence. With a car, I can go on dates. I can drive myself to school. By the end of the summer, I will have turned sixteen and will be able to find a part-time job to pay for gas and dates. With a car, I can leave the house and my dad anytime I choose. For eight weeks of sacrifice, I see many future benefits.

I call Mr. Nelson and tell him I am interested, and we arrange a meeting time. I ride my bike to the interview.

Mr. Nelson asks, "How old are you, son?"

"Fifteen, but I'll be sixteen in July."

He says, "Well, I usually like to hire boys who are at least sixteen, but I guess I could make an exception for you."

The interview goes well, and at the end, Mr. Nelson says, "I think you will do fine in this job. Would you like to work for me this summer?"

"Yes, I would. Do you need anything else from me?"

"I just need to talk with one of your parents to confirm they are okay with you taking the job."

"Ok. I will have my mom give you a call."

"That sounds good.

I am excited that I have just been hired for my first job. My mom is surprised but says she will talk to Dad, who not surprisingly, has no problem with it. One less mouth to feed.

Mom says, "I just want to make sure you know that you will be on your own for the summer. There won't be anyone around that you know."

"I understand, but I will be okay. Can I go?"

She says, "Let me call Mr. Nelson and confirm everything." I give her his phone number, and after the call, she says, "Well, the job is just as you described it. You can go."

"Thanks, Mom!"

On June 23, 1967, Mr. Nelson picks me up at my house. He has one RV motorhome and one panel truck. Each vehicle tows a food service trailer. Mr. Nelson drives the truck, and his wife drives the RV. Mr. Nelson introduces me to two boys in the RV I will be working with, then says to me, "Hop in the truck and ride with me."

It's about an hour's drive to the Paulding County Fairgrounds, our first stop on the county fair circuit. We don't talk much during the drive. Mr. Nelson listens to radio station CKLW, and I finally hear the song "Love is Here and Now You're Gone" by the Supremes that Diane's brother said was cool. It's got a good beat and I bet I could dance to it.

The setup is easy. The trailer towed by the panel truck is equipped to sell hotdogs and drinks. Mr. Nelson says, "You will likely work all of the stations this summer, but let's start you in this trailer."

He plugs the trailer into an electrical outlet and hooks it up to the water spigot. He sets up the hotdog roller that can grill twenty footlong hotdogs at a time. A warming tray is below the grill that holds another twenty footlong hotdogs. He then fills the condiments tray.

He explains, "Mrs. Nelson makes the coney dog chili each day and dices the raw onion. All you need to do is make sure you keep the condiment trays full. The footlong hotdog options are simple: mustard, ketchup, chili, onions, and relish. The drink options are iced tea and lemonade. Both drinks are made from a powder that you mix with water and dump into a clear bubbler dispenser. The ice chest over there is for the drinks along with cups, lids, and straws," he says, pointing to a large white chest in the corner. "And that's it."

Mr. Nelson shows me how to put the bun in a white cardboard holder, pick up a footlong hotdog and place the hotdog in the bun, using a pair of tongs for each step. Add the condiments requested by the customer and collect the money. The whole process takes less than a minute. For a drink, dip the cup into the ice bin, fill it half full, then add either iced tea or lemonade by pulling down the lever on the bubbler.

My "training" takes less than thirty minutes.

Mr. Nelson wheels the snow cone and cotton candy carts down a ramp from the panel truck. Both carts are on wheels, so again, the setup is easy. Just plug the cart into the power outlet, and it is ready to go. Snow cones are easy to make. The snow cone machine grinds a block of ice into tiny bits. I grab some ice with an ice cream scoop, round it off, and put it into a paper cone. I pull down a lever to dispense cherry, grape, orange, or lime syrup over the ice, and that's it.

The cotton candy process is even simpler. Turn on the machine containing a large stainless-steel tub, which blows air through a spinning tube in the center of the tub. Pour flavored sugar into the tube, take a long paper cone, and collect the spun sugar. Pretty easy.

Mr. Nelson said the final trailer sells candy apples, caramel apples, popcorn, Coke, and Sprite, and will normally be operated by Mrs. Nelson and him.

By 3:00, we are finished setting up, and I am trained. "Set up your tents and then you're free for the rest of the day," Mr. Nelson tells us. The two tents each sleep two guys. The other guys decide to share a tent, so I have the second one to myself. The modest canvas tent has a zippered flap in the front. Nothing fancy. I lay out my sleeping bag on the floor of the tent and bring in my small duffle bag containing my clothes and toiletries. This is home for the next eight weeks.

I take off to explore the Paulding County fairgrounds. I find the showers and restrooms. Good to know. I also locate a church tent that serves home-cooked meals, and since nothing else is open, I decide that will be my dinner for the evening. Walking back toward the footlong trailer, I see the cane ring toss game being set up. It looks like the same game I see every summer at the Allen County Fair. You get six rings for a quarter and try to toss a wooden ring onto a decorative wooden cane. If your ring lands over the top of the cane, you win and get to keep the cane. As kids, we loved this game and would always come home with several canes and use them for pretend sword fights. As I walk by, a girl about my age struggles to carry a box from a truck.

"Do you need some help?"

She turns around and looks at me. "Sure. Thanks."

I help her carry that box and several others and then help her set up some of the canes. She introduces herself. "I'm Lynette. Are you working at the fair?"

"Yes, I'm Johnny and I'm working this summer for Mr. Nelson at the footlong stand. How about you? Are you working here this week?"

"Yes. My dad owns this stand. I'll be working here all summer."

"Great. I'm sure I will see you around. It was nice meeting you, Lynette."

She says, "You too. See you later."

Lynette is very pretty. She has large brown eyes and shoulder-length brown hair that flips up in the back. She looks about my age and is definitely someone I want to get to know better. It's a good first day at work.

Selling footlong hotdogs, snow cones, and cotton candy is interesting at first, but soon becomes repetitive. The most interesting part of the job is the customers, especially how they dress and speak. The best part of the job is that I will see Lynette almost every day this summer. It turns out that we will be at the same fairs.

Lynette and I get to know each other, and when I take a break for lunch or dinner, I go over to her stand to see if she wants to take a walk. She introduces me to her dad, and he seems okay for a dad.

The following Friday, after we move to the next county fair and I finish set up with Mr. Nelson, I help Lynette and her dad set up their stand. Afterward, Lynette invites me to their trailer for dinner. She is making spaghetti and says it will be ready at 6:00. Their trailer is near where I set up my tent. Dinner is a nice change from the footlongs I've been eating for a week. After dinner, Lynette asks her father if she can go for a walk with me.

"Just don't stay out too late," he says.

"I won't," she tells him. We walk all around the fairgrounds. She's been here before with her father, so she knows where everything is located.

"Where are you from?" I ask her.

"I live with my dad live in Findlay, Ohio, and will be a rising junior at Findlay High in the fall. I'm an only child. My mom died from cancer two years ago." Findlay and Lima are roughly forty miles apart and have about the same-sized population.

"I'm sorry to hear that about your mom." I say and tell her about my situation.

She says, "It must be hard being away from your family."

"Not really, now that I have a new friend."

She smiles, I lean in, and we kiss. The kiss is sweet but reserved. I can tell she has not kissed many boys. We hold hands and continue our tour of the fairgrounds.

It turns out that the two other guys that Mr. Nelson hired for the summer are best friends. One of the guys quits after the first week, the second guy lasts two weeks. I am now on my own. Mr. Nelson hires temporary local workers at each location to fill in for the guys who left. I eat a lot of footlongs and drink a lot of lemonade. Each day, that is my go-to meal. Otherwise, I am spending my hard-earned money on food. Some of the fairs have an all-you-can-eat pancake and sausage breakfast sponsored by a church or a Rotary Club. I like those breakfasts and always fill up.

On Sunday mornings, I attend church service at each fairground. The interesting thing about those services is that one week it will be a Baptist minister, and the next week, a Methodist minister, or a pastor from a Church of Christ. I find out that each denomination has a set of beliefs that may be different from the others, but all have one thing in common: the belief in Jesus Christ.

Rainy days are always slow at the fairgrounds. Sometimes, if it is raining hard, Mr. Nelson will close early and give us a break. The tent becomes problematic on rainy days. It leaks, and sometimes water runoff floods my tent. After the second week on the road, I abandon the tent and sleep every night in the back of the panel truck, which is always dry. I store my duffle bag and sleeping bag in the truck and can easily pull down the roll-top door at night. I feel much safer than I did in the tent.

Fair life has a seedy side. Some people call all of us who work at the fair "Carnies," short for carnival workers. However, I quickly learn that the real Carnies are the guys who set up the rides and run the games of chance and sideshows. Those Carnies are not to be trusted. Most of the games are rigged in some way so that only a few players win. The Carnies usually have a bottle of liquor stashed under the counter, and after hours, many of them get drunk. I steer clear of all of them.

In early July, my sixteenth birthday comes and goes without

fanfare. I tell Lynette it's my birthday, but nobody else knows or cares. Mr. and Mrs. Nelson are fine employers, but employees are temporary, and the Nelsons make no attempt to invite me into their family circle.

Lynette continues to be the best part of my summer on the road. During my breaks, we stroll the fair or chat while she works the cane toss booth. Fridays are the best. After setup, Lynette and I always find time to share our hopes and dreams. She is a good listener, and I enjoy being with her. She cooks dinner every Friday when the fair is closed and invites me to join them. She is a great cook. After dinner, we find time alone, inevitably leading to kissing and cuddling.

One surprise occurs on Saturday, July 22, 1967. I am by myself working the hotdog stand at the Clark County Fair in Springfield, Ohio. I look up to take the next customer's order, and my mom says, "Hello, stranger."

I am shocked. Even more shocking, my dad is there with her. Henry, Kevin, and Brian are also in line with them.

I smile. "Hi. What are you guys doing here?"

Mom says, "We came to see you, and we're hungry. What do you have back there?"

"Footlong hotdogs and more footlong hotdogs, iced tea and lemonade."

"Well, I guess we will each have a footlong."

I fix the hotdogs just the way they like them and give each of them a drink. Other people are waiting in line, so I tell Mom, "I'm by myself right now, but I have a break in about an hour. Do you think you will still be here then?"

Mom says, "We will meet you back here in an hour."

When they return an hour later, Mr. Nelson returns to relieve me. I introduce everyone to him, and he tells my mom, "You've got a good boy there. He's been working hard this summer."

Mom thanks him, and while we walk around the fairgrounds, my brothers jump around and bombard me with questions.

"Johnny, how many hotdogs have you eaten so far?"

"Did you play the cane game? Do you have any canes for us?"

"When are you coming home?"

An hour later, I say goodbye. It was nice seeing everyone. Even my dad seemed cordial to me. I don't exactly miss them when they leave. Well, maybe I miss my mom.

It's 9:00 p.m. on August 24, 1967, the last day of the Allen County Fair and the last day of my first job. I have been working six, sometimes seven, days a week, at least ten hours a day, with only two thirty-minute breaks each day. It's been a long eight weeks.

Mr. Nelson comes inside the hotdog stand. "You've been a good worker this summer," he says. "Thank you. If you need an employment reference, please feel free to give them my number. I'll give you a good review."

"Thank you. Much appreciated," I say.

He then hands me an envelope. "Here's this week's salary and your bonus. You've earned it. Plus, I put in a little extra."

"Thanks, Mr. Nelson, and thanks for the extra money. I hope to buy a car with this bonus."

"Good luck, son. Do you need a ride home tonight?"

"No. My neighbor is working at the fair, and I'll get a ride home with him. Thanks, anyway."

He says, "Ok. You are free to leave. Take care."

I say goodbye and then walk over to the cane ring toss stand to say goodbye to Lynette. She can take a break, so we go for a walk. We exchange addresses and phone numbers. She then gives me a kiss that will not be forgotten. I say to her, "Wow! Where did that come from?"

She laughs and says, "It's always been there. It just took a special person to bring it out."

I smile and say, "I'm going to miss you. I hope I can visit you in Findlay once I get my driver's license and a car."

She says, "I would like that." I walk her back to the cane stand and wave goodbye.

I gather my stuff from the panel truck and put it in my duffle bag. Before I leave, I look inside the envelope Mr. Nelson gave me. I stare open-mouthed at three crisp new one-hundred-dollar bills and a new fifty-dollar bill. I feel a sense of accomplishment.

I did it. I have enough money to buy a car.

Life & Love

24

During the three-hour bus ride to Lima for Christmas break, I think about spending twenty long days at my childhood home. Being in my room on Truman Street brings back memories I would just as soon forget. A gaping hole remains in the wall going into the kitchen, where my dad took a drunken swing at me over five years ago. He's the same mean old man he was when I left in September. Henry must temporarily surrender his bedroom so that I can have my old room back. I had loaned him my 1964 Chevy Chevelle while I was at Kent, and he has to give me back my wheels too.

I take the Chevelle out for a spin. I'm on Elida Road heading west, and for some reason, the car in front of me decides to change lanes without warning and cuts me off. I hit the brakes hard and avoid a collision, but when I do so a plastic baggie falls from underneath the dashboard. I reach down and pick it up. It's filled with marijuana and rolling papers. Well, I guess some things have changed since I was away. Looks like Henry now smokes weed.

My first Saturday night back is different. No parties to go to. All my friends are living their everyday lives. The guys and girls I had hung out with seem to have moved on. Some married right after high school. Others moved away from Lima, some went to college, some were drafted and went to Vietnam, but most stayed right here and found low-paying jobs to survive. That is life in a blue-collar town in northwest Ohio.

Around 7:00, I decide to cruise hamburger alley, the same thing I had done many other Saturday nights in Lima. I pull into the King Burger drive-in on North Street and cruise through to see if I know anyone. Nope. I travel west on North Street and circle through Frisch's Big Boy, thinking I surely will see someone I know. Nothing, no one. I drive back onto North Street and head west to the Red Barn. I drive through the parking lot. Nada. No one. I drive back onto North Street, continue west, and head for McDonald's. A lot of people are there, but no one I know. If it had been summertime, I would have headed to the Dairy Queen, but they're closed for the winter.

I turn around and head back on North Street. This time I visit the same burger places in reverse order. After driving through the King Burger, I continue east on North Street until I reach Spykers. I pull up to the drive-thru window and order a large fresh-squeezed lemonade. Delicious. Then I do what I had done so many Saturday nights in high school: I repeat the loop through hamburger alley.

After my second run, it all seems so pointless now. In high school, we would cruise all night long and think nothing of it. Whatever allure it held for me then is gone. I decide to get something to eat but skip the hamburger alley hangouts and drive downtown to my favorite burger joint. The Kewpee is a Lima tradition. Inside, a sign on the wall reads: YOUR GRANDPAPPY ATE HERE. I eat inside rather than get curb service.

I order my usual: a special with cheese and a Frosty. The special is a hamburger with lettuce, tomato, and Miracle Whip. A Frosty is a smooth chocolate soft-serve ice cream in a tall, old-fashioned, swirled glass. Both are delicious. French fries would have been nice, but so far, the Kewpee has yet to follow the hamburger alley trend. No french fries are on the menu.

With nothing better to do, I see the new James Bond movie, *On Her Majesty's Secret Service,* at the Sigma Theater on the northwest corner of the square. It is easy to find a parking spot. I buy a large popcorn and a Coke and find a seat. James Bond shoots the bad guys, drives a fast car, and has flings with some of the most beautiful women in Hollywood.

The movie is over shortly before 10:00 and I'm not ready to go home to my dad or our run-down house so, even though it will likely be pointless, I decide to make one last run through hamburger alley. As I am cruising through Frisch's Big Boy, I see a car on the other side of the lot flash their lights and honk their horn. I don't recognize the car but roll down my window to get a better look. A girl steps out of the passenger side and waves at me. I immediately recognize Barbara who I dated a couple of times and gave me my first french kiss at a house party at her home. I wave back and drive around to the other side of the parking lot and pull up next to her car.

Barbara immediately hops into the passenger seat of my car. "Hi Johnny. How have you been? I saw you drive by twice earlier tonight, but you went by so fast I couldn't get your attention."

"Barbara, it's great to see you. I didn't recognize the car you were in, or I would have stopped earlier."

"That's okay. I'm just out with a girlfriend of mine. Are you home from Kent State for Christmas?"

"Yep. I like Kent State and think I did pretty well the first quarter. How about you? How is the Ohio State Branch in Lima?"

"It's good, but I think I am ready to go to the main campus in Columbus. I'm going to apply to transfer next fall. I'd like to talk with you some more. Would you mind giving me a ride home? I'll let my girlfriend know that she can leave without me."

"Sure. It would be great to catch up with you."

Barbara lets her girlfriend know what is happening and gets back in my car. I order Cokes and french fries for us from the carhop and we start to catch up on our lives. After that party where I got my first french kiss and my introduction to petting, we dated a few times, but it didn't quite have the thrill of that initial encounter. Barbara then started going steady with a guy from Lima Central Catholic, but we remained friends.

Our conversation is easy, and Barbara seems to scoot closer to me the more we talk. We don't talk about boyfriends or girlfriends and so I never have a chance to tell her that I am dating Katie. We leave Frisch's and I'm driving her home when she suggests that I stop on a dark street just before her house so that we can talk some more. I'm not sure where this is going, but I pull over and set the parking brake. Barbara slides towards me and before I can say anything her lips are on mine and her tongue is in my mouth. I pull away and say, "Sorry, I should have told you I have a girlfriend at Kent State and it's pretty serious."

Barbara says, "That's okay. I just thought you might like to have a little fun."

"It's very tempting, you are very tempting, but I think I'm going to pass. You still know how to turn a guy on."

Barbara laughs. "Okay, Mr. Boy Scout, you can take me home."

The next morning after church, I take the grand tour of Lima and reminisce a bit. I first drive by Lima Senior. It looks the same as does the root beer stand, Dogs 'N Suds, on the corner by the school. Next, I drive to Main Street and head north, past Lee's Drive-In Hamburgers, across "Hog Crick" (aka the Ottawa River), and past the square. I drive past J.J. Newberry's and S.S. Kresge's and then past the Ranger Theater on my right. When I was a kid, we would walk to the Ranger from home on Saturday mornings, and for a quarter could watch a double feature of westerns with a Coke and popcorn.

I drive by the Ohio Theatre, where I used to fly flattened popcorn boxes from the balcony, and past Robb Park, where I played Pop Warner football. I drive to the Lima Mall and past Westgate Bowling Lanes. I head home, having completed the grand tour in less than fifteen minutes. Lima used to seem much bigger.

On Monday morning, December 15, 1969, I get ready for work at a temporary job. I had contacted the head guy to see if he needed extra help during the Christmas season. He told me before I left for college that a job was waiting for me whenever I was back in town, and he was as good as his word. I need the extra money, so I put on a coat and tie and drive to the main office on Elizabeth Street. I am warmly greeted by the full-time staff. I enjoyed working there last year, and it feels good to be back.

After work, I call Katie from the telephone at the nearby Sinclair gas station. Inside the phone booth, I fish a handful of nickels, dimes, and quarters from my pocket. I put a dime in the slot and dial the number for Katie's home in Cleveland. The operator comes on the line and tells me to deposit sixty-five cents for three minutes. I deposit the money, and an older woman answers the phone.

"This is Johnny. Is Katie home?"

The woman says, "This is her mother. I will see if I can find her." Her tone is chilly. I guess that iceberg hasn't thawed yet.

After a minute, Katie comes on the line. "I was hoping you would call soon. I miss you."

"I miss you too. Is this a good time to talk?"

She says, "Anytime you call is a perfect time to talk."

That makes me feel good, and the conversation is easy, except that every couple of minutes, the operator comes on the line and says, "Deposit sixty-five cents for three additional minutes." After briefly catching up on what each other has been up to, we arrange a time to talk again on Saturday.

During my exile in Lima, I speak to Katie once a week, and those are the happiest moments of my Christmas break.

Life & Love

25

This morning I took the bus from Lima to Kent. I survived the rest of my time in Lima, but it feels great to be back home on campus. During our last phone call, Katie said she thought she would be back around 3:00 today. I told her my bus arrived in Kent at noon, so I would be waiting in my room for her call when she got to campus.

Shortly after 3:00, Katie calls. "Are you ready to see me?" she asks.

"I've been waiting for almost three weeks to see you. It can't happen soon enough."

"Is your roommate back in the dorm yet?"

"Carl arrived about an hour ago and just went to the cafeteria."

Katie says, "My roommate is back too."

"Too bad. I was looking forward to some alone time with you."

She sighs. "Me too, but I guess that is not going to happen today. Where do you want to meet?"

"How about Eastway Center lounge?"

"Perfect, see you in about twenty minutes."

"Can you make it fifteen?" I ask.

She laughs. "Good things come to those who wait. See you soon."

When Katie walks through the door of Eastway, my world lights up. She looks great. She's wearing a cute yellow sweater with small white polka dots that hugs her body in just the right way. We embrace, and I get the sweetest, hottest kiss that immediately reminds me of our time together on that Friday night after finals. It makes me hot just thinking about it.

"I missed you. You look gorgeous," I say.

"Thanks, I really missed you too."

"How was your time in Cleveland?"

"Let's get something to drink, and I'll tell you about it."

We find two lounge chairs together, and I get us a couple of Cokes. I am about to hand Katie her Coke when she stands, wraps her arms around me, looks into my eyes, and says, "I love you."

"I love you more," I say and lean in and kiss her.

She smiles. "Not possible."

"So," I say, "how was your mom? Has she come around yet about me?"

Katie says, "Not quite. In fact, the first weekend I was home, she invited Chuck over for dinner without telling me."

"You've got to be kidding."

"Nope, and it was awkward. After dinner, I spoke with Chuck alone and told him that my feelings about him had not changed and that I still wanted to be friends, but nothing more. Chuck said, 'I hear you're seeing someone at Kent.' I said, 'My mom must be your little bird. Yes, I am dating someone.' Then my mom came in the room, and said, 'How are you two lovebirds doing? Do you need anything?' I said, 'Chuck is just leaving.' He thanked my mom for dinner and left. My mom said, 'Why can't you see that you two are perfect for each other?' I said, 'Chuck may be perfect for you, but my heart is with Johnny in Kent.' My mom said, 'But you only just met him.' I said, 'Mom, you need to let it go. Chuck and I are never going to be together again.' She looked at me and said, 'We'll see.' So now you see what I am dealing with at home."

"Wow! That's a lot. I'm sorry I'm causing such problems between you and your mother."

Katie looks into my eyes and says, "You're worth it." She smiles and gives me another special kiss.

We continue to talk about what we each did during the Christmas break, and I continue to look at Katie and be amazed that someone so beautiful could be in love with me.

"Do you have any plans for this evening?" I ask her.

"Being with you is my plan," she says. What do you have in mind?"

"I thought we might walk downtown to Big Daddy's. Their pizza is the best, and they usually have a live band on Saturday nights. Have you been there before?"

"That sounds like fun. The last time you planned for us to go to Big Daddy's, I think I distracted you," Katie says with a wink.

"Yes, you were extremely distracting, and I loved every minute of it."

Katie smiles her naughty smile. "Me too, but I've never been to Big Daddy's or any bar downtown."

I say, "Well, it's time to initiate you into the Kent bar scene. I don't think the band starts playing until around 8:00. How about if I walk you back to your dorm and come back and pick you up at 8:00? It's only about a fifteen-minute walk."

"It's a date," Katie says.

It's dark when we leave Eastway Center. We hold hands as we walk to her dorm, stopping for some passionate kisses every few minutes, then continue on our way. It takes a lot longer to get there, but every extra minute is one I get to spend kissing Katie.

Shortly before 8:00, I'm back in the Terrace Hall lobby. Katie gets off the elevator and somehow looks even more spectacular than she did just a couple of hours earlier. She changed into a skirt that shows off her legs and a different sweater that accentuates her body. I take her hand, kiss her, and say, "Ready to go?"

She nods, and we walk down the Terrace Hall steps and turn left onto Main Street. On the way to the bar, we pass fraternity row—two city blocks of large Victorian-style houses on Main Street that now house most of the KSU fraternities. They are off campus, so the rules about parties and drinking don't apply. Almost every Friday and Saturday night, a party happens at one or two of the fraternities. Several of the guys from the third floor of Clark Hall pledged Sigma Chi, and as we pass that fraternity house on Main Street, I tell Katie that some of the guys from Sigma Chi are encouraging me to pledge. "I've been to a few of their open rush parties. They seem like good guys, but I want to make sure my academics are solid before committing to a fraternity."

Katie agrees, "That's smart."

The bouncer at Big Daddy's checks our IDs. Katie and I are both eighteen and get our LO stamp, which limits us to drinking only beer with 3.2 percent alcohol. The band starts playing as we arrive. We run into a couple of guys from the third floor of my dorm. I introduce them to Katie, and we join them at their picnic table.

"What do you like on your pizza?" I ask Katie. "And how about beer? Do you have a preference?"

Katie says, "I like pepperoni pizza, but anything is fine. I've only tried beer a couple of times, so I'm going to let you decide."

"Okay, pepperoni pizza it is, and I will order us a pitcher of Rolling Rock." A few minutes later, we have the beer, and in about twenty minutes, the pizza. Both are really good.

"How do you like the beer?" I ask Katie.

"It's a bit smoother than the ones I've tried before. I like it better."

The music is fine. My girl is very fine. I am in good company. It is cold outside, but warm and cozy sitting beside Katie. I am in love and feel loved by the only person in the world that matters. It's a new year and a new decade. My insecurities of the 1960s are gone.

This is going to be the best year of my life.

Bayonets & Bullets

26

Sunday afternoon, May 3, 1970 • Kent State University, Kent, Ohio

Katie and I hold hands and walk around Front Campus, enjoying the sunny day, and taking in the spectacle. Jeeps and guardsmen are everywhere. Armored personnel carriers sit at every intersection and have torn up the asphalt with their tank treads.

"I heard this morning in the cafeteria that over eight hundred National Guardsmen are on campus, and I believe it. It just seems like an overreaction," I tell Katie.

Students chat with the guardsmen. I don't witness any tension, just students and guardsmen talking. Both want to know when the guardsmen are going home. No one seems to know. I notice the guardsmen really like to talk to the pretty female students. Who can blame them?

As Katie and I walk past a guardsman talking to two students, Katie says, "I know that girl, that's Allison, and she's with her boyfriend. I wonder what they're talking to that guardsman about." Katie says, "Hi, Allison."

Allison holds a flower in her hand and looks our way. "Hi, Katie. It's a beautiful day, isn't it?"

"Sure is," Katie says.

Allison puts the flower in the barrel of the guardsman's rifle. The guardsman smiles at her. Then an older guardsman, who looks like an officer, says, "Private, this is not a party. There will be no fraternizing with the students." The officer removes the flower from the rifle's barrel and throws it on the ground.

Allison says to the officer, "What's the matter with peace? Flowers are better than bullets."

After the officer leaves, the guardsman smiles, and flashes Allison the peace sign.

"Too bad all the guardsmen aren't like that one," I say to Katie, "We need guardsmen who want peace not violence on this campus."

As we walk down the street, I notice more cars on the road than usual, and most of the people in them don't appear to be students. "Looks like people are coming onto campus just to see what's going on," I say.

Katie says, "Sure looks that way."

Shortly after 1:00, some of the guardsmen start challenging people coming onto campus who don't look like they belong here. I watch as a guardsman stops four guys that came on campus from Main Street and seem to be in their mid-twenties. "Where do you guys think you are going?" he asks them.

One guy answers, "We just want to see what all the fuss is all about and what is left of the ROTC building."

"Only students and others with official business are permitted to be on campus. Unless you can show me a Kent State student ID, you need to leave this campus immediately." The guys mumble something to each other, then turn around and go back the way they came.

An officer tells a couple of younger guardsmen leaning against their jeep and smoking cigarettes, "Guard, maintain control of your weapons and keep them at the ready position at all times. You need to be in control and ready to move out."

"The guardsmen are starting to act differently," I say. "They seem much more uptight than they were an hour ago. They must have gotten new orders."

I'm starting to get concerned about this change in demeanor by the guardsmen and say to Katie, "Let's head over to The Hub for a Coke."

As we walk into the Student Union, a pile of flyers sits on a side table. It's a new flyer from Robert Matson, vice president for student affairs, and Frank Frisina, student body president, and it reads:

A Special Message to the University Community:

During the last two days, the disruptive and destructive activities of a dissident group comprising students and non-students and numbering 500 to 600, escalated from a peaceful rally through illegal threat to life plus property damage leading eventually to the Governor's imposition of a state of emergency encompassing both the city of Kent and the University.

The Governor, through the National Guard, has assumed legal control of the campus and the city of Kent. As currently defined, the state of emergency has established the following

1. Prohibited all forms of outdoor demonstrations and rallies, peaceful or otherwise;
2. Empowered the National Guard to make arrests;
3. A curfew is in effect for the city from 8 p.m. to 6 a.m. and an on-campus, a curfew of 1:00 a.m. has been ordered by the National Guard.

THE ABOVE WILL REMAIN IN EFFECT UNTIL ALTERED OR REMOVED BY ORDER OF THE GOVERNOR.

THE CAMPUS AT PRESENT IS CALM. SEVERAL HUNDRED NATIONAL GUARD AND STATE POLICE ARE PRESENTLY ON CAMPUS TO MAINTAIN ORDER. THEY ARE UNDER THE DIRECTION OF GOVERNOR JAMES A. RHODES AND WILL REMAIN ON ALERT ON AND AROUND THE CAMPUS UNTIL NORMAL CONDITIONS RETURN.

WE ARE MOST THANKFUL THAT THUS FAR THERE HAS BEEN NO LOSS OF LIFE. HOWEVER, FIVE STUDENTS AND SEVERAL LAW ENFORCEMENT OFFICERS DID REPORT INJURIES THAT WERE APPARENTLY NOT SERIOUS.

WE PLAN TO RESUME OUR NORMAL CLASS SCHEDULE ON MONDAY WITH THE EXCEPTION OF CLASSES SCHEDULED FOR THE FLOOR OF MEMORIAL GYMNASIUM. CURRENTLY, THE GYM FLOOR IS BEING USED TO PROVIDE BARRACK FACILITIES FOR THE NATIONAL GUARD TROOPS.

MORE THAN 40 PERSONS WERE ARRESTED SATURDAY NIGHT BY LAW ENFORCEMENT OFFICERS FOR VIOLATION OF THE CITY CURFEW. ALL FACE COURT ACTION.

CONSEQUENTLY, THERE IS GRAVEST CONCERN IN ALL QUARTERS OF THE UNIVERSITY COMMUNITY OVER THE CAMPUS VIOLENCE AND THE DESTRUCTION OF PROPERTY.

WE URGENTLY REQUEST ANYONE WITH INFORMA-
TION CONCERNING THE IDENTIFICATION OF
PARTICIPANTS IN THE VIOLENT AND DISRUPTIVE
ACTIONS OF THIS WEEKEND TO COME FORWARD.
ANY INFORMATION YOU HAVE MAY BE REPORTED TO
EITHER THE STUDENT ACTIVITIES CENTER (2480)
OR THE UNIVERSITY POLICE (2212) BY PHONE,
LETTER, OR IN PERSON.

WE CONGRATULATE THE MANY STUDENTS WHO
CONTINUE TO VOLUNTEER THEIR TIME AND
EFFORTS TO RETURN THE CAMPUS TO NORMAL.

NATURALLY WE WILL MAKE EVERY EFFORT TO KEEP
YOU FULLY INFORMED AS THE SITUATION MAY
CHANGE.

"This is not good," I say. "No one is going to be happy about not being able to rally and protest. We have the right to free speech and to peaceably assemble under the First Amendment of the Constitution. They can't stop us from attending a rally."

Katie says, "That's true, but they have the guns, and we don't."

"I heard the guns aren't loaded."

"That may be true, but the bayonets look pretty sharp."

"Also, I can't believe Student Body President Frank Frisina, would sign off on this crap, urging students to rat on their fellow students. Our student government sounds like it's just a patsy for the administration and Governor Rhodes."

After we sit down at a table, I get a Sprite for Katie, and a Coke for me. A radio station plays over the public address system, but it doesn't sound like WKSU. An announcer says:

"We have a Special Report. Governor Rhodes held a press conference in Kent, Ohio, this morning with General DelCorso from the Ohio National Guard. The Mayor of

Kent, LeRoy Satrom, also attended. We have learned that at 5:00 p.m. yesterday, it was Mayor Satrom who called the governor's office and requested the assistance of the Ohio National Guard. The National Guard was mobilized and arrived in Kent around 10:00 p.m. last night and shortly thereafter came onto the Kent State University campus. Governor Rhodes, who is currently running against Robert Taft for the Republican nomination for the U.S. Senate, attended a political campaign event in Cleveland yesterday and took a helicopter to Kent this morning. The governor visited the KSU campus and saw the remains of the ROTC building that was burned to the ground by KSU student protesters last evening.

"What follows is a recording from the governor's press conference this morning. As the recording begins you will hear Governor Rhodes pound his fist on the table when talking about the student demonstrators at Kent State University:

"They're worse than the Brownshirts and the communist element, and also the Night Riders and the vigilantes. They're the worst type of people we harbor in America. And I want to say that they're not going to take over campus. And the campus now is going to be part of the County and State of Ohio. There is no sanctuary for these people to burn buildings down of private citizens, of businesses in a community, and then run into a sanctuary. It is over in Ohio."

The governor says that throwing a rock at a National Guardsman is a felony. *"We are going to disperse crowds and we are going to help the mayor enforce the curfew,"* he said.

General DelCorso, the commanding officer of the Ohio National Guard troops at Kent State then speaks. *"It was fortunate that we had troops here assembled for another mission. At the request of the mayor of Kent, we moved our forces here and were able to contain the fire to one building."*

Governor Rhodes ends the press conference by stating, *"We will provide whatever degree of force is necessary to protect our citizens' lives and property."*

"No wonder the guardsmen are getting more serious," I say. "It looks like the governor gave the Ohio National Guard new marching orders. Instead of just keeping the peace, the governor is now telling the general he wants action."

Katie says, "We need to be careful. There's no telling how these guardsmen will react after hearing the governor's 'law-and-order' rhetoric."

"I agree. We should be careful tonight."

We finish our pops and I walk Katie back to Terrace Hall. Several guardsmen are leaning against their jeeps as we approach her dorm. They still look relaxed, so I ask the one nearest me, "How's it going? Any idea how long you're going to have to stay here?"

He looks at me, smiles at Katie, and says, "No orders yet. We're just killing time."

"Where are you from?"

"Stow. I got called up two weeks ago to deal with that trucker strike in Akron. Union members were interfering with freight deliveries, and we provided security for the non-union truckers. We came here last night."

"Well, I hope this is over soon, and you can go home."

"Me too," he says.

We say goodbye and walk up the steps to Terrace Hall. Inside the lobby, Katie says, "I know you want to see what's going to happen tonight, but please be careful. Everything is cool right now, but it can change quickly."

"I will steer clear of any trouble," I promise her. "See you tomorrow."

We kiss, and Katie says, "See you tomorrow." She smiles and waves goodbye.

As I walk back to Clark Hall, I pass by the administration

building on Front Campus. Several types of military vehicles are parked out front.

"Is this your headquarters or something?" I ask one of the guardsmen standing there.

He says, "Yeah. Something like that. We've commandeered the old Wills Gym behind the administration building."

"Are you expecting any trouble tonight?"

"I hope not."

Teens & Dreams

27

Saturday, November 18, 1967 • Lima, Ohio

I'm working an 11:00 to 4:00 shift today at McDonald's today. During the week, I work the after-school shift from 5:00 to closing at 10:00. I average thirty hours a week and make $1.10 per hour. After taxes and Social Security deductions, my weekly take-home pay is $25.00. I've told my boss that I prefer not to work on Sundays because I go to church and believe it should be a day of rest. He has no problem with that.

I'm up early, as usual, even though it's Saturday, and decide to give my baby blue 1960 Renault Dauphine a wash and vacuum at the car wash on North Street. With the money I earned working at the county fairs last summer, I bought the Renault in early September.

The Dauphine is the French version of the compact German Volkswagen beetle. The Dauphine is in pretty good shape except for the battery, which keeps dying on me. Fortunately, you can start this car three ways: by turning the key, for an electric start, (when the battery is working); by popping the clutch (if you can get someone to give you a push); or by using the lug wrench as a hand crank to start the engine. A hand crank was used to start the old Model T Ford back in the early 1900s but has not been used for any American car in decades.

Like the beetle, the Dauphine's engine is at the back of the car

179

where the trunk normally would be. To hand crank the car, you use the same lug wrench that you use for changing a tire. Put the head of the lug wrench through a hole in the bumper and push it in until it is seated in the engine block. Make sure the ignition key is in the "on" position and the stick shift is in neutral, then give it a crank or two or three. Usually, the engine will start after the first or second crank. It is a bit embarrassing if you're on a date and need to get out and crank the engine. I'm going to have to spring for a new battery soon.

This morning, however, the battery is working fine, and I drive to the car wash, put in my quarter, and use the hand sprayer to give her a nice bath. After the car wash, I drive to The Huddle on High Street for my favorite breakfast: pancakes and a Coke. Parking is more convenient at The Huddle, but I like the pancakes at S.S. Kresge's better.

I had given my paper route to Henry just before I left to work the county fairs last summer. As I'm pulling out of The Huddle, I see him using my old Schwinn to deliver the papers. He now has a double route—his old paper route, plus mine. I honk the horn at him as I drive by, and he waves back.

Tonight, I have a date. Unfortunately, it is not with Lynette.

In September, after I got my driver's license and my car, I gave Lynette a call and we arranged a date in Findlay. She gave me directions to her house, so I drive forty miles and knock on the front door. Her dad answers and greets me warmly. "Lynette is getting ready and will be down shortly."

"Okay. Thanks," I say.

He invites me into the living room and says, "Have a seat. What are you two doing tonight?"

"I'm not sure. Since I'm not familiar with Findlay, I asked Lynette if she would plan our date."

Just then Lynette enters the room. She has heard our conversation and says, "We're going to a movie, Daddy."

He turns to me. "Just make sure she is home by eleven."

"No problem," I assure him. "I have a midnight curfew, so I will need to leave Findlay by 11:00 to get home by midnight."

He says, "Okay, you two. Have fun."

I open the car door for Lynette, and she gets in. I join her and she says, "I thought we might get a hamburger and Coke before we go to the movies. Wilson's Hamburger Shop is not too far away and it's pretty good."

"That sounds great. What movie are we going to see?"

"*Bonnie and Clyde*. Have you seen it?"

"No, I've been wanting to, though. That sounds perfect." The burgers at Wilson's are good, although not as good as the Kewpee's in Lima. We leave the restaurant and go back to my car.

Lynette says, "We still have some time before the movie starts, do you want to just sit here and talk for a bit?"

"Sure." I say, "How have you been?"

"Pretty good. I've met some new friends at school."

"That's good."

"Yeah, it's a good group. Both girls and guys and we all get along well."

We talk about our schools and classes, and I tell her about my new job at McDonald's. Then she says, "We'd better head to the movies."

"Just show me the way."

After the movie we get back into my car. "*Bonnie and Clyde* was really good," I say. "Well, until the end when they both got shot to pieces."

She laughs. "I enjoyed it. Thanks for driving all the way to Findlay. I guess I'd better get home."

"Oh, okay." It's only 9:30 and her curfew is still ninety minutes away. The date has gone fine, but all night I feel like something is off. We don't have the easygoing conversation that we had at the county fairs during the summer, and I have not gotten any signals that she wants to kiss me. I'm not sure what is going on, but it does not feel right.

As I drive up to her house, she says, "Thanks for the hamburger and movie."

I say, "You're welcome" and lean in to give her a kiss. She turns and gives me her cheek and says, "Goodnight. No need to walk me to my door."

I am a bit stunned. "Oh, okay. Goodnight." She opens the car door, runs up the steps to her front door, and waves goodbye.

On the way home, I mull over our date. Something is going on that she is not telling me. It is like the Lynette from a few months ago and the Lynette from tonight are two different people. Our conversation was stilted, and there was none of the affection present during the summer.

I have not heard from Lynette since our date and decide that if she wants to see me, she will let me know.

Enough reflections. It's time to head to my shift at McDonald's and think about my date with Stephanie tonight.

About three weeks ago, the manager, who is also the owner of the McDonald's franchise, asked if I would like to be an assistant manager and learn to bag and call the shots. Of course, I said yes, and now I usually call all the shots or help the manager bag while he does it. It's a fun job and I enjoy it.

Today is no different. I arrive at 11:00 and call the shots during the lunch rush. The manager is very particular about making sure the customer receives hot food. Occasionally, I overestimate the number of burgers or fries needed and, if they sit too long in a warming bin, they must be thrown away. I hate doing that, but the manager explains that if we serve stale or cold food, we will likely lose a customer forever. He would rather throw food away than lose a customer.

At the end of my shift, I drive home to get cleaned up for my date tonight. The odor of french fries and hamburger grease permeates everything I wear, so I need a quick bath and change of clothes.

Three weeks ago, Diane introduced me to Stephanie, one of her girlfriends from Shawnee High School. It was a blind date, a first for me. Diane told me that I would like Stephanie. "Stephanie is pretty and very nice. I know you two will hit it off."

Diane was right. We went on a double date with her and Jack. I drove and we went bowling at Westgate Lanes. Stephanie is intelligent, cute, and funny and we have an instant attraction.

At the end of the night, I drive Stephanie home and say, "I had a great time tonight and would like to see you again."

Stephanie says, "I was hoping you would say that. I feel the same way." She leans over and gives me a long kiss. She has very soft lips and when she starts to pull back, I lean in and kiss her again. We kiss several times.

"When can I see you again?" I ask.

Stephanie laughs and says, "How about next Saturday?"

I say, "It's a date." I walk her to her front door and kiss her goodnight. Wow! The best blind date ever. Diane really called that one right.

Tonight, Stephanie is having a party at her house. I have not yet met her parents, so this should be interesting. It turns out Stephanie only invited couples to the party and so the interactions and dynamics are completely different than most parties I've attended. Stephanie introduces me to her parents who are very nice. I'm not sure what I had expected but they are easygoing and don't seem worried or intense about anything.

Stephanie's mom prepared a variety of snacks and set out Cokes and Sprites on the dining room table. Around 9:00, she says goodnight to everyone and goes upstairs to where Stephanie's dad had retreated earlier in the evening.

Stephanie puts on the *Up-Up and Away* album by The 5th Dimension and turns down the living room lights. Each couple snuggles up and soon everyone is making out. I look at Stephanie and she leans in and starts kissing me passionately. I reciprocate and soon we are in our own make-out session.

No one seems to want the night to end, including me, but when the album finishes, Stephanie says, "I'd better start cleaning up." I help and soon everyone gets the message that the make-out session is over. Stephanie turns on the lights and everyone gets ready to leave.

After everyone is gone, I tell her, "I had a wonderful time. Thank you."

Stephanie smiles and says, "You're welcome. It was a very special night." She walks me to the door, and we have one last passionate embrace before I reluctantly walk to my car.

Teens & Dreams

28

Saturday, December 23, 1967 • Lima, Ohio

Earlier this year, my cousin Jim and I met Beth at a Saturday morning bowling league at Northland Lanes. Beth is a beautiful girl from Bath High School, and I enjoyed seeing her every Saturday morning until the league ended in April. Our team came in second place and we each received a trophy for that achievement.

Bowling ended, but my friendship with Beth did not. We meet almost every Saturday or Sunday and discuss anything and everything over a hamburger and Coke at the Kewpee or Frisch's Big Boy. Sometimes Jim joins us, but most of the time, it's just Beth and me talking about life, love, politics, and anything else on our minds. The only weeks we miss are those when I worked at the county fairs last summer.

I talk about the girls I am dating, and Beth gives me some great tips on what girls like and don't like. We also talk a lot about the war in Vietnam. I hate the war, and Beth feels the same way. Her boyfriend had just been shipped to Vietnam when I first met her in January. Beth gets a letter from him almost every week. His one-year tour of duty is scheduled to end on January 5, 1968. Beth is counting down the days.

Today I'm waiting for Beth in a booth at Frisch's Big Boy. I have a small Christmas present for her. Thirty minutes pass, and then another thirty. Beth doesn't show. This has never happened. She always meets me at our agreed-upon time and place. It's snowing, but only an inch or so has accumulated. Still, I am afraid Beth has been in an accident.

I find a pay phone, call her home number and Beth's mom answers. I've met her mom, so when I ask for Beth and tell her my name, she knows me. I tell her Beth was supposed to meet me for lunch and ask if she's home. Beth's mom tells me the news. Earlier this morning, Beth received a call from her boyfriend's father telling her that her boyfriend had been killed in action in Vietnam.

A hot flush comes over me, and I am speechless. Her mom tells me Beth is overcome with grief and is in her room. She thinks it's best that I talk with her another time.

"Please let Beth know that I called and tell her I'm sorry for her loss." That phrase seems so inept, but my brain is in a fog, and I can't think of more comforting words.

I hate this damn war. Beth's boyfriend had only two weeks left of his tour of duty in Vietnam. Every day, mothers, wives, daughters, and girlfriends get the same news that Beth heard today. Tomorrow, another nineteen-year-old boy will be drafted, and a couple of months from now, he will be fighting in Vietnam and killed in action. When will the madness end?

Life & Love

29

Katie is snuggled up against me in her twin bed. Her roommate went home for the weekend so last night was really special. It was the first time we had been alone together since that night in December after finals. Katie had once again metamorphosed into a sexual goddess. She did things to me I'd only dreamed of, and it only made me want her more. It was passionate and intense, and then after a short intermezzo, it was passionate and intense again. I was satiated and slept soundly.

I feel Katie stir. "Good morning," I say.

She rolls over and kisses me lightly. "Good morning to you too. Did you sleep well?"

"Best sleep ever. Did I tell you that I love you lately?"

"Not since last night. You said it maybe once or twice or a hundred times."

"I love you. I love you. I love you. I will always love you."

She smiles. "I love you too. I hope you will still love me later today. Are you ready?"

I know what she's referring to. "I've been ready to meet your mom. Of course, I will still love you, no matter what happens tonight or tomorrow."

Katie says, "Well, she wants to meet you, and I was surprised when she said she wanted you to come to Cleveland. I'm not sure if she's just curious or if she has another agenda."

"Don't worry. I plan to be on my best behavior and woo her."

"We'll see. She's a tough nut to crack. My Uncle Gene is picking us up here at 11:00. Do you want to go to your dorm, pack an overnight bag and meet me back here?"

"I do, but first I want to have breakfast with you. I thought we could walk down to Captain Brady's."

"That sounds like a great idea. I hear their Brady Roll is out of this world."

"It's my favorite. A large cinnamon roll, split on its side, buttered, and grilled. It's almost as delicious as you were last night."

"You're bad," she says, lightly punching my shoulder. "We should be careful leaving my dorm. Since overnight visits are still technically not permitted, it would be best for you to leave first, go down the back stairs, and out the back door. Then go to the front door and I will meet you there."

"Sounds like a good plan."

Katie says, "I need ten minutes to get ready, so you can leave any time after I head to the restroom."

"Okay. See you soon."

I do as Katie suggested without incident and sit in the lobby to wait for her. No one is around. It's Saturday morning, and every typical college coed is sleeping in.

Katie comes down shortly. "Good morning," I say. "Did you have a pleasant evening last night?"

She pushes me lightly and whispers, "It was wonderful, and you know it."

I smile, and we walk down Main Street to Captain Brady's, across from Prentice Gate on the corner of Main and Lincoln Streets.

Only a few customers are inside. I order two grilled, split, and buttered Brady Rolls, plus orange juice for me and coffee with cream and sugar for Katie. While waiting for our order, I spot a copy of the

Daily Kent Stater lying on a table beside us. It's from the previous Wednesday, January 14, 1970.

I hold up the paper for Katie to see. "Did you see this article about the New Mobilization Committee to End the War in Vietnam, the group they call New Mobe?"

"No, what's it about?"

"Well, you know New Mobe is planning several national days of anti-Vietnam War protests, right? This adjutant general of the Ohio National Guard named DelCorso is quoted as saying that New Mobe is part of an international communist conspiracy against the U.S. government. Where do they get these guys? That is such bullshit. New Mobe has nothing to do with communism. Their sole goal is to end the war in Vietnam. Generals like DelCorso are dangerous to all of us."

"It's amazing, the kind of people they put in charge of our military," Katie says.

Our order is ready, so I put down the newspaper and pick up our food from the counter. I watch Katie take her first bite of a Brady Roll. "*Mmmm*, that is delicious," she says. "I didn't realize what I was missing." I take a bite of mine and agree. It is delicious.

After breakfast, we go our separate ways, and as we part, I say, "I love you. See you soon."

"Ditto. See you soon."

I clean up and pack for the one-night stay at Katie's house in Cleveland. I know this will be a big step in our relationship. I want her family to like me, and I want to like her family. I stuff everything I need into my backpack and return to her dorm shortly before 11:00. Katie is waiting in the lobby talking with her uncle.

She sees me and says, "Uncle Gene, this is Johnny. Johnny, this is my uncle Gene."

"Nice to meet you," I say, shaking his hand. "Katie has told me a lot about you and your family."

"It's good to meet you too. Are you ready to go?"

I say, "Yes. Thank you for picking us up."

Uncle Gene grabs Katie's bag before I can, and we walk to his car.

The ride to Cleveland is cordial. Gene asks me about Lima and how I am doing at Kent State. He talks about his seven children and job as a firefighter. Being one of six kids, I know seven kids is way too many for one family, but don't say so. The ride only takes about an hour, and soon we pull up in front of an older two-story house on a busy street on Cleveland's west side. The house and landscaping are perfectly maintained.

Katie introduces me to her mother, Ruth, and her grandmother, Nanna.

"I've been looking forward to meeting you," I say to her mother." You have a very special daughter."

"Thank you. She is my very special baby girl."

"Mom, I'm not quite a baby anymore," Katie says.

"You will always be my baby," Ruth replies.

I smile and tell Nanna, "It's great to finally meet you. Katie tells me you are an excellent cook and that she learned everything about cooking from you."

Nanna smiles. "Thank you." She is very sweet. Katie told me she emigrated from Germany when she was only sixteen and speaks fluent English but doesn't talk much.

I say goodbye to Gene and thank him for the ride to Cleveland. He replies that he will see me tomorrow for the return trip. Katie then shows me the bedroom I will be using.

I whisper, "I thought I was going to be sleeping with you."

She bumps my shoulder with hers. "Behave." I smile and she laughs."My brother's away for the weekend so you get to use his room."

Katie shows me her room and her mom's room and then shows me around the rest of the house. The inside is as well maintained as the outside. It's obvious that Nanna has a lot of pride in her home.

After the tour, Katie says, "How about if I make us some lunch?"

I say, "That sounds good, can I help?"

Katie says, "Sure."

I set the table while Katie gets cold meatloaf from the refrigerator and makes us all sliced meatloaf sandwiches with potato chips and a pickle. It's delicious. During lunch, her mom grills me with questions about my parents and where I grew up. I give her the basics, leaving out the trauma of my childhood. No need to have her dislike me right off the bat.

After lunch, Katie gives me a tour of her neighborhood and we talk about her childhood here in Cleveland. All her reminisces are about her mom and her grandmother. She had previously told me that her mom and dad divorced when she was nine years old and that she has not seen her dad much since then. Katie says very little about him. She shows me St. Mark Catholic Church where she went to grade school and middle school.

Katie says, "I'm sure my mom will want us all to go to the 11:00 Mass tomorrow morning."

"That's okay with me."

She smiles. "You're so easy."

I smile too. "Yep, you can take advantage of me anytime you want."

She gives me a side-eye. "You'd better behave. You're right next to a church and Jesus is watching you."

"Me and Jesus are close buds, so no problem." She laughs and we walk back toward her house.

Living in a big city seems so different from Lima. Lots of people, lots of cars, everything seems busy. I'm not sure I could ever live in a big city, but that's an opinion I won't share with Katie. At least, not yet.

When we return to her house, Katie sets up the Scrabble game. I am immediately outmatched by both Katie and her mom. They are getting multiple four- and five-letter words each turn, and some-times a six-letter word, and I am lucky to play a single four-letter word but more often only manage one with three letters. Katie wins the game, with her mother coming in a close second. I bring up the rear very far behind. We then play gin rummy and I do a lot better, winning most of the games.

Nanna makes pork roast for dinner with mashed potatoes, gravy, homemade applesauce, and green beans. It is delicious, much better than anything my mom could make. After dinner, I can tell Ruth wants to have a serious conversation. I sit on the couch with Katie next to me, and her mom sits in a chair across from us.

"So, what are your intentions with my daughter?"

Katie is surprised. "Mom, we don't need to talk about that."

I interrupt Katie. "It's not a problem. I intend to love Katie for as long as she will let me," I tell her mom. Katie beams.

Ruth says, "Well, you know she has another guy who loves her. He's very nice and comes from a very good family."

I say, "I understand, but that was the past, and I am the present."

I can tell by the pinched look on Ruth's face that she does not much like that answer. "I just want Katie to find someone she can be happy with," she says.

Katie decides that the conversation has gone in this direction long enough. "Mom, I'm eighteen and an adult. I can decide for myself who makes me happy, and I'm happy with Johnny." She turns to me. "I have a five-hundred-piece jigsaw puzzle upstairs. Do you want to help me finish it?"

"Sure."

Katie takes me by the hand and leads me upstairs to a sewing room where the puzzle has been started on a card table. As we sit down, she kisses me lightly. "Are you ok?"

I say, "As long as I am with you, everything is perfect." She smiles.

We finish the puzzle around 11:00. Katie leads me to my room and kisses me goodnight. "See you in the morning," she says.

I don't want to let go of her hand, but I do. "Goodnight."

Katie crosses the hallway and I watch as she closes her bedroom door. I'm tempted to tiptoe across the hallway to her room but think better of it.

The next morning, we get ready for church, and the three of us walk up the street to St. Mark's. Katie tells me Nanna likes to get up early and has already been to the 8:15 Mass.

We enter the church, and as we walk down the center aisle toward the altar, a guy from a pew on the right reaches out and taps Katie lightly on the arm. "Hi, Katie."

Katie is a bit startled. "Oh, hi, Chuck."

Ruth's face lights up, and she smiles at him. "Hi, Chuck. It's good to see you here."

Katie turns to me and says, "Johnny, this is Chuck. Chuck, this is Johnny."

"Good to meet you," I say. "I've heard a lot about you."

Chuck says, "Yeah, okay."

We continue toward the front pews. Katie and her mom genuflect and sit down. I follow them and just sit down. Katie whispers something to her mom that I cannot hear. The Mass lasts about forty-five minutes. We do not see Chuck again on our way out.

When we get back to Nanna's house, she has Sunday dinner waiting for us. She has made roast chicken with roasted potatoes and carrots along with fresh, buttered dinner rolls. I tell Nanna it's the best roast chicken I have ever had and mean it. She smiles and thanks me warmly.

After dinner, Gene arrives to take us back to Kent. I thank Ruth and Nanna for their hospitality and tell them I look forward to seeing them again soon. Gene drops us off at Terrace Hall and we thank him for the ride then take the elevator up to her room. Fortunately, her roommate is not back yet, so we have a short, but intense lovemaking session. Afterward, we discuss the visit with her mom.

Katie says, "You were very cordial with my mom and the visit went better than I expected. But running into Chuck at church was a setup. He usually attends a different church closer to where he lives. My mom probably told him I was coming home this weekend and would be attending 11:00 Mass. I confronted her when we sat down in the pew, but she denied it and said I was being paranoid. I still think she set the whole thing up."

"What do you think she hoped to gain by doing that?"

"She thinks that if I see Chuck, I will realize what I am missing and want him back. Just the opposite happened. Once I realized it was a setup, I resented her interference and resented Chuck for participating in her scheme."

"Well, I'm happy to be back at KSU and I'm happy you are back in my arms. I love you."

Katie says, "I love you more. You are too sweet."

Bayonets & Bullets

30

Sunday evening, May 3, 1970 • Kent State University, Kent, Ohio

While eating dinner in Eastway cafeteria with several guys from the third floor of Clark Hall, our only topic of conversation is the Ohio National Guard. The questions being asked are: Why are they here? When are they leaving? Are their guns really loaded with bullets? Who is in charge? Why haven't we heard anything from President White?

No one has any answers, only speculations. Resentment toward the Guard is growing. The Guard is occupying our campus and doesn't seem to be leaving anytime soon. We are all young adults and are being ordered around like children. This is our home. The military has taken over our home. How can we not resent them?

I hate the feeling of not being in control of my destiny. My defiance of authority is probably the result of my dad's tyrannical control over me for the first eighteen years of my life. I am now on my own and will make my own decisions. I don't need the National Guard telling me what I can and cannot do. The occupation force needs to leave campus now!

Many of us at dinner have heard that a rally is happening on the Commons at 8:00 tonight. Rather than staying in our dorm room and feeling helpless, several of us decide to attend.

Shortly before 8:00, we approach the Commons. From the top of Blanket Hill next to Taylor Hall, we see students congregating around the Victory Bell, but nothing organized is happening. We walk down Blanket Hill and join the crowd. Guardsmen are on the other side of the Commons by the burnt-out ROTC building.

Everyone asks the same questions we asked at dinner, but the crowd is peaceful. Some coeds kick a soccer ball around. As night falls, the crowd grows and seems to get more restless. Shortly before 9:00, a National Guard jeep comes speeding across the Commons. A National Guard officer with a bullhorn tells us that our assembly violates the Ohio Riot Act and that we have five minutes to disperse.

Students loudly protest that we have a Constitutional right to assemble peaceably, but the guardsmen ignore us. After five minutes, the guardsmen pull their gas masks down over their faces and fire tear gas into the crowd. The tear gas burns my eyes and rubbing them only makes it worse. We have no choice but to move away from the Commons.

Some students shout, "Let's protest at President White's house." Others shout, "Let's go to Prentice Gate." The crowd splits, and I follow the group heading to Prentice Gate on Front Campus.

On Front Campus, about three hundred students join the protest. We know an 8:00 curfew is in effect tonight for the City of Kent, and it's now after 8:00. National Guard helicopters circle above us shining spotlights on the crowd. Guardsmen block the Main and Lincoln streets intersection, preventing the crowd from moving downtown. Instead of confronting guardsmen armed with M1 rifles and bayonets, we sit down in the middle of Main Street before the intersection with Lincoln Street.

No one in the crowd threatens the guardsmen or anyone else. We are exercising our right to assemble peacefully with a sit-in. I see several people I know in the crowd, including Allison, who earlier today had told a guardsman that flowers are better than bullets, and her boyfriend. I also see several people I met the previous Friday at the rally to bury the Constitution, including Jeff, Alan and his sister Chic, and fellow freshman Joe.

The crowd is angry but not violent. One of the student leaders reads off a list of demands and tells a police officer that we want to speak with President White and Mayor Satrom. It's hard to hear what the student leaders are saying because the *whup, whup, whup* of the helicopter blades overhead drowns out most of the speeches. After a while, one student gets permission to use the police public address system and tells the crowd that Mayor Satrom is coming to discuss their concerns and that President White is also being contacted. The student says that if we move back onto campus, the guardsmen at the scene will reciprocate by moving off campus. I then move with the group off the street and back onto campus. Initially, the guardsman back off and retreat to the road.

Around 11:00, a National Guard officer with a bullhorn announces, *"Neither Mayor Satrom nor President White is coming to address you. A new 11:00 p.m. curfew is in effect and all students are required to return to their dorms immediately. You are violating the Ohio Riot Act and must disperse immediately. Go to your dormitories immediately or be arrested."*

I am stunned. I am not alone in that feeling. We feel double-crossed. We were told if we moved onto campus, the mayor and President White would address our concerns. Now, we are told neither President White, nor the mayor is coming. Several students curse the guardsmen, and several others hurl rocks at them. I watch with amazement at how quickly a peaceful demonstration turns violent once the guardsmen use their authority against the students.

Within minutes after the announcement to disperse, the guardsmen don their gas masks and start lobbing tear gas canisters into the crowd of students. The helicopters hover lower, illuminating students with their spotlights. The wash of the helicopter blades helps to engulf the students with tear gas, and I suddenly feel the burn in my eyes again. The guardsmen point their bayonets toward us and advance. Two students are stabbed in the back. I'm not waiting around to be bayonetted by a guardsman. I take off running across campus.

I feel like I'm in the middle of a war movie. Helicopters drone overhead with their roving spotlights, the guardsmen charge the students with their bayonets, and I hear the screams and protests of students running for their lives. It all seems surreal. Students run toward the closest building, Rockwell Library, but at this time of night, it's likely locked. Instead, I run up Hilltop Drive and cut between McGilvrey Hall and Kent Hall. I stay away from the Commons and run past Bowman Hall toward the Eastway complex. Fortunately, I don't encounter any more guardsmen and arrive safely back at Clark Hall.

In the lobby, I take a minute to catch my breath and calm down. I am really rattled by what just happened. Once again, things turned violent before I recognized what was happening. I'm fortunate to be back in my dorm and uninjured, but I'm angry with the KSU administration and the Ohio National Guard. Why isn't the KSU administration protecting us from the National Guard?

I am in occupied territory and can do nothing about it. I feel helpless.

Teens & Dreams

31

Prom tonight! Stephanie asked if I would take her to the Shawnee High School prom. It's my first prom, and I'm excited to go.

Last Saturday, I went to the Varsity Shop on Main Street to get measured for my tux—a white dinner jacket with a black bow tie and black cummerbund. I am going to look so cool. The Varsity Shop closes at 5:00 today. My shift at McDonald's is done at 4:00, so I will have just enough time to pick up my tux and get ready before I pick up Stephanie for our pre-prom dinner at the Thunderbird Restaurant.

I'm up early to wash and vacuum my car so it will be perfect for Stephanie. Well, as perfect as a cherry red 1960 Pontiac Catalina convertible can be. I purchased the Catalina in January to replace my Renault Dauphine. The white top is discolored but works fine. The only problem is the plastic rear window, which is cracked and broken so I use duct tape to hold it together and keep out rain and snow. I like the car a lot. It has a powerful 389-cubic-inch engine with a four-barrel carburetor that really roars and throws you back in your seat when you floor it. The downside is the gas mileage— about eight miles per gallon—so I don't plan to take it on any long trips.

After it's washed and vacuumed, the Catalina looks fantastic. It is a beautiful day, so I'll be able to put the top down for my prom date tonight.

I finish my shift at McDonald's and drive to the Varsity Shop to pick up my tux, arriving with less than ten minutes to spare before they close. The clerk asks if I want to try it on, and I say, "No, I'm sure it will be fine." I pay for the tux and hang it on a hook in the back seat of my car.

I drive home, take a quick bath, and splash Hai Karate cologne on my face. I put on the pants and shirt. Both fit fine. I look for the bow tie and cummerbund, but don't find them. I try on the dinner jacket, and something is very wrong. It's huge. My receipt says they fitted me for a thirty-eight regular. I look at the label inside the jacket. Forty-eight regular. They gave me a jacket ten sizes too big and forgot to include a bow tie and cummerbund. Crap. I call the Varsity Shop hoping someone is still there, but no one answers. It's 5:30. I'm picking up Stephanie in thirty minutes and have no idea what to do. Maybe I can buy a bow tie at the mall. I race over there and find a black bow tie at Sears, but they have no cummerbunds.

I drive to Stephanie's house feeling somewhat distressed. Her mom answers the door and asks, "What's wrong?" I tell her about the tux, and she chuckles and says, "Well, let's see what we can do."

Stephanie's dad says, "I have a cummerbund you can borrow, so that solves that problem, but I'm afraid I'm not going to be able to help you with a jacket. I'm about the same size as the one you're wearing."

Stephanie comes down the stairs and she looks magnificent. She's wearing a pale-yellow, floor-length dress with matching high heels, and a pearl necklace. Her hair is up in a French twist. I smile at her. "You look beautiful," I say handing her a wrist corsage made with yellow and white carnations. "This is for you." She thanks me and gives me a kiss on my cheek.

I explain my tux fiasco to her and apologize. Meanwhile, her mom has pinned up both sides of the jacket from the inside to make it smaller. It still looks enormous, but not as bad. I resolve that nothing else can be done and that the stupid-looking jacket will not stop me from having a good time with Stephanie at our first prom.

Her dad takes some photos, and we walk out to my car. I open the door for Stephanie, and she gets in. I say, "How about if I put the top down?"

She stares at me wide-eyed. "I don't think so! I just spent all afternoon at the beauty salon getting my hair done."

I laugh. "Oh, I guess your hair would get messed up with the top down." The top stays up as we drive to dinner.

The Thunderbird is only ten minutes from Stephanie's house. I've never been to the Thunderbird or any other fancy sit-down restaurant. My restaurant experiences are McDonald's, Red Barn, Big Boy, and Kewpee. Not quite the same. Upon Stephanie's instructions, I called and made a reservation for two. After we are seated, I again apologize to her for the mix-up with the tux.

"Don't worry about it. Let's have a good time at the prom and the after-prom party."

The prom is scheduled to last until 11:00 and then one of Stephanie's friends is hosting a party that will go until at least 1:00 in the morning. Our meals are delicious, and the waiters are friendly and attentive.

After dinner, I drive us to Shawnee High School gym with the convertible top still up. I leave my tent-sized jacket hanging on my chair. I'm sure her friends notice it, but no one says anything. The prom theme is "Somewhere Over the Rainbow." A bit corny, but the prom committee has done a great job dressing up the gym with rainbow-colored decorations. A band plays Top 40 hits. We boogie to "Dance to the Music" by Sly and the Family Stone, "Young Girl" by Gary Puckett and The Union Gap, "Mony Mony" by Tommy James and the Shondells.

We take a break and Stephanie introduces me to some of her friends and they seem cool. One of her friends has a flask and passes it around. I pour a bit into my punch glass and pass it to Stephanie. She hesitates for a moment and then does the same to hers. It's not enough to get us drunk, but I do feel a bit more pep in my step when we start dancing again. We have a great time at the prom. After a disastrous start, it's been a beautiful evening.

When we leave the gym, Stephanie and I linger a while in my car, kissing, before we drive to the after-prom party. I would like to do more, but every time I try, she firmly pushes my hand away. I get the message and we stick to kissing.

The after-prom party is in the finished basement at the home of a friend of Stephanie's, only a short drive from the high school. About thirty people are there when we arrive. "Cry Like a Baby" by the Box Tops plays on the record player and several couples are dancing as we enter the room. Rainbow-colored crepe paper streamers and balloons hang from the ceiling adding to the festive atmosphere. We each get a Coke and dance to the next song, "Tighten Up" by Archie Bell & the Drells. After dancing for a couple of hours, we are spent.

"It's been a wonderful night," I tell Stephanie. "Thank you for inviting me to your prom."

"It has been fun. I'm glad your wardrobe problem didn't spoil it for you," she says.

I take Stephanie home shortly after 1:00 and thank her again for a nice evening. We kiss goodnight and I drive home.

Prom night had a disastrous beginning but lived up to its hype. What a night to remember.

Teens & Dreams

32

School's out, I've got new wheels and I'm ready to ride. I bought a 1964 Chevy Chevelle with a 327-cubic-inch engine and a four-speed manual transmission. The exterior color is desert beige, and the interior has light brown seats. It's too cool for school. I loved my 1960 Pontiac Catalina, but the transmission was slipping. It probably had something to do with me revving the engine and then throwing the automatic gear shifter into drive so the car would peel out. It was fun while it lasted, but very tough on the transmission. So, I traded up for my new ride.

At the end of May, Stephanie and I broke up. Her idea, not mine. Once again, I got the line, "I think we should see other people." It came totally out of the blue. We had been going steady for six months and I thought things were going well between us. I guess Stephanie had something else or, more accurately, someone else on her mind. That was only two weeks ago, and then last night at Russells Point I saw her walking around the amusement park with another guy.

I'm not too broken up about it. I was also on a date at Russells Point. I finally got up the courage to ask Lisa, a pretty girl from Lima Senior, to go out with me after my cousin Jim introduced us. It was the first time I had asked someone from Lima Senior on a date.

I pick Lisa up at her house on West Elm Street at 7:00. She is a year older than me and graduated from Lima Senior last week. She is cute with short blond hair and a perky nose. She is slender but with a very nice figure. When we first met, I thought she was shy and reserved.

We drive to the amusement park at Russells Point on Indian Lake, forty-minutes southeast of Lima. It's a beautiful, warm summer night. I'm wearing shorts with a collared short-sleeve shirt and sandals. Lisa wears baby blue short-shorts, a pale-yellow blouse, and strappy sandals. After we get in my car and are pulling away, I notice Lisa unbutton an additional button on her blouse and a bit of cleavage peeks out of the "V" in her blouse. I'm not complaining, I love the look.

We arrive at Russells Point and I hurry around the car and open the door for Lisa. She takes my hand as she gets out and doesn't let it go. Her hand is smooth and soft. As we walk toward the rides, she starts rubbing the side of my hand with her thumb. It feels wonderful.

"Are you ready to go on the Silver Streak?" I ask.

"I'm ready for anything," she replies.

I'm unsure how to take that answer, but say, "Okay, let's go."

The Silver Streak is an old wooden roller coaster. It's exciting, but it creaks and moans on every ride, and you think for sure that this time it's going to fall apart. Of course, it never does. We are first in line for the next ride, and I ask Lisa, "Do you want to take the front car?"

"Of course," she says, and we climb in.

As the coaster pulls us up the big hill, Lisa takes my left hand with her right, raises our hands over our heads, and yells, "Both hands in the air!"

I know what she wants to do, but I've never had the courage to do it. Now I have no choice. I raise my other hand holding onto the safety bar in front of us and Lisa does the same. As we crest the top and accelerate downhill, I am both exhilarated and terrified, but manage not to grab the safety bar. Lisa screams, and after the downhill rush, we both grab the bar. As the ride comes to an end, Lisa snuggles next to me, looks up, and kisses me.

Her face is flushed and she's smiling. "Thank you. That was fun."

"You are too much. I can't believe we took the first dip with our hands in the air."

We walk around the amusement park holding hands and sharing cotton candy. That's when I see Stephanie and her date. Stephanie doesn't stop, and neither do I, but we both say, "Hi." Lisa looks questioningly at me. "That was my former girlfriend, Stephanie."

Lisa smiles and kisses me again. "Her loss is my gain."

We sit on a bench and finish our cotton candy. "Are you ready for the Wild Mouse ride?" I ask.

"Yes! Let's go." She pulls me off the seat and we run down the midway to the Wild Mouse. We climb into the front seat of a car and the ride takes off. Lisa slides into me with each outside turn and does not attempt to move back to her side of the seat. When the ride ends, she's almost in my lap and kisses me again.

"Thank you. That was fun," she says.

"My pleasure," I say, and really mean it. I am having a great time with Lisa. We eat a snow cone and then ride the Ferris wheel.

We walk a bit more, and Lisa suggests, "How about if we go for a drive around the lake?"

"It's a beautiful night, great idea."

We leave the amusement park and drive around the lake. As we pass a parking lot that leads to a public beach, Lisa says, "Why don't you pull in here and park? I think we will be able to see the lake from the car."

"Sounds perfect."

I park facing the beach and see no other cars in the lot. Lisa takes my hand, looks up at me and then kisses me lightly at first, and then her tongue flicks the inside of my mouth. I reciprocate. Her kisses are passionate, and I immediately feel the stirrings in my shorts.

Lisa pulls back, looks into my eyes and holding my gaze, unbuttons another button of her blouse. I can see the top of her white lace bra and a whole lot of cleavage. I kiss her lips and her neck and then the top of her breasts. She moans. I brush my thumb across her nipple, and she moans again. She unbuttons another button and I slip my hand under her bra and over her bare breast. It is soft and luscious. I lower my mouth to her nipple and lightly suck. She moans with pleasure. I pull down the strap of her bra covering her other breast and see the most beautiful sight—two milky white breasts with perfect light brown hard nipples. I kiss both nipples and then unbutton the rest of her blouse. She is gorgeous.

I kiss her navel and then unbutton her shorts. I slip my hand inside and over her lacy panties. I can feel her wetness through her panties. I kiss her passionately and then slide my hand beneath her panties and feel her pubic hair and the lips of her vagina. I push my middle finger inside of her and she moans even louder. Lisa then places her hand on the outside of my shorts over my erect penis and rubs it softly. While I am rubbing her, she is rubbing me. I am about to explode, and she knows it. Reluctantly, I pull her hand away.

She looks at me, kisses me and whispers, "I'm still a virgin and want to remain a virgin for now. Is that okay?" I nod and pull my hand away from her vagina. She says, "Everything you are doing feels really good. I just don't want you to think we will go all the way."

I kiss her and say, "Everything you are doing turns me on. I too am a virgin, so this is all new for me."

She kisses me again. "You don't need to stop what you were doing if you want to do more."

I kiss her hard then kiss and suck her nipples, which are now hard and erect. She rubs my penis again through my shorts and then pulls on my earlobe with her teeth. I again pull her hand from my penis and say, "If you keep that up, we will have a mess."

She smiles a knowing smile and kisses me passionately. We continue kissing and touching each other until I say, "As much as I hate to say it, we'd better head back so that I can get you home before your curfew."

We both put ourselves back together as best we can. I drive Lisa home and stop in front of the walkway to her house.

"What are you doing next Saturday?" I ask her.

"I think I have a date with you."

I smile and kiss her. "Yes, you do. I will call you tomorrow."

"I would like that."

I walk her to her front door and kiss her goodbye. "It was a wonderful date. Thank you."

She says, "You are one special guy. Thank you."

As I drive away, I realize this was my first sexual encounter. No, we didn't have sex, but we did almost everything else. It was the first time I had seen and felt a naked breast. It was the first time I had touched a vagina. I brought my fingers to my nose and breathed in. The smell of her sex engulfs me, and I am immediately turned on again. This is the first time a girl has touched my penis. Wow! What a night.

It's Sunday afternoon, and I am at the Kettlersville Drag Strip in Kettlersville, Ohio. I've been here before with some friends and watched them race their cars. Last Sunday, I decided to go by myself and race my Chevelle. I want to see how my car will do on the quarter-mile dragstrip. I had raced illegally on Lima's streets but never raced at a drag strip.

The first thing I do is get my car rated so I know my racing class. The Chevelle is rated JPS for Class J Pure Stock. After I pay my entry fee, they write JPS with white shoe polish on the passenger side upper corner of my windshield.

After watching other cars race for about an hour, my name is called over the public address system, and I drive up to the staging area behind the Christmas tree light stand. The light stand controls the start of the race and the race tower behind us controls the light stand. Once both cars are in position, the light stand starts a countdown by flashing the first yellow light, then the second yellow light, then the third yellow light, then the fourth yellow light, then the fifth yellow light, and then the green light. Once you see the green light, the race is on, and you take off. If you leave too soon, you get a red light and are disqualified. The other driver automatically wins.

I pull forward and peel out a little to warm up my tires. I know from my buddies to roll up my windows now and shut down my car's heating and cooling system to reduce drag and get maximum horsepower. I slowly pull up to the light stand, and a white light indicates I'm in the proper position. I know what to do: depress the clutch pedal, rev the engine to 4000 rpm, hold it steady. When the light stand goes to green, I'll slide my foot off the clutch pedal to pop the clutch and get the most power while simultaneously flooring the gas pedal. Once I reach the red line in first gear at 6000 rpm, I'll power shift into second gear by keeping the gas to the floor and shifting. It's a dangerous procedure and if you don't do it right, you can tear up your transmission.

The guy in the Mustang beside me is ready to go too. The light stand starts its yellow light countdown. I rev the engine to 4000 rpm, put the transmission into first gear, and when the light goes to green, I floor it and shift into neutral at the same time. I get a loud roar from my engine, but nothing else happens because the car is in neutral. The Mustang takes off and I realize my stupid mistake. I put my car in first gear and floor it. Of course, it's too late. The Mustang wins. It's a rookie error. Too much adrenaline, not enough experience. I lose my first official drag race.

That was last week. Today, I'm determined to do better. I'm still a bit pumped up from my date last night with Lisa, but this time I'm going to focus and do it right. I pay my fee and wait for my turn.

When my name is called, I drive to the staging area, peel out and pull up to the Christmas tree light stand. I get into position and glance sideways to see a Mercury Cougar next to me. I roll up my window, turn off the A/C fan, put my car into first gear, and rev the engine to 4000 rpm. The tree stand countdown starts. It's hot inside the car. My hand is on the gearshift knob, but this time I'm not going to shift until after the race starts. I've done this many times on Wayne Street. This is no different. The fifth yellow light comes on. I don't wait for the green light but rather pop the clutch and floor it. My Chevelle leaps forward and I'm immediately ahead of the Cougar. I do a smooth power shift into second gear, and then a smooth shift into third gear, and then fourth gear, and the race is over. I win!

I now move on to race against the other cars in my class and win all my races. At the end of the day, I'm presented with a two-foot-tall silver trophy.

It's been a pretty good weekend.

Life & Love

33

Sociology 101 meets at 9:55 this morning in University Auditorium for me and four hundred of my fellow class-mates, including Katie. At the beginning of the quarter, we decided to take another course together. I signed up for it during winter quarter registration and Katie was able to pick it up in Drop and Add. Last Friday, we took our midterm, a multiple-choice exam with fifty questions. I'm getting pretty good at taking tests. I surprised myself during fall quarter. I pulled up my history grade from the D- I received in that awful first midterm to a final grade of B and made the Dean's List with a 3.41 GPA.

This morning I received a letter from my mom enclosing an article from the *Lima News* announcing that I had made the Dean's List. Mom said she was proud of me. That was a first. I can't recall a time when she said she was proud of me about anything. Mom never put me down like Dad did, but her praises were sparse. Mom also enclosed two other articles from the newspaper. The first was an article about a girl from my high school class who died from a drug overdose at Bowling Green State University, and the second was an article about a guy from my high school class who had been killed in action in Vietnam. My mom must be sending me messages. The first message is: drugs can kill. Stay away from drugs. The second message is: war can kill. Stay away from Vietnam.

Before class today, the professor posted our midterm grades at the rear of the auditorium. I am waiting for Katie outside the auditorium when she arrives.

"Are you ready to see our grades on our midterms?" I ask.

"I'm ready when you are," she says.

Taped to the back wall of the auditorium is a computerized printout of our grades listed in numerical order with number one being the top grade in the class and four hundred being the worst. Other columns list the student ID number, the raw score on the exam, and finally the letter grade for each student. Since there were fifty questions on the exam, fifty would be a perfect raw score. The student ID number is your Social Security number with an additional number at the end.

Katie and I make our way to the front of the group crowded around the printout. It takes a bit of scanning to find a grade, but I know Katie's Social Security number, so I look for hers. She received an A. I smile and think, "Way to go." Next, I look for my grade. I too received an A. My raw score is forty-nine and my rank in the class is three, meaning only two students ahead of me received perfect scores of fifty. I am happy to be ranked third out of four hundred.

We back away from the group, and I smile at Katie. "I guess we're doing something right. We both got As."

Katie smiles. "You should be very proud of yourself. Number three in the class. How do you do that?"

"A lot of studying and a little luck, I guess."

"Or you are just plain smart."

I laugh it off and we walk down to our favorite seats in the second row toward the center of the auditorium.

After sociology class, Katie has an English class in Satterfield, and I have Geology 102 in McGilvrey. Before we go our separate ways, I say to Katie, "Tonight is the first night that they are selling beer on campus. They've converted the Portage Room at the Student Union into a Rathskeller. I thought it might be fun to check it out. Do you want to go?"

Katie says "Sure. What time do you want to meet?

"How about I pick you up at your dorm at 8:00?"

"I'll be ready," she promises.

My geology class is much smaller than last quarter's intro course, Geology 101, with Professor Glenn Frank. I thoroughly enjoyed that class, so I enrolled in his Geology 102 course to complete my science requirement. Professor Frank is a fabulous teacher and makes every class meeting interesting. I thought seriously about changing my major to geology but could not quite see myself working for an oil company or a mineral exploration company, so I decided to stick with my plan to teach high school math and social studies.

I walk back to my dorm after class. It has been very cold all week and today is no different. The highs will only be in the low thirties.

On Tuesday afternoon, snow had begun falling and by early evening we had eight inches. At dinner that night, word circulated through the cafeteria that the Eastway dorms had challenged the Tri-Tower dorms to a snowball fight at 8:00.

The snow is wet and heavy and perfect for making snowballs. Shortly before 8:00, the Eastway team, mostly guys but also a few girls, gather in the courtyard outside Clark. We load the pockets of our winter coats with as many snowballs as possible. Promptly at 8:00, at least a hundred fifty of us, maybe two hundred, make the short trek to Tri-Towers. Our group greatly outnumbers the forty or fifty guys waiting behind a snowbank in front of Tri-Towers. We get within thirty feet and stop. We shout out a pre-launch countdown of five, four, three, two, one, then simultaneously throw two hundred snowballs at the Tri-Tower guys. They lob a measly forty or fifty at us, an anemic effort by the Tri-Towers team. We deploy our snowball reserves until we have none left and must make new ones.

A loud cry from behind interrupts our efforts to replenish our snowball inventory. We turn to see hundreds of snowballs coming at us. Two hundred Tri-Tower guys had been lying in wait. They had waited until we used up all our snowballs, then start pelting us from behind. We are outflanked and outsmarted. It is a massacre, and we all take several snowball hits. We immediately retreat to Eastway, acknowledging our defeat.

Even though we lost the snowball fight on Tuesday, it was a blast. Today it's still frigid, and most of the snow has thawed and refrozen. It is a typical winter day at KSU.

When I get to the Clark Hall lobby, I find several newspapers in the first-floor lounge and decide to catch up on current events. An article on the war in Vietnam catches my eye. The Pentagon is calling for the drafting of an additional nineteen thousand men in March 1970 and expects a total of 225 thousand men to be drafted this year. That is fewer than the number of men drafted in 1969, but any number greater than zero is too many. Nixon claims to have a plan to end the war, yet U.S. servicemen are dying daily. Heavy fighting continues without abatement. I can see no end to the war in Vietnam.

I spend the afternoon in my dorm room to catch up on reading for my classes. At 6:00, I walk to the Eastway cafeteria for dinner. It's packed and takes a while to get through the line. I choose spaghetti, the main entrée for today, and sit with a group of guys I know from the third floor of Clark. I've eaten a few bites when everyone starts complaining that the spaghetti is dry and tasteless. Usually, the cafeteria food is pretty good, but tonight it is clear that the spaghetti is reheated and overcooked.

Almost spontaneously, everyone in the cafeteria starts chanting, "*We want real food! We want real food! We want real food!*" Someone at the table next to us takes a handful of spaghetti and throws it at our table. We immediately retaliate and hurl handfuls of spaghetti back at them. Pretty soon, everyone in the cafeteria throws spaghetti, and I hear: "*Food fight!*" The chant grows louder as everyone joins in. "*Food fight! Food fight! Food fight!*" Everything on everyone's tray is thrown back and forth: noodles, salad, french fries, garlic bread. It doesn't matter. Everything is thrown and re-thrown, again and again.

After a few minutes, someone from the cafeteria announces over the public address system: *"The cafeteria is closed. Please return to your dorm rooms."* No one gets hurt, but we are all a mess. I have spaghetti sauce in my hair, noodles on my face, and salad all over my shirt. I wipe as much off my face and clothes as I can and leave it on the dining table.

With food trailing behind us, we make our way back to Clark. I hit the communal showers to wash off the spaghetti sauce and all the other food sticking to me. Even after shampooing my hair twice, I can still smell garlic and Italian spices.

I walk to Terrace Hall to meet Katie. Shortly before 8:00, she comes down to the lobby. She looks hot in her tight jeans and form-fitting sweater. I kiss her. "Where is your roommate tonight?"

Katie gives me a big grin. "You always have only one thing on your mind. She is upstairs reading."

"That's true. I always have you on my mind."

Katie smiles and kisses me again. "You are too smooth. Are you ready to go?"

I help her on with her winter coat and we take the short walk to the Student Union. On the way, we talk about new movies in the theaters. "I'd like to see *Butch Cassidy and the Sundance Kid*. I hear Paul Newman and Robert Redford are excellent together," I say.

Katie says, "I want to see *Funny Girl* with Barbara Streisand. It just came out last week."

"Let's make a date for Saturday. We'll see what's playing at the theater downtown."

Katie leans over, kisses me, and says, "You have a date."

As we enter the Portage Room, we are both pleasantly surprised. It looks just like a downtown bar. Heavy tables and chairs are scattered around the room. A jukebox in the corner plays one of my favorite songs, "Raindrops Keep Falling on My Head" by B.J. Thomas. It's crowded but we are lucky and find a vacant table for two. A bar serving beer and soft drinks is set up against the far wall.

We can't order a beer from the bar, though. We must be served at our table by a waiter. It seems silly, but I guess those are the conditions placed on their liquor license. The beer choices on tap are Budweiser and Miller High Life. Of course, both have only 3.2 percent alcohol. We each order a Miller.

The jukebox keeps spinning the 45s. We hear "Psychedelic Shack" by the Temptations and "Bridge over Troubled Water" by Simon and Garfunkel. Then we listen to "Without Love There is Nothing" by Tom Jones.

I raise my cup to Katie. "To us, forever and ever."

Bayonets & Bullets

34

Last night was shocking. I ran for my life on my own campus. Students were bayoneted. Dozens of students were arrested. It was as if someone had flipped a switch and suddenly the guardsmen turned from being peacemakers to participants in a blood sport. The occupiers were in control. They had guns. They had bayonets. They had tear gas. We have the moral imperative. The war in Vietnam is wrong. The National Guard on the KSU campus is wrong.

We still have heard nothing from KSU President White. Two flyers from Vice President Matson and Student Body President Frank Frisina on over the weekend have been the only communications from the university. Last night President White refused to engage in a discussion with his students. The Sunday flyer said classes were still on for today. This morning, I have a 7:45 Integral Calculus class at Merrill Hall on Front Campus. Things are not normal, but what else is there to do except go to class?

At breakfast in Eastway cafeteria, everyone talks about the guardsmen on campus, and the tear gas last night, the burning of the ROTC building on Saturday night, and the damage to downtown Kent on Friday night. A lot has happened since we attended classes on Friday. Yet, we still don't know for sure that President

White is even on campus. We heard that he was at some boondoggle in Iowa over the weekend. Who is in charge at KSU? No one knows.

The noon rally on the Commons is a hot topic too. Is it still on? Sunday's flyer stated that all rallies were banned, but the U.S. Constitution grants us the rights of freedom of speech and peaceable assembly. The guardsmen can't blindly ignore the Constitution. And neither can that bastard, Governor Rhodes. It is his fault the guardsmen are on our campus.

Today's rally was scheduled to protest the invasion of Cambodia and the war in Vietnam. Now, the main concern is the occupation of KSU by the Ohio National Guard. We want our campus back. Period!

After breakfast, I walk to Merrill Hall on Front Campus for my calculus class. This morning is beautiful, and this afternoon promises to be even better with temps in the high seventies. The most direct route is across the Commons. As I reach the top of Blanket Hill and stand next to the Pagoda, I look down at the war scene before me. National Guardsmen still ring the burnt-out ROTC building, which is now cordoned off with a wooden picket fence. Jeeps, trucks, and armored personnel carriers are parked everywhere.

I walk down Blanket Hill and across the Commons. No guardsmen confront me. What will they do, challenge every one of the twenty thousand students attending classes today? That's not practical or possible. So, what are the guardsmen here for?

When I get to Front Campus, the scene is even worse. Almost all of Hilltop Drive is lined with army vehicles. Do they really think the campus is going to be invaded by non-student instigators? If it weren't so serious it would seem preposterous.

I make it without incident to calculus, a relatively small class of about thirty students. The professor welcomes us and notes that several students are missing. She addresses the elephant in the room, by saying, "The absences are probably due to the presence of the National Guard on campus. Before we get into our classwork today, I want to tell you what I know about what's going on. Apparently,

Governor Rhodes has declared a state of emergency for the City of Kent and Kent State University thereby giving control of the campus to the Ohio National Guard. The National Guard has prohibited all rallies whether peaceful or otherwise. I understand that the Executive Committee of the Faculty Senate is meeting at 8:00 this morning to discuss this situation and that President White will meet with the entire faculty this afternoon. That's about all I know, but I am happy to try and answer any questions you may have."

I raise my hand. "Why haven't we heard anything from President White? I hear he was not even on campus last weekend."

The professor replies, "President White is on campus. He was out of town attending a professional conference but returned Sunday afternoon. It is my understanding that he met with Governor Rhodes at that time. I do not know the substance of that conversation."

Another student asks, "So, who's in charge of the campus?"

The professor says, "Right now, academics are still being run by the faculty and KSU administration. Campus facilities are under the control of the Ohio National Guard."

We have no other questions, so class continues as though nothing unusual is going on right outside the doors of Merrill Hall.

Teens & Dreams

35

Saturday, August 3, 1968 • Lima, Ohio

Lisa and I have been seeing each other at least two to three times a week since our first date in June. I love being with her, and the non-sex sex gets better all the time. We talk about everything. We often agree on politics, but when we don't, she is not shy about letting me know her position. I like that she has her own opinions, and isn't going to be submissive to any man, including me.

On Wednesday, I didn't have to work at McDonald's until 5:00, so I pick up Lisa at noon, and we drive to Faurot Park in Lima. I bring a blanket, and we sit on the side of a hill in the shade of a tree and talk all afternoon. I tell her that I am opposed to the war in Vietnam and that I cannot see the logic of sending over five hundred thousand U.S. soldiers to Vietnam to protect the U.S. from, what? So that another Asian country will not be subject to a communist form of government? Every month, more than one thousand U.S. soldiers are killed, a high price to pay for a war nobody wants. Lisa agrees and knows guys from her high school class that will soon be heading to Vietnam. She says it all seems so senseless. I agree.

We talk about civil rights leader Martin Luther King Jr. being shot and killed on April 4 and Bobby Kennedy being shot and killed on June 5 while running for U.S. president. We agree that since President Lyndon Johnson decided not to run for re-election,

Bobby Kennedy easily would have won the Democratic primary and the presidential election in November. My hunch is that Richard Nixon will win the Republican nomination next week. His campaign promise to end the war in Vietnam will carry him through and he will win the presidency. Lisa thinks Hubert Humphrey will win the Democratic nomination later this month and the election. We disagree, and that's fine.

I ask Lisa, "Are you planning to go to college?"

Lisa says, "I've been accepted at Miami University in Oxford, Ohio, and will be moving there in early September."

"Congratulations. What are you going to study?"

"I'd like to teach history or civics or maybe even go on to law school if my grades are good enough. How about you? Any thoughts of going to college after you graduate next year?"

"I have thought a lot about it. I do not want to go to Vietnam, but I do want to get out of Lima. The only way to accomplish both goals is to go to college. No one in my family has ever graduated from college, so I'm not quite sure how to apply, but hopefully I can figure it out."

Lisa says, "I'm happy to help you with your college applications if you need it."

I say, "Thanks. I might have to take a trip to Miami University for some personal consulting."

Lisa smiles, leans over, kisses me, and says, "I would love to give you close personal attention."

Tonight, Lisa and I are going out again, back to Russells Point at Indian Lake. We haven't been there since our first date and decided that a reprise is in order. I pick her up at 8:00. She is wearing a short khaki skirt and a white sleeveless shirt with a low, scooped neck accentuating her prominent breasts.

"You look hot," I tell her.

"Thank you. I hoped you would like it."

I open the door for her, and she kisses me before getting into the car. That's sweet.

On the way to Russells Point, Lisa says "How about if we skip the amusement park and head to the beach instead? Do you still have the blanket we used at Faurot Park on Wednesday?"

"I do and think that is a perfect idea." We pull into the same parking lot as last time just as the sky is turning from yellow to orange to purple. The view is stunning. "I like how you think. It's a beautiful sunset."

We spread the blanket on the sand at the back of the beach away from the parking lot but protected by some bushes and trees. I sit down and Lisa lays down on her back in front of me and puts her head in my lap. One other couple is on the beach watching the colorful display, and after the sun dips below the horizon, they walk back to their car. We now have the beach to ourselves.

Lisa pulls me to her and kisses me. Her first kiss is very tender and sweet. She then opens her mouth and is searching for my tongue. She finds it and I get hot very quickly. She rolls me onto my back and bends down to kiss me. Her scoop neck shirt falls open, and I see her lacy light-yellow bra.

She sees me looking. "Do you like what you see?"

"Very much," and I reach up to cup her breasts with my hands.

"Not so fast, Mister. You just lay there and watch."

I lie back down, and Lisa takes the bottom of her blouse and in one smooth motion pulls it over her head. It is a sexy move, and I am stunned. Her magnificent breasts peek from the top of her bra. She leans down and brushes her breasts against me and gives me a very wet kiss. She sits back up and unbuttons my shirt. She leans down again and this time instead of kissing me, she wraps her mouth around my nipple and flicks it with her tongue. I've never experienced that before, and it really turns me on. I moan and she flicks my other nipple.

I move to sit up to kiss her, but she gently pushes me back down with one hand and with the other she runs her fingers over the top of my shorts and my now erect penis. Each time she does this, it drives me crazy. This time, however, instead of stopping, she bends down and kisses my penis through my shorts. She then unbuckles my belt and unzips my shorts. I reach up for her and she bends down and gives me another deep kiss. She sits back up and then slowly pulls down my shorts, then my underwear, and frees my erect penis. I am both surprised and excited. This is definitely new territory. I've always been covered when she touches me. Lisa grasps my naked penis and starts stroking it. I know what is about to happen, but before it does Lisa bends over and takes my entire penis into her mouth and moves her lips over the head of my penis. I immediately moan and explode inside her mouth. She does not pull away, but rather swallows and licks my penis. Very soon I am hard again. She pulls my penis out of her mouth but does not let go. She bends over and whispers in my ear "Did you enjoy that?" I manage a *yes* between moans as she once again strokes my penis. She knows I am getting ready to come again and brings her lips down over me. My whole body stiffens as she slows down the rhythm of her mouth and flicks her tongue up and down my penis. I want her to do it faster, but she makes me wait, prolonging my ecstasy. Then just when I think the longing for more will never end, she grasps my penis with her hand, moves up and down twice, and wraps her mouth around my penis as she once again drains me dry.

With my penis still throbbing, I flip Lisa onto her back, unsnap her bra and take her breasts into my mouth. Her nipples grow erect on my tongue. I unzip her skirt and pull it down over her legs. She is wearing light yellow panties that match her bra. She looks magnificent. I kiss her and whisper to her, "Tell me what you want me to do."

"I want you to touch me and make me feel good."

"I want to do that. Can you show me how?"

She takes my hand and together we pull down her panties. I am astounded by her naked beauty. She grasps my hand and places my middle finger toward the top of her vagina. She moves my finger back and forth over the lip of her vagina. Soon, I get the rhythm and she removes her hand and starts to moan. I move my finger back and forth faster and faster. I bend over and take her nipple in my mouth while my finger is still moving over her vagina and suddenly, she moans loudly, goes rigid, and I stop.

She frantically says, "Don't stop! Keep going." I do and she moans loudly again and lets out a sigh. "That was perfect."

I smile and snuggle next to her. "No, you are perfect and amazing. Thank you."

She smiles and kisses me. "I'm glad you enjoyed it."

"I enjoyed it twice. I didn't even know that was possible."

"I enjoyed it twice too. You are very good."

"I have a really good teacher."

She kisses me, and says, "I have the very best student."

After a little while, she says, "We'd better get dressed before we get caught."

After we're dressed, I say, "I think I'm falling in love with you."

"I know. I feel the same way." She gives me a very sweet kiss and we walk back to the car.

The drive back to Lima goes way too fast. I don't want to leave her and can tell that she feels the same, but we are approaching her curfew, so I drive her home.

"Thank you. You were wonderful," she says.

"I will never forget this night," I say.

We walk up to her front door and kiss. I don't want to leave but say, "See you soon,"

"I hope so," she says.

Teens & Dreams

36

Friday, September 13, 1968 • Lima, Ohio

I 'm finally a senior at Lima Senior High. Last Saturday was my last day at McDonald's. I enjoyed working there, but now I have a new job that I think I will like even better. I just completed my first week.

I signed up for the Cooperative Office Education (COE) program, at Lima Senior. It's a vocational education program usually taken by students not planning to attend college. I'm the anomaly.

In the COE program, students go to class for half a day and work the other half in an office environment. In the mornings, I have classes in college English, college math, bookkeeping, and COE. The COE program placed me in a job as a teller at the main branch of Metropolitan Bank on Elizabeth Street in Lima where I work in the afternoons. I earn $1.60 per hour rather than the $1.10 per hour I made at McDonald's. The whole thing is a sweet deal. I go to school for only a half day, make more money than I did before, and finish work at 4:30 in the afternoon rather than 10:30 at night. I dress up every day in a coat and tie and am treated like a professional rather than a day laborer. I like it.

On the first day I shadow the head teller. On the second day, he sets me up at my own teller window and coaches me throughout the day on the various types of transactions that customers request. He also shows me what to do and what not to do if someone tries to rob the bank. Do give the robber all the money in your drawer, including the marked bills with the exploding dye. Do press the silent alarm button under the counter. Don't try to be a hero and resist the robber. The bank is insured, so don't worry about handing over the money. We want to keep everyone in the bank safe and let the police and the FBI deal with the bank robber after he leaves the building.

The other tellers at the bank are friendly and helpful. I'm not sure what I expected, but working at the bank is fun and I'm treated like an adult, rather than a kid. All the tellers process the same types of transactions and interact directly with the bank's clients. At the end of every day, we must balance our cash drawer, ensuring the cash and check transactions match up. The first day, I am off by one penny. The head teller says if I get that close every day, then I'm a keeper. I plan on being at the bank for the rest of the school year.

I'm the only guy in the COE program. The other fifteen students are all girls. It's not a bad ratio for a guy. My bookkeeping class is the same: thirty students and two guys. It's the dichotomy between bookkeeping and my college math class, the Theory of Functions, that is most striking. Bookkeeping is ministerial—record the debits and credits to a ledger and make sure they balance. It's boring stuff. Functions is highly theoretical and requires a lot of thinking and process learning. Other than me, none of the students in my bookkeeping class plan to go to college. In Functions, everyone plans to go to college.

The students in both my college prep classes can't quite understand how I can be in both vocational ed and college prep at the same time. Of course, parents of the college prep kids always assumed they would go to college. At my house, my parents always assumed I would go to work. When my mom graduated from high school, she immediately began work as a clerk in a five-and-dime store. My dad finished fourth grade and never went back to school. His parents put him to work. If I'm going to go the college route, I will have to figure out how to apply and pay for it myself. No one on my dad's side of the family or my mom's side ever graduated from college. I'll be breaking new ground if I can figure out how to do it.

I'm determined to get a college degree. Doing so will allow me to be as far away from my dad as possible and get the 2-S college deferment so I don't get drafted and sent to Vietnam for at least another four years.

Metropolitan Bank closes at 4:00. By the time I clean up my work area and balance my transactions, it's 4:30. I'm picking up Lisa at 6:00 and we're going to the Lima Senior football game. I've always enjoyed football under the Friday night lights at Lima Stadium, and with Lisa by my side, I will like it even better.

I pull up to Lisa's house and start to walk up her sidewalk to knock on her door. She must have seen me coming because she opens the door and runs to me, throws her arms around me, and gives me a kiss.

"Well, hello to you too," I say.

She beams. "I've been looking forward to seeing you all day."

I smile at her and take a good look. She's wearing a Kelly-green sweater that looks great with her blond hair. A short, black pencil skirt and black boots complete her outfit. "You look smashing tonight."

She tips her head to the side, smiles, and says, "Well, thank you fine sir."

I laugh and open the car door for her. It's only a short drive to the football stadium.

Lisa asks, "How was the bank today?"

"I really enjoy working there. How was your day?"

"I packed all day. I leave for Miami University tomorrow morning."

"I know. This is our last night together, and I don't want to be sad. I know I will miss you, but I want you to have fun on your last night in Lima before going to college."

"It's not like I'm never coming back. I'll be home for Thanksgiving and Christmas."

"I know, but we have agreed that neither of us should be tied down while you are at Miami. That would never work. You are going to conquer the world and I will try and survive another year in Lima."

She says, "I'm going to miss you too. I don't know what life will be like at Miami, but it will be hard to beat the summer I've spent with you. You make me happy every time I see you."

"Well, let's make it another happy night. There's nothing quite like a Friday night football game on a crisp fall evening."

The Lima Senior Spartans play a good game and win. After the game, we decide to go out for pizza. We talk. We laugh. We have a good time and avoid the inevitable.

I drive her home, and as much as I try to be happy for Lisa, I am one sad puppy that she is leaving tomorrow. I pull up in front of her house and look over at her.

She looks sad, too, and says, "I've had a perfect summer. Thank you."

"I've loved every minute we have spent together. I hope you have the best time at Miami."

She pulls me to her and gives me a kiss that I will not soon forget. And then another kiss and another kiss and more kisses. I don't want to let her go, but her curfew is just a few minutes away and I know her mom will be looking out the window. I exit my car, open her door, and walk her up to her house. I say, "I'm not saying goodbye, but rather au revoir until we meet again."

Lisa says, "Au revoir," kisses me, and walks into her house.

I make it to my car before the tears start to fall. She is not only my lover, but also my best friend. I've known for months this day was coming, but it still doesn't make it any easier.

Life & Love

37

Today is going to be another cold, overcast day with a high only in the twenties. A good day to catch up on my reading assignments. I plan to read in the morning, watch some college basketball on TV in the Eastway lounge this afternoon, and then meet Katie at 7:00 and go watch the KSU men's basketball team play the Western Michigan Broncos in Memorial Gym. After the game, we're going to a Sigma Chi fraternity party. It should be a fun evening.

I'm at Terrace Hall shortly before 7:00 and wait for Katie in the lounge. She walks off the elevator a few minutes after I arrive, and my mouth drops open. She is wearing a very short black straight skirt with the peach-colored cashmere sweater that I like, and black leather boots that come up just below her knees. Her auburn hair is done in a flip, and her green eye shadow highlights her crystal blue eyes. I give her a catcall whistle, and she smiles.

"You look delicious, I tell her. "Let's skip the basketball game and go to your room."

"Behave. You know my roommate is here this weekend."

"We'll let her watch."

She gives me a light push. "You are a naughty boy. Let's go."

We show our student IDs to get into Memorial Gym, already about three-quarters full. In the pre-game warm-ups, a cheer goes up every time one of the Golden Flashes basketball players jumps above the rim and acts like he is going to dunk the ball, but instead drops it in the net. Since 1967 dunking has been illegal in college basketball, even in warm-up drills. It's amusing to watch these guys act like they are going to dunk but then drop the ball in from above the rim.

The KSU Golden Flashes are always competitive even though they have not had much success this year. They are 6–16 overall and 1–8 in the Mid-American Conference, and clearly not heading to either the NCAA Tournament or the National Invitational Tournament. We've been to several home games. They are fun to watch, and the four thousand or so fans at the games agree with me. The Western Michigan Broncos have a similar record, so it should be a good game.

The players from Western Michigan are introduced first to some light applause. When the KSU players are introduced, Katie and I join in as the crowd goes wild—cheering, clapping, and whistling.

Western Michigan takes the tip and has a fast start hitting eighteen of their first twenty-three shots. Kent goes down by twenty points but rallies toward the end of the first half to close the gap and is only down by thirteen at the half. The score is 48–35.

I turn to Katie. "It's going to be tough for the guys to dig out of this hole, we can leave if you like."

"I'm enjoying the game but if you want to leave, that's okay with me."

"No, I would like to stay and see what happens, if you're okay watching what could be a massacre." We get Cokes from the concession stand and share a box of popcorn.

Just before the beginning of the second half, Katie says, "I believe Kent has a comeback in them and it's going to end up closer than you think."

I smile. "We'll see."

At the beginning of the second half, the Broncos have another fast start and, with twelve minutes to go in the game, KSU is losing, 65–46.

Then, Kent does the impossible and ties the game 67–67 with four minutes and forty-eight seconds remaining. The Golden Flashes allow Western Michigan to score only two points in the last seven minutes. It's a close game right to the end, but the Flashes prevail, 85–82. Katie reminds me that she had predicted their incredible comeback all along.

After the game, I hold Katie's hand as we walk toward Main Street and head downtown. It's a cold night, but the wind is calm, and walking feels good.

Several of the guys on the third floor of Clark Hall survived pledging and initiation and are now members of Sigma Chi. They keep encouraging me to pledge, and I keep telling them I want to wait until next year. They invited me to an open party tonight to meet some of the other fraternity brothers. I'm sure the leaders want to check me out too. The guys I know told me if I had a date to bring her along, but I didn't need to bring any food or drinks.

The two-story Victorian-style Sigma Chi house is located off campus on Main Street. It sits on a hill and is enormous. All the lights are on in the house and on the front porch. We walk up the driveway, and I am about to knock when the door opens, and Jay, one of my friends from Clark, says, "Welcome. Come on in." In the living room and dining room, at least fifty students are talking, drinking, and dancing.

Jay and Katie have previously met, so no introductions are necessary. Jay says, "Help yourself to something to drink. We have a keg in the kitchen and Hairy Buffalo right over there." He points to the corner where partyers are gathered around a twenty-gallon round plastic trash can lined with a black garbage bag.

Katie and I stare at Jay. "Hairy Buffalo. What's that?" I ask.

Jay says, "That's a Sigma Chi special. We start with two bottles of one-hundred-fifty proof grain alcohol and then add a couple of bottles of fruit punch, and as people arrive, they add whatever they bring to the party: wine, beer, whiskey, vodka, gin. Everything is dumped in. It's not bad. Have a taste."

I look at Katie, and she says, "Let's try it."

"Okay, but I hope it doesn't make us sick."

We each take a cup and dip it into the reddish-purple mixture. I taste it first and say, "Not bad. It's sort of fruity."

Katie tries it next. "I like it," she says.

I say, "Go slow with it. Remember, the mixture started with one-hundred-fifty proof grain alcohol."

"Got it," Katie says.

A stereo system with three-foot-tall speakers has been set up in the parlor, a reception area right inside the front door. A Temptations album is playing, and couples are grooving to the music.

Jay introduces us to several of his fraternity brothers, who all seem like good guys. We're having a great time talking to some of them and their dates when we hear shouts of "Jay! Jay! Jay!" Jay has a reputation as a wild man. He is the guy that started the Slip 'N Slide on the third floor of Clark Hall last fall.

Jay raises his hand, and someone turns the music down low. He takes an empty beer glass that looks like it came from one of the bars downtown. He holds it in the air for everyone to see, and we hear the *ting, ting, ting* as he taps it with a butter knife. He sticks the glass in the corner of his mouth and takes a bite. Of course, the glass breaks, and he now has a mouth full of glass. He starts chewing the glass, and everyone cheers, "*Jay! Jay! Jay!*" He chews the glass for at least a couple of minutes, then goes to the kitchen to spit it out. He comes back and opens his mouth—no cuts, no blood.

"Amazing and crazy," I say to Katie.

Katie says, "I can think of a couple of other adjectives." We both laugh while Jay guzzles a plastic cup of beer.

The music resumes, and Katie and I join those dancing in the dining room, where the table and chairs have been pushed against the outer wall. Throughout the evening, we drink Hairy Buffalo, dance, drink some more Hairy Buffalo, dance, talk to some Sigma Chi brothers, and dance. It's loads of fun, and I can see Katie is enjoying herself.

I ask Katie what she thinks of the people she met tonight. She agrees everyone is friendly and interesting, including the girls. Right before we're ready to find our coats and walk back to campus, the brothers ask the girls, including Katie, to stand in the middle of the living room. The brothers stand in a circle around them with their arms around each other's shoulders and sway as they sing:

"The girl of my dreams is the sweetest girl
Of all the girls I know
Each sweet co-ed like a rainbow trail
Fades in the afterglow.

The blue of her eye and the gold of her hair
Are a blend of the western sky
And the moonlight beams on the girl of my dreams
She's the sweetheart of Sigma Chi.

Oh, the blue of her eye and the gold of her hair
Are a blend of the western sky
And the moonlight beams on the girl of my dreams
She's the sweetheart of Sigma Chi."

When they finish singing "The Sweetheart of Sigma Chi," Katie walks over to me smiling and kisses me softly. "Thank you for bringing me tonight," she says. "That was very special."

"I thought they were singing about you," I say. She smiles, which sort of seals the deal for me.

I know I will pledge Sigma Chi next fall.

Bayonets & Bullets

38

After calculus class, I look out over the once-beautiful Front Campus landscape and see occupation and oppression. Military vehicles are parked everywhere. How are we supposed to study with the National Guard pointing their bayonetted rifles at our faces?

I decide I can do nothing but persevere so I head to my next class, History of Ohio, at Bowman Hall with Katie. I intentionally avoid the Commons because I know there will be a heavy National Guard presence there so take an alternate route past the Student Union and Van Deusen Hall. I arrive at Bowman early and look for Katie. I have not spoken to her about what happened last night.

I find Katie outside the door of our classroom. She drops her books and gives me a kiss and a big hug like I haven't seen her in months rather than yesterday afternoon. She looks distraught.

"What's wrong?" I say.

Katie says, "I was accosted by a guardsman on the way to class, and I've been so worried about you."

I'm alarmed. "Are you okay? What happened?"

"I was walking to class and when I got to Memorial Gym, a guardsman who was standing next to his jeep, stepped in front of me, placed the flat side of his bayonet across my chest next to my face, and said, 'Just where do you think you're going?'"

"I was so startled I couldn't talk. I felt the cold blade of his bayonet and I flinched. It was very frightening. I told him I was going to my history class in Bowman. He demanded to know which building that was. I pointed toward Bowman and told him it was just up the way.

"He said, 'When you're finished with class, go straight to your dorm. No congregating is permitted.'

"I nodded, and he moved to the side to let me pass."

"What a prick. He had no right to do that to you. He was just on a power trip. Fuck him!"

Katie says, "What about you? I heard several students were injured last night in a clash with the National Guard on Front Campus. Were you there? Are you okay?"

"Yes, and yes. Let's find a seat in the classroom, and I will tell you about it."

Class is held in a lecture hall that holds about a hundred students. We walk toward the front and take the first two seats in the second row.

"It turned ugly, really fast last night. I was with about three hundred students just outside Prentice Gate. The guardsmen blocked us from going downtown, so we all sat down in the middle of the street at the corner of Main and Lincoln. We really wanted to hear from President White. We heard he would talk to us if we moved back onto campus. We complied, then were told that President White would not talk with us. The National Guard gave the order to disperse and started lobbing tear gas canisters at us. It was crazy. Helicopters hovered overhead, their rotors slicing through the air and their spotlights shining on us. It was loud and chaotic.

"Without warning, the guardsmen charged us, and we all ran. I took off toward McGilvrey Hall. Most everyone else headed toward Rockwell Library. I saw guardsmen stab several students in the back with bayonets and arrest dozens of others. It looked like a war scene."

Katie said, "It must have been terrifying."

I said, "It really shook me up. I thought the National Guard was going to kill us. How about you? Did you stay in last night?"

Katie says, "Yes, I went to bed early and knew nothing about what happened until this morning when I heard students talking about it in the cafeteria. What are you going to do after class today? I heard the rally at noon on the Commons is still on."

"I want to attend the rally, but I'm worried about you. The National Guard has flipped from being our protector to being our intimidator. Anything can happen."

Katie says, "I hate the war in Vietnam, and I hate that the National Guard is occupying our campus, but I don't want to get caught in a skirmish with them. I'll stay close to you, and if things start to turn ugly, I'll head back to my dorm."

"I don't want you to get hurt. If the Guard gives the order to disperse or starts lobbing tear gas at us, run up Blanket Hill, head toward Prentice Hall, and take Midway Drive back to your dorm. Don't worry about me. Just get away fast if things turn bad. Okay?"

Katie says, "Okay."

Class is getting ready to start but only about half the usual number of students are here.

The professor begins, stating, "We are in uncharted territory. The Ohio National Guard on campus has never happened in the history of KSU and we don't know how long they will stay. We are in a state of emergency and the Guard appears to have unlimited powers. All rallies and outdoor assemblies have been declared by the Guard to be unlawful. I know that many of you are considering whether to attend the noon rally on the Commons. I'm not going to tell you what to do, but if you decide to attend, I encourage you to listen to the advice of the faculty marshals led by Professor Glenn Frank and Professor Jerry Lewis. The marshals will be wearing light blue armbands. I encourage everyone to stay safe during these troubled times. I have a short lecture of thirty minutes, and then we will end class for today."

After class, I ask Katie, "Do you still want to attend the rally?"

Katie says, "Yes, but I want you to promise me that you will be extra careful and follow the faculty marshals' instructions. You know Professor Frank. You've had him for two courses, And I think you respect him."

"Okay, but you have to promise to do exactly what we discussed and return to your dorm if things turn bad."

She says, "I will."

I say, "Let's drop our backpacks off at your room before we head to the Commons."

"Good idea," Katie says and gives me a kiss to remember.

"Wow, what was that for?"

"I love you, and don't you forget it. If things turn crazy on the Commons today, if we get separated, I want you to come to my dorm as soon as you can. Promise?"

"I promise, and I love you," I say, and seal it with another kiss.

Teens & Dreams

39

The day after Thanksgiving is the busiest shopping day of the year. Metropolitan Bank is open, and the head teller asked me if I could work a full day today. They expect to be very busy. I told him I would be happy to and that I could work full days over the Christmas break if he needed me. I can use the extra money.

The bank opened at 9:00, and it's been nonstop since then. Many small businesses have come in to get extra coins and one-dollar bills for the busy weekend. Toward the end of the day, many business customers make their largest deposits of the year. I enjoy chatting with the regulars and ask them how business is going. Some show me pictures of their children or grandchildren, and I gush over them.

We are in a lull around 2:00, when one of my favorite customers walks into the bank. Her name is Debbie, and she is stunning. She has shiny dark hair that reaches the middle of her back, big dark brown eyes, and olive skin. She's about five foot six and is always impeccably dressed in a stylish outfit. Debbie graduated from Shawnee High School last year and works at her family's jewelry store while deciding whether she wants to go to college. She always comes to my teller window. Even if another one is available, she waits for me.

"Good afternoon, Debbie. Did you have a good Thanksgiving?"

"I did, but I ate too much. How about you?"

"I ate way too much turkey and stuffing and pumpkin pie."

She laughs and hands me her deposit slip with the cash and checks. I count the cash, verify the amounts on the checks and enter the deposit on my teller machine. I hand her the deposit receipt and am just about to tell her to have a good weekend when she says, "I'm having a few friends over at my house tonight for a small party. I thought you might like to come."

I am surprised but manage to say, "Thanks. That would be great. What time?"

"Around 7:00. Here's my address." She hands me a small piece of paper from the jewelry store with her address and phone number. She turns to go and waves at me. "See you then."

The last time I was on a date was with Lisa the night before she left for Miami University. It's not an intentional thing. It's just that compared to Lisa, no one interests me. Lisa and I had agreed we wouldn't call each other but write letters instead. She wrote me a letter soon after arriving at Miami telling me how great everything was and saying she missed me. I wrote back to her. About a week after my letter, she wrote to me again telling me about her classes. I replied but have heard nothing more. Her last letter was over eight weeks ago. I'm sure she is home for Thanksgiving, but she hasn't called or stopped by the bank to see me. I assume she is dating someone at Miami, and we are history. It's a tough pill to swallow.

Debbie's invitation came at exactly the right time, and I'm looking forward to her party.

Occasionally, my COE teacher, Mrs. Carter, will stop by the bank to see how I am doing in my job. I told her I would be working today, even though it was a school holiday. Around 3:00, I spot her walking through the lobby door. I like Mrs. Carter a lot. She is the grandmotherly type, always supportive, and never critical of anything or anybody. She sees me and walks up to my open window.

"How is work going? Have you been busy today?" she asks.

"Hi Mrs. Carter. Very busy. Are you out doing some holiday shopping?"

"I am. I just thought I would stop by and say hello."

"Thank you," I say. "That's very nice of you."

She says, "Are you ready for the COE district meeting in Dayton next Thursday?"

I was elected president of my COE class and am now running for district president. I have to give a speech at the meeting next week. "I'm still working on my speech, but I think it will be good," I say.

Mrs. Carter says, "Well, I know you will do fine. Have a good weekend, and I'll see you Monday in class."

"Thank you," I tell her. "Have a good day."

Mrs. Carter has been a positive influence in my life. She has encouraged me and helped me see my self-worth. For a long time, I believed my dad when he said I was a stupid son of a bitch. And I had an inferiority complex because we lived in a run-down house next to railroad tracks. Mrs. Carter assures me that I am smart, personable, and funny. She is the first teacher to tell me I can do anything I put my mind to.

With Mrs. Carter's support, I agreed to run for COE district president. Voting will occur after the dinner and speeches next Thursday. COE students from all over Western Ohio will be there and will vote on the candidates. I've been working on a speech that takes its cue from President Kennedy's inaugural address, which included his famous saying, "Ask not what your country can do for you, ask what you can do for your country." The opening line of my COE speech will be: "Ask not what COE can do for you, but what you can do for COE." I think it's good, but we shall see.

We do have one ace up our sleeve for the COE district meeting. Everything at the meeting will occur at a catered, sit-down dinner. One of my COE classmates said her family is good friends with the owner of the Chinese restaurant in Lima. She said she thought she could get us fortune cookies we could hand out along with a flyer at the meeting.

I had a thought. Let's stuff the fortune cookies with a message that reads: "Vote for Johnny." She brought a few fortune cookies to class to see if it would work. I typed up a sample sheet, and we cut the messages into small strips of paper. There is just enough room to insert the "fortune" into each cookie. It will work. Next Monday, the whole class is going to stuff two hundred fortune cookies. We plan to place a fortune cookie on each attendee's dinner plate before the start of the district meeting.

The COE class has been holding fundraisers. We've sold book covers and bumper stickers and hosted a bake sale. We've raised enough money to take seven children from the Allen County Children's Home on a shopping spree the week before Christmas. It is the first time in my life I've thought about doing something for someone else. Before that, I was just trying to survive, and my thoughts were always just about me.

I am busy with customers the rest of the afternoon and have no time to think about Lisa or Debbie. The bank closes at 4:00 and my cash drawer balances perfectly. I drive home thinking about the party tonight. I really don't know what to expect or who will be there. Debbie knows about my part-time status at the bank and that I am a senior at Lima Senior High. She also knows I am a year younger than her. Apparently, that doesn't bother her, nor am I concerned that she is a year older than me. Anyway, this isn't a date, just a party I've been invited to attend.

Debbie lives in Shawnee, and when I pull up in front of her house, I am surprised at its size and grandeur. It is a dark brick home with a circular driveway. Other cars are parked in the driveway, so I park behind one and walk to the front door. I didn't know if I should bring anything, but at the last minute, I stopped at a florist and picked up a small bouquet of flowers. I ring the doorbell, and Debbie answers. Wow! She looks gorgeous. She's wearing a form-fitting, black cocktail dress with spaghetti straps and a scoop neckline. A diamond and gold necklace brings the whole look together. She is stunning and I feel underdressed.

"Hi, "she says and kisses me on the cheek.

"Hi. These are for you," I say, handing her the flowers.

"Thanks. Let me introduce you to my parents." Debbie takes the bouquet and welcomes me into the foyer.

Her parents are talking in the lavish living room, decorated with fine antiques and artwork. She introduces them to me and hands her mom the flowers. "Mom, Johnny brought these for me. Would you mind putting them in some water?"

Her mom says, "That's very nice. I would be happy to take care of them."

We walk downstairs to a large, beautifully furnished rec room. About ten people, both girls and guys, are in the room and everyone is talking. A stereo plays a Supremes album in the background. Debbie has good taste in music.

She takes me over to a wet bar and says, "We have beer, wine, and soft drinks. Can I get you something?"

"A beer would be good, thanks." She hands me my first Heineken.

Debbie takes my hand and says, "Let me introduce you to some people."

They all are her former high school classmates. All attend different colleges and are home for Thanksgiving weekend. Most of them are not coupled up but have dated each other at one time or another. Some are still dating.

The atmosphere at the party is laid back and I join a small group of Debbie's friends by the wet bar. They talk about college life but also about current events and what is happening in the world. We talk about Richard Nixon winning the presidential election and what that might mean for ending the war in Vietnam. I mention that I had read that as one of his last acts, President Johnson is involuntarily sending back to Vietnam twenty-four thousand troops that had already done one tour of duty. This is the first time that has happened. One of Debbie's friends, attends Brown University in Rhode Island, says he supported the actions of the two Black athletes who had given a Black Power salute this past October while the U.S. national anthem was playing during the Mexico Olympics medal ceremony.

Someone mentions the news program, *60 Minutes*, which debuted on CBS in September, and how they are impressed by the quality of the programming. I've seen the show and agree with them.

We talk about sports, particularly, the NFL. Most of us are Cleveland Browns fans. Their record is 8–3 so far this season, and we all hope the winning streak continues. Our conversation then grows animated as we talk about the Heidi Bowl that took place on November 7. The New York Jets were playing the Oakland Raiders, and the Jets were ahead. With just one minute and five seconds left in the game, NBC cut away to broadcast the movie, *Heidi*. In the last minute of the game, the Raiders scored two touchdowns and won the game. Outraged fans flooded the NBC studios with protest calls.

All the conversations are engaging, and no one seems pretentious or uncomfortable around me, even though we have just met.

After about an hour, Debbie takes my hand and says, "Let's take a walk." We go outside through the sliding glass doors that lead to the inground pool, covered with a tarp for the winter. The landscaping is immaculately tended and illuminated by soft lighting.

"Are you enjoying the party?" she asks me.

"You have some really cool friends," I say.

"They are cool. I've known most of them for a long time. I'm glad you came tonight. I've wanted to get to know you better since I first met you at the bank."

"Me too, but I didn't know if you had a boyfriend or something."

"No boyfriend. My last relationship ended about six months ago. How about you, any girlfriend?"

"Nope. My last relationship ended about three months ago."

"Well, I'm glad we have that settled."

I say, "Me too," and move closer to her. She comes toward me, and we kiss. A light kiss at first, then another light kiss, then a more urgent kiss as though another kiss might never happen. Then she slips her tongue into my mouth and presses her body against mine. That kiss tells me this is something special.

We finally separate, and she says, "I liked that."

"I liked it more," I say.

She laughs and puts her arms around me. "I'm glad you're here."

"Me too. Thanks for inviting me. Sometimes I can be a little dense when it comes to dating."

She says, "So we're dating now?"

I say, "After that kiss, I hope so."

She smiles. "Me too."

Teens & Dreams

40

Tuesday, December 31, 1968 • Lima, Ohio

Today is New Year's Eve, and Metropolitan Bank is open, so I am working. The head teller had asked me to work every day that the bank is open during my Christmas break. I am happy that they took me up on my offer. The morning has been very busy, but many of the shops and businesses are closing early for New Year's Eve and so it slowed considerably this afternoon.

When things are slow at the bank, we take the time to roll the loose change that we receive during the day. Using the bank's sorting and counting machine, you dump the loose change into a bin at the top, and the machine sorts and stacks the coins by value. Quarters drop into one slot, and dimes, nickels, and pennies drop into their respective slots. You place a paper sleeve under the appropriate stack, which fills with the correct number of coins. Pretty neat.

Before the sorting starts, if you look in the bin closely, you can see differences in some of the coins. Based on their color, I can tell which quarters and dimes were minted in 1964 or earlier. Those coins are one-hundred-percent silver coins and brighter than those minted after 1964. The U.S. Mint is taking the pre-1965 coins out of circulation, so they've become scarce. With scarcity comes an increase in value. The silver coins are worth more than their face value due to the value of the silver alone. When I find a silver coin in the bin, I set it aside. I then alert the head teller that I want to exchange my money for the silver coins. The head teller verifies the transaction, and I pocket the silver coins, collecting them to start my own savings account.

I do something similar with pennies. Some pennies are worth more than a penny, particularly some of the wheat pennies minted between 1909 and 1958. Two stalks of wheat are on the "tails" side. After 1958, the stalks were replaced by the Lincoln Memorial.

In 1943, due to the copper shortage during World War II, the U.S. Mint made steel pennies with a zinc coating, so they appear silver or gray. It's easy to spot steel pennies in the coin sorting bin, so when I see one, I always set it aside. Wheat pennies are more challenging. If I spot one, I take it out of the bin to later determine whether I want to keep it, based on its mint date and mint location. The head teller also must verify my purchase of the pennies. This is the first time I have collected anything, and it feels good to have a little savings that also doubles as a hobby.

Around 2:00, my favorite customer enters the bank and walks up to my teller window. "How is my favorite teller doing today?" Debbie asks. We've been dating for a month, and every time I see her, I feel butterflies in my stomach.

"I'm doing great now that you are here. How is my favorite customer doing?"

She leans toward me and whispers, "I will be better tonight when I can wrap my arms around you and kiss you."

I blush, and say a bit formally, "Thank you. I feel the same way."

She laughs and hands me the deposit for her parents' jewelry store. I verify everything and enter the deposit into my teller machine. "Is 8:00 still good for me to pick you up tonight?" I ask her.

"Yes, I'm looking forward to ringing in the New Year with you."

"Me too. See you tonight."

She smiles and says, "See you later."

Shortly after Debbie leaves, another regular customer steps up to my window. He owns a local business, and his deposits are almost always in cash. It takes time to verify his deposit, since I count the bills once and then count them again. Everything is in order, so I enter his deposit into my teller machine and give him a deposit receipt.

He hands me a five-dollar bill and says, "This is for you. Thank you for always giving me very prompt service."

I look at him, push the five-dollar bill back toward him, and say, "I'm happy to be of service. Your business with the bank is my reward."

He pushes the bill back toward me and, as he walks away, says, "Happy New Year!"

"Happy New Year to you too." I am stunned. No one has ever given me a tip, and I don't know if I can accept it. I call the head teller over and explain what happened. He tells me the bank has no policy against accepting a gratuity and that I should keep it. I thank him and pocket the five-dollar bill.

Shortly before closing, Mrs. Carter walks up to my teller window. I did not see her come in and am surprised when I look up and she's standing before me. She says, "I just wanted to stop by and wish you a Happy New Year. How is everything going?"

"It's great," I say. Happy New Year to you too. Also, I want to thank you for finding this job for me. I've learned a lot, and really enjoy it."

"You're welcome, and I hope 1969 will be an even better year for you." She continues, "I'm so proud of you for winning the COE district presidential election. Your speech was well done, and the fortune cookie idea was inspired."

"Thanks, but I could not have done any of it without your help."

"I see bigger and better things for you in your future, Johnny. After Christmas break, let's talk about what you plan to do after you graduate from Lima Senior."

"Thanks. I would like that."

She waves goodbye and says, "Happy New Year!"

"Happy New Year to you too."

I pick Debbie up at her house at 8:00. "How was your day?" I ask her.

"Great. After I left the jewelry store, I went home, finished my college applications, and put them in the mail."

"So, you've decided to attend college next year?"

She says, "Yes, my mom and dad really want me to go. I took the ACT and did well, and my grades were pretty good at Shawnee, so I'm hoping I have a decent chance of getting into a good college."

"I'm surprised. I knew you were thinking about college, but I guess I didn't know you had decided to go."

Debbie says, "I know. I thought I could wait and decide later, but then I found out that some colleges have an end of the year application deadline. I decided to go ahead and apply and see what happens."

I say, "Good luck. Where did you apply?"

"Georgetown, Duke, Cornell and Ohio State."

"That's a lot of schools."

"My dad told me to apply to several schools to increase my odds of getting accepted at a good one."

"What's your first choice?"

"Duke, then Georgetown."

"Have you actually visited those schools?"

"I have. In the fall of my senior year at Shawnee, my mom took me to all of them plus a couple of others. I really liked Duke the best. It has a beautiful campus, and everyone seemed so friendly. I just wasn't ready to go to college right after high school but I'm ready now. How about you? Any thoughts about college?"

"Yes, but I'm not sure how to go about applying. I should talk to my guidance counselor."

"Yes, your guidance counselor should have the applications and guidebooks for most colleges. I could also help you with your application if you'd like."

"Thanks. I'll look into it."

I should have seen this coming, but the reality of it smacks me in the face. Debbie had said she was thinking about college, but I had no idea that some colleges had year-end application deadlines. I thought we both still had plenty of time to apply. The impact on me of Debbie going to college has also been influenced by what happened with Lisa when she went to Miami University. I still have heard nothing from her since her last letter in September.

I like Debbie a lot. We've gone out every weekend since her party right after Thanksgiving. She's fun and intelligent, and we have a good time together. I decide that I'm not going to think about her going away. We still have nine months before college starts and a lot can happen during that time. I'm going to enjoy whatever time we have left together.

Tonight's party is at the home of a high school friend of Debbie's. This is my first New Year's Eve party, but I am not about to admit that to Debbie. At least seventy-five people are already here and more arrive every few minutes. I'm glad some of Debbie's friends from her Thanksgiving party are here. Debbie reintroduces me to them and introduces me to new people.

Debbie and I stick close together. I talk to one of her friends, and I can hear Debbie behind me talking to some other people. She takes my arm, and as I turn toward her, she says, "Johnny, I want to introduce you to my friend, Lisa, and her boyfriend, Chase, who is visiting from Columbus."

I look up and am surprised to see *my* Lisa. Debbie and I have never talked about our exes, so she is surprised when I say flatly, "Lisa and I know each other. We were at Lima Senior together."

Chase looks at me a little funny, then shakes my hand and says, "So, you are *that*, Johnny. You and Lisa dated before she went to Miami University, right?"

I look at Lisa and say, "I guess my reputation precedes me."

Debbie looks at Lisa and then at me and says, "Wait. I didn't know you guys knew each other."

Lisa says, "Johnny is the guy I told you about that I met just before we graduated last year."

Then Debbie says, "And Johnny is also the guy I told you about that I met at Metropolitan Bank, and we've been dating since Thanksgiving."

"Well, I hope we have that settled," I say. "It was good seeing you again, Lisa."

I turn away when I hear Debbie say to Lisa, "Let's catch up before you go back to college."

Lisa says, "Sure thing."

I ask Debbie, "Do you want to go out on the patio and get some air?"

Debbie smiles at me. "Good idea." I open the French doors onto a bricked patio, and we step outside.

"Sorry about that. I didn't know you and Lisa had dated," Debbie says.

"We've never talked about our past girlfriends and boyfriends, so you couldn't have known. How do you and Lisa know each other?"

"Our parents have known each other since we were in junior high. We had family cookouts at each other's homes. Lisa and I became good friends."

I say, "Lisa and I were dating right up to the time she went to Miami University. I haven't spoken to or heard from her since last September."

Debbie pulls me to her and kisses me and then kisses me again. She says, "I'm starting to get the picture of why you were upset when I told you I had applied to colleges. It must have felt like déjà vu."

"A little, but I've decided to focus on the here and now, and to me, what's standing in front of me looks pretty good."

Debbie says, "I like that, and I like you."

I take Debbie in my arms and kiss her hard. "We better go back in before you freeze to death."

She says, "I need one more kiss before we go in." I oblige.

Life & Love

41

Monday, March 30, 1970 • Kent State University, Kent, Ohio

Classes for spring quarter start today, but it doesn't feel like spring. Frost is on the ground this morning and the high today will only be in the forties. It's been a brutal winter.

I would like to have gone to Fort Lauderdale, Florida, for spring break with my friends but didn't have the funds. Even if I shared money for gas and a hotel room, it just wasn't going to happen. Instead, I stay on campus and pick up some extra cash working in the AV department repairing films from 8:00 to noon, Monday through Friday.

Katie went home to Cleveland, so when I'm not working, I play pool or ping pong at the Eastway Rec Center with other similarly situated students. I am also recovering from winter finals. I studied hard and believe I did well on all my exams. My English 161 paper was a different story. I'm just not writing well enough to get a decent grade. My first paper was a B, but I received a C on my second paper. I had written the final paper during finals week and handed it in, but I am not confident in the result. I just don't know what I don't know about writing a paper. Katie receives As on all her English papers and has offered to give me a writing tutorial. If I don't get a decent grade in English 161, I'm going to take her up on it.

I've been checking my dorm mailbox daily for my final grades. The university was late in mailing them and I just learned that

School of Education students can pick them up in person in the Terrace Hall lounge.

I have three classes today: calculus at 7:45 in Merrill Hall, History of Ohio at 8:50 with Katie in Bowman Hall, and English 162 at 11:00 in Satterfield Hall. History of Ohio is the only course that fit both our schedules and satisfied a requirement for each of our majors. I hustle to get from Merrill to Bowman but make it on time. Katie is in the second row waiting for me.

I sit down give her a kiss. "How is your first day of classes so far?"

Katie says, "Unlike you, I do not get up before dawn for my classes. This is my first class of the day."

"Yeah, I guess I knew that. Well, anyway, it's good to see you. When is your next class?"

Katie says, "Not until eleven. How about you?"

"The same. I have English 162 in Satterfield. I can pick my grades up in the Terrace Hall lounge today, so I thought after class, I could walk you back to your dorm unless you need to do something else."

She says, "That's fine. After we get your grades, do you want to walk with me to Tri-Towers to get mine? Arts and Sciences students pick theirs up in Tri-Towers lounge."

"Sure, that sounds like a plan."

The History of Ohio course is interesting. The professor starts class by giving us little-known facts about Ohio. Ohio was declared a state in 1803 and Thomas Jefferson, the President, approved its constitution and boundaries, but failed to give it the presidential stamp of approval. That did not happen until 1953 when President Eisenhower signed and backdated Ohio's admittance to the United States of America. Of the eight U.S. presidents to come from Ohio, seven U.S. presidents were born in Ohio and the eighth, William Henry Harrison, was born in Virginia. Ohio's flag is not a rectangle like all the other state flags, but rather is pennant shaped.

Katie turns to me and whispers, "Well, who knew?"

I smile and whisper, "Not me."

After class, I present my student ID at Terrace Hall and the clerk hands me an envelope. I tear it open. Four As, and a C in English 161. My GPA for the quarter is 3.60 and my cumulative GPA is 3.52. I made the Dean's List again, but the C in English really bothers me.

I show Katie my grades, "I'm going to need that English tutorial that you offered."

She says, "Anytime."

"Let's do it this coming weekend."

"Perfect," she says.

Katie drops off her books in her room and we walk to Tri-Towers. She shows her student ID and gets her envelope. She is happy with her 3.32 GPA for the quarter and cumulative GPA of 3.25.

Katie's next class is on Front Campus and mine is in Satterfield so we're going in opposite directions. I ask, "Do you want to meet at the Student Union for a Coke around 3:00 this afternoon?"

Katie says, "That sounds good. See you there."

Katie is already seated and drinking a pop when I arrive. "How was your class?"

"Very interesting. It was Psychology 101. How about your English class?"

"Frustrating. I just don't get it. I understand what I'm reading, but when I put it on paper, somehow, it just doesn't work. I hope you can help."

She says, "When we meet this weekend, be sure to bring all your English papers from the last two quarters so that I can see the comments and try to figure out where you need help."

"That sounds like a good idea," I say. We sip our pops, and I continue, "I need to think about what I am going to do this summer. If I go back and live at home in Lima, I have a guaranteed job at Metropolitan Bank, but I will have to live with my dad again and I really don't want to do that. If I stay in Kent, I will need to find off-campus housing and a job and figure out what to do about meals. Any advice?"

Katie says, "Do what makes you the happiest. Plus remember that Kent is a lot closer to me than Lima."

"Good advice and a good point. Lima does not make me happy. I would hate living at home again with my dad, but I liked working at Metropolitan Bank."

Katie says, "Maybe you can find a job at a bank here in Kent."

I say, "That is a really good idea. I hadn't thought of that. I'm sure I can get a good recommendation from the head teller at Metropolitan Bank. That might make a difference in an interview. Thanks."

Katie says, "Happy I can help."

I lean over and kiss her.

She says, "There should be plenty of sublets available close to campus. You might want to check Glen Morris or College Tower apartments."

I say, "I'm liking the idea of summer in Kent better and better."

Katie says, "Me too."

Bayonets & Bullets

42

10:00 a.m., Monday, May 4, 1970 • Kent State University, Kent, Ohio

During our walk from Bowman Hall to Terrace Hall to drop off our backpacks at Katie's dorm, we encounter several National Guardsmen marching in formation toward the Commons. None of them are smiling. We move off the sidewalk to get out of their way and let them pass.

"Looks like reinforcements to support the Guard on the Commons," I say.

Katie says, "They should walk on the grass and let us walk on the sidewalks. It's our campus. It's like we're a nuisance and keeping them from doing their job. Their job is to protect us, not intimidate us."

On the way to Katie's dorm, we walk by the Student Union where a group of students stands outside.

"Let's stop and ask them if they have any information on the noon rally," I say.

"Good idea."

They haven't heard anything, so we go inside. It's more crowded than on a normal day. We find out from some students that the rally is still on. The flyer we picked up yesterday prohibits all gatherings of any kind, though, and the lobby is abuzz with speculation about what the National Guard might do. There's no talk about the invasion of Cambodia or the war in Vietnam. We have our own war to worry about right here on campus.

As we leave the Student Union, we see another group of guardsmen heading for the Commons led by several Army officers in jeeps.

"More reinforcements," Katie says. "They must be expecting trouble on the Commons at noon."

I nod. "Looks that way."

On our way to Terrace Hall, we see more military vehicles and guardsmen stationed at the intersection of Main Street and Terrace Drive. They are all business with their helmets on and rifles in the ready position. No flowers in their guns today.

I wait for Katie in the lobby while she takes our backpacks up to her room. Out of the corner of my eye, I see sudden movement at the Education Building across the street. People are pouring out of the building and moving far away from it. I leave Terrace Hall and run across the street to see what's happening. I ask a student why she's leaving the building, and she says, "There's been a bomb threat, and they're evacuating the building to search for it."

I hurry back to Terrace Hall, where Katie is waiting for me with a worried look. "What's happening?"

I tell her what I know. "It's probably just a hoax, but they need to clear and search the building to make sure."

"Why would somebody do that? I don't understand how that will help get the Guard off campus."

"I don't get it either. With the guardsmen occupying campus, we must expect the unexpected. Your confrontation with a guardsman this morning shows that some of them are on a power trip. They know with a rifle in their hands they hold the power of life and death. That makes them feel important. Now someone has called in a bomb threat. I think someone wants to take back that power and reassert control over their life."

Katie says, "Let's wait here until things calm down outside before we go to the Commons."

Teens & Dreams

43

Sunday, January 19, 1969 • Lima, Ohio

While I get ready for church, I think about the good time I had last night. I had mentioned to Jack and Diane that I was seeing someone from Shawnee whom I met at the bank. Diane and Debbie went to the same high school, but Debbie was a year ahead of Diane. Diane knew of Debbie, but they had never met. We decide to double date and go bowling at Westgate Lanes. I drive across the street to pick up Jack then we pick up Diane.

"You're going to like Debbie. She's very sweet and has restored my faith in dating," I tell them.

Diane says, "I'm glad you found someone. I know your breakup in September was rough on you."

As I pull into the circular driveway in front of Debbie's house, Jack says, "Very nice. What do her parents do?"

"They own a jewelry store." I was just about to walk up to Debbie's house when I see her come out her front door. I open the passenger door for her.

"Thank you," she says and gives me a kiss before getting in. I introduce everybody, and then the twenty questions flow while we drive to the bowling alley. Jack and Diane want to know everything about Debbie, and Debbie wants to know everything about them.

Saturday night is party night at Westgate Lanes. They turn

down the lights and turn up the music all night long. We talk and bowl. Jack is by far the best bowler among the four of us. Debbie holds her own, and both Debbie and Diane score over a hundred. Afterward, we have pizza at the bowling alley's restaurant, and play eight-ball pool. Debbie and I win the first game because Jack scratches when trying to sink the eight ball. We switch partners, and Jack and Debbie win the second game. It's a fun night.

On the way back to her house, I mention to Debbie that I attend Shawnee Church of Christ every Sunday with Jack and Diane. I changed churches about six months ago. I pull up in front of Debbie's house, open the car door for her and walk her to her front door.

We kiss several times and, Debbie says, "Thank you. I had a wonderful time tonight. I like Jack and Diane."

"They like you too."

"I would like to go to church with you sometime."

"How about tomorrow?"

"Perfect."

"I'll pick you up tomorrow morning at 9:30. Is that okay?"

She kisses me again and says, "I'll be ready."

Back in the car, Diane gushes over Debbie and says she is sweet. I agree with Diane and tell them she is joining us for church tomorrow. Both Jack and Diane like that.

Sunday mornings always seem like such a blessing. Whether it's cold or hot outside, sunshine or rain, Sundays always bring peace and serenity to my world.

On the drive to pick up Debbie this morning, I think about my meeting with Mrs. Carter last week. She had asked, "What do you plan to do after you graduate?"

"That's a good question. I like working at the bank. It's a great job, but I hate living at home with my dad, and I do not want to get drafted and go to Vietnam. I need another plan. Going away to college might be the answer. What do you think?"

She says, "I have no doubt that you will do well in college. You can do whatever you put your mind to. If you commit to doing the work needed to succeed in college, you will excel."

"I have no idea how to go about applying to college or how to pay for college. I also don't know what college I could get into."

"Well," Mrs. Carter says, "I can help you with that, and your guidance counselor can help too."

"Great. How do I start?" I ask.

"The first thing you need to decide is whether you want to go to college in Ohio or elsewhere. Staying in Ohio will be your most affordable option."

"Then I want to stay in Ohio but get as far away from my dad as I can."

"You may want to think about colleges and universities in Northeastern Ohio. Several very good ones are in that area. I will talk to your guidance counselor and have her give you some options to consider."

"Great. Thank you."

Now, on this beautiful Sunday morning, I'm going to pick up a beautiful girl and I get to spend most of the day and night with her. Tonight, we are going to my first concert—Diana Ross and the Supremes at the University of Dayton Fieldhouse at 8:30.

I pull up in front of Debbie's house, walk up the front steps and ring the doorbell. She answers the door quickly. "Good morning," she says.

"Good morning. You look great." She is wearing a wrap-around dress that hugs her slender body and a string of pearls that sets everything off.

"Thank you. You don't look so bad yourself," she says as we head to the car.

At church, everyone welcomes Debbie and says they're glad she came. We spot Jack and Diane and sit with them. The minister's sermon is inspiring. It is based on 1 Corinthians, Chapter 13, Verses 4–8a: *"Love is patient, love is kind. It does not envy, it does not boast, it is not proud. It does not dishonor others, it is not self-seeking, it is not easily angered, it keeps no record of wrongs. Love does not delight in evil but rejoices with the truth. It always protects, always trusts, always hopes, always perseveres. Love never fails.*" It just happens to be my favorite verse.

Outside, Debbie says, "Everyone is so friendly, and the minister's message was one of love and encouragement."

"The congregation makes me feel welcome," I say, "and the minister always has an uplifting message. I feel good every Sunday when I leave."

Back in the car, Diane says, "That was a lot of fun last night. We should do it again soon."

Debbie says, "Johnny needs to work on his pool game, first." I agree and we all laugh.

I take Debbie home and we agree that I will pick her up at 6:00 for the concert tonight.

Debbie is waiting when I arrive for our drive to the concert. On our way to Dayton, I tell her about my meeting with Mrs. Carter and my decision to apply to college.

She asks, "Do you know where you will apply?"

I shake my head. "Mrs. Carter is going to set up a meeting with my guidance counselor to discuss my options, but it most likely will be a school in Ohio."

"Have you taken the ACT?

"Nope. I need to do that."

"Good to do it as soon as possible. Almost all colleges in Ohio require the ACT and it takes about six to eight weeks to get your scores. You have time, though. Most schools in Ohio will allow applications until March 31.

We find the University of Dayton Fieldhouse. The parking lot is packed, but we manage to find a spot way in the back. I already have the tickets. When I heard on the radio that Diana Ross and the Supremes were coming to Dayton, I drove down to buy them the first day they went on sale. We have excellent seats on the floor, fifth row from the stage.

Diana Ross is even more magnificent in person than she is on TV. The Supremes sing all their greatest hits and we both sing along to "Stop! In the Name of Love" and "Baby Love" when she points her mic toward the audience. The concert is sold out, and the audience applauds and roars their approval after each song. It is the first rock concert for both of us, and one I will never forget.

In the parking lot, Debbie gives me a big kiss, and thanks me profusely for bringing her. We are mellow on the drive home. When we pull up in front of her house and she says, "I love every minute I spend with you. You always make me feel so special."

"I enjoy our time together too," I say. "Every time I leave you, I can't wait until the next time I see you."

We get out of the car. Debbie wraps her arms around my neck, kisses me, and says, "You are a special guy."

I smile. "Thank you. Goodnight."

When she reaches her front door, she turns and blows me a kiss. I know, as much as I try not to, that I am falling for that girl.

Teens & Dreams

44

Friday, March 28, 1969 • Lima, Ohio

College decision time is fast approaching. I have no idea where I will be in September. Waiting to hear is torturous.

Mrs. Carter set up a meeting in February with my guidance counselor who is surprised that I am considering going to college. She says, "Most students in the vocational education programs don't go to college. Some get further vocational training at a community college. Have you considered that?"

"I am not interested in vocational training," I reply. "If I don't go to college I will stick with my job at Metropolitan Bank. It's a good job and all the employees are good to me."

The guidance counselor says, "Then why do you want to go to college?"

"First, I want to get as far away from my dad as possible. I hate him. Second, I do not want to go to Vietnam. If I don't go to college, then I will be drafted. My third and more practical reason is that I want to make more than $1.60 an hour. A college education allows me to do that."

She looks at me and thinks for a moment. "I understand. Let's review your school record at Lima Senior. You have a 3.2 GPA. That puts you in about the top third of your class. That's good. I also see that you are taking college prep classes in English and math. That's unusual for someone in a vocational ed program, but also good.

And you've taken two years of French. That is important for many colleges. Mrs. Carter thinks you are college material and a recommendation from her will help your application. Have you thought about what college you would like to attend?

"I was hoping you could help me with that."

"Well, for financial reasons you should stick to in-state public colleges. Do you know if you want to go to a big city or a smaller town?"

I say, "A smaller town would work best for me."

She says, "Well, two schools come to mind: Kent State University in Kent, which is in northeastern Ohio, and Ohio University in Athens, which is in southeastern Ohio. I have handbooks for both schools. Would you like to look at them?"

"Yes, thank you."

The guidance counselor says, "Mrs. Carter told me about your family's financial situation, so I know you will need to apply for financial aid. One of your parents will need to fill out and sign a financial aid application. It is likely that you will qualify for federal grant-in-aid programs. Additionally, the federal Work-Study program allows you to work up to fifteen hours per week while you are in school to help pay for incidentals, entertainment, and other costs. If the grants and Work-Study don't provide enough funds, you can take out a student loan to cover the remaining costs."

"So, you are saying that I could have enough money to go to college?"

"Yes, provided your parents are willing to sign the financial aid application and their finances are as dire as Mrs. Carter thinks they are."

"Okay. That's a big deal for me."

The guidance counselor says "You will need to take the American College Testing exam which everyone calls the ACT. It's required to complete a college application in Ohio. The test is offered five times a year, and the next test date is Saturday, March 22. You will need to sign up within the next week to make the deadline for that test date."

"It sounds like I have a lot to do and need to make a decision quickly."

"That's true if you want to start college this fall. If you are willing to wait until next year, you have more time to apply and take the ACT."

"I definitely want to start college in September."

She says, "Okay then. Look at the handbooks and let me know what you would like to do. I have applications for both colleges."

"Thanks for your help." I leave her office and walk to my car. I can't believe there's a way for me to go to college, and one that's far away from Lima.

I look at the handbooks for Kent State and Ohio University. Both are about a three-hour drive from Lima. Both qualify as being far enough away from my dad. Both are small-town schools with big universities. Both have a student population of about twenty thousand. Kent State started out as a teacher's college, and I'm leaning toward teaching as a career. I also like the fact that Kent State isn't in a big city but is close to Cleveland and Akron. Ohio U. is in Athens, which is in the middle of nowhere. I decide to apply to Kent State. I thought about applying to both colleges, but I'm the one who will have to pay both application fees. Kent State is where I really want to go, so I don't need to apply to both colleges.

The next day I obtain the applications for the ACT and Kent State from my guidance counselor. I will have to pay a fee to take the ACT. I complete the ACT application, enclose a money order I bought from the post office for the fee and mail it the day after I get it from my guidance counselor.

I want to talk with Mrs. Carter before making a final decision about Kent State. The day after I mail my ACT test application, I sit down with Mrs. Carter after COE class and tell her my reasons for favoring Kent State over Ohio University.

"Those are all good reasons," she says. I also think that Kent State will give you a fresh start. I know of only one other student applying to Kent State this year. However, at least a dozen students from Lima Senior are applying to Ohio University. Going to a school where no one knows you allows you to leave behind every-thing that bothers you about your dad and about students here at Lima Senior. With a fresh start you, and only you, determine your future success."

"I like that," I say. "Would you write a recommendation for me to Kent State?"

"Of course."

"Thank you."

"Good luck. I hope you're accepted."

Last Saturday I took the ACT. Parts of it were difficult, but I think I did okay. Yesterday I completed the Kent State application, then went to the post office and purchased a money order for the application fee.

My mom agreed to fill out the financial aid portion of the appli-cation. After completing it, she says, "I don't know anything about college applications, but I hope they give you enough money so that you can go to college. I filled in as much information as I could about our finances and savings, which isn't much. I wish I could help you pay for college, but we just don't have the money."

"I know, Mom. That is why the financial aid application is so important. We'll just wait and see what Kent State has to say. Thanks for completing your part."

"Good luck, honey."

"Thanks, Mom."

I sign the Kent State application, put it in the envelope with the financial aid form and the money order for the application fee, and drop it in the mail at the post office.

Now, I'll just have to wait and see what happens.

Life & Love

45

I t's cold. It's rainy. It's Katie's birthday. A lot is going on today. Too bad it's crappy outside.

I have a 7:45 Introduction to Psych class in Lowry Hall on Front Campus and an 8:50 Introduction to Teaching class in the Education building. Then, no more classes until golf at 11:00 at the KSU golf course. I plan to attend the Student Mobilization Committee march against the war in Vietnam at 11:00, so I will have to skip golf or hope it's canceled because of the bad weather.

First, some breakfast at the Eastway cafeteria. I pick up a copy of the *Daily Kent Stater* from the rack as I get in line for food. The headline announces, APOLLO 13 CRISIS ENDANGERS CREW; MOON LANDING MISSION CANCELLED. I get some cereal, toast, and juice and start reading. *Apollo 13* is in trouble on the dark side of the Moon with three astronauts onboard: Jim Lovell, the commander, along with Jack Swigert and Fred Haise. Last night, they heard a loud bang, the command ship sank into partial darkness, and warning lights came on. A fuel cell might have exploded, leaving the spaceship without electricity and oxygen in the main cabin.

After taking a spoonful of cereal and a bite of toast, I am about to continue reading when a cafeteria worker wheels a TV on a cart into the cafeteria. He plugs it in and turns it on. A special report is relaying the troubles with the *Apollo 13* mission. I move closer to the TV.

The reporter says, "Right after the power went off, Commander Lovell radioed mission control and said, 'Houston, we've got a problem here.'"

I say to myself, that's an understatement. The astronauts are 250 thousand miles from home, the spaceship *Odyssey* is in a roll, and mission control needs a plan to stop it. The command module is essentially dead, with only enough battery power and oxygen to re-enter the Earth's atmosphere. All power and oxygen to survive until re-entry must come from the lunar module *Aquarius*.

Mission control has ordered the astronauts to shut down nonessential systems in the command module and transfer to *Aquarius*. Houston believes they may be able to fire the lunar module engines to give the command module a boost toward Earth. The astronauts will return to the command module and jettison the lunar module before re-entry.

A landing in the Pacific Ocean just north of New Zealand is planned for 1:04 p.m. on Friday, April 17. I need to get to class, so I'll have to wait for more news.

After my psych and ed classes, I walk to Terrace Hall to meet Katie. We had planned to meet in the lobby at 10:00 and join the peace march on the Commons at 11:00. The weather is getting worse and I'm not sure the march will happen.

Katie comes down to the lounge right on time. I hug her and say, "Happy Birthday, old woman!"

She smiles and gives me a push. "Just because I'm nineteen and you're still eighteen, does not make me an old woman."

"You're right. You're just robbing the cradle."

She pushes my shoulder. "You'd better be careful, Mister."

I smile, give her a kiss, and say, without a smirk this time, "Happy Birthday. I love you."

Katie says, "Thank you. How are you doing today? Did you hear about *Apollo 13*?"

I say, "I did. Isn't that crazy? They could be 'Lost in Space'," I say, using air quotes.

Katie says, "I hope not. Smart people work at mission control in Houston. I hope they can figure out how to get them back to Earth safely."

I say, "Have you heard if the peace march is still happening today?"

"I've heard nothing, but I'm not sure I want to stand in the rain for three hours."

"I get it. I'll head to the Commons to find out. I'm not sure if I'll last the whole March either. We're still on for your birthday dinner tonight at 6:00, right?"

Katie smiles and says, "Of course, where are we going?"

"It's a surprise. Just dress nicely and bring your raincoat. I'll pick you up here at 6:00."

"Okay. See you tonight."

I kiss her. "Happy Birthday. See you later, alligator."

She smiles. "After while, crocodile."

"Real soon, raccoon." She laughs and we wave goodbye.

Before I leave Terrace Hall, I use the house phone to call the KSU golf course and learn that golf has been canceled. Perfect. Now I don't have to skip class.

I walk to the Commons. It is a miserable day in the low forties, raining and the wind is blowing like hell. Maybe two hundred people in raincoats mingle there. No one seems to be in charge, and no one knows if the peace march is still on. After about fifteen minutes, five people show up with a banner. Apparently, they are the leaders of the march. Despite the weather, the march is still on. We will walk the same route that we did during the march last October. I'm already cold and wet, but I think about the U.S. soldiers in Vietnam. Last week, 138 U.S. servicemen died in Vietnam. Almost fifty thousand have been killed since the start of the war. Even more have been wounded. Some have lost their legs and arms. Others are wheelchair bound. I decide I can survive a couple of hours in the rain if it might help bring our soldiers home sooner.

The Peace March starts shortly after 11:00. We recruit more students at dorms along the way, gaining about fifty more marchers. We head down Midway Drive past President White's house, down Main Street past the Sigma Chi house, and down to North Water Street. We make our way back to Summit Street and onto campus. There is no violence, just a small group of peace marchers fighting the wind and rain. The march seems anemic compared to the fifteen hundred people who were on Front Campus to listen to Jerry Rubin last Friday. Jerry Rubin talked of revolution. The marchers today talk about how cold and wet they are.

I complete the march and walk back to the Commons to listen to several students try to shout over the wind and rain about how Nixon broke his promise to end the war in Vietnam and stop the draft. Neither is close to happening. After a while, people start to drift away and head back to their dorms. I join them.

Back in my dorm, I take a shower and after warming up, I walk back downtown to the Music City record store on North Water Street to buy Katie a birthday present. She has a record player in her room and likes the Moody Blues, so I want to buy her their new album, *Days of Future Passed*. It's a cool album, which includes the best-selling single, "Nights in White Satin." A guy on my floor owns a copy, so I've heard it several times. The record store has the album on sale for two dollars and ninety-nine cents. I buy it. I could have also bought the album on cassette or eight-track cartridge, but I'm pretty sure she doesn't have a player for either one. I stop by the drugstore on the way back to campus and purchase some wrapping paper, ribbon, and a Hallmark birthday card. It's still raining so I put my purchases under my raincoat and manage to keep everything dry on the way back to my room.

I wrap the album and get ready for my date with Katie. I've made a reservation at the Brown Derby in Kent, a steak and seafood restaurant that's supposed to be the nicest restaurant in town. It is only about half a mile from Terrace Hall, so it will be an easy walk. I head over to pick up Katie. It's finally stopped raining and the wind has died down.

Katie steps off the elevator wearing a royal blue miniskirt and a shear white blouse and carrying her raincoat. She looks beautiful and I remind myself what a lucky guy I am to have her in my life. "Wow! You look delicious," I say.

Her eyes twinkle and she smiles. "Thank you."

We kiss, and I say, "Let me give you your birthday present before we leave."

We sit on a couch in the lobby. She opens the card first, reads it, and says, "That is sweet. Thank you." She opens her gift and her face lights up. "I've been wanting this album. How did you know?"

"I guess I'm just psychic."

She laughs, and says, "I guess so." She gives me a long kiss, which I enjoy very much "Let me put this in my room before we go."

She is only gone for a couple of minutes. "So, where are we going?" she asks.

"I made us a reservation at the Brown Derby."

She says, "Isn't that expensive?"

"Only the best for my girl. Are you ready to go?"

"Yes, I am." I help Katie with her coat and hold the door open for her. As we turn right onto Main Street, she loops her arm through mine, and we walk arm-in-arm for the short trip to the restaurant.

When we arrive, we are escorted to a candlelit table with a white tablecloth, white cloth napkins, and a bud vase of daisies. The lighting is dim and classical music plays softly in the background.

"Fancy," Katie whispers.

The waiter hands us the menus, and upon his recommendation, we both order filet mignon. I excuse myself to go to the restroom, but instead, I find our waiter.

"Today is my girlfriend's birthday. Is it possible to get a slice of cake with a lit candle at the end of our meal?"

"Not to worry," he says. "I will take care of everything.

Katie and I agree that the steak, baked potato, and green bean almondine were the perfect choice. After our waiter clears away our dishes, he says he will be back shortly with dessert menus. Instead, a couple of minutes later he returns with a small chocolate cake topped with five lit candles. He's accompanied by other waiters, and they all sing "Happy Birthday" to Katie.

She is surprised and a bit embarrassed by all the attention but says to me, "Thank you. This has been a wonderful birthday, one that I will always remember."

"You're welcome. I love you."

Bayonets & Bullets

46

11:00 a.m., Monday, May 4, 1970 • Kent State University, Kent, Ohio

After police and fire authorities investigate the bomb threat and declare the Education building all clear, Katie and I leave her dorm and walk toward the Commons.

"Let's be careful," I say. "Based on what I saw last night at Prentice Gate, the guardsmen are unpredictable, and I think some of them are on a power trip. If they start firing tear gas, let's head to the Prentice Hall parking lot and then, as we discussed, you take Midway Drive back to your dorm. Is that still okay with you?"

Katie says, "Yes, but remember you promised to follow the directions of the faculty marshals and not to engage with the guardsmen. Is that still okay with you?"

"Definitely. I want to support the protest of the invasion of Cambodia and the war in Vietnam, and I want to protest the National Guard taking over our campus, but I'm no radical. I'm not going to be a part of any violence against the Guard or anyone else. My priority is to make sure you are safe."

Katie says, "I think we have a plan." She turns toward me, takes my hands, pulls me to her, and says, "I love you," and kisses me.

"I love you too," I say.

The quickest way to the Commons is to walk back up Terrace Drive to the Student Union, past the burnt-out ROTC building, and across the Commons to the Victory Bell at the base of Blanket

Hill. The Victory Bell is always the epicenter of any rally on the Commons. It is where the rally was held last Friday afternoon, and where students first gathered on Saturday and Sunday nights.

I turn to Katie. "We can try to approach the Commons from the Student Union, but the National Guard probably will block off the area between the Commons and the ROTC building and not let students on the Commons. Our best bet is to go out the back door of Terrace Hall and take Midway Drive up to the Prentice Hall parking lot and cut across the parking lot to the top of Blanket Hill."

Katie says, "You're right. Let's go that way."

As we walk out the back door, we see an armored personnel carrier still parked at the corner of Midway and Main Street, and quite a few guardsmen at the Midway Drive entrance to campus. We walk in the opposite direction up Midway Drive toward Prentice Hall and Taylor Hall. No guardsmen occupy the Prentice Hall parking lot, nor can I see any guardsmen next to Taylor Hall. We walk to the south side of Taylor, stand next to the Pagoda, and look out over the Commons. As I suspected, a line of guardsmen with jeeps is stationed in front of what's left of the ROTC building blocking any access to the Commons or the Victory Bell from Front Campus.

It's only 11:15, but a couple of hundred students already stand around the Victory Bell and another couple of hundred students, like Katie and me, stand on Blanket Hill.

"Let's get a little closer," I say.

We walk about halfway down Blanket Hill. It seems with every passing minute, more students arrive. The crowd by the Victory Bell grows too. The spring day is beautiful, and I think many students are outside just to enjoy the warm weather.

I see several students I know from the weekend protests mingling by the Victory Bell, including Allison and her boyfriend, Jeff, and Joe. Everyone is milling about talking with each other like it's a social gathering. The guardsmen are on the other side of the Commons, and no one seems worried or concerned.

I turn to Katie. "There doesn't seem to be any leader or any organized protest. It's still early, but I bet many people here are like us. They want to show support, but don't want any violence. I hope the guardsmen keep their distance and leave everyone alone."

Katie looks worried. "Let's hope everyone remains calm."

Teens & Dreams

47

Monday, April 21, 1969 • Lima, Ohio

Last Wednesday I flew on an airplane for the first time, which was pretty cool. Almost everything about last week was pretty cool. Well, there was one thing that was not cool. Being elected district COE president qualified me to run for national president at the COE national convention in Fort Worth, Texas. Mrs. Carter thought that I should run and said Lima Senior would pay my travel expenses to the convention. I told Mrs. Carter that I would love to go. We leave Wednesday, April 16, 1969, and return Sunday, April 20, 1969. I'm excited. I've never flown on a plane or stayed in a hotel.

I will have to give another speech and Mrs. Carter feels that my district speech is so good that I can easily enhance it for the national convention. I revise my speech and show it to Mrs. Carter. She makes a few suggestions but thinks it's very good.

Mrs. Carter escorts me on the trip. She drives us to the Dayton airport for a late morning nonstop American Airlines flight to Love Field in Dallas. I'm excited as we board. I have a window seat so I can watch as we take off and see everything between Dayton and Dallas. The airplane is a Boeing 727 with a capacity of 131 passengers. It has three jet engines and takes off like a rocket. It seems in no time at all, the plane lifts off the ground and we are flying. I am truly amazed. It seems almost impossible that this big and heavy plane can fly.

We have clear weather all the way to Dallas. The captain tells us that we will fly 748 nautical miles to Love Field in two hours and fifteen minutes. Since Dayton is in the Eastern time zone and Dallas is in the Central time zone, the time when we land will be only one hour and fifteen minutes after the time we took off. Amazing!

The plane landing is very smooth. I hear a chirp when the wheels touch the tarmac and then the roar of the engines as the captain uses reverse thrusters to slow down the plane. We retrieve our luggage and find the Hertz rental car desk. Mrs. Carter drives us to our hotel in Fort Worth, thirty-three miles away.

I've stayed in a roadside motel before with my parents, but this is my first stay in a *real* hotel, and I am impressed. The hotel has a cavernous lobby made of marble and granite, and fresh flowers on a pedestal table at the entrance. I have my own room with a king-sized bed and a color TV. All, pretty cool.

Mrs. Carter says that we don't have anything on our schedule tonight so we will have dinner together, and then the rest of the evening, I am free to swim in the hotel pool or relax in the lobby, but I cannot leave the hotel grounds. Tomorrow, COE has reserved buses to take all COE attendees to Six Flags Over Texas, a huge amusement park located between Dallas and Fort Worth. We will have our first COE meeting and dinner tomorrow night.

The next morning, we load into the buses for the short drive to Six Flags. It turns out all the COE attendees are staying at the same hotel. Mrs. Carter sits with another teacher, a friend of hers, so I sit by myself a couple of rows behind them.

A few minutes later, a really striking girl with auburn hair and blond streaks sits down beside me. She looks right at me and says, "Hi. I'm Cindy"

"Good to meet you. I'm Johnny," I say. "Where are you from?"

"Kettering. It's a suburb of Dayton, Ohio."

I say, "I'm from Lima, Ohio."

"That's just up the road from us."

"Yep. About seventy-five miles north on I-75."

We chat on the way to Six Flags. As we get off the bus, she says, "Are you here with anyone?"

"Just my teacher." I point her out.

"If you'd like, you're welcome to walk around with us. I'm here with five other girls."

"That sounds great. Let me check with my teacher."

Mrs. Carter says, "That's fine. Just make sure you return to this same bus by 4:00 for the ride back to the hotel."

"I will," I assure her. "See you later."

I join the group from Kettering, and we enjoy the rides and experience everything the park has to offer.

Cindy and I ride most of the rides together. She is sweet and cute. On one scary roller coaster, she takes my hand as the car climbs to the top of the hill and doesn't let go the whole ride. She is very "hot," as the guys in the locker room say. I have trouble keeping myself from staring at her and know I'm in trouble. I'm still dating Debbie back home, but I'm attracted to Cindy. This has never happened to me and I'm not sure how to handle the situation.

We go on a haunted house ride. As we enter the dark tunnel, Cindy takes my hand again and this time scoots over and sits right next to me with our legs and sides touching. During one very scary part of the ride she buries her head against my chest. I am having a hard time keeping my hands off her and she seems to be having the same problem.

After the ride ends, she says, "Do you want to get something to eat and catch up with the group later?"

I don't know what this means, but say, "Sure."

Cindy tells her friends we are going off on our own and we walk toward the concession stands. Cindy takes my hand, and we find a food line that's not too busy. We each get a Coke and sit down at a picnic table away from other people.

We talk about our schools and our COE programs. Then we talk about our jobs. Cindy asks, "Do you have a girlfriend?"

I'm unsure how to answer, but say, "Yes, how about you? Do you have a boyfriend?"

"Yes."

I raise our hands which are still clasped together and ask, "What are we going to do about this?"

She smiles at me and says, "I think we should just have fun together while we are in Texas. Are you okay with that?"

Again, I'm not sure what to think or feel, but say, "Yes."

She looks at me with her big blue eyes, leans over, and kisses me. I'm surprised, but not surprised. We've been moving toward a kiss all day. As she starts to pull away, I kiss her, and this time linger with my kiss.

"You're a good kisser," she says.

"Thank you, but it takes two for a great kiss, and I need another one to make sure I have it right."

She smiles, put her arms around my neck, and gives me a full-on French kiss. I participate fully then say to her, "I think I'm smitten."

She laughs and says, "Me too."

Now I know I am in trouble. I just don't know how much trouble. We exchange kisses for several more minutes, then walk hand-in-hand to ride more rides. I like her kind of fun.

When we only have an hour before we need to be back at the bus Cindy says, "We should find my friends."

I nod and say, "Let's go." We catch up to the group but continue to hold hands.

A little while later, Mrs. Carter sees us and asks, "Are you all enjoying Six Flags?" We all say yes, and I see that Mrs. Carter spots me holding Cindy's hand. Mrs. Carter looks at me and says, "I will see you back at the bus in about thirty minutes."

"See you there," I say.

After she leaves, Cindy holds up our hands and whispers to me, "Is this going to be a problem with your teacher?"

I whisper back, "I don't know."

On the bus ride back to the hotel, Cindy and I again sit together. When we get inside the lobby of the hotel, Mrs. Carter says to me, "Let's meet in the hotel lobby at 6:00 sharp and we will go to dinner together."

I nod and say, "Okay. See you at 6:00." I tell Cindy about my pre-arranged dinner plans. "Do you want to try and meet here in the lobby after dinner?"

Cindy says, "That sounds good. See you later."

Dinner is fine, but I'm preoccupied with thoughts of Cindy. I only half listen to the speakers. Just before dinner is over, Mrs. Carter says, "Same rules as last night, please don't leave the hotel grounds. Also, tomorrow will be a full day of programs and you will give your speech at lunch."

I nod and say, "I'm ready."

Mrs. Carter says, "You are going to do very well." We say good-night and I walk toward the hotel lobby. Cindy is sitting alone on a sofa, and she rises as I come over. "Hi," I say. "How was your dinner?"

"Good. How about yours?"

"I don't know. I couldn't think about anything but you."

She smiles. "Sorry I'm so distracting."

I laugh. "You are not sorry."

She gives me a naughty look. "Do you want to go for a walk?"

"Yes, but I need to stay on the hotel grounds. School rules."

"I saw some nice walking paths when we arrived," she says.

As we exit the front door of the hotel, Cindy takes my hand. It's dark, but landscape lighting illuminates the path, and we see no one else as we walk.

Ornate iron park benches are scattered along the way. Cindy asks, "Do you want to sit for a while?"

"Sure," I say, and we sit down.

We both know what we want and within a few seconds, we are kissing. Not a few little kisses, but a full-on, make-out session. I get hot very quicky. Then we hear someone coming. We stay seated but stop kissing. As soon as an older couple passes by, we kiss again. I quickly know that I have a problem inside the front of my pants that is not going to go away until we stop kissing.

"We need to walk so I can cool off." We stand and Cindy wraps her arms around me, pulls me to her, presses her breasts against my chest, and gives me another hot kiss. Her body feels great and I'm sure she can feel my erection.

"You are not helping my situation," I tell her.

She smiles, takes my hand, and we start walking.

When we arrive back at the hotel. Cindy says, "I'd better head up to my room before my roommate sends a search party out to look for me."

"Okay. See you tomorrow. I'm going to walk a bit more so that I can cool off before I head up to my room."

She gives me another long kiss with a lot of tongue and says, "Don't forget about me. See you tomorrow."

I say, "Not a chance of that. Goodnight."

I spend the next morning preparing for my luncheon speech. I think I'm ready and head downstairs. Cindy walks up to me just before I sit down for lunch and says, "Good luck with your speech. I'm sure you will be great."

"Thanks," I say.

The speech does go well, and I receive enthusiastic applause for my speech. Mrs. Carter congratulates me on a job well done.

In the afternoon several hundred COE attendees, including students and teachers, attend a joint session. Cindy and I sit together at the end of a row toward the back. After an hour of listening to speakers drone on about nothing that is interesting, Cindy leans over and whispers, "I'm going to the restroom. In about five minutes meet me in the hallway outside this room. Okay?"

I nod and say, "Okay."

Cindy leaves and about five minutes later, I leave. I see Cindy in the hallway, and she says, "Let's go to your room."

I nod and we head to the elevators. I'm not sure what she has in mind, but I'm not thinking with my head right now. We get to my room and start kissing and the kisses are even hotter than they were last night. Cindy begins to unbutton her sheer black blouse. No more incentive is needed, and I undo the rest of the buttons on her blouse. She is wearing a lacy black bra and I cup one breast and then the other. I then kiss her nipples through her bra, and she moans. I'm not sure how far she wants to go but I'm ready for anything she wants to do. She pulls down the bra strap of her right breast and takes my right hand and puts it underneath her bra. Her breast is so soft, and her nipple is so hard. I start sucking her nipple. She then reaches behind her back and unclips her bra. The bra falls away and two beautiful slightly upturned breasts with perky nipples are in front of me. They are magnificent. I reach out and touch both breasts. They are so soft and luscious. We kiss some more, and I kiss her breasts and roll my tongue around her nipples. She moans but does not make a move to touch me and does not take off her skirt.

I am loving every minute of being with her, but I'm not sure where this is going, if anywhere. She kisses me and says we'd better head back downstairs. Reluctantly, I say, "Okay."

She puts herself back together and I say, "You'd better go first. I will come down in a bit."

She smiles and says, "Okay." She kisses me again and leaves.

It takes a good ten minutes for me to get to the point where I can leave my room without embarrassment. I take the elevator back down to the lobby and start to head back toward the ballroom where the COE conference is being held. As I approach the doors, everyone starts coming out of the ballroom. I guess the afternoon session is over.

Our next event is dinner tonight at 6:00. I head back up to my room. Around 5:00, I get a call from Mrs. Carter. She says we need to talk. "Can you meet me in the lobby in five minutes?

"Sure. What is this about?" I'm worried by the tone of her voice.

She says, "Let's talk downstairs."

I find Mrs. Carter in the lobby, and she says to follow her to one of the small conference rooms. We sit down and Mrs. Carter says, "One of the other COE teachers saw you leave the afternoon session early. She knew who you were because she had listened to your speech at lunch. She said you did not return to the afternoon session. Is all that true?"

"Yes, I was bored and decided to leave."

Mrs. Carter asks, "Where did you go?"

"Up to my room. I stayed there the whole time."

Mrs. Carter says, "This is going to be a problem. All national COE office candidates are required to attend all meetings of all conference sessions. They may disqualify you because you left the session early.

"I'm sorry. I didn't know."

"I understand, but I don't think that is going to help your situation. I will see you at dinner and let you know what the COE administrators decide to do."

"Okay."

At 6:00, I head to dinner and find our assigned table. Mrs. Carter sees me and pulls me aside. She says, "They have disqualified you."

"I'm sorry. I take full responsibility. I know I've disappointed you and that is the last thing I wanted to do."

She says, "I understand. Just make sure you attend all the meetings tomorrow."

"I will."

After dinner, I meet up with Cindy and tell her what happened. She is surprised and says, "I'm sorry. I know how much you wanted to win the election. Is there anything I can do?"

I shake my head. "No. The decision has been made. Neither of us can do anything about it now." We take another walk, but my heart isn't in it. I walk her back to the hotel and say, "I'll see you tomorrow."

She tells me goodnight and we part ways.

The next day, I attend all the sessions. It is our last day. I can tell Mrs. Carter is upset, but she says nothing more about my disqualification. At the end of the day, I take another walk with Cindy. We sit on a bench and kiss, but it does not have the same passion as the day before. Neither she nor I suggest that we go back to my room.

At the end of the night, I say "I really enjoyed our time together. I know you have a life in Kettering, but if you would ever like to get together, just let me know." We exchange addresses and telephone numbers and say goodbye. It's a bittersweet parting.

The flight back to Dayton was uneventful and the car ride to Lima was quiet.

Today is my first day of classes after our trip. I'm not sure what I'm going to say to the COE class about the convention. Mrs. Carter takes the lead and simply says that I was not elected to national CEO president. She says nothing about the disqualification and neither do I. Her grace has saved me from embarrassment.

Teens & Dreams

48

Friday, May 23, 1969 • Lima, Ohio

Mrs. Carter recommended that I arrange a personal interview with the Kent State University admissions office. I call and schedule an appointment for Monday, May 5, 1969, at 2:00. I'm not sure what to expect in the interview, but Mrs. Carter assures me that I will do fine.

On the Saturday before my interview, I am challenged to drag race my Chevelle on Wayne Street against a 1965 Mustang. We take off, side-by-side. I do a power shift from first to second gear and mistime the shift. I let the clutch out too soon and hear a grinding noise as I try again to shift into second gear. The Mustang races on and disappears. I am still in first gear. I drive forward and try again to shift into second gear, but the transmission will not engage. I am stuck in first gear.

I drive home in first gear and park it. My friend, Jack, knows a lot about cars so I ask him to take a look. He concludes that I need to rebuild my transmission or replace it. I've chewed up some gears.

I tell Jack about my interview at Kent State on Monday. He says, "If you can find a used transmission at a junkyard, I can help you put it in, and we might be able to get you back on the road by Monday."

"Can you help me find the right transmission?"

"I'll ask my dad if we can take his Ford pick-up." An hour later, we are headed to the junkyard. The owner helps us find the correct transmission and we load it onto the truck. It's heavy and takes both of us to lift it.

On the way home, Jack says, "This is a messy job and will take both of us to do it. At best, it is an all-day job. I can't guarantee we will be done by Monday morning, though."

"I understand and appreciate your help."

Jack says, "I have a date with Diane in a little while, so let's start on it first thing tomorrow morning. I'll meet you at your car at 8:00 tomorrow."

"Great. See you tomorrow morning and thanks again."

"No problem."

On Sunday morning we jack up the car, slide underneath and start unscrewing bolts from the transmission. Some of them are rusty and hard to remove. After several hours we're finally able to pull the transmission. Jack compares my old transmission to the one we picked up at the junkyard. It doesn't match. Fortunately, the junkyard is open on Sunday, but not until noon. We load up the old and the new transmissions and take them to the junkyard. The owner sees the problem and finds us a transmission that matches my Chevelle. By the time we get back to my house, it's 3:00.

"We can try, but I don't think we will be able to install the new transmission before dark," Jack says.

It's not what I want to hear but I have no other solution. "Let's give it our best shot and see what happens," I say.

We work all afternoon and into the evening until it is too dark to see what we're doing, and Jack says, "We still have a couple of hours of work. If we get up at sunrise tomorrow, we should be able to finish before I leave for school."

"Thanks, Jack. See you tomorrow."

On Monday, May 5, we get started on my car a little later than we had planned and run into some problems. Jack says, "I need to go to school, but I can show you what you need to do to finish the job. You should be okay." Jack leaves, and I'm on my own. I'm not the most mechanically inclined person, but I can follow directions. Of course, it takes longer than expected. I finish at 11:00 and take it for a test drive. Everything works.

I still need to get cleaned up and then drive to Kent State. It's a three-hour drive, and my appointment is at 2:00. I know I'm going to be late. I don't know if the admissions office will be able to see me if I'm late, but I decide to make the drive anyway. Even if I don't have the interview, at least I can see what the Kent State campus looks like.

It's noon when I get on the road. I arrive on campus shortly after 3:00 and by the time I locate the admissions office, it's 3:20. I tell the receptionist that I had car trouble on my way to Kent and apologize for being late for my appointment. She tells me she will ask the admissions officer if it's possible to see me.

The admissions officer walks out of her office, introduces herself, and says, "I understand you had some car trouble. I have another appointment in fifteen minutes, but if you would like to talk until then, I would be happy to speak with you."

I'm relieved. "That will be fine. Thank you." The shortened interview goes okay, but I'm unsure whether I hurt or helped my application by showing up late. The admissions officer does confirm that they had just received my ACT scores and they should be able to decide on my application by the end of May. Her next appointment arrives, so I thank her for her time and leave. I drive around campus and am surprised by its size. It's much bigger and more spread out than I expected, but I like what I see.

It's Friday, May 23, 1969, and I have good news for Mrs. Carter. After I got home from working at the bank yesterday, a big brown envelope from Kent State is waiting for me. I open it and read that I have been accepted and will start classes in September 1969. I have been awarded federal grants sufficient to cover my tuition and room and board for the 1969-70 school year. I have also been granted a job in the Work-Study Program for up to fifteen hours per week. I whoop and holler. My mom comes rushing into my room and asks what's wrong. I tell her I've been accepted at Kent State. She gives me a hug and tells me congratulations. It's the first time in a long time that I can remember my mom giving me a hug.

I arrive at COE class and see Mrs. Carter with a big smile on her face. She says, "I just heard from your guidance counselor that you've been accepted to Kent State. Congratulations!"

"I just found out last night. I'm surprised that you've already heard the news."

"Are you excited?"

"I sure am," I say, "and thank you so much for your recommendation and everything you've done for me this year. Without your help and support, I would not be attending college in the fall."

"You're welcome. Good things come to good people, and you are one of the good ones."

At the bank, I tell everyone my good news and they congratulate me. Debbie arrives to make her afternoon deposit and I tell her my news. "Congratulations," she says, then asks, "Are we still on for dinner tonight?"

"Yes. I will pick you up at your house at 7:00."

"See you tonight."

She does not linger at my teller window, and though she does congratulate me, her praise seems less than effusive. I wonder if something else is going on that I don't know about. We have continued to date since I returned from Fort Worth a month ago, but our relationship seems less intense, less complete. I don't know if it is me or her, but we are different. I did not tell her about what happened with Cindy in Fort Worth, and I have not seen or spoken to Cindy since the day before we left to come home.

At the end of April, Debbie had told me that she had been accepted at Duke, her first choice of colleges. Before Debbie mentioned that she had applied there, I had never heard of Duke University. Now I know it's located in Durham, North Carolina, and is one of the top universities in the U.S. After that news, Debbie also told me she had been accepted at all the other colleges where she applied. We celebrated her acceptance at Duke even though I knew that it meant the end of us.

Tonight, we have a dinner reservation at the Milano Club on Market Street in Lima. It has the reputation of being the finest restaurant in Lima. I have never been there, but Debbie has and says it's her favorite restaurant. I can see why when we walk in. The atmosphere is romantic. The lighting is dim, tealight candles in shiny gold dishes sit in the center of each table covered by white linen tablecloths. A waiter in a black suit and tie escorts us to a table in the corner and pulls the chair out for Debbie to be seated. We raise our water glasses and toast to Debbie's acceptance to Duke and my acceptance at Kent State.

Debbie says, "I have some news about Duke I've decided to attend their summer session and get a head start on my classes."

I'm surprised but ask, "Will that help you graduate earlier?"

"Maybe. It depends on whether I take classes during summer session next year."

"When do you start?" I ask.

"Monday, June 2. I am driving to Duke this Sunday with my parents to get settled in before classes begin. I know this is a surprise to you and I'm sorry, but I just found out this past week that I could attend summer session."

"We've known that sooner or later we would go our separate ways to college. Yours just happens to be sooner. I'm glad for you."

"Thanks, but I want tonight to be about you and your success. I'm so excited that you were accepted at Kent State."

"It doesn't have the reputation of Duke, but I think I'll be happy there."

Dinner is very good. We make small talk as we eat, and I try not to be subdued, but I am only partially successful. After dinner, I drive Debbie home. We park in her driveway, and I say, "So this is it. Our last date."

"For now. Who knows what the future may bring," she says.

I lean toward her, she meets me halfway, and we kiss.

"I'm going to miss you," I say.

"Me too," she says. I walk her to her door, and we embrace one last time.

Life & Love

49

Today is Earth Day, the first one ever. It is the idea of Senator Gaylord Nelson of Wisconsin that at least one day each year, Americans will focus on saving our environment. Thousands of schools, colleges, and universities are expected to offer programs today to discuss pollution, air quality, and other environmental concerns. Corporations spew chemicals into our air and pollute our water. Insufficient laws exist to limit or control these activities, and corporations have no incentive to change because change costs money and reduces profits.

KSU has scheduled a full day of programs and speakers. At 3:30 I plan to attend "Crisis in the Environment," and tonight at 8:00 in the University Auditorium, environmentalist and consumer rights advocate, Ralph Nader, will speak on "Chemical Pollution." Katie and I plan to attend his speech together.

Since Monday, KSU has offered programs on the environment and other issues affecting society as part of Think Week. Last night Katie and I listened to former Secretary of the Interior Stewart Udall, who served in the Kennedy and Johnson administrations, talk about what will be needed for environmental change in the United States. Secretary Udall said Congress and society severely underestimate the magnitude of the clean-up required in the U.S. He said pollution must become a political imperative before Congress acts.

Udall said the irony of the environmental problem in the U.S. was evident when he flew over Michigan, the Wolverine State but saw no wolverines; when he flew over New Jersey, the Garden State, but saw gardens choked with smog; and when he flew over Orange County, Florida, and saw orange trees covered with swamps.

The last couple of weeks have been quite active on campus with political speakers. Last Thursday, former astronaut, John Glenn, spoke as a candidate for senator from Ohio. He was the first American to orbit the Earth, circling it three times in 1962. His appearance was timely, as the crew of the disabled *Apollo 13* was still making its way back to Earth at the time of his speech. They landed safely in the Pacific Ocean the next day, Friday, April 10, 1970.

John Glenn spoke before a packed house in Cunningham Hall, room 101. When asked about his views on pollution in America, he said that uniform federal standards are needed across the nation to address the problem rather than letting the states enact ad hoc legislation.

I meet Katie at the Terrace Hall lounge at 7:00. A big crowd is expected to listen to Ralph Nader, so we want to get to University Auditorium early.

On the way over Katie says, "How was the program on Crisis in the Environment that you attended this afternoon?"

"Did you know that the last eighteen miles of the Cuyahoga River in Cleveland before it dumps into Lake Erie are totally devoid of life? The pollution in the water has killed everything. And when the Cuyahoga River caught fire last June, the flames reached five stories high. That was not the first time it caught fire, but it did get the most publicity. Lake Erie is dying. Raw sewage is still being pumped into the lake."

Katie says, "Wow! I had no idea the river and lake were that bad, and I've lived close to them most of my life."

The auditorium is already starting to fill up when we arrive. We're lucky to find seats toward the front. Shortly before 8:00, they direct students to Wills Gym where loudspeakers will broadcast Ralph Nader's talk.

Nader begins his speech by saying, "Concerned about pollution? Don't wring your hands but be prepared to do something about it!" This call to action is a wake-up call for me and others. He predicts that within the next couple of years, the voting age will be lowered to eighteen and when that occurs, all college students will need to wield their political power by voting. Mr. Nader blames big corporations as our primary polluters, and until substantial financial disincentives are enacted, they will continue to pollute.

Nader's speech is a good end to the first Earth Day. I hope all Americans can become as enlightened as I feel.

Bayonets & Bullets

50

11:30 a.m., Monday, May 4, 1970 • Kent State University, Kent, Ohio

By 11:30, more people have gathered on the Commons by the Victory Bell and on Blanket Hill, and more stream in every minute. Students stand on the outdoor terrace of Taylor Hall overlooking the Commons, and along the side of Johnson Hall, and on the rooftop of both Johnson Hall and Stopher Hall. More students seem to be on Blanket Hill than on the Commons by the Victory Bell.

At the other end of the Commons, roughly five hundred people are standing behind the National Guardsmen and next to the burnt-out ROTC building. Another crowd of students begin gathering in front of the tennis courts, also at the other end of the Commons. Everyone on both sides of the Commons just seems to be waiting and watching to see what will happen. By 11:45, at least fifteen hundred students are mingling around not sure what will happen next.

At 11:48, someone starts ringing the Victory Bell apparently trying to call even more people to the Commons for the rally. Students immediately chant:

"One, two, three, four, we don't want your fucking war!"

"Pigs off campus!"

"Guards go home!"

Within a minute or two, a campus police officer using a bullhorn at the other end of the Commons orders students to leave the area immediately. The chanting and crowd noise are so loud, it's hard to hear anything he says.

I turn to Katie. "Are you still, okay?"

"Yes, but can you believe how many people are here?"

"I know. I think most students are here because they don't want the guardsmen on campus. Don't you think it's strange that no one from the KSU administration is here to talk to the students? Not President White or any vice presidents or deans. They have totally abandoned us."

Katie says, "They've surrendered the campus to the National Guard."

"Exactly."

No one moves a foot in response to the campus cop's command. The cop climbs into the front seat of a jeep with three National Guardsmen and drives toward the crowd at the Victory Bell. Two guardsmen in the backseat hold their M1 rifles at the ready with their bayonets fixed. The cop again with a megaphone tells the students their presence on the Commons constitutes an illegal assembly, and for their own safety, they must disperse immediately. He gets close to the crowd, and I hear him say, "This assembly is unlawful. The crowd must disperse at this time. *This is an order!*" The campus cop repeats the announcement several times as the jeep loops in front of the students and then back around again.

The students chant louder: "*One, two, three, four, we don't want your fucking war! One, two, three, four, we don't want your fucking war!*" Several cheers go up, and then more chanting. "*Pigs off campus! Pigs off campus! Pigs off campus!*" Someone throws a rock at the jeep, but it bounces harmlessly off the hood.

There's a short break in the chanting. Then a student addresses the other students by the Victory Bell. They are too far away for me to hear what he is saying. Suddenly, a cheer goes up, and the students on the Commons chant: "*Strike! Strike! Strike!*" Something must have been said about a student strike.

For a third time, the campus cop and the guardsmen circle back around in the jeep and again come close to the students and shout into their bullhorn, "*Attention! Attention! This is an order! Leave this area immediately!*"

The students respond: "*Fuck you! Fuck you!*" The order is given again, and the students respond again with "*Pigs off campus! Pigs off campus! Pigs off campus!*"

It is clear the message coming from the jeep is having the opposite of its intended effect and is further enraging the students. When the jeep loops close to the line of guardsmen, an officer steps forward and talks to the men in the jeep. He must have given an order to desist because the jeep immediately stops looping the Commons and joins the line of guardsmen.

Suddenly, all the guardsmen don their gas masks and several of them pick up what look like grenade launchers, then move forward toward the crowd. They fire tear gas canisters at the students forcing them up Blanket Hill.

"Let's go!" I shout. I take Katie's hand and start a fast walk toward the top of Blanket Hill. There's a lot of confusion. Students try to get away from the tear gas. As Katie and I move up the hill, we both get a whiff of it, immediately stinging our eyes. Fortunately, the wind is blowing away from us and toward the National Guardsmen. As the tear gas disperses around us, we're able to continue up Blanket Hill. I look back and see several students pick up tear gas canisters and hurl them toward the guardsmen.

Katie and I stop at the top of Blanket Hill near the Pagoda to see what will happen next. More students than before seem to be at the top of the hill. I can't tell if it's just that we are all now concentrated in a smaller area or if more students have joined us. I conclude it's probably a little of both. The 11:00 classes have let out and many students are heading to lunch.

I say to Katie, "It looks like over two thousand students are here now."

"It's hard to tell who the protesters are and who have just come to see what is going on," she says.

Some students are using the Taylor Hall restrooms to rinse their eyes. Others are wetting tee shirts or the sleeves of sweatshirts to hold over their noses and mouths as protection from the tear gas.

Almost every tear gas canister launched by the National Guard is picked up and lobbed back by students. The wind continues to be in our favor and much of the tear gas blows back toward the guardsmen.

Something seems to be happening with the guardsmen. They line up in formation in three distinct groups. One group lines up to our left directly in front of the burnt-out ROTC building. Another group lines up in the center of the Commons almost directly across from the Victory Bell, and a third group lines up to our right and toward the north side of Taylor Hall. It doesn't look good. They all have M1 rifles with bayonets pointing at us.

It looks like they will be given orders shortly to move out and head up Blanket Hill.

Teens & Dreams

51

Wednesday, June 11, 1969 • Lima, Ohio

Graduation day is finally here. After thirteen years in Lima Public Schools, I have earned a diploma. Yesterday afternoon, at a party on the front lawn of the YWCA, members of the Class of 1969 signed each other's yearbooks and added a short note of remembrance. Some were funny. Some were sad. All were heartfelt.

I was invited to a graduation party last night and another one tonight. My friend's parents rented out the pool area of the Springbrook Country Club for the party last night. I'd never been there.

A variety of food selections is laid out on two long tables, and soft drinks are on ice in several huge tubs. A couple of the guys smuggled in a bottle of vodka and spiked one of the two punch bowls. Everyone knows which one is spiked and the vodka guys keep it loaded. I try a cup of spiked punch and decide it's not bad.

I'm at the party alone and talk to several girls about what they are doing after graduation. All but one are going to college. Some are going to Ohio State. Others to Miami University or Bowling Green State University. None say they are going to Kent State, and most don't even know it's in Ohio. That's okay. I am ready for a fresh start. Some of the guys in my math and English classes are also at the party. Most of them are heading to Ohio State. Again, none are going to Kent State.

I picked up my cap and gown earlier in the week. My mom is coming to graduation. My dad is not. That is fine with me. My dad and I only talk when necessary. He has yet to say anything about me going to college.

The principal calls my name, and I walk on stage. I hear some light applause as I accept my diploma. I then watch Jack receive his. He gets a robust round of applause from his whole family, and Diane too. Her graduation was last night.

After the ceremony, I find my mom and thank her for coming. She gives me a hug. "Johnny, I'm so proud of you."

"Thanks, Mom." I tell her I'm going to a graduation party with some friends and won't be home until late tonight.

"Honey, you stay out as long as you want."

I love my mom even though I've never told her, and I know she loves me, even though she has never spoken those words to me. As I've grown up, I've come to better understand that her life has not been easy. She is the sole breadwinner and sole caretaker of the house and her six children. She has a husband who abuses her children physically and emotionally and she can do little about it. He doesn't work. He's an alcoholic and probably a philanderer. Yet my mom has provided us with a roof over our heads and food on our table. I've come to appreciate that she is quite a woman.

Jack and Diane have invited me to a graduation party at Diane's house tonight. Jack said there will be big news at the party and hoped I could attend. When I arrive, about thirty people are already there. Beer and wine are available, but Diane encourages everyone who drinks to stay at her house tonight. She has plenty of blankets and sleeping bags. Unlike last night, most people at this party have no plans to go to college. I am in the minority.

At 10:00 on the dot, Jack asks everyone to quiet down. Diane is confused and asks him what's going on. He doesn't answer, but puts his arm around her waist and says, "I want to thank you all for coming tonight. This is graduation weekend for most of us, so first,

I want to thank you for being our friends, and then I want to raise a glass and toast all of you who graduated this week. To the new high school graduates!"

We raise our glasses and take a drink. Jack says, "As most of you know, Diane and I have been dating for over three years. She is the best thing that has ever happened to me, and I want all of us to thank our hostess and toast her." He raises his glass and says, "To Diane!"

Jack continues, "Some of you have asked what I am going to do after graduation. Of course, Diane and I talked about what we might want to do in the future, but we made no definite plans. That is about to change."

Jack lets go of Diane and gets down on one knee. He reaches into his pocket and pulls out a small black jewelry box, opens it, and says, "Diane, I love you and will always love you. Will you marry me?"

Diane is caught completely off guard by the question but manages to say, "Yes, I love you too."

Jack slides a solitaire diamond ring set in gold onto her left ring finger. Diane blushes and wraps her arms around Jack, kisses him, and then starts crying. I can tell these are tears of joy.

I step up and say, "Well, it's time for another toast. To Jack and Diane. May their love last forever." Everyone raises a glass and toasts, "To Jack and Diane!"

All the girls immediately encircle Diane and want to see her diamond. All the guys, pat Jack on the back and congratulate him. After a few minutes, I see Jack standing alone and walk over to him. "Well done. I don't think Diane or anyone else saw that coming."

Jack says, "I've been thinking about asking her to marry me for a long time and tonight seemed like the perfect time."

"Good luck to both of you," I say. He thanks me as we shake hands.

On my drive home later that night, I reflect on how my world is changing. My friends are getting married, and I am heading to college. Life will never be the same.

Teens & Dreams

52

Sunday, July 20, 1969 • Lima, Ohio

Since graduation I've been working full time at the bank, mostly at the branches substituting for bank tellers who are on vacation. I like working the drive-up window. The other tellers don't like it, but I think it's great. I get to see the kind of car each customer drives and because my seat is higher than most cars, I also see and hear what's happening inside the car. Most drivers and passengers must think the outdoor microphone only works when I am talking with them, but that isn't so. It's on all the time and I often hear things that are meant to be said in private.

The bank has generously offered me a week of paid vacation, even though I've only worked full time for a month. The head teller at the main office told me about the vacation and said, "You've worked hard all year. You deserve it." I thanked him and this past week I took my first ever paid vacation. I didn't do much on vacation. I spent a day on the beaches at Indian Lake and Lake St. Mary's and a couple of days at Long's Quarry reading and relaxing in the sun.

During my vacation, I have a lot of time to think about what life will be like at Kent State. I know I will live in a triple and have two roommates, but I have no idea who they are or where they're from. I think about what major to declare. Teaching high school history or math would be interesting. Math teachers are more in demand than history teachers, so majoring in math makes sense. One benefit of being a teacher is not working during summers but still getting paid. That's a good deal. Work for nine months and get paid for twelve.

Today is the last day of my vacation and tonight a historic event is supposed to happen—U.S. astronauts will walk on the Moon. It sounds like the stuff of Jules Verne or Flash Gordon.

On July 16, 1969, a *Saturn V* rocket launched *Apollo 11* from Kennedy Space Center on the east coast of Florida and it's now in lunar orbit. Tonight, Commander Neil Armstrong and Lunar Module Pilot Buzz Aldrin will steer the lunar module *Eagle* as it detaches from the command module *Columbia*, descends, and lands on the Moon's surface. If everything goes as planned, they will walk on the Moon while Michael Collins, the third astronaut aboard *Apollo 11*, pilots *Columbia*.

I'm meeting Jack and Diane at her house to watch the Moon landing with them, her parents, and her brother. Jack and Diane have been so cute together since their engagement. They were always a cute couple, but now they are all over each other, all the time. Every time I see them, they are holding hands or kissing. Maybe I'm a little jealous. Since Debbie left for Duke, I haven't dated anyone, and I don't want to start a relationship that will end in September. For now, I'm flying solo.

I arrive at Diane's house shortly after 3:00. The TV is on, and everyone is watching as Walter Cronkite, the CBS news anchor, explains what's happening. At exactly 4:05, *Eagle* separates from *Columbia* and begins its descent toward the Moon. We're on the edge of our seats holding our breath as Commander Armstrong looks for a place to land in the smooth, level crater called the Sea of Tranquility. At 4:18 p.m., we hear Armstrong say, "The Eagle has landed." We jump up from our seats, cheering and hollering. I can't believe it. Man is on the Moon.

We watch for a little longer, but nothing significant will happen until after 10:00 tonight when the Moon walk is scheduled so we enjoy a barbecue party while we wait. Jack cooks hotdogs and hamburgers on their Weber charcoal grill. Diane serves her homemade baked beans and potato salad. Her mom brings out brownies, and her dad brings out Cokes and beers. We have a real feast.

Shortly before 10:00 we go back inside and turn on the TV. Walter Cronkite tells us that the astronauts have gone through all the preparations needed to open the *Eagle's* hatch and Armstrong will be the first one out. It's cool that Neil Armstrong is from Wapakoneta, Ohio, only sixteen miles southwest of Lima. Just shows it's possible even for a small-town kid to grow up and make history.

At exactly 10:56 p.m. we watch via an external camera attached to the lunar module as Neil Armstrong descends the ladder and takes his first step on the Moon's powdery surface. He tells the hundreds of millions of people watching television from around the globe, "One small step for man, one giant leap for mankind." We all cheer wildly.

Nineteen minutes later, Buzz Aldrin leaves *Eagle* and joins Armstrong on the surface of the Moon. For more than two hours, they walk and jump in the reduced-gravity atmosphere, and explore the area around the lunar module, which they name Tranquility Base. The gravity of the Moon is only one-sixth the gravity of Earth. They collect surface samples, set up scientific equipment, and take photographs, but the coolest thing these space explorers do is plant the U.S. flag on the surface of the Moon. New explorers plant the United States flag on another celestial body. Incredible. They ascend the stairs, climb back into *Eagle,* and prepare to rejoin *Columbia.*

I heard President Kennedy in 1961 say that the U.S. has a goal "before this decade is out, of landing a man on the Moon and returning him safely to the Earth." The first part of that goal has been achieved and the return trip to Earth will begin on July 22, 1969.

I thank Jack and Diane for allowing me to experience with them an event that I know I will remember for the rest of my life.

Life & Love

53

President Nixon wants more men for his war machine because he's running out of bodies to throw at the Viet Cong. He clearly doesn't comprehend that much of America opposes the war in Vietnam. Today he asked Congress for the authority to eliminate most draft deferments, including occupational, agricultural, and fatherhood deferments. He also proposes that all student deferments, like the 2-S deferment I have, be eliminated. Everyone currently holding a student deferment would be permitted to finish college before being drafted. The rest of male high school students in America are out of luck.

The military has issued 1.8 million student deferments, four million dependent deferments and twenty-three thousand agricultural deferments. Nixon wants to kill off the best and brightest minds in America, then kill off fathers and leave thousands of children orphans, then take our farmers so that all of us starve.

Nixon also wants to replace the draft with an all-volunteer army. Who in their right mind would volunteer to go to Vietnam to fight for a losing cause that is not a threat to the security of the United States? He says he will award army enlistees more money and benefits, which, of course, they will not be able to use when they are transported back home in body bags.

What will the president who campaigned to end the war in Vietnam do next?

Bayonets & Bullets

54

Katie and I stand at the top of Blanket Hill next to the Pagoda and watch the guardsmen form into three groups at the end of the Commons near the destroyed ROTC building. An order must have been given because, a few minutes before noon, all three Guard units wearing gas masks simultaneously march toward Blanket Hill, launching tear gas canisters in front of them as they advance.

"You'd better head back to Terrace Hall," I tell Katie. "This doesn't look good."

"I agree," she says, her voice worried. "I'll walk across the Prentice Hall parking lot and take Midway Drive back to Terrace Hall. Please be very careful. I don't want you to get hurt."

"Okay. You head back now. Don't worry about me. I'm not going near the guardsmen."

I hurriedly kiss her, and she says, "Come to my dorm as soon as the protest rally is over, okay?"

"I will. See you soon."

I watch Katie cross the Prentice Hall parking lot and then lose her in the crowd. The Guard continues to advance and is now halfway up Blanket Hill. I move down the back side of Blanket Hill toward Prentice Hall. In a few minutes, the center and south units of the guardsmen merge at the top of Blanket Hill and stop next to the Pagoda. Behind me, the north unit of guardsmen has come up the other side of Blanket Hill and formed a line between Taylor Hall and Prentice Hall.

Students are scattered everywhere. Some are in front of Taylor Hall, others are on the Taylor Hall terrace. Some stand in the Prentice Hall parking lot. Some are with me between the Prentice Hall parking lot and Taylor Hall. Others move down to the football practice field. Some, like Katie, left or are leaving the area.

Maybe fifty or so students closest to the Guard taunt them by spewing epithets and giving them the middle finger. A few find rocks and throw them at the Guard. Even the most courageous students, who are closest to the guardsmen, are too far away and most of their rocks fall short. I see a few guardsmen get hit, but they fail to react to the epithets or the rocks. It's hard to tell how the students find rocks to throw. The entire area is either paved or covered with grass. It's not like a pile of rocks is lying around some-where. A construction site is nearby. I guess they could have picked up the rocks from the debris and carried them here.

The guardsmen still wear their gas masks and have an almost alien look to them. It must be hot inside those masks. It's in the seventies and I'm hot just standing here watching. I keep wondering what the Guard is going to do next. They don't seem to have a plan. What is their endgame? They have already dispersed the students from the Commons. Are they going to escort students back to their dorms? Are they going to start making arrests? Neither seems likely or possible. It looks like there are maybe one hundred guardsmen. Every time they move forward, the students retreat. The guardsmen have no way to surround the students or make arrests. They don't have enough manpower to do that.

The guardsmen stop for a couple minutes at the Pagoda at the top of Blanket Hill, but then must have been given the order to disperse the students on the football practice field, because the guardsmen move in unison in that direction. The students on the practice field have only two options: either move toward Midway Drive and the Prentice parking lot, or exit through a narrow, single-person-wide gate in the fence and head toward Memorial Gym. Students bunch up trying to get through the gate before the guardsmen arrive. The last student makes it through just before the guardsmen arrive. The guardsmen on the north flank between Taylor Hall and Prentice Hall hold their position. They probably did this to prevent students from moving back toward the Commons.

I walk along the edge of the Prentice parking lot to see what the guardsmen are doing. They cleared the students from the practice field and stopped. A fence encloses three sides, so they really have nowhere to go. They could head toward me and the other disorganized group of students in the Prentice Hall parking lot and on Midway Drive, but cars are in the lot, and if they did that, everyone would simply move further down Midway Drive. The only other thing for the guardsmen to do is to return to the Commons. I watch them meander around the practice field. Initially, they look confused and without direction or purpose, but then line up along the edge of the practice field fence.

Some of the students on Midway Drive, seeing that the guardsmen have stopped, move into the Prentice Hall parking lot and back toward the guardsmen. Several students grab rocks from the construction site and throw them at the guardsmen. Other students gather in front of Taylor Hall. I watch one guardsman on the practice field pick up a rock and throw it back toward the students.

Students continue to regroup in the Prentice Hall parking lot and on the hill in front of Taylor Hall. I move toward the group in front of Taylor Hall and stand next to the metal sculpture in front of the building.

Some students continue yelling epithets and throwing rocks, but I don't join them. I too want the Guard off campus, but violence isn't the answer.

I still see no one from the KSU administration. Where is President White? Having tea in his big office in the administration building while his campus is under siege and his students are being chased by the National Guard?

Teens & Dreams

55

My favorite couple, Jack and Diane, got married at Shawnee Church of Christ last night. It was the first wedding I'd ever attended. Jack looks spiffy in his baby blue tuxedo and Diane looks radiant in her white lace wedding dress. She is so slender; Jack could wrap his hands around her waist. The organist is playing the wedding march as Diane walks down the center aisle of the Church. Everyone stands as she walks past. She really is one of the most beautiful girls I've ever seen. Jack is a lucky guy, and he knows it.

The minister knows them well and says a few words about their love and affection for each other and for Jesus Christ. They exchange wedding vows and then give each other a kiss that is probably too long, but who cares? It's their first kiss as a married couple. They are in love. After the wedding photos are taken, they emerge from the church to a shower of rice. I help prepare Jack's car for their departure. We tie tin cans on strings to the back of his car bumper and I write "Just Married" in white shoe polish on the rear window. They climb in Jack's car and take off to cheers, whistles, and the clatter of tin cans. We will meet them at the Eagles Club downtown for their reception.

On my way to the reception, I reflect on all the events of the past two months. Jack had no plans to go to college and was concerned that he would be drafted into the Army and go to Vietnam. He liked the idea of military service but wanted to avoid Vietnam. Jack's dad is an Army veteran and encouraged him to talk with the Army recruiter in Lima before deciding to enlist. The recruiter said he could make no promises, but he thought Jack had a good chance of being assigned to Germany rather than Vietnam after he finished basic training. Jack and Diane talked everything over and decided to get married in August and take a short honeymoon. Jack would report to basic training in early September.

They had a lot to do to plan a wedding in two months, but Diane and her mom made it happen. The reception is cool. Beer and pop are on ice and champagne is at each table. Jack starts the reception with a champagne toast to his new bride and we all clink glasses. We help ourselves to some delicious food from a huge buffet. During dinner, a DJ spins 45s and everyone dances. I ask a few girls I know to dance, and we all have a good time. The party lasts late into the evening and is still going strong when I leave around 11:00.

The Allen County Fair opens today. At 7:00 p.m. I pick up my cousin, Jim, and we drive to the fairgrounds. Jim graduated from Lima Senior with me but still wasn't sure what he wanted to do. Jim is one of the smartest people I know and would do well in college. I ask him about his plans on the way to the fair.

"I need a break from school and want to get out of Lima and do something exciting with my life," he says. "I've always admired the Marines because they go in first when a conflict occurs. Last week I talked to the Marines recruiter and signed up. I head to Parris Island, South Carolina, for Basic Training on September 8."

"Congratulations. I'm just surprised everything can happen so fast."

"Once I decided to go, I thought, why wait? Sign me up for the next boot camp."

"Wow, you are something else."

"You're heading to Kent State in September, right?"

"Yeah. Classes start September 29. I'll move to campus the week before for New Student Orientation."

Jim says, "I'm sure you will do really well in college."

"Thanks."

The Allen County Fair is always a good time and tonight is no exception. The rides light up the night sky and the midway is hopping. After we walk around for a while, Jim sees a girl he knows and stops to talk with her. He tells me he's going on rides with her so I'm on my own. I decide to visit a few friends I know will be here.

My first stop is the footlong hotdog stand. "Hi Mr. Nelson. It's Johnny. I worked for you two summers ago."

"Of course, I remember you, Johnny. You were one of my best employees ever."

"Thanks. It's good to see you. How has business been this summer?"

He says, "Great, but it's always a struggle to get good employees. Any chance you need a job this week?"

"No, thanks. I'm working full time as a teller at Metropolitan Bank and then I'm off to college at the end of September."

"Well, good for you. Good luck, Johnny."

"Thanks. See you later."

I walk over to the cane ring toss and see Lynette standing on the other side of the booth taking money and giving customers rings to toss toward the canes. I watch her for a few minutes. She looks good. Better than I remembered. She has a break between customers and so I go over to her and say, "Hi there, stranger."

She looks up, surprised. "Hi, Johnny. It's good to see you. Are you working at the fair this week?"

"No, I'm here with my cousin who is riding some rides with a girl. I just thought I'd stop by and say hello."

"I'm glad you did. Did you graduate from Lima Senior this year?"

"Yes, and I'm going to Kent State next month. How about you?"

"I graduated from Findlay, and next month I'm headed to Bowling Green State University."

"Congratulations. I just wanted to say hello. You have customers waiting. Take care and have fun at Bowling Green."

"Thanks, and good luck to you at Kent."

I run into Jim, and he tells me the girl he's with is giving him a ride home.

I take one last look around the Allen County Fair and realize that this could be the last time I walk these grounds.

Teens & Dreams

56

Friday, September 19, 1969 • Lima, Ohio

Today's my last day at Metropolitan Bank. The people I work with have been good to me and today is no different. I'm working at the main office and this afternoon they are having a going-away party for me. They bought me a fancy cake that says, "GOOD LUCK! WE WILL MISS YOU!" They all pitched in and got me a backpack. Tellers and other employees I know signed a card and wrote nice messages. Toward the end of the party, the bank president stops by and wishes me good luck. I had met him a couple of times when he stopped by to see how the tellers were doing, but it is still a surprise that he takes the time to wish me well.

A few weeks ago, the head teller also had me sit down with a loan officer at the bank to discuss my financial situation for college. I show her my financial aid letter. She says it is a good package, but she recommends that I take out a student loan for emergencies or unexpected expenses. She says $300 should be enough, but to let her know if I need more. I also think $300 is the right amount. The student loan will accrue interest, but I won't have to start paying it back until after I graduate. I sign the paperwork and the loan officer hands me a $300 check.

After the going-away party is over, two hours remain before closing. The head teller approaches me and says, "Close your window and balance out. You can leave early today." I thank him and do that.

Before I leave the head teller says to me "If you need a job next summer or during Christmas break, just let me know. I'm sure we can work something out."

"Thanks. I appreciate everything you've done for me."

"You are a great employee. Thanks for working for us."

I say my goodbyes to everyone and walk to my car.

I leave for Kent State tomorrow morning. I'm hitching a ride with the only other graduating senior from Lima Senior who is going to Kent State. Freshmen are not allowed to have cars on campus and so my Chevelle is staying home. My brother, Henry, who just got his driver's license, has promised to take care of it for me. I told my mom about my moving plans. Neither she nor my dad offered to drive me, and I had no expectation that they would. My dad is still a bastard. No way will I ride in a car with him for three hours. My mom would have to figure out who would stay with my brothers, and I would be concerned about her driving home by herself. So, riding with a fellow Kent Stater is the perfect option for me.

Life & Love

57

Spring is here! We have had a very cold winter and, until this week, a chilly spring. Temps have been in the seventies, and it's forecasted to reach eighty today. It's about time.

Campus extracurricular activities got a little crazy with the warm weather. On Monday night, students staged an epic mud fight by residents of Korb, Beall-McDowell, and the Tri-Towers dorms. Residents from the upper floors of Tri-Towers dropped plastic university bookstore bags filled with water onto three hundred students gathered on the grass below. Mud started flying and it soon became an all-out fight. Students hurled clumps of mud at the students dumping water from above. One student, apparently thinking that he had a handful of mud, threw it at a student dumping water but, oops, it was a rock covered in mud, which broke a dorm window.

The students all had fun. Beer bottles, whiskey bottles, paper cups, plastic bags, and other trash littered the front lawn of Tri-Towers. Drains in the dorm lavatories and showers were clogged with mud. A third of the lawn in front of Korb is torn up and needs to be rebuilt and reseeded. The unhappy KSU maintenance staff was left to clean up the mess.

It was good that the students could get outside and have some fun. Study hard and play harder is a good rule to live by. I'm sad I missed all the fun. I didn't hear about the mud fight until it was all over.

Midterms are coming so last night I studied. I'm also studying tonight, but President Nixon is going to address the nation about Vietnam, so I'm in the Clark Hall lounge waiting for him to come on TV. I hope he will tell us that he is withdrawing more troops from Vietnam sooner than predicted and that the U.S. will no longer draft men to fight in the war.

"This is not an invasion of Cambodia. We take this action . . . for the purpose of ending the war in Vietnam." I listen to Nixon try to tell us the opposite of what is occurring right now in Vietnam and Cambodia. Nixon has ordered U.S. troops into Cambodia and yet he says, "This is not an invasion of Cambodia." Nixon is expanding the geographic scope of the Vietnam War but tells us he is doing this for the purpose of ending the war. Every escalation in the war has been for the purpose of ending the war through a victory. When will the madness end? With fifty thousand U.S. soldiers dead and hundreds of thousands wounded, we know there can be no victory in Vietnam. Only more dead and wounded. How many more body bags will we have to see before this war is over?

An invasion of Cambodia is not the answer. If Nixon thinks his "moral majority" will save him from criticism, he is mistaken. I'm sure there will be outrage across America. My only hope is that the protests to come will be peaceful. There can be no honor in using violence to protest for peace.

Bayonets & Bullets

58

12:15 p.m., Monday, May 4, 1970 • Kent State University, Kent, Ohio

Guardsmen on the practice football field try to decide what to do next. More students start to move back into the Prentice Hall parking lot from Midway Drive. A low metal fence lies between the guardsmen and the students coming off Midway Drive. Several students find more rocks and throw them over the fence at the guardsmen. Most fall short, but some find their mark. A few guardsmen throw the rocks back at the students. It's like there's a tennis match between the guardsmen and students, with the metal fence being the net.

Students now fill in the space by the Pagoda at the top of Blanket Hill and gather on all the unfenced sides of the guardsmen. A lull in the activity ends when a female student shouts, "Put down your guns and go home, you're surrounded." A cheer from the students erupts and then some laughter. The guardsmen have guns and bayonets. The students have a few rocks and aren't even close enough to the guardsmen to pose a serious threat.

A fence is behind and on both sides of the guardsmen. Two of the most activist students, Jeff and Alan, intentionally try to antagonize the guards. I see Jeff retrieve a tear gas canister and lob it over the fence at the guardsmen. Alan goes around the fence and is closest to the guardsmen, waving his Black Anarchy flag with KENT painted in red across the front.

Suddenly a group of about a dozen guardsmen kneel and aim their rifles directly at the nearest students who are over one hundred feet away and separated from the guardsmen by a fence. The guardsmen do not fire. It seems a scare tactic to remind the students who holds the advantage in this skirmish.

An officer from another group of guardsmen standing between Taylor and Prentice halls walks toward me but continues past and heads toward the guardsmen kneeling on the practice field. I watch as he huddles with four other officers. After a short palaver, the officers split up and approach the kneeling guardsmen. The officers must have given them orders because they form into lines and start to move from the practice field back toward the top of Blanket Hill and the Pagoda. A cheer goes up from the students. The students must view the retreating guardsmen as some sort of victory because the cheers grow louder as the guardsmen approach the top of Blanket Hill.

I watch guardsmen walk back up the hill, but I don't cheer, and I don't see the victory. The guardsmen still hold their guns and occupy our campus. All they've done is move a couple of hundred yards one way and then back the other way, moving the students off the Commons and the front side of Blanket Hill. Why is there a reason to cheer?

As the guardsmen move up Blanket Hill, the students clear a path and let them pass without interference. It looks like the guardsmen are heading back to the Commons. Many students think the party is over and walk toward Midway Drive to go to lunch or their classes. I decide to stay a little longer to see what happens when the guardsmen descend the other side of Blanket Hill toward the Commons. Will the students follow them? Other than verbally harassing the guardsmen, I don't see the point of following them back to the Commons.

The guardsmen continue to climb Blanket Hill, and I mirror their movements until I'm standing in front of Taylor Hall next to the metal sculpture. I have a clear view of the guardsmen with nothing between me and them other than the metal sculpture. A student off to my right is taking photos with a small disposable camera. Joe, whom I met at the sit-in on Main Street last night, is about ten yards in front of me. He gives the guardsmen the middle finger as they pass the Pagoda. Several students are between me and the Prentice Hall parking lot. Alan waves his black flag below me but closer to the guardsmen. Jeff in his distinctive white headband stands downhill from me in the northwest corner of the Prentice Hall parking lot. Allison and her boyfriend stand just a little farther downhill in the front section of the parking lot.

The students are no longer in groups, but are scattered in front of Taylor Hall, between the cars in Prentice Hall parking lot, on the grass next to the parking lot, and along Midway Drive. Hundreds of students want to see what the Guard will do next.

I watch the guardsmen crest Blanket Hill in front of the Pagoda and begin to march down the frontside of Blanket Hill toward the Commons. Students stand around watching. Without any additional provocation by the students and without any warning, I hear a guardsman shout, *"Guard! Prepare to fire!"* In one swift movement, the guardsmen turn in unison, crouch, and aim their weapons at the students. A split second later, the same guardsman shouts, *"Guard! Fire!"* It all happens so fast, there is no time to react other than to dive for the ground.

The guardsmen unleash a fusillade of bullets.

I feel a bullet whiz past my ear and ricochet off a car behind me. A millisecond later, I hear *ping* as another bullet hits the metal sculpture in front of me.

The student taking photos falls, moaning.

An officer of the Guard yells, *"Cease fire! Cease fire! Cease Fire!"* The firing stops. I'm alive and unharmed. But the air is filled with the anguished sounds of screams and crying.

I crawl toward the wounded student. He has been shot in the chest. His blood runs down my leg and pools on the ground below me. He is still alive and conscious. I say, "It's okay, man. We are going to get you some help." I rip off my shirt and try to staunch the flow of blood. "It's going to be okay, buddy. What's your name?"

"John." He can barely speak.

"Okay, John. Stay with me. My name is also John, but my friends call me Johnny. Hang in there. We're going to find someone who can help you." I think, but for the grace of God, I could be the "John" lying in this pool of blood.

At least for now, the bullets have stopped. I look up and see countless students face down on the ground, but I can't tell if they've been shot or are lying still, afraid that the guardsmen will resume shooting. Another student on the hill just below me is in agony. He has also been shot. Several people from Taylor Hall venture out from the safety of the building and run up to us.

Students start to surround us, and one shouts, "Stay back. Stay back. Somebody call an ambulance." One guy crouches down beside me and says, "I can help this guy. I know first aid."

"Okay. This is John. Stay with him until an ambulance arrives."

I stay low and run to the other student a few yards downhill. His shoe is gone. He's been shot and part of his left foot is missing. Bones stick out from the bottom of his foot. "Let's get out of here and get you some help before they start shooting again," I tell him. "What's your name?"

"Tom."

"Okay, Tom, I'm Johnny. I'm going to take you to someone who can help you." He is losing a lot of blood and needs help fast. Reaching down, I grab him, put him face down over my shoulder in a fireman's carry, and shuffle him to Prentice Hall, the closest dorm. I see several other shooting victims along the way.

Two girls rush to Tom's aid inside the dorm as I lay him down. One girl says, "He needs a tourniquet. Give me your belt!" I hesitate, and she shouts, "Now! I'm a nursing student."

I quickly pull off my belt and hand it to her. She wraps it around Tom's lower leg and pulls it tight. She tells the other girl watching, "Hold this belt and pull as hard as you can. We need to stop the bleeding." The girl does as instructed. The blood flowing from Tom's foot starts to slow, but he's fading in and out of consciousness.

"This is Tom," I tell them. "Please take good care of him. More students have been shot. I'm going to see if I can help."

The nursing student says, "We'll stay with him until we can get him into an ambulance."

I push my way through the crowd gathering inside Prentice Hall. Outside, the parking lot is in utter chaos. The acrid smell of gun smoke assaults my nostrils. Tear gas still lingers in the air and burns my eyes. I blink as I try to take in the scene. Students are crying and shouting. Guardsmen are regrouping on the hill, holding at the ready their M1 rifles with bayonets fixed. Disbelief shows on the faces of everyone. Students who were not wounded cautiously get up from the ground and tend to those who are bleeding.

A few feet away, a guy holds a girl in his arms. She's been shot. I know her. It's Allison, and the guy cradling her is her boyfriend. Students surround them, trying to provide aid.

Suddenly, I hear someone scream, "Help me!" I turn and run toward the call for help. Across the parking lot, a young brown-haired girl kneels next to the unmoving body of a boy lying face down in a pool of blood. As I get closer, I see he's been shot through the mouth. My God. It's Jeff. Just a few minutes ago, he had been full of life and shouting at the guardsmen. Now, he's not moving, and a lot of blood is on the pavement, I know he is dead.

An ambulance must have been on standby because within a few minutes, I hear the wail of a siren and it stops at the top of Blanket Hill next to the Pagoda.

Someone shouts, "*Call another ambulance! People are dying down here! Get another ambulance down here!*" I hear the siren screams of approaching ambulances grow louder. In the parking lot, other students lie on the ground who have either been wounded or killed.

The gravity of what has just happened begins to settle on me and makes me angry. I look up at the guardsmen and then at the carnage before me. Why did American soldiers fire on unarmed American students on American soil? They were brought here to protect us, not kill us. Will they open fire again on the rest of us?

One student shouts, "Unbelievable!"

Another says, "I can't believe they fired."

Then a chant starts, "*Pigs off campus! Pigs off campus! Pigs off campus!*" Another ambulance arrives. The chanting stops.

I look out over the war scene. The guardsmen have discharged more tear gas. I can't tell whether the smoke in the air is from the tear gas or the guardsmen's rifles. The guardsmen who shot the students still stand by the Pagoda. Several of them who were lined up between Taylor and Prentice halls come toward Jeff, apparently to help, but are jeered at and chased off by angry students.

Several students carry Allison and other injured students toward the ambulance next to Taylor Hall. Professor Frank, wearing his light blue faculty marshal armband, tells the students to put them down. The ambulance is full. Other ambulances are on the way.

Guardsmen on both sides of Taylor Hall march across the Commons toward the burnt-out ROTC building.

I am in utter shock over what has happened. I can still hear the words of the dean of students during freshman orientation last September saying, "Welcome to Kent State University!" The incongruity of that welcome and the horrific scene in front of me leave me wiping tears from my eyes.

I stop, bow my head, and pray for the wounded students.

Bayonets & Bullets

59

More ambulances arrive. Within a few minutes, the injured students are driven away amid a cacophony of blaring sirens. I feel empty. I'm sure other students feel the same way. Are the guardsmen going to shoot us all? Those guardsmen responsible for this massacre should be punished.

I walk to the top of Blanket Hill next to the Pagoda. Bullet casings litter the ground. Guardsmen are lined up across the Commons next to the burnt-out ROTC building. They hold their rifles at the ready position. Students gathering around the Pagoda demand: why did the National Guard open fire on unarmed students? Outrage surges as the shock wears off and anger takes its place. I'm angry too and want answers.

A faculty marshal walks up to the students by the Pagoda and pleads, *"I want to protect your lives. I wish you could understand me. They have live ammo. We've made our point. If we walk down the hill there, they are going to shoot."* He pauses a few moments then continues, *"If you want to strike, strike the fucking school, but I will tell you this, they are going to kill you. You could be black. You could be white. They don't give a shit who you are they are going to kill you. I've got one more thing to tell you. You know who these guys are? These guys are weekend soldiers. They've got guns."*

No one can make sense of the situation right now. Everyone is enraged. Everyone is in shock.

Helicopters hover overhead. The *whup, whup, whup* of their blades intersperses with the shouts of students about what to do next.

I walk down Blanket Hill with other students and join the group facing the guardsmen. Some students talk about charging them. That's crazy talk. The guardsmen have guns and have clearly demonstrated they will use them.

One faculty member with a megaphone urges the gathered students, *"Don't let anybody start you again going across this campus. We've had bloodshed. It's a hell of a thing that's happened here today. This campus will never forget, but don't start chasing across this field again."*

Students voice their outrage over the day's events and demand accountability. The same faculty member interrupts, *"I want you to understand that the faculty is with you in regard to this Vietnam thing. We're with you. We're with you."*

Another graduate student faculty marshal takes the megaphone. *"I recommend—you can do what you want—I recommend the students on this campus undertake a total boycott, a total strike against this university."*

We all cheer wildly in agreement.

Faculty Marshal Dr. Jerry Lewis, a sociology professor, now has the bullhorn and urges everyone to sit down and remain calm. He pleads several times for everyone to sit down. Multiple people yelling for everyone to sit down causes confusion. I sit down. Some students remain standing. A chant begins. *"Sit. Sit. Sit."* Soon other students follow and now most sit down on the Commons.

An attempt to have everyone sing, "We Shall Overcome" quickly falls apart. Dr. Lewis says, *"Let's sit for a moment in silence. Then for heaven's sake, let's get up and slowly and in a reasonable way march out of here away from those men with the guns."*

That suggestion is met with *"No! No! No!"* then loud drawn-out *"Nooos!"* and angry protest.

About five hundred students are now on the Commons. Like myself, most are not radicals but students who want the guardsmen who fired their weapons to be held accountable. Dr. Lewis is urging everyone to remain calm. I look behind me up toward the top of Blanket Hill and see another line of guardsmen behind us. They now surround us.

While Dr. Lewis is talking, I see my geology professor Dr. Glenn Frank speak to an officer of the Guard. He appears to be trying to convince him to back off. Apparently, it doesn't work. The guardsmen do not move and Professor Frank walks toward us looking dejected.

Professor Frank takes the megaphone from Professor Lewis and implores the students, "*Please listen to me right now! I don't care whether you've listened to anyone before in your lives. I am begging you right now. If you don't disperse right now, they're going to move in and there can only be a slaughter. Would you please listen to me! Jesus Christ, I don't want to be a part of this!*"

I think about what I promised Katie. That I would listen to and do anything that Professor Frank tells me to do. I'm also worried about Katie. She probably made it back to her dorm before the shooting started, but I'm not sure. I see the logic behind Professor Frank's plea that only more violence can result from us staying on the Commons. I rise along with several others and walk back up Blanket Hill and away from the Commons. The guardsmen part and let us pass. Some students point at the guardsmen and yell, "*Fuckers! Fuck you! Eat shit!*"

A guardsman with a megaphone orders, "*You have five minutes to clear the area. If you do not clear the area in five minutes, you will be arrested.*"

That announcement is met with boos, swears, and jeers from the students. Someone from the retreating group shouts, "*They're animals, not humans. Get out of here. You don't want to get killed. Let's go.*"

As I crest the top of Blanket Hill, I see the Highway State Patrol, followed by the National Guard start moving across the Commons. I hear a student shout, "*Everybody back to the dorms!*"

With my head down and tears in my eyes, I walk toward Terrace Hall.

Bayonets & Bullets

60

1:30 p.m., Monday, May 4, 1970 • Kent State University, Kent, Ohio

As I walk down the backside of Blanket Hill in front of Taylor Hall, I see the blood of Joe on the ground. I see the blood of John on the ground near the metal sculpture where I held him. I see the blood of Tom where I picked him up and carried him to Prentice Hall. In the corner of the Prentice Hall parking lot, I see a river of blood from Jeff. Walking across the Prentice Hall parking lot, I see the blood of Allison and other wounded students.

I look down at my shirt and jeans. I am covered in blood, the blood of those who were shot because they dared voice their disapproval to the National Guard. Freedom of speech was on trial today and lost. If guardsmen can shoot us with impunity, our basic freedoms have been stripped away.

I enter the back door of Terrace Hall and immediately look for Katie. The lobby is packed, and I don't see her. Some people are crying. Some appear to be in shock, blank looks on their faces. Others with bloodstained clothes look like they've been in a war. They must have helped the wounded too. We're all saturated with smells of blood, sweat, tear gas, and gun smoke.

Katie sees me and I see her at the same time. We run toward each other. I open my arms and she falls into them. She leans back with her arms around me and sobs, "Are you okay?"

"Yes, the blood is from students who were shot."

With tears streaming down her face, she says, "I've been waiting for you here in the lobby since I left you. I was terrified when I heard the shots. I didn't know if you were alive or dead. I've been praying that you weren't shot.

I say, "But for the grace of God, I would be dead right now. The person beside me was shot in the chest and the person just below me was shot in the foot. I know at least one guy is dead. He was shot in the head."

Katie can barely speak between sobs. "I'm glad you are okay. I don't know what I would have done if you had been injured."

"I'm okay. Don't cry. I'm sorry I couldn't return sooner. After the wounded were taken away in ambulances, some of us went back to the Commons. We wanted the guardsmen who had shot the students to be held accountable. Professor Frank was there and pleaded with us to go back to our dorms before more of us got shot. I remembered my promise to you and came back here."

Katie reaches up and puts her palm to my face. "Thank you. I love you, Johnny."

"I love you too."

We sit holding each other close for a few minutes. I look around the lobby and see other distraught students crying and sobbing. None of us can understand how unarmed students could be shot during a peaceful protest.

An announcement is made over the loudspeaker of Terrace Hall: "*Kent State University is now closed. The Ohio National Guard requires that all students leave the campus by 5:00 p.m. today. I repeat. All students must leave Kent State University by 5:00 p.m. today.*"

I look at Katie. "Now what are we going to do?"

"I'll call my uncle Gene and ask if he can come and get us. You can stay at my house until you figure out what you want to do."

"That sounds like a good plan. While you make your call, I'll go back to my dorm to shower and pack. Please call my room when you have news."

Katie says, "Okay. I'll talk with you soon. Be careful.

"I will." We kiss and Katie takes the elevator up to her room.

About forty-five minutes later Katie calls. "I had some trouble making the call to my uncle. I could not get through on my room phone, so I went across Main Street and used the pay phone at Burger Chef. I'm calling you from there. My uncle is on his way. I also called my mom and let her know I am safe. She wants us both to come to Cleveland as soon as possible. Uncle Gene should be here right around five. Do you want to meet us at Terrace Hall?"

"I'm glad you were able to get through. That's a good plan. I'll be there by 5:00."

After I hang up, I try to call my mom to let her know I am okay, but every time I try to make an outgoing call, I get a busy signal. I give up and will try her again when I get to Katie's house in Cleveland.

Katie's uncle Gene finally arrives at Terrace Hall shortly before 5:30. "I'm glad you both are okay," he says. "What happened here is beyond comprehension. The town is in total chaos. It was quite a trip to get to your dorm. I just had my first police escort."

"Why did you need a police escort?" I ask.

"When I got near the KSU golf course, I was stopped by the Kent police. After explaining that I was here to pick you up, the officer ordered me to wait in my car for an escort. I had to wait for twenty minutes. That's why I'm late."

Katie says, "We're so glad you're here. We have our luggage and are ready to go."

As we leave campus, I look back at the Midway Drive entrance, not knowing if or when I will be allowed back on campus. I also don't know if I want to go to a university where they shoot their students.

Epilogue

On Monday, May 4, 1970, at 12:24 p.m. on the campus of Kent State University, twenty-eight Ohio National Guardsmen pivoted in unison toward hundreds of unarmed students at an anti-Vietnam War rally, readied their loaded M1 rifles and side arms, aimed, and fired sixty-seven shots in thirteen seconds, killing four and wounding nine others. All were full-time Kent State students.

Allison Krause, Jeffrey Miller, Sandy Scheuer, and Bill Schroeder were killed. Allison Krause and Jeffrey Miller were protestors at the rally. Sandy Scheuer and Bill Schroeder were onlookers. Allison, a freshman, was shot in the chest from 343 feet away. Jeff, a sophomore, was shot in the mouth from 270 feet away. Sandy, a junior, was shot in the back of the neck from 390 feet away as she was walking away from the rally and heading to class. Bill, a sophomore, was shot in the back from 382 feet away.

The wounded students—Joe Lewis, John Cleary, Tom Grace, Alan Canfora, Doug Wrentmore, James Russell, Robert Stamps, Donald Mackenzie, and Dean Kahler—will never forget the terror they experienced that day. They were 60 to 750 feet away when they were shot. Dean Kahler, a freshman, has a bullet lodged in his spine, is paralyzed from the waist down, and will never walk again. He was 300 feet away.

Joe Lewis, who was closest to the guardsmen when the firing started, heard an officer give the command, *"Fire!"* Others say they heard an officer give the command, *"Guard! Ready to fire!"* No one disputes that the guardsmen took aim at the students. No one disputes that the guardsmen fired, and thirteen students were killed or wounded by their bullets.

Like me, hundreds, if not thousands, of innocents witnessed the carnage of May 4 and will forever be scarred by it.

Kent State shut down for six weeks immediately after the shootings. Over four million students at hundreds of universities, colleges, and high schools nationwide participated in strikes, rallies, and demonstrations forcing hundreds of schools to close. On May 10, 1970, the Ohio National Guard finally left campus and returned to their everyday jobs.

After we evacuated from campus, I stayed with Katie at her home in Cleveland for three days and then took a bus to Lima. I stayed there until I confirmed that the Ohio National Guard no longer occupied KSU, then drove my Chevelle to Kent and found an inexpensive, one-bedroom sublet at College Towers, a high-rise apartment building just off campus.

As I drove into Kent, I saw a lawn sign in front of a house that read: 4 DOWN, 20,000 TO GO. That sums up the attitude of Kent residents and businesses. They blame the students for everything that happened in Kent and on the KSU campus during the first four days of May 1970. The prevailing attitude among the locals and many Ohioans is that *they got what they deserved.*

No business in the City of Kent or Portage County had any

interest in hiring KSU students for summer work, but there was much less animosity just a few miles away in Summit County. In Stow, five miles west of campus, I was able to find a job as a temporary teller for a local bank.

Cleveland is only an hour away, so I saw Katie almost every weekend.

The President's Commission on Campus Unrest, which convened in June to study dissent, disorder, and violence on college campuses, submitted its 419-page report two days ago. It concluded that "The indiscriminate firing of rifles into a crowd of students and the deaths that followed were unnecessary, unwarranted, and inexcusable."

Today is the first day of fall quarter classes at Kent State for the 1970-71 academic year. I'm now a sophomore, living back on campus in a single room in Stopher Hall. Katie lives just across the green in Lake Hall. Only by God's grace did Katie and I escape being casualties that day.

Life goes on for most of us, but not for the four students killed by the Ohio National Guard. The four dead in Ohio will live in our hearts forever as will the nine who were wounded on the day the Vietnam War came home to America.

Acknowledgements

First and foremost, I would like to extend my deepest gratitude to my wife, Laura. The countless hours you spent researching, editing, and enhancing *Flowers Are Better Than Bullets* have been invaluable. Your unwavering support and keen eye for detail have been the backbone of this project.

To my beta readers—John Burke, Betty Cothran, Louis Cox, Alan Dillman, Kenneth Dillman, Bob Opotzner, Ann Orr, and Pam Peters—your feedback was instrumental in refining this novel. Your thoroughness and insights truly elevated the story.

I am also immensely grateful to Joel Brigham, Linda Cardillo, Jeannie Daniels, Ryan Dillman, Michele Kerbow, Ryan Kerbow, Diane Pohorylo, Brittany Schwertberger and Rick Stidley. Your input and suggestions have enriched portions of the book, adding depth and authenticity to the story.

Last, but certainly not least, my heartfelt thanks go to Liz Campion, and the dedicated Kent State University Library staff at the May 4 Special Collections Archive. Your assistance in my research was pivotal, ensuring the historical accuracy and depth of the narrative.

To all who have been a part of this journey, thank you. Your contributions, big and small, have made *Flowers Are Better Than Bullets* a reality.

About the Author

Rodney Dillman grew up in Lima, Ohio. His deep connection to Kent State University and its infamy stems from his enrollment there while earning a B.S. in education and an M.A. in economics. He also holds a law degree from Duke University.

Before venturing into the world of creative writing, Rodney enjoyed a career as an investment lawyer and corporate executive. His expertise led him to author a legal treatise in 2007, published by The American Bar Association Press. He co-authored a second edition of the same book in 2022.

Flowers Are Better Than Bullets is Rodney's debut novel.

Connect with Rodney!

Author website — www.rodneydillman.com
Facebook — https://tinyurl.com/AuthorRD1
X (Twitter) — @rodneydillman
Instagram and Threads — @roddillman